Three stubborn women, each of which made a promise. Who will yield, and who will break?

Abigail made a vow to her husband before he passed, one she could not, would not break. But life hasn't been easy without him by her side, and her children grow more with each passing day. Sometimes it feels like she'll be alone forever.

Amanda is tired of being a mess. She wants to achieve, to impress, to excel. If that means changing who she is, even changing her entire life, then so be it.

Donna has learned the truth about the world the hard way. You either attack, or you're attacked yourself. She doesn't like being the villain, but she's done being a patsy. She's determined to carve out a place for herself, no matter what.

These women have all returned to Birch Creek with big plans, but the future loves to surprise us. Can their vows keep them on target? Or will they decide it's more important to follow their hearts, no matter how bad the fallout?

THE VOW

B. E. BAKER

For Anna

Once I thought someone needed help at church.
But really, God knew I needed a friend.

A true friend is a treasure, no matter when you meet.
I'm glad I found you.

PROLOGUE: ABIGAIL

When I was twelve, every mom my sister and I knew (including our own) drove a minivan. They were underpowered—the size and space of a van, with the efficiency of a car. They were low cost—made to be an efficient option for moms on a budget. Worst of all, they were always treated badly by the driver and the occupants. It made them an embarrassing cliché, and we both knew we wanted nothing to do with them.

We made a sacred pact to never drive minivans ourselves.

I laugh at how serious we were about that promise. We still joke about it today. I, of course, drive a minivan, and my sister has mocked me for it mercilessly. Although my failure to keep our vow has featured in many jokes, the promise we made was never something that altered the course of my life.

Humans make promises all the time. Our futures aren't very secure, and promising things is our way of trying to exert some control over the chaos and doubt and fear that threaten to consume us.

We make promises to ourselves: to work out daily, to get more rest, to give up soda.

We make promises to others: to finish projects, to get together more often, to incentivize certain behavior.

We make promises that are legally binding: house notes, car notes, employment contracts.

Some promises, though, can alter the course of our entire life. These vows often have higher stakes. Do you take this man to be your lawfully wedded husband? You are aware that you'll be using your home as collateral?

On the other hand, before I gave birth to my son Ethan, I signed no papers, I answered no questions, and I made no promises, except to pay my hospital bill. And yet, from the time he was born, nothing and no one mattered as much as he did. It was the same with all four of my children. I'd do anything, sacrifice anything, burn down literally everything, if that's what it took to bring them peace, joy, and safety.

Humans aren't actually that original when you think about it. All of us long for the same things: safety, success, and love. Our fear of losing those things drives all our actions, including our promises. But sometimes, in order to be healthy and happy and strong, we have to break a vow.

Then we just hope that we survive the fallout.

🐦 I 🐿

AMANDA

lmost everything in our lives happens because of an interconnected chain of events. Sometimes it's hard to know where it starts. Sometimes, it's something small—inconsequential.

Ethan always slams the door when he leaves. It must be a teenage boy thing. But this morning, that door slam woke Roscoe.

If Roscoe hadn't started barking, Gabe might still be asleep.

If Abby hadn't been on a work call, Gabe wouldn't have woken me.

If Whitney hadn't finished the last of the Lucky Charms, Gabe might not have woken Maren by demanding them at the top of his lungs.

If she was still asleep, Maren wouldn't be reading Emery the riot act.

And if Emery hadn't started bawling louder than the dog barks, Abigail's conference call probably wouldn't have been interrupted.

Although I've never heard her yell at them, all four of Abby's kids live in abject terror that they might anger her.

Or perhaps it's more that they worry they'll disappoint her.

Either way, when she yanks her door open, all it takes is one stormy look. Izzy starts hissing at the others like a cat whose tail has been stepped on. Whitney's entire face scrunches into a storm cloud. Gabe sticks his fingers in his ears and starts saying "la la la" at the top of his voice. Meanwhile Maren's ranting at Emery to stop being such a big fat baby, which is only doubling the rate of tears streaming down her little sister's face.

Maybe it's just a bad morning. They do happen, and when this many people are in one place, they spiral quickly. But here's my takeaway: this house is much, much too small.

We cannot live like this.

I'm not on an active work conference call, so I'm stuck running interference on everything. I've become much more capable at handling the chaos than I was a few months back, thankfully. I add a handful of marshmallows to his Rice Crispies and Gabe unplugs his ears and beams. I ask Whitney and Izzy to hold hands and sing, and they do. Within two rounds of "*Jesus Said Love Everyone*," they're smiling instead of scowling. (For the record, this would never work with Maren. She'd probably eat the other person's face before she'd voluntarily sing while holding hands.) Finally, for my last act, I ask my non-angelic children to take their fight to my bedroom so it won't be as loud.

I'm improving. I didn't claim to be perfect.

They're still in there, Maren grumping and Emery sobbing, when Abigail emerges from her bedroom. Her hair's pulled into a high ponytail at the back of her head, not one single dark blonde strand out of place. She's already put on the same basic makeup she wears every day —shimmery golden-beige eye shadow and mascara with a nice pinky-neutral lipstick. It was clearly a video call, because she's wearing a beautiful sky blue suit.

"What in the world was going on with you three today?" Her head swivels like an owl tracking a group of mice. "You knew I had a call. I told you that last night." She doesn't say a word about the ongoing howling coming from my room. I've noticed that she almost never comments on my children's behavior, at least, not when I'm around. She directs all her prickly motherly energy at her own.

Gabe's lip quivers. "I'm sorry."

"I'm sorry we ran out of Lucky Charms," Abby says. "I'll buy more today, but you can't freak out when we run out of things. You're too old for that."

"It wasn't only us," Izzy says, more than ready to throw her cousins under the bus. Apparently I'm not the only one who has noticed that Abby only parents her own children, overlooking the shortcomings of mine.

Emery's sobbing escalates in the background, adding support to her accusation.

"You're the only three who answer to *me*."

They all blink, but they don't complain, they don't argue, and they don't bawl or bicker or defend.

"It won't happen again," Izzy says. "It might have been my fault. I tried to mother them again."

Abby rounds on Whitney and Gabe. "Why do you get upset at her for mothering you? Oh, it's because she's not your mother. But when you act like children, she has no choice. Either behave properly, or don't complain when she tells you what to do." She puts her hands on her hips. "Got it?"

They all nod.

"This family only works when we all do our part, and you three aren't doing yours."

They hop up and race around the kitchen, Whitney

emptying the dishwasher, Izzy taking out the trash, and Gabe helping Whitney by unloading the silverware.

I swear, some days I wonder whether Abby made some deal with a demon and had her children replaced with cyborgs. Meanwhile, the ruckus in my room is still punctuated by sharp shrieks and melodramatic sobs. Abigail glances back at the door, as if to ask, "Aren't you going to deal with yours?"

"We need to talk," I say. "And I don't want to pick a fight here, but I've been thinking about this over the past few days." I'd have brought it up sooner, but I've been worried she'll suggest that one of us move, and I actually like living with her huge brood.

Abby frowns. "About what?"

"This house is too small."

She opens her mouth, and my heart sinks. She's going to offer to move out. She always does the right thing, the good thing, the generous thing, even when it inconveniences her.

"I should explain that I like living together, but I think we need more space."

Her mouth snaps closed.

"I think we should expand the farmhouse, or at the very least, remodel the space we have."

"You want to put our own money into a house we may not keep?"

I swallow and try to gather my thoughts. It's not as easy for me to explain things as it is for her, and sometimes her questions make me feel like I'm testifying in court. Not that I've ever done that, but it kind of feels like I imagine it would. "I called Mr. Swift, and he said that although it's not yet certain that we'll inherit, he thinks any remodeling we do that will improve the value of the home would be fine, and we can use the 'household fund' associated with the estate to do it."

6

She blinks. "The household fund?"

"It's what we've been using to pay the bills that don't depend on our usage, like the taxes and upkeep or repairs."

"Is there enough to cover something like a remodel? We do need to make sure it can cover the fixed costs of the ranch through disposition."

"Mr. Swift said there's more than sixty thousand dollars beyond what he anticipates we'll need for the other routine expenses."

"Sixty thousand isn't bad," Abby says. "It's not a fortune, but if we're smart with it, we could improve a lot."

"Have you done much remodeling in the past?" I ask.

She shrugs. "A few things here and there. You?"

I shake my head.

"In my experience, success depends largely on who you know in the area. You really need to work with people you trust, unless you're handling things yourself. Our first line of business would be finding a good contractor." Abby taps her lip. "We should only change things we can finish quickly, or what's the point?" Her eyes widen. "Maybe we could convert the big garage area to living space and then build a carport. The garage door's broken anyway, so it's already unusable for day-to-day driving and parking. Instead of repairing it, we could convert that contiguous square footage to another room and bathroom. It'll need insulation and electrical, not to mention plumbing, but the slab's already there. The extra weight shouldn't be a problem. It's not like we're adding another floor."

I should have known—if she's not arguing with me, she's already sprinting halfway down the road. "I think our first task would be determining what things we most want to change or add."

"A bathroom!" Izzy's bouncing up and down.

"With a shower," Whitney says. "Not a crummy, old tub-shower combo, but a real shower with good water pressure."

Living in an old home sure changes your perspective. "You're right," I agree. "Another bathroom, or even two, should be our number one priority."

"A movie room!" Gabe says. "Like the one we had back home, with a fridge and a microwave for making popcorn."

"What about a workout room?" Abby asks.

"We can run outside," I say.

"Not when the snow starts," she says. "And the living room doesn't have enough seating right now for everyone who lives here. If we add another sofa or some chairs in there, there won't be room for anything else."

I hadn't given much thought to what circumstances they left in Texas. New York was hard to leave, with takeout at my fingertips and people always moving and churning. There were a million fun and exciting things to do, but it was small. Even with this many people, our living space isn't much more cramped than what we left. Living in the suburbs of a large city like Houston, they probably had a massive house with a lot of space. I hadn't even considered adding a movie room, more than one extra bathroom, or a workout room.

"Did someone say something about a new bathroom?" Emery may still be bawling in my room, but Maren looks totally unconcerned, her face desperately hopeful. "Because I vote yes to that, and I think there should be a girls' bathroom and a boys' one."

"There are four girls and only two boys," Izzy says. "That's a stupid idea."

"Fine, then one for you guys, and one for us." Maren

crosses her arms. "Ethan stinks up the whole place, and I'm sick of it."

"You poop too," Gabe says. "Everyone's poop stinks." Even his scowl is cute.

"Amanda and I clearly have some things to discuss," Abby says briskly. "But rest assured, the adults will make informed decisions. Once we're ready to move ahead with anything, we'll let you know what we've decided."

Maren huffs, but she accepts it and walks away. Why does *everyone* always listen to Abby? Her kids don't argue and complain like mine do, and none of hers are bawling in her bedroom, either.

I want to be more like Abby. I *need* to be more like her.

And I hate my pathetic longing, but it's persistent.

Abby grabs her purse from the kitchen counter. "Kids, I'm headed to the school. I'm really sorry you missed the teacher meet and greet, but if you come with me when I enroll you, you can at least see the school."

"I'm helping Jeff and Kevin trim the horses' hooves," Izzy says. "Kevin says he can teach me how, starting with rasping."

"Me too." Whitney shrugs. "And I don't really care about missing the teacher thing. School is school."

"It's my last day of being free," Gabe says. "Can I just watch *Pokémon?*"

Abby frowns. "We have the weekend left."

"But today's the last day when we'd usually have school during the week," Izzy clarifies.

"Actually." Abby looks a little uncomfortable. "The Daggett County schools don't have class on Fridays."

"Whoa," Izzy says. "No school on Fridays?"

"That's right. None at all, except one Friday in May, but I think that's exams or something."

"I'm so glad we moved." Gabe plops down on the sofa and grabs the remote.

"Hey," Abby says. "What are you doing?"

Gabe's eyes slowly rise. "I asked."

"But I didn't give you permission. You're supposed to pick up sticks in the side pasture, remember?"

He sighs heavily, but he hops off the sofa and walks to the door, pausing in the doorway to grab his boots. "But when I'm done?"

"Yes, then you can watch TV." She turns toward me. "You coming along? Or did you already register yours?" Abby slings her purse over her shoulder, and I notice there are papers poking out of the top.

I haven't even looked up where to go to register, but I can't admit that. What kind of mother doesn't think about enrolling her kids? I figured since it's a public school—they could just go. It didn't occur to me I had to do something to get them on a list. "I'd love to come," I say, before she notices that my private school privilege is showing. "But can you hold off just a moment while I find my birth certificates and vaccination records?"

It ends up taking almost half an hour for me to find them, partly because it takes me a while to find the documents, and partly because I change clothes first. I can't bring myself to climb into the car in yoga pants and a t-shirt when Abby's dressed so professionally. Luckily, Abby doesn't seem annoyed.

She does pause before opening her car door. "I need to enroll Gabe and Whitney at the elementary school first. It's right next to the high school, but you're welcome to drive separately if you'd rather just go to the high school."

Seeing as she just waited half an hour for me, I'm not likely to mind a few extra minutes at the elementary school. Even so, I'm surprised to realize that I don't even mind the idea of spending more time with Abby. "Oh, that's fine. Let's go together."

We spend a few minutes talking about ideas for the remodel first, but then I can't help circling back to the Fridays off thing. "Why don't they have school on Fridays?"

Abby grimaces, and I realize I didn't misinterpret her expression earlier. "It was a funding thing, I think. Some information mentioned that for farmers and ranchers, having an extra work day was helpful, but it gave them a chance to reduce teacher salaries by twenty percent."

My jaw drops.

"I'm sure you're thinking the same thing as I am—how does that save them money? Their fixed costs are the same, and surely they receive commensurately less from the government agency matches for the year, with fewer instructional days, but. . ." She shrugs. "I guess it was worth it to them. I can't comprehend prioritizing slightly lower taxes over the quality of my children's education."

I was definitely not thinking the same thing—I'm going to have to look up the word 'commensurately' later. "Actually, I was thinking it's too bad they have an extra day here, where there's so little to do, instead of in New York or Houston, where there are more activities and locations to visit and learn about. I could have made Friday into a regular museum day. What will we do here? Shovel more cow poop?"

Abby's arched eyebrow shows her judging me for judging the tiny town we live in, but I'm not going to back down. I was excited to come back, and I've also been a little concerned about whether my decision was a good one.

"At least we're not living in Flaming Gorge," she says. "Then we'd need to drive forty-five minutes to school each way."

"They can ride the bus, right?"

Abby laughs. "Yes, they can ride the bus, but it's still a long drive for the kiddos."

We pass the Brownings restaurant on our left, easy to pick out with its tin walls and bright red roof, and then make a right just before the fairgrounds. We reach the elementary school first, and it takes us almost five minutes to track down someone who can help us. Once we do, she's super quick, and super chatty. I'm pretty sure she now knows everything there is to know about Gabe and Whitney. Even I didn't know that Gabe can ride a unicycle.

The high school's just across the street, so we don't bother moving the car. It's a quick walk from the elementary school office to the orange brick high school building. I don't say anything about it, but the elementary school building itself is borderline depressing. There aren't the usual cutesy playgrounds and bright colors. At least the high school has some nice oak trees in front of it, and a scrub brush covered mountain behind it.

When we walk through the door, unlike at the elementary school, the secretary greets us like a bouncer. "Who are you?" She looks us over from head to toe. "What do you need?"

"I'm Abigail Brooks." Ever the charging bull, Abby seizes control. "This is my sister-in-law, Amanda Brooks. We just moved into the Birch Creek Ranch, Jedediah Brooks' place. We're here to enroll our children." She whips Izzy's birth certificate and immunizations out and brandishes them like a dagger.

"Oh." The secretary-bouncer stands down. "Great, then come on in." She circles around the reception desk and sits down, her fingers already clacking over the keyboard. "I'm Donna. I'll need to get some basic information from you, and then make some copies of your documentation."

Donna's not the friendliest person, but at least she's competent. She prints off the forms, and then takes our papers to copy while we're filling them out. She fights a little with the copier, which appears to have been manufactured shortly after the typeset press was first invented, but that actually makes me like her a little more. "This fudge ripple fracking machine always does this." She opens a side flap and tugs and tugs. "If the district doesn't approve a replacement on you soon, you razzle frazzit pile of rubbish, I'm going to—"

Abby snickers.

Donna, her dark brown, bobbed hair falling across the side of her face, turns toward us with a half smile. "Sorry. This thing is the bane of my existence right now."

"I'm guessing you have a few kids at home," Abby says.

"One," Donna says. "He just turned six, and he picked up some bad habits from his father, so I try to make sure he doesn't learn any more from me." Once the copies have been made, she proffers the originals. "You're all set. I'm sure your children will be the talk of Manila High. We don't get a lot of new students around here. It's too bad you don't have younger kids. As far as I know, my son's the only new kid at the elementary school."

Abby's head tilts, reminding me of an owl again. "I have two kids I just enrolled over there, so he won't be alone. What grade will he be in? First?"

Donna nods.

"My son Gabe will be in second."

Donna's exhale sounds relieved. "Too bad they aren't in the same grade, but having a few more new kids will be great. Especially another boy."

"We should have you over so they can meet," Abby suggests.

"I would love that," Donna says.

"What about tomorrow?" Abby doesn't waste time. At least she's not one of those women who says she'll do something and never does.

Donna's eyes widen, clearly thinking she was just being polite. "Oh. Well, my niece is coming over tomorrow—I promised her I'd teach her to crochet. But I could take her home early—"

"How old is your niece?" I ask.

"She's a senior in high school. She turns eighteen in a few months."

"Maren's fifteen," I say. "You're welcome to bring her. Maybe they'll get along as well."

"Oh," Donna says. "That's so nice of you to offer. I can ask her and see what she says. What time did you have in mind?"

"I have some work to catch up on in the morning," Abby says, "thanks to our recent move back out. But if you come around four-thirty, the kids can play for a while before dinner."

"I'd love to do that," Donna says.

On the walk back to our car, I feel quite a sense of accomplishment. I snap a nice, scenic photo of the corner of the high school with the mountain behind it and can't help smiling.

"It's nice to meet some new people," Abby says.

Before I can even respond, my phone rings. "It's Amanda Saddler," I say to Abby. "The neighbor who lives down the road."

"The one with the pet pig," she says.

I swipe to answer. "Hello?"

"Amanda?" She loves that we have the same name.

"Yes, it's me."

"I found the best show." She practically cackles. "It was really hard for me to stop after the first episode, but I think you're going to love it. Wanna watch it together?"

She cracks me up.

"Did I mention that I bought a bottle of champagne?" This time, she giggles like she's twenty, not eighty plus.

"I'd love to come watch it," I say. "When did you have in mind?"

"How soon can you get over?"

I laugh. "Is after dinner alright?"

"You must think I'm crazy to be pushing you to come right away, but when you're pushing ninety, you don't have time to wait. I might die before we finish watching this if you don't hurry."

She's the healthiest old lady I've ever met, always working in her garden, playing with her pig, and cleaning things without being asked. But she constantly makes jokes about her age. I suppose that's what you have to do, if you want to keep a good outlook about it. "I look forward to it. I'll bring some cheese and crackers."

"Cheese and crackers?" She whistles. "Your New York is showing." She definitely cackles this time. "You do that, and I'll have a big bag of spits."

She hangs up before I can even ask what in the world that means.

"Feel like a girls' night?" I ask.

"I would *love* a girls' night," Abby says, her eyes on the road. "But remember how I'm working on a Saturday? I'm not sure quite how long this petition is going to take, so I better start it tonight."

Which is how I wind up at Amanda's all alone, Gouda cheese and Wheat Thins in hand. She drags me through the door with a smile and pushes me toward a large, striped sofa. True to her word, there are two bottles of champagne with flutes in the center of the coffee table.

Surrounding them, there are three enormous ceramic bowls full of sunflower seeds and two empty bowls.

"What are the empty bowls for?" I ask, a little bewildered.

"Where you think you gonna spit?" She lifts one eyebrow. "Not on my floor."

And I've now figured out why she apparently calls sunflower seeds 'spits.' Sometimes I can't tell if she's the most awesome person I've ever met. . .or the grossest.

"There's barbecue, ranch, and original." She points at the lowest spot on the sofa. "I sit there, remember?"

I drop into my seat on the other side, expecting her to join me, but she's too busy hitting play and uncorking the champagne. By the time the credits have ended, I've got a handful of 'spits' and a glass of champagne.

After a few glasses of champagne, I feel like I finally get it.

Spits are downright delicious.

By the time the first bottle is empty, we've watched two full episodes, and things in my life feel pretty clear. "You know how Emily in the show loves her job?" I lean back on the sofa. "I've never loved my job. Not even a little bit."

Amanda hits pause and turns around on the sofa. "Don't you just take photos? You don't like that?"

I shake my head, and it feels like the room shifts a little bit, like we're on a boat. I don't drink very often. I probably should stop right now. But Amanda's already handing me another glass. I'll just hold it, not drink anything. "It's not the photos I don't like. It's how I constantly have to be living my life so that I have these beautiful moments to capture. And everything I post is only a little bit of the truth." I lean closer to her. "I cropped most of the high school out of the photo today and added some filters so it looks like my girls are going to school in an off-season ski village or something." I sigh.

"If your job is the only part of your life you wish was different, I think you're doing pretty well." Amanda beams at me and refills my glass. When did I drink it?

"It's not only my job." I close my eyes. "My love life is disastrous—and the only guy I like, my boss says I can't date." I sit upright and open my eyes. "And my kids don't listen to anything I say. Not that I know what to say when they start fighting anyway."

Amanda spits a mouthful of shells into her bowl. "Well, I didn't have kids, and my love life wasn't very good. But I think if you want something different than what you got, you gotta do something different than what you're doing."

How is she so wise? Maybe it's because she's old. But she's totally right—if I want a better love life, if I want a better job, if I want to be a better mom, I need to change all that stuff. "You're smarter than the Dalai Lama. Actually." My brain feels foggy. "I'm not sure who the Dalai Lama is. It might be a character from a kids' movie with llamas in it."

Amanda laughs.

"But how do I change?" I sigh. "I mean, how do I *get* two men to fall all over me at a party, for instance? Or how do I get my kids to listen to what I say?"

"You should find someone who has all those things, and then do what they do." Amanda nods. "I learned ranching from my parents. They were excellent ranchers." She refills my glass.

I have a rare moment of total clarity: Abigail. One year after her husband died, she had two men chasing her. She has a successful career she seems to love. She has children who listen and hang on her every word.

I need to be like Abigail.

Amanda gets me a piece of paper and a pencil, and we start writing down all the ways I'm about to change my life forever. . .by turning myself into Abigail.

When I wake up the next morning, my exact memories of the night before are a little fuzzy, but as I scan the list we made, clearly at a point that was a little past tipsy, I'm surprised. It's actually spot on. In our drunken bumbling, I may have come up with the best life plan I've ever seen.

Amanda Brooks is about to turn her life around and have everything she ever wanted, by becoming a better person in every way. And my model for this new life happens to live right here in this house. I rewrite the list to be a little more clear, and then I race outside, ready to begin.

ABIGAIL

My phone is mocking me.

Coward. Coward. Coward.

Before we left Utah, I went on my first two dates since losing my husband almost a year and a half ago, and they were pretty good dates, my dunking in an ice-cold lake aside. The guy who took me out lives right down the road, and is easily the most eligible bachelor in the area.

But now that I'm here, I can't seem to bring myself to call him—or even to text.

Amanda did tell me that he knows I'm here. Or at least, that I'm coming. He drove past when she and her kids were moving in a week ago, and he stopped to help them move. We hadn't left yet, so she couldn't tell him *when* we were coming, but he knows it's soon.

Two and a half days have passed since we finally reached the ranch, and I'm officially using work as an excuse to avoid reaching out.

Which is ironic, since I've now spent about three times as long researching and writing this petition as I should have. Since lawyer's time is our money, and I can't overbill the client for my own inability to focus, I'm really just wasting time. Which means I'm wasting money.

My brain is spinning round and round like a Ferris wheel.

"Mom!" Ethan bursts through the front door. I know, even though I'm in my room, because the door whamming against the wall sounds like the report of a gunshot. His boots, clumping on the wood floor, are nearly as loud.

My almost-eighteen-year-old son bursts through every door, really. Maybe it's a teenage boy thing. I've tried to break him of it, but it never works.

"I'm coming." I close my laptop and jog into the family room before he tracks mud anywhere else. I check the floor without thinking, assessing the damage, but blessedly his boots were actually clean. Thank goodness.

He's definitely excited about something—his eyes are bright. "Izzy was outside, trimming hooves—"

"She said she would be—"

"And she said that you guys may be remodeling the house?" Has everyone been desperate for us to change things?

I would personally love a more modern feel, as well as a workout room and another bathroom, but I've also been happy living closer to all my little people. Even if their interruptions and complaints sometimes make working from home harder, I love having them around. "We are looking into it," I say.

"Guess what?" He's bouncing on his toes. I always thought his little boy excitement would fade as he grew up, but he still practically vibrates when he gets excited, like one of those tiny, yappy dogs.

"You bought a lottery ticket and you won?"

Small wrinkles form between his eyes. "Mom, it has to do with the remodel, obviously."

I can't help poking at him. "Obviously. Do share."

"Kevin's a remodeler guy! Like, he's apparently the best in town. He's been working part time on the house they're in. Jeff said it was part of his deal with Jed. They got a percentage knocked off their boarding costs, because he agreed to fix things up."

That's been my biggest hesitation. I don't know anyone here, so how could I find someone I trust? But if Kevin can do it—and he lives close. I also hear the winter is the slowest time for ranchers. If he's doing work next door, I can even get a feel for what his jobs look like. But. . . "He's like twenty-one, isn't he?"

"Mom." Ethan rolls his eyes. "He's twenty-four, and he's been working on houses with his dad for ten years already."

"Wow, so he's basically an expert." I try my hardest to suppress my sarcasm.

Ethan's shoulders droop and the buzzy vibration evaporates. "Fine. I thought you'd be happy, but whatever."

I hate raining on his parades. Like, really hate it. Poking him is one thing, but when he gives up, it wrecks me. "I was only kidding. I'd love to come see his place and hear what ideas he may have."

I find Amanda and catch her up to speed. "If we aren't happy with the work he does, it's going to be awkward," she warns.

"I agree." I bite my lip. "With a town this small, that risk is probably inevitable."

"He's living next door, though," she says.

"Which will make things way easier, assuming he's good."

"Assuming that, yeah."

Fifteen minutes later, Kevin's racing from room to room, picking up piles of socks and paint cans. "Paint is the second to last thing you do," he says. "Then it's just floors and trim and you're done." He waves around the room. "But you can get a good feel, even at this point, how much better the room looks." His buzzy excitement almost rivals Ethan's.

Assuming the small house looked like ours before he started, he's scraped off the popcorn ceilings, redone the texturing on the walls, replaced all the lights, and brightened it up quite a lot with lighter colors. "What floors are you considering?"

He shows us the new laminate floors he chose, and then he walks us through the bathroom he's already finished, which I love, and the kitchen he's nearly completed. "The backsplash is obviously not done." He swallows, and I realize that he's nervous.

If the clean, modern subway tile in the bathroom hadn't already won me over, the light, wood-look floors and the silvery glass tile backsplash in the kitchen would have.

"I'd have preferred stainless appliances, but with the budget Jed set, I had to find these white ones used." He shrugs. "It's still a lot better than the faux wooden ones it had before. They were from the seventies." He grimaces.

"What's your schedule like?" Amanda asks.

"Some of that depends on my bosses." He grins. "They can be real slave-drivers."

"Do you have time now to check things out?" I ask.

"Like, right now?" Kevin sets the paint can down. "What exactly did you have in mind?"

"We have a wish list," I say, "but we need someone with a little more knowledge to tell us what's reasonable."

"Do you have a budget?"

"Sixty," I say. "For everything."

"Alright. I wasn't really expecting to go over today, but sure. Let's do it."

"Abby doesn't mess around," Amanda says.

I'm impressed with his ideas—he thinks we can do a

large bonus room, a storage room, and an extra bathroom. "It's an oversized three-car garage," he says. "And if we knock out this wall, we can connect to it in a much more natural space, and allow the bathroom to be accessed from the add-on as well as the main house hallway much more easily."

We're going over a rough blueprint when I realize dinner's almost upon us, and I've done nothing at all on the memorandum I promised Lance for tomorrow.

"Would you have time to go look at tile and flooring in the morning?" he asks. "If we pick the bathroom tile and fixtures, I could give you a much better cost estimate."

"Sure," I say. "But if we're going to do that, I'd better get caught up on my work."

With a goal in mind that excites me—selecting things for the renovation—I'm finally able to focus. That, combined with a few strokes of luck on my case law research, and I manage to finish up just before midnight.

The next day, Amanda's as excited as I am. We talk about colors on the drive to Green River, and through it, all the way to the Home Depot in Rock Springs. By the time we arrive, we have quite a few ideas in mind. Kevin parks and cuts the engine. "Now." He doesn't open his door or get out. Instead, he spins in his seat until he can see both Amanda on the passenger side and me in the back. "You two, listen real good."

What could he possibly need to say that he didn't say on the long drive we just had?

"This is where things usually fall apart."

"Huh?" Amanda looks as confused as I am.

"It's usually married couples I bring, but sometimes it's moms and their kids or whatnot. Any which way, people get along when we are talking about what they want done, usually. Then we get to the little stuff, like tile colors and light fixtures, and these people who love each other turn into crazy folks. So when we walk in there, just remember that the color of the tile and the shape of the light bulbs doesn't really matter."

I laugh. "That's ridiculous." It's not like Amanda and I will fight over what color the bathroom tile is! We're both desperate for an extra toilet, shower, and sink. "You don't need to worry," I say. "I'm not overly attached to anything, and besides. For the remodel component, we can each pick the details of our own bathrooms separately. If we disagree on this new one, I'll let Amanda choose."

"That's not a great plan." Amanda's head swivels to face me. "The entire house needs to be done in a consistent style so that if it is resold soon, it won't look patchwork or disconnected."

I groan. "Then you can just pick everything. How's that?" Typical, that's what it is. The person who can't control her own children is going to throw a tantrum if she can't pick the tile? Fine. I can live with anything. "Let's just go. Maybe we'll get lucky and like the same things."

Amanda doesn't argue, but she looks like I feel: much less excited, thanks to Kevin's condescending warning.

In the end, it's actually good that he warned us. Or maybe it wouldn't have made a difference. "Every single tile you like is the most expensive tile on the wall." Amanda arches one eyebrow, accusing me. "We'll never be able to stick to a budget if you insist on everything being high end."

She's right—but I've always been like this. I can walk into practically any shop, anywhere on earth, know nothing about what they sell, and still pick the most expensive option. "Let's try this, then." I point at the wall. "From here on out, you pick a top three that are in our budget, and then I'll select the final one from among them."

"So I never get to make any final decisions at all?"

If God waltzed into this store and offered Amanda three wishes, she'd complain that he was late and that three wishes wasn't enough. "What do you propose?"

She shakes her head. "I don't know, but I don't think that's fair."

"We aren't even confirming final selections," I say. "We're merely here to get an idea of what we want and a ballpark price."

"I hate to say this," Kevin says, "but including my estimates for electrical, framing, windows, drywall, paint, trim, and plumbing, you're already over the sixty grand, and that's without any remodeling of the current home. It's just for the extra 1200 square feet you're adding when we convert the garage area."

"Fantastic," I snap, knowing I'm being a jerk. I inhale and exhale slowly, trying to get my irrational emotions under control. So much for this being fun. "I'm sure you'll disagree, but I don't mind chipping in some of my own money to help offset the costs of the remodel. Especially if we can get things done quickly and improve our quality of living."

"What exactly were you thinking of doing with your own funds?" Amanda seems *more* annoyed, not less.

"The hall bathroom first," I say. "Having two sinks and some storage in there would be tremendous. My kids are still keeping their things on that wobbly wire rack. Plus, the shower pressure is terrible. At a baseline, a plumber needs to diagnose and repair that issue. I'd love to get new appliances in the kitchen, like true convection ovens, for one, but even new enough ovens that they bake properly would be a big improvement."

"There's only one oven in there now," Amanda says. "I've never seen much point in having a second."

"If you were baking a triple batch of cookies, you would."

"A triple batch?" Amanda looks horrified.

"New counters that don't take forever to clean and aren't stained would also be nice. But then I'd probably want new cabinets to put them on."

"Not all of us have millions in savings," Amanda says.

"Do any of us have millions?" Kevin laughs, clearly trying to dispel the tension. "Remember what I said, guys?"

Judging by Amanda's expression, we both remember, and we're both annoyed. But at least it gives us a common enemy.

"Let's just price out some basic options," I say. "If you don't want to pick them, Kevin can select some middle of the road stuff, and then we can make more decisions as we firm up our plans."

She huffs, but she points at a few tile options and Kevin writes the prices down. We move along, from one category to another, even taking the time to check out the true convection oven options.

"Why is it so great, exactly?" Amanda asks. "I mean, what makes it true, as opposed to, say, a false convection oven?"

"Cute," I say. "But it's pretty simple. Convection means the movement of heat. Most supposed convection ovens made for residential purposes have little fans in the back to circulate air. That means they're still hotter on top when it's actively heating than anywhere else. A true convection oven has heating coils on all sides in addition to the fan, so the heating is actually as consistent as it can get. It also means that it can effectively cook more than one pan of cookies, for instance, instead of burning the top and bottom of each."

She doesn't roll her eyes, but I can tell from her sigh that she'd like to.

Amanda drags Kevin ahead two rows to look at faucets, leaving me behind to peruse the lower cost countertop options. That's when I hear a familiar voice.

"Kevin! What are you working on these days? Finally done with the old house?"

I hear a startled, "Oh," from Amanda. And then she says, "He's helping Abby and me."

My heart kicks into high gear, my pulse pounding in my ears.

"Abby?" Steve's voice is as deep as ever, and hearing him say my name. . .half of me wants to sprint around the corner and catch up to them. The other half wants to turn tail and run. Why am I so split? What is so confusing about this?

If I'm a viable option, I'll never get the green light. Dating me is too dangerous.

Steve's words from the summer come back to me. Is that really it? Am I afraid to see him again, afraid that if we date, I'm betraying Nate? Of course not. I'm not that confused.

But for some reason, when I hear Amanda say, "Yeah, she's here somewhere. She was looking at countertops—" I duck.

I crouch down low and crawl on my hands and knees under one of the fake display countertops.

My heart really takes off then, like I'm an ingenúe in a slasher movie, and the terrible serial killer is coming for me with a chainsaw.

"Abby?"

Worse even than one of those idiotic teenagers, I'm facing inward, my eyes focused on the cabinet in front of me. Did I think if I couldn't see him, he wouldn't recognize me?

This is worse than when I fell in the lake.

I spin around and stand up, plastering a smile on my face. "Steve?"

His expression is bemused. "What were you doing down there?"

There are many things I can't do, but I've never had trouble talking my way out of something. "The last time I chose granite, it wasn't very well processed." *Very well processed?* What is wrong with my brain? Move on, move on. "Flakes kept falling off the bottom. I was. . ." I clear my throat. "Um, I was checking this one."

"That's silestone," he says, his gorgeous eyes sparkling with suppressed mirth. "It's manmade, so I think you can be pretty sure it won't ever flake off."

He knows. Of course he knows. He's not a drunken horse trainer, like I thought. He's an emergency room doctor. People probably lie to him all day long, more elegantly than I just did.

But that reminds me of something, a way to turn the tables on him. It's the best defense if you're scrambling— put the other side on defense instead. It's a total hunch, but not a terrible one. After all, Amanda told Steve I was coming, and he probably knows school starts Monday. "Don't you work in Green River? What are you doing here?" I glance over at Kevin.

He looks down at his shoes. It's not conclusive proof, but people often look down when they're lying or hiding something, and Steve's not in scrubs. He *could* have changed, but I doubt it.

"I work fifteen minutes away," Steve says.

He notably did *not* tell me he just got off work. I'm a lawyer. Did he think he could throw me off with that kind of non-statement? "So, you just got off work?"

Steve's brows draw together. "I needed sandpaper and some zip ties."

He didn't just get off work, or he'd have said that. "You drove all the way from your property out here for zip ties?" I bob my head. "That makes sense. I'm sure they don't have them at the True Value, you know, the one you drove right past."

"They cost less out here," Steve says doggedly.

Amanda snorts from behind him.

"Do you know how hard it is to bump into someone who never leaves the house?" Steve crosses his arms.

"Calling or texting might have been easier," I say.

"We're going to go look at the shower options," Kevin says.

"You can," Amanda mutters. "I'm not going anywhere. This is the most fun I've had since the Fourth of July."

"Your sister-in-law is scary," Steve says.

"Don't I know it." Amanda smirks.

"You didn't call me, either." Steve leans against the counter, the muscle in his arm bunching as it shifts to hold his weight. In faded blue jeans, worn cowboy boots, and a dark blue shirt, he's basically lethal. In that moment, I have no idea why I didn't call him.

"Why didn't you call him?" Amanda asks. "Are you blind?"

I'm going to kill her when we get back home.

"At least you should have texted him," she says.

With my bare hands.

"I've been swamped," I say. "Between packing, and the move back, and catching up with my work, and enrolling the kids—"

"You're happy to see me again, then?" Steve smiles slowly, one dimple showing up like a sneaky little heart assassin.

Happy feels like an inadequate word. Delighted?

Giddy? Overjoyed? "Kevin has to get back soon," I say. "He still has to make a run with Ethan to check on the herd."

"They went out without me." Apparently Kevin only moved an aisle over. Far enough away that we can't see him, but close enough to hear every word.

"Great," I shout. "Fabulous." Why is no one on my side? "But we do need to get back so we can throw something decent together for dinner. We have people coming over."

Steve straightens like a puppet being yanked, and his eyes flash. "People? What people?"

I point at the back of the store. "I'm pretty sure the sandpaper is on aisle 24 and the zip ties are on aisle 22." I have no idea where they are, but it seems likely enough. That's when I realize Steve's already holding both items. "Wait, if you have what you came for, what were you doing back here?"

He chucks them under the counter where I was hiding. "Abby, I didn't need anything. I drove out here because Kevin said you'd be here." He steps closer. "I figured if you drove a few thousand miles, the least I could do was drive sixty." His voice drops a bit more. "And I would walk five hundred more, if that would help."

Classic love songs. For an old guy, Steve has some game. I can barely breathe right now.

"If you two could talk a little louder, that would be great. I can barely hear you, so I'm guessing Kevin's missing most of it," Amanda says.

I spin around. "Were you in on this too?" My hands naturally go to my hips.

She inhales sharply. "Well, Kevin wasn't sure if he should tell Steve to come or not."

For the love. "Look, we're busy tonight, and then tomorrow—"

"Do you know Donna?" Amanda asks. "She has a son named—"

"Aiden." Steve's cocky grin is back. "I've known her for decades, now."

"Would you feel comfortable having dinner with all of us?"

Oh, Amanda won't be at the dinner. I'm going to kill her on the way home.

"What can I bring?" he asks.

"Hey," I say. "I'm standing right here."

Steve shrugs. "The only thing worse than having allies is not having them."

"If you think quoting Winston Churchill is going to impress me. . ." Well. He'd be right. "Fine. Bring rolls. And a dessert." I cross my arms. If you ambush me, you get to do some heavy lifting. "And sodas."

Steve laughs. "Anything else?"

"And it's not a date," I say. "It's just a dinner with friends."

"Rome wasn't built in a day. I'm a patient man," he says.

"See you at five-thirty," I say.

"You told Donna four-thirty." Amanda's a sell-out.

"So the kids can play." I shake my head. "Did you want to play Twister, Steve?"

His smile is basically wicked.

"Scratch that question."

"See you at four-thirty." Steve's smirking when he spins on the heel of his boot and turns to walk away. I'm still staring when he turns around.

And also when he looks over his shoulder and catches me watching him.

But his wink. . . It's almost worth it.

Amanda whistles once he's out of sight. "Now that was impressive. Most men won't get up to get the remote.

He drove all the way out here so that he could line up a date, and he settled for some kind of potluck without any complaint."

"Oh, please," I say. "He came all the way out here because he was too nervous to call me."

"You don't make a shaky pass when you need a touchdown. That's when the quarterback has to run it himself." Kevin's looking very pleased with himself.

"*Stare decisis*," I say.

"Huh?" Amanda and Kevin both say at the same time.

"Oh, I'm sorry. That's the Latin phrase for lower courts needing to follow the precedent set by higher courts. I thought we were all saying things that the other people in the conversation wouldn't understand."

Kevin snorts. "You're strange."

"She's right, though. What were you saying about a touchdown?"

"Steve couldn't risk fumbling the ball—not when he knows she's skittish as a spring deer."

"You're saying he drove out here instead of calling. . .because he cares about her that much?"

"Yes." Kevin nods. "That's exactly what I'm saying."

✣ 3 ✣

DONNA

My very first love in life was art. I think I started with finger paints, but I quickly progressed to paint books with paint dried on the paper that I activated with water. I worked my way up from there to the little white watercolor trays, filled with dried paint. Finally, once I was old enough to take care of my own brushes, I graduated to the kinds of paints you squeezed out onto a palette.

But in school, I often couldn't get my hands on paints. Other kids took them, and teachers declared they were too messy or that they cost too much.

With the benefit of an adult perspective, I can admit that I'm not the best artist. In fact, I may not have much natural talent there at all, but it still speaks to me. It always has. From poems to paintings to songs, that's how I understand the world, people's pain, and my own growth. When I had a bad day, the only thing that made me feel better was to express it via a picture of some kind. The adult coloring books have been a godsend, but back in school, my options were limited. Often, my only real tools were notebook paper and pencils.

One day in particular, Dad had yelled at Mom. Patrick sided with Dad, and it felt like the whole world was against Mom and me. When I walked outside to meet the bus, it looked like it was about to rain. Only, it never rained. The sky just sat like that, all grey and overcast and rumbly. At recess, they ushered us all outside, eager to have the kids get their wiggles out before the rain poured down. We shivered and stared at the sky for the entire thirty minutes, but no rain ever fell.

When I reached art a few moments later, I knew that I *had* to recreate that sky. It was how I felt inside.

But the world conspired against me. Phillip Edwards took the only decent paint set. Carolyn Thorpe stole the crayons. The colored pencils were scattered all over—no one thief to even target. Stamps and pens wouldn't do it justice.

So I gathered as many pencils as I owned, of every shape and variety and brand, and I sharpened them all until they were ready to jab out someone's eye, and I set to work. The only way I could make the lined notebook paper into the sky rumbling outside and aching in my heart was to shade every inch of the page with graphite.

It took me more than an hour, but I never flagged. I carefully sketched, shaded, and shaped the dark clouds. I darkened the bottom side of the threatening storm clouds that never gave way, that never followed through on their threats. They just ruined everyone's day, everyone's life, never getting the misery over with so the world could move past it to sunshine.

When my teacher finally came by my desk, she froze. "What is that, Donna?"

I cleared my throat, but nothing emerged. How could I explain? How could the woman who always wore pink sweaters possibly understand?

"Donna? What did you draw? Is it a cave?"

A cave? I pointed at the dark clouds. "It's the sky."

She turned her head slightly and then her lips parted. "Oh. The sky outside right now." A half smile formed on her face, because that was something she could understand. That was something familiar, something not-scary. Something she wouldn't need to tell the guidance counselor about or bring to the attention of my parents. She was turning to leave when she stopped and looked back at me. "Sweetheart, you did a wonderful job, but did you notice what happened to your hands? Look at your arm."

Shaping something as dark as I felt, as dark as the day outside, took a lot of graphite. And that day I learned something new—something I should have paid more attention to.

When you spend a lot of time around something dirty, it leaves a mark.

I washed my hands for several minutes, reapplying soap, scrubbing and rubbing and abrading my skin, but when I went home that day, there was still a faint trace of dark grey on the sides of my hands, on my wrist and forearms, and on the edge of my jacket.

When you endure darkness in life, it's the same. You can scrub and scrub, but the stains never disappear entirely. It adheres to and changes your very soul.

Charles Windsor the Fourth wasn't the best-looking guy I'd ever met, but he was the smartest and probably the coolest, and his family was shiny and beautiful and impressive. From the moment our eyes locked in Econ 101 at Stanford, I couldn't look away. No part of our meeting set off alarm bells. He didn't remind me of that dark day or the tumultuous sky or the darkness in my soul. He certainly never spoke to me the way Dad talked to Mom. In fact, their entire family was as opposite from ours as I could ever have imagined. They were light, and bright, and airy.

But sometimes what we see on the surface isn't the whole story.

I wonder what I'd have done differently if I knew the truth then that I know now. I wonder how far and how fast I'd have run, if I knew that Charles Windsor the Fourth had learned more than how to run a business from his esteemed family. How would I have reacted if I knew that all that brightness, all that grace and elegance, covered up something darker than graphite, darker even than that heavy sky?

The women I'm going to visit are both widows. According to Patrick, one died in a car accident, and the other died of cancer only a year and a half ago. I could never admit this out loud, but I've often dreamed of how much better my life would be if Charlie had just died.

"Mom?" Aiden tugs on my sleeve.

"Right."

"Are we going inside?" Beth asks. "Aren't we here?"

"Yes, of course we are." I shove all my morose thoughts away and slide my Happy Donna face into place so that I'm ready to perform. Lately, it seems like it's almost always performance time. "I really hope their son is nice."

"It's okay, Mom." Aiden's voice is cheerful, and I don't think he knows how to fake it yet. "School's going to be fine."

"It won't be like San Francisco," I say. "There won't be hundreds of kids at your school. According to Judy, there are only thirty-six second graders and twenty-nine first graders. I hope you make friends because—"

"Yes, yes," Beth says. "You're a concerned mother, bringing her son home to a strange place. We get it, but the only way you'll find out is if we actually go inside and meet them." She's a bit snotty, but considering her parents, I'm grateful she's not worse.

I can't help my sigh as I open the door and make the walk toward the front porch. I feel a little guilty about coming here like this, essentially using my son as an excuse to spy on these women, but if I've learned anything from being with Charles, it's that kindness gets me nowhere.

No one else will take care of me, so I'd better do what needs to be done myself.

I'm not a chump, not anymore.

I clean up my own messes.

I make my own luck.

And I refuse to feel bad about what happens to other people. It's not like I'm doing it for myself anyway—it's all for Aiden. And I'd do anything, deal with any stains I pick up, if it keeps my darling Aiden safe and healthy and standing in the warmth of the sunlight.

I pick up my hand to knock, but before my knuckles connect with the door, it swings open.

The little boy behind the door is darling—tousled blond hair, deep blue eyes, and the most pathetically eager face I've ever seen. "Are you my new friend?"

If I had a warm, beating heart instead of a block of dark ice, his eager smile might melt it.

"Okay. Why not?" Aiden shrugs.

"Wanna see my room? My big brother has a lot of really cool stuff."

My reserved giant of a child bobs his head. "Sure."

"I'm Gabe. What's your name?"

"Aiden."

"I'm really, really good at legos, even though my mom hates them."

"I don't have any." Aiden's brow furrows.

"You can have some of mine, then. My mom would be happy." Gabe takes Aiden's hand and tugs him down the hall, unconcerned that the front door's still hanging wide open.

"I think he'll be alright," Beth says.

"I am so sorry." Abigail rushes toward the front entryway, rubbing her hands together. "I didn't even hear a knock."

"Your sweet little son must have seen us," I say. "He opened the door before we could—"

The most exuberant barking I've ever heard starts in one of the back rooms and comes hurtling at us in the form of a black and white dog. Abigail body checks him. "Roscoe. Down." He stops barking, but the rumbling growl is almost more ominous. "Down, Roscoe. Now." He drops this time, his belly on the floor, but his eyes are telling me that he knows the truth. I'm a black-hearted devil, and he won't let me harm his people.

Good luck, Roscoe. If I can't beat a dog, I deserve to lose.

"I'm so sorry. He's usually really friendly with all the people coming and going on the farm."

Does she suspect me?

"He only gets aggressive when someone comes into the house without him noticing." The beleaguered look on her face says it all. "We're remodeling right now, so he's kind of on high alert."

"That's good—I'm sure he just wants to keep his family safe," I say. "How long have you had him?"

"Actually, he came with the house." Abigail smirks. "At least he kills the rats."

Ah, rats. "Not many dogs do that—cats are usually much better."

"You country people handle this stuff a lot more calmly than I do." Abigail's eyes sparkle. "The one time we saw mice back home, I couldn't sleep all night. I called the exterminator the next day and paid a small fortune to get the top of the line rodent elimination plan."

"Our top of the line plan is named Lynx," I say. "And he costs a case of tuna each month."

She has a nice laugh. "This must be your niece." Abigail offers her hand. "I've heard good things, young lady."

"I'm Beth." My brother's daughter almost never looks shy, but I suppose Abigail is a little intimidating.

"You're a little older than my Izzy," Abigail says, "but I hope you'll keep an eye out for her, and Amanda's two daughters as well."

"Of course," Beth says. "I'm sure they won't need help finding anything. Manila High School's not exactly large."

"I could hardly believe it when I found out they had six grades at the same school," she says, "but Izzy's happy that she and Emery will be at the same place, with Whitney joining them next year."

"You have three kids?" Beth asks. "Is that right?"

"Four." A tall young man with a deep voice exits the room Gabe and Aiden just entered. "I'm Ethan, the black sheep of my family."

"More like a black ox," Abigail says.

"But I know what noise a sheep makes." Ethan baas. "What sound would an ox make?"

"Oxen complain about everything and break stuff all the time," a blonde girl with a cute bob says from the kitchen. "And they don't go to college like they should."

"Hey, I'm taking online classes," Ethan says.

"We all know. You haven't gone a single day without whining about them," Abigail says.

"I can't wait for college," Beth says. "Like, I'm literally counting down the days."

"You don't say." Abigail's face breaks out into a lovely

smile. "Well, come right in, Beth. How do you feel about handsome oxen?"

Beth laughs. "Can't say that I've met one before now. Mostly here, we just grow pigs."

They're all laughing as they walk through the entry hall and into the family room. I thought it was smart to come, when Abigail invited me to dinner. Suss out the enemy, find out their weaknesses, and evaluate their strengths. But now that I'm here, in an old farmhouse that somehow feels like a bright and sunny day, I realize it was a mistake. People with black hearts, people who are stained, we never fit in. And bringing Aiden over, showing him this family, letting him make a friend—I never should have done that either. You don't realize what you're lacking until you see someone who has it.

"Donna?" a man's voice asks.

The weather outside was so gorgeous that no one thought to close the door. I spin around toward the doorway. "Steve?" What's he doing here? "Are you checking on their horses or something?"

He beams. "You must not have spoken to many people since moving back."

I've been busy. "Dad's quite a handful. I don't get out much."

"Whoa, you got stuck taking care of him? What about Patrick?"

"Amelia happened."

Steve doesn't say another word. His lips just press together until they turn white. It says something about my sister-in-law that just her name can serve as an answer to a question. Like, if someone asked me, 'Did you have a good day?' I could reply, 'Amelia.' People would nod knowingly.

Which still doesn't tell me what he's doing. "Why are you here?"

"I ran into Abby and Amanda at Home Depot today—"

"Home Depot in *Rock Springs*?" I ask. "What in the world were you doing there?"

A door in the hall a few feet away flies open, and Amanda emerges. "He was stalking my sister-in-law." Amanda's smile is smug. "And I was helping him do it."

"Stalking might be a strong word to use," Steve says. "I needed zip ties."

Wait. Steve Archer. . .and the poised mother of four? Really? I can't see that at all. Then again, my earliest memory of Steve is the time he made a sword out of a rake and practically put Patrick's eye out. I thought my dad's head was going to explode. That vein kept throbbing, all through Steve's explanation.

"He's not really stalking her," Amanda says. "They've been on a date—that she agreed to go on."

"Actually, two dates," Steve says. "If you count family dinner."

"Which you really shouldn't." Amanda's face is scrunched up in a hilarious way.

"No, she's right. A family dinner is not a date," I say. "But I'm glad you're not stalking her. I doubt Clyde would be super keen on arresting you."

"Uncle Dex would never," Steve says.

"Wait, your Uncle is the. . .what? A sheriff?" Amanda asks.

"He sure is." Steve straightens his already broad shoulders. "That'll make you think twice about throwing accusations around, won't it? I might sue you for libel."

"Actually," Abigail's voice carries across the room from the kitchen. "Libel's for written statements. I think your best bet would be to bring an action for slander. However, unless you're talking about filing a civil suit, it would be a prosecutor, not a sheriff, who made the decision of how to proceed."

I can't stop my laugh. "Oh, Steve. She's way out of your league."

"Hush," he hisses. "I'm hoping she won't notice." He lifts two bags up in the air, the muscles in his chest and arms rippling a little. For a country boy, he's not bad to look at, at least. "I brought drinks *and* rolls, just like you said."

Amanda walks past us both, snatching the rolls right out of Steve's hands. "What about dessert? Did you forget that?"

"I went by The Gorge, but they didn't have anything good left. And Brownings only had brownies." He shrugs. "They're in the car."

"That was a test," Amanda says. "And you failed. Luckily, Abby made cowboy cookies." I can't tell whether she's making a joke.

"They do have pecans and coconut in them," Abigail says. "I hope no one has allergies. But if you do, assuming the brownies are nut free, then you'll have that option."

"You made cowboy cookies?" Steve's eyebrow arches. "Did anyone in particular inspire those?" He walks—no, wait—he saunters into the kitchen, his boots sliding a bit as he moves. "Or have you always been a fan of cowboys?"

"Oh my word," I say. "Please tell me you're kidding right now."

Steve scowls at me over his shoulder.

"It's a good thing you weren't this cheesy in high school." I chuckle. "I mean, nachos aren't this cheesy. *Have you always been a fan of cowboys?*" I belly laugh. And then, for some strange reason, I can't stop. Tears actually form in the corners of my eyes.

"I'm glad you find me so amusing."

Abby's glancing from me to Steve and then back to me. "How long did the two of you date?"

My laughter cuts off with a choked sound. "What?"

"I'm assuming it was a while back, and I'm assuming it didn't last very long." The corner of her mouth twitches. "And now you behave more like siblings, no?"

I open my mouth to argue, but Steve beats me to it. "You were right, Dee. She is out of my league." It doesn't stop him from slinging an arm around her shoulders.

A pang of something contracts in my heart. Am I jealous of Steve paying her all his attention? No way. I'm afraid the more pathetic answer is the truthful one. I'm jealous of *anyone* having someone who seems to truly like them. That means I'm jealous of both of them and all their bubbly joy.

Which is probably precisely the reason I don't deserve any myself.

"Dinner's ready," Abby says. "If you're all hungry."

If I felt a little intimidated by her at first, with her perfectly tailored business suit, and her beautifully streaked hair, and her complete command of the English language, by the time dinner's over, I feel even worse. Her kids are borderline angelic. She's a competent lawyer who gave up being made partner to move out here and support her oldest son. And on top of all that, she's the best woman at faking kindness that I've ever met. She hasn't said a single mean thing to me or anyone else. Not even a backhanded compliment.

Now Amanda? She's someone I might actually get along with. She's smart and pretty, but she looks like she doesn't believe it. She says catty things with some frequency, and she ducks and dodges when any parenting issues arise. Plus, her kids are prone to throwing fits and petulantly whining, so that makes me feel better. When

Aiden squeezes two cups worth of ketchup on his plate for ten or eleven French fries, she just laughs.

"I'm so sorry," I say. "I can buy you more ketchup."

Amanda waves me off. "You should see how much milk we pour down the drain every morning."

I almost feel bad for asking her the questions I came to ask. Not enough to rethink my plans, but almost.

When I find out that Abigail made dinner herself, after working this morning and driving all the way to Rock Springs and back, I insist on loading the dishwasher.

"Please," Abigail says. "Don't bother. My kids will do that. It's important that they learn how to work."

And true to her word, they actually do. Disgustingly, they all hop up and start working on their assigned chores without complaint. Abby sets a plate of chewy, crunchy-on-the-edges cowboy cookies on the coffee table and waves her hand. "Aiden and Gabe are back in his room, breaking more of Ethan's Pokémon figurine collection, so we can actually pretend to be real adults for a minute."

I tense. "Breaking? Oh, no. I'll go see—"

Ethan's headed out the door, but he turns around. "I pretend to care, since Gabe feels like he's getting away with something, but really?" He shrugs. "I'd have just given them to him. Don't worry about it."

See? Disgustingly angelic. Patrick never did or said or gave a single thing to me when we were kids unless there was something in it for him. "If you're sure."

"Don't give it another thought." He grabs the door handle. "I'm just glad he's got a friend. It's hard in a new place."

Before he can close the door, Beth darts toward it. "Where are you going?"

"Feeding the animals," he says. "Or at least, monitoring the girls to make sure they do it right."

"I'll help." Beth beams.

"It's something about being close to good kids," Amanda stage whispers. "Mine are better when Abby's are around, too."

"They are?" Abby quickly suppresses her shock. "I mean, that's great."

Amanda frowns. "Well, they're not perfect, but there's less hair pulling and shrieking than there used to be."

"Sometimes I really regret that Aiden's all alone." The second the words leave my mouth, I wish I could yank them right back. Could I sound any more pathetic?

"You've got plenty of time," Abby says. "I'm sure that even with an age gap, Aiden would love a little brother or sister."

"Sure," I say. "Maybe after they let his dad out of jail, I can make one more before divorcing him."

Even Steve's jaw drops, and he must have heard the story around town. It's like my brain has hit the pause button and my normal filter is just broken.

"I'm sorry. I guess you probably haven't heard, and that's not the best way for me to tell new people." I shrug. "My husband's in jail right now, facing felony charges for embezzlement."

4

AMANDA

Every time I think I know someone, wham. Some new piece of information comes out and I realize that I know nothing at all.

"Aunt Mandy," Izzy says.

"Yes?" I squint at the recipe. It went fuzzy while I was busy thinking.

"Um." Izzy scratches her nose. "You just added a fifth cup of flour."

"What does that mean?" I glance from Izzy to the recipe book and back again.

"Well, the recipe said to add four, and now we have five."

Thanks to the incessant spinning of the old, reliable Kitchen Aid mixer, it's too late to try and scoop it back out. Now our beautifully smooth cookie dough is clumpy and powdery. "What do we do?"

"No big deal," Izzy says. "Trust me. I've made all the mistakes in the book."

I glance down at the book with awe. "There are mistakes in here? That's brilliant. Where is that? And what does it say we should do if we add too much flour?"

Izzy laughs. My twelve-year-old niece is actually laughing at me. "You're so funny. I swear, I didn't like you at first, but I totally didn't know how funny you were."

She didn't like me at first?

"Mom wasn't always this funny," Emery says. "Back in New York, she was grouchy a lot more."

"That makes sense," Izzy says.

And they're still talking, as if they don't even realize I'm standing *right* here. "But really, though, where's the section on mistakes?"

Izzy laughs much harder this time. "I added too much flour like right after I started baking. The good thing is, we can fix it. The bad thing is, the only way to do it is. . ." She swivels the metal lever and the bowl drops from the mixer. "Can you grab the other bowl?"

Emery snags it from the upper shelf, thanks to the use of a small wooden stool, and hands it to Izzy.

"We just make another batch real quick, and then add only three cups of flour. Then we combine them. The good news is—"

"We're about to have a *lot* of cookies." Emery beams.

We end up using all but about two cups of flour in the house, but at least all the cookies turn out perfectly. And no one notices that I totally *wasn't* kidding about the cookbook having a common mistakes section. Which is lucky, but it makes me wonder. Why isn't there a common mistakes section? Manuals for assembly have stuff like that. Software and hardware and electronics come with a troubleshooting section. Cookbooks totally should have a section about common baking errors, or at the very least, some recommendations at the bottom of each recipe.

"—at least, not until Mom gets home."

"What about Abby?" I ask.

Izzy blinks. "Oh, I was just saying we can't make

anything else until she gets home and we can let her know we're out of flour."

I'm an adult. Why do they have to tell Abby? "Do we need more cookies?"

"No, not cookies," Izzy says. "But mom always makes these amazing knot cinnamon rolls for our first day of school."

Of course she does. She probably squeezes that right in, between her daily yoga and knitting them a quilt. Are quilts knitted? If anyone can knit a quilt, it's freaking Abby. "Well, I can certainly drive to the store and buy more flour. Do we need anything else?"

"We should take Miss Venetia some cookies," Izzy says. "She's like the nicest person ever."

"Who?" How much of their conversation did I miss?

"You know, she runs the True Value."

"Wait, you know the grocery store lady?"

"Don't you? She's always giving us extra stuff, like spotty bananas, and meat that just expired." Izzy grabs a paper plate and starts stacking cookies on it. "She's so nice."

My stomach turns a bit at the thought of the meat she kindly gave us. Because it's rotten.

"Are you making that face about the meat thing?" Izzy asks.

I nod.

She rolls her eyes. "The meat's totally fine for days after the sell-by date, but they just can't sell it is all." Izzy has never looked or sounded more like her mom.

"The thing is, I've probably never said two words to her, so taking her cookies would be weird."

My niece finds this deeply disappointing, clearly. "Well, that can all change today. I'll introduce you."

But I don't want to be introduced. I want to go down

there in pajamas and slippers and not care whether I'm being judged. I want to be an anonymous shopper of whom no one takes note. I want to buy my guilty pleasure candy and my ice cream vats without anyone noticing who's bought it or speculating as to why. "Uh. Pass."

It must be exhausting being saintly.

"Come on! I've already put some on a plate." Sadly, she's really not kidding. Izzy, a miniature version of her mother, carries the plate of chocolate chip cookies, warm from the oven, for the lady who runs the only grocery/hardware store in town. We compile a surprisingly long list of grocery items on the drive over, and worst of all, it turns out that Izzy's right. Venetia is a wonderfully kind woman.

Who already knew my name.

"Amanda! Izzy! Emery!" She beams. "It's so nice to see you all."

So much for making anonymous trips in my bathrobe. "We made you some cookies," Izzy says. "Chocolate chip."

"Maybe I'll have a chance with these." She shakes her head. "My husband ate every last one of the snickerdoodles."

"That rascal," Izzy says.

She actually said rascal. Like we're living in the 1950s. "Golly gee, I'm just glad to hear he liked them," I say.

Emery lifts one eyebrow and glares at me like I've sprouted horns.

Izzy freezes, clearly wondering whether I'm actually evil enough to mock the world's kindest saleslady.

"Did you help make the snickerdoodles?" Venetia sounds annoyed, like she *knows* I'm mocking her.

What's wrong with me? I can't keep my internal dialogue to myself like a normal crazy person? "Um, no, but I'm a big moral supporter of all cookies, and also, all cookie sharing. In fact, I'm here today to replenish the supply cabinet so we can make more cookies."

Venetia points toward the far corner. "That's the baking aisle."

"Is the bakery behind it?" I ask. "Because that makes sense."

"We don't have a bakery here," she says, "but the bread aisle is just past it."

They don't have a bakery? How did I never notice that? "Does Brownings have a fresh bakery counter?" I ask.

She shakes her head. "No, folks pretty much make their own treats around here, or they eat the packaged kind." She points at the Chips Ahoy cookies on the endcap of the snack food aisle.

That's just depressing. "Why isn't there a bakery?"

She shrugs. "I guess a town this small don't really need a bakery all the time. I think over in Flaming Gorge there's a cupcake and event cakes business, but it's only open certain hours."

Just like lighting striking dry ground, an idea hits me. "I should open a bakery," I say. "I could start with cookies."

Emery laughs.

Izzy marches past me toward the baking aisle.

"I'm serious." I trot after them. "It was fun today, and your mom has amazing recipes. I can learn to make them really well, and then I can sell cookies." And then I'll have revenue that's not tied to keeping Lololime, or anyone else, happy. Well, except for the customers, I suppose.

"Uh, sure." Izzy may as well pat me on the head and offer me a dog biscuit. "That sounds like a great idea."

Just for that, I drag the girls back home, load up two

more plates of cookies, and drive all the way back to Brownings. "Now, we're going inside, and we're going to take them a plate of cookies to sample."

"For what?" Emery asks. "You were just asking if the recipe book had a section for mistakes." She doesn't even bother trying to suppress her laughter.

"Go ahead and laugh." I'm not going to admit that it stings. "I can make and sell cookies, and I think this town actually needs them."

"All four hundred people who live here," Emery says.

"Four hundred and eight, now," Izzy says.

"Donna and her son are new too," Emery says. "Four hundred and ten."

They are still laughing.

"People drive through too," I say. "There are three hotels in town, for heaven's sake. Especially during the summer, Flaming Gorge is a decent draw."

Izzy and Emery exchange a look.

"Just get out of the car."

"Is it professional to take your daughter with you on business calls?" Emery's tone is kind of snotty, but her words are actually fairly true.

"Get back in the car."

They don't argue, which is nice. I really shouldn't haul them in, if I want to talk business, but I feel practically naked, marching into Brownings with nothing but a paper plate of cookies in my hand. And now that I'm inside, alone, holding a plate in a place that probably already serves cookies, everyone in the room swivels to face me. I've been here a few times now, and I've never bothered to meet anyone who works here, much less learn their names. Maybe I should have brought the girls. Izzy probably already knows everyone's shoe sizes.

"Amanda?" A woman with red hair streaked with grey

walks toward me. "Amanda Brooks, right? Paul's wife?" She grimaces. "Widow. Sorry."

I nod. "That's me. Have we met?"

She shakes her head. "We haven't, but your husband was something of a holy terror when he came to visit for the summer, and your oldest girl looks just like him."

Maren really does. "Well, you're absolutely right. I am Amanda Brooks, and Maren does resemble her father heavily. I'm sorry he was such a disaster, but I promise to keep my kids on their best behavior."

"Nonsense is practically expected when boys come visit without their parents."

"I'm sorry, but I'm not sure I caught your name."

The redheaded woman holds out her hand. It's wiry and her fingers are quite long, with short, clean nails. "Greta. Greta Davis. My sister Linda and I own Brownings."

"It's a pleasure to meet you, Greta. I know you're a hard-working woman, and your sister too, I'm sure, so I won't keep you. Venetia over at True Value mentioned to me that there's not a bakery in town. I know you offer desserts already, but I thought you might be interested in supporting a brand new local business, Double or Nothing Cookies."

"Double or Nothing?" Her eyebrows rise.

"The first time I made these cookies." I hand her the plate. "I added too much flour, and had to double the batch to keep from ruining them." I don't mention that it was these actual cookies.

She smiles. "That's a cute story. I'd love to give them a try."

I expect her to wait until I've left, but instead she snags a cookie from under the Saran-Wrap and takes a bite right in front of me.

"These are amazing." Her smile broadens. "If we can

work something out on pricing, I'd be interested. How many varieties of cookie do you offer?"

"It's a brand new business," I say. "I'll need a little more time to put together an ordering menu and a delivery timetable."

"That sounds fine," Greta says. "I'd be very interested in samples of each kind, and I'd love samples of how they'll be served too. What type of packaging are you thinking? What's the anticipated shelf life? I'm assuming they're preservative free."

My head's spinning about now, and I can barely feel my feet. I had no idea that these people in this tiny little town would be such savvy businesswomen. "Right. Of course. I have a few more places to visit, and then I'll start working on the details. I'll try and bring you a proposal late this week or early the next."

"A proposal?" She chuckles. "A simple pricing sheet, a few samples, and a delivery calendar would be more than enough."

"Right, that's what I meant."

"Perfect." She leans a little closer. "Peanut butter's my favorite."

"Noted," I say.

I'm almost back to the door, and I haven't tripped over my own feet yet, when I hear my name being called again. "Amanda?" This time, it's a man. "Is that what she said?"

I turn around a little too fast and bump the door-frame. A strong hand shoots out and grabs my shoulder, righting me fully.

Large hands. A light grey, button-down shirt. Black slacks. And shiny, black cowboy boots. I drag my eyes up to his face, finally. I'm disappointed when he's not unbearably beautiful, and his eyes aren't as green as grass.

That shouldn't be my barometer. I know that.

But somehow, it is now. He's not Eddy, so even though he has a craggy, ruggedly handsome face, with five o'clock shadow to spare, my heart barely accelerates. In New York, this man would have a dozen women pawing him already, especially if he wasn't half-broke. Judging by his designer boots, he's not even close to broke.

"I'm Derek Bills. It's nice to meet you."

"Uh, well, normally I'd offer my name, but you seem to already have made note of it."

"Amanda is a nice name, but pardon my brash nature, it's not nearly striking enough for a woman with your looks."

Oh, no. Is he kidding? That's his opening line? "Uh. Thanks." Plus, did he just insult my name?

"I went too far. Sometimes I have trouble knowing how much of what I'm thinking I should share." He sighs, and it's kind of adorable. "Look, I'm only in town for a few weeks, at least, for now, but I'd love to take you to dinner."

"This is the one dinner spot in town," I say, "and it looks like you've just had lunch here."

"I'll be bouncing back and forth between here and Flaming Gorge," he says. "I'd be happy to take you up there. I hear the resort has a reasonably nice restaurant."

"I haven't tried it yet," I admit. "But tonight's not great. My kids both start school tomorrow morning, and two of them are waiting in the car right now." One isn't mine, but that's probably not critical information at the moment.

"Tomorrow then? Or the next day? It's not like I have a lot of social events on my calendar."

"Why are you here?" I ask. "Unless it's top secret information?" I lift both eyebrows. If he says he's with the secret service or something, I'm going to push past him and never look back.

"I'm a talent scout," he says.

"Excuse me?"

"I'm looking for models, and I think you'd be wonderful."

Okay, that was actually worse. I can't keep from muttering as I shove past him. "You have got to be kidding me."

He laughs. "I'm totally kidding. Geez." He jogs behind me, catching me just outside the door. "I'm the vice president in charge of the processing and supply for Highborn Leather. We supply a half dozen designer brands with their leather goods. We also partner with Jonquil meats, the leading supplier of beef to Michelin three-star restaurants in America."

Now that I might believe.

"I'm looking into the possibility of putting in a processing plant out here. I'm assembling a report on three different locations, and we'll select the most cost-effective one that meets all our requirements."

"And if you chose this area?" I lift one eyebrow.

"We'd need at least two hundred employees to run our leather processing plant. We'd need another hundred and fifty at least for the butchering and meat processing. They'd all need to locate housing, and the school system and other infrastructure would need to be sufficient to support those needs in the short run, allowing room for expansion. Our biggest concern here is shipping costs and reliability during winter months."

And I thought my head was spinning about calculating business costs to sell cookies. "Right. Well, it sounds like you have things under control."

"You're selling cookies?"

"Actually, I'm a social media influencer," I say. "But I've always thought about starting a little business on the side."

"An entrepreneur. Now I'm even more impressed. Do you mind sharing your social media handle?"

"Champagne for Less," I say. "But I really do need to get going."

He puts one hand over his heart. "So is that a no to dinner?" His eyes plead with me silently.

"How about this?" I ask. "I'll give you my number, and you can try to convince me via text to grab some coffee."

"I'll take your offer, and raise you a phone call." His grin is sly and full of confidence. "I do my best work in person, but I'm not bad on the phone either."

"What kind of work are you talking about?" Another masculine voice asks from the street.

I was so caught up in my conversation with Mr. Leather that I didn't even notice Eddy crossing the street. The second I turn his way, our eyes lock and my heart hammers in my chest.

"Eddy."

"Please tell me this isn't the boyfriend," Derek says, "because that will make my work a lot harder."

Eddy glowers at him. "What's your work? Are you a gigolo or something?"

A muscle works in Derek's jaw. "This guy is rude. Is that how I can expect everyone out here to behave?"

"No, just the local veterinarian," Eddy says. "Working with animals all the time helps me spot them among the human population."

Surprisingly, Derek laughs. "Touché."

Eddy lifts one eyebrow. "I'm not sure you used that word right."

Derek inhales slowly and then exhales. "Amanda, I think it's time for me to head over to Flaming Gorge. Why don't you give me your number, and I'll go."

I hold out my hand for his phone, and he hands it

over. It takes me about ten seconds to save my number, but the tension in that ten seconds is terrible. Eddy hasn't moved an inch, like he's worried if he does, Derek will pounce or something.

"Thanks." Derek smiles. "I'll definitely be calling. And if you need anyone to bounce ideas off of for that business plan, I'm your guy." He's good looking, and he's clearly got his life together, but I'm relieved when he finally walks to his shiny black BMW and opens the door.

Eddy swallows, the muscles in his throat working soundlessly while Mr. Bills turns his car on and pulls out of the parking lot.

"So."

"Business plan?" His voice is all forced cheerfulness. "What business plan?"

"Aunt Mandy's making cookies!" Izzy's voice floats toward us from four cars down. I forgot they had the windows rolled down and are likely soaking up every word like tiny sponges. Ah, the joys of kids.

"Cookies?"

"Want some?" Emery opens the door and carries the other plate over.

"I never turn down cookies," Eddy says.

I almost object—they were meant for the Gorge, after all. But it became clear to me in Brownings that I have a little more work to do before I'm ready to solicit customers. "I had a lot of fun making them today with the girls, and I've been trying to come up with a business plan." I shrug. "Paul always said the best businesses are the ones where the person noticed a need and filled it, as opposed to developing a product and trying to find a market for it."

"I think it's a great idea," Eddy says. "Tell me how I can help."

I really don't know where to begin, but if this business takes off and I really don't need social media to pay all my bills, Eddy's not off the table anymore. If I'm being honest with myself, that's my true motivation.

❧ 5 ❧

ABIGAIL

Novelists sell books. Shopkeepers sell their wares. Amanda sells her tips and thoughts and lifestyle. Restaurateurs sell food, or if it's a fancy enough place, an experience.

As a lawyer, my only valuable commodity is my time. I'm forced to keep track of it down to a tenth of an hour. Sometimes it feels like I live my life in six-minute increments.

Review and analyze case law regarding unpaid claims. 1.5

That's an hour and a half I'll never see again.

Draft correspondence regarding same. 0.2

Twelve minutes gone.

Research the impact of violations of the FTCA on Unisafe. 2.9

Two hours and fifty-four minutes vaporized.

And on and on and on.

Most of those projects have been snatched, in the past few months, in between horseback rides, work in the barn or on Forestry Service land, and the cooking of dinner. I squeeze in a contract review between bathing

Gabe, and reading him stories, and talking to Ethan about future plans. I email my boss in between mediating fights among children and their cousins, teaching Izzy to bake, and mopping the never-ending wood floors.

A mother's work isn't ever quite done. Neither is a lawyer's, it seems.

It's probably an occupational hazard, but I spent most of the summer counting down days until school would resume. In many ways, summer's the most exhausting time of the entire year. I'm expected to get all my work done, and yet I want to spend time with my beautiful children. I want to play games. I want to cook and bake and talk and sing and dance.

But the more I do those things, the further I fall behind, and the less I can do them the next day, week, and month. With all the demands on my time, I never seem to find a moment to do anything that *I* want to do. I watch no television. I read no books. I barely have time to brush my teeth. I can't even think about how horrifying my toenails must look.

In light of that, the first day of school should be delightful. I'll finally be able to enjoy a day of silence, a day of uninterrupted work time, and maybe, if I'm willing to drive all the way to Green River, a pedicure. The start of school also marks the beginning of a more organized and predictable schedule, which allows the control freak inside of me to breathe a sigh of relief.

Yet, it's also sad.

Another year has come and gone. Another summer of unplotted and unmarked time that will never return. When my children were babies, I counted the minutes in a different way, each one an agonizing barrage of diapers, bottles, crying, naps, feeding, and washing, and starting all over again. The idea of one of them going to school was thrilling. The thought of them leaving for college?

Nirvana! I might have a home to myself. I could take a bath or go to the bathroom without someone interrupting to ask where the blocks had been put, or to complain that a sibling had bitten them on the calf.

Now that Ethan could literally leave my home at any moment, now that Izzy draws nearer to departing with every breath, it saddens me in a way I can't easily express. My children, my darling little fuzzy-headed, awkward chicks, will fly away soon.

Sometimes I wonder whether the bulk of my fear comes from Nate's death.

After all, when I envisioned this stage before, the chicks spreading their wings and flying away, I wasn't sitting in this nest by myself. I had a companion, a best friend.

A lover.

Now when they leave, I'll be utterly and completely alone.

Once I see the kids off for the day, and Ethan and Jeff and Kevin leave to harvest another hayfield, I set to work. It's the best way to distract myself.

I finish my memorandum, two letters, and petition in record time, and then I stare at the screen. When I burst into tears for no reason, I decide it's time for a new distraction, something I haven't had time for in months.

"Abby?" Amanda's voice is soft, almost like she's hoping I won't answer. "You closed the door. Are you. . .taking a nap?"

I laugh out loud.

It's been *years* since I've taken a nap. I swing the door open, and she jumps back a step. "Oh."

"I'm going for a run. Want to come with me?"

She shakes her head slowly.

"I've seen you go running before." I look her up and

down. "You're in great shape. Did you already work out today?"

"You couldn't pay me to go running with you."

"That's rude." My hand goes to my hip without thinking. "Why ever not?"

"You've seen me go for a *jog*. There's a big difference between what you do, and what I do."

"How would you know? I haven't been out all summer. I'll be lucky to make it five miles."

She starts laughing. "Lucky to make it five miles?" She's still laughing. "I don't think I've ever gone five miles."

I blink.

"I jog a mile. Maybe two. If I've had a Redbull or something, I might walk one more for a total of three. That's a big day for me."

"Oh."

"I love you Abby, I really do, but if you want me to keep loving you, don't try to convince me to work out with you. 'Kay?"

At least she's not afraid to tell me what she's thinking. I'm not sure that was always the case. "See you in a bit."

"Five miles?" She shakes her head. "Don't drop dead out there. Or at least take your phone so you can call me when you do."

"How could I call you if I was dead?" The thought makes me laugh in a way only another widow would possibly understand.

She's grinning in a we're-so-broken-no-one-else-could-ever-understand-us kind of way when I leave. The sun's shining awfully bright when I reach the main drag, which is a small country road with an almost imperceptible shoulder. In Houston this would barely qualify as a road, but here, it's the main thoroughfare.

Do I turn left and go past Amanda Saddler's and up

into the canyon? It's the more scenic route. It's the greater elevation, and consequently, it'll do my thighs the most good. Or do I turn right and head toward town? There's not a lot to see that direction. The road's mostly flat, almost straight, and trees line the majority of it.

But Steve's that direction.

Not that he's likely to be home.

I wonder if he'd talk to me, even if he was. I avoided him last night like a chicken running from a circling hawk. Every time he came close, I'd shove something in between us. A salad bowl. A bag of chips. A small child.

As if there was ever any real question of what I'd do, I hang a right.

The first mile is always the worst.

And this isn't a normal first mile of a run. It's my first mile since June. It's my first mile in Utah, ever. It's my first mile since my kids all left the house and went back to being tiny adults. It's my first mile in a new home, a home where there's no Nate. No future for *us*.

But in the middle of that first mile, my exhaustion kicks in, and the pavement beneath me levels out and I *breathe* and I let go of all of it.

Okay, maybe not all of it. I am awfully out of shape. I could really use some reason to stop and take a little break.

"Just my luck. Not a single street light in all of Daggett County," I wheeze.

My armpits are sweaty. My brow is sweaty. I've sweated clear through my sports bra, and my shirt, and now I wish I'd worn something a little less bulky, like my integrated sports bra tank top. Of course, when a certain little white farmhouse comes into view, I get a second wind.

I could race the Flash himself.

I could show Hermes how to do his job.

Now that I'm almost forty, that second wind lasts approximately eleven seconds. Ah, well. It was nice while it lasted. Anticlimactically, Steve doesn't appear to be home. He's not mowing the lawn without a shirt on, like I've relived in my mind a dozen times. He's not grilling burgers in his swimsuit, a sight I've never actually seen. He's not even sitting on the porch swing fully clothed, drinking an ice-cold beer.

It's then that I finally admit to myself that I had my hopes up. I may be hiding under counters in random stores. I may be dodging him and blocking him with anything I can find when he comes looking for me, but that's all for show. It's posturing. Apparently I can miss Nate, and worry about my future, and get hung up on Steve all at the same time.

Humans are interesting creatures.

Steve's house is about three miles from mine.

Apparently my desperate hope that he'd be home and happen to see me jogging past in this stupidly cute outfit I picked with Amanda's help from her dumb old sporting goods company fueled me for the first three miles. But now that I've passed his house and nothing has happened, it begins to feel like torture. I'm suddenly acutely aware that every single step I take is a step I'll need to retrace to get home.

Unless I have the guts to call Amanda.

But she'd figure out from where I am what I was hoping for when I jogged this far. She'll laugh, or at least, her eyes will sparkle. And she won't let it go any time soon, either.

I've passed two and a half houses, with admittedly large yards, when I turn around and head back. This time, my Flash-esque energy is sadly lacking. In fact, if I'm being honest with myself, I might even call what I'm doing right now *hobbling*. How pathetic. Not even four miles, and I'm winded, footsore, and zapped of all energy. Apparently at this age, I can't skip running for extended periods of time and just pick it right back up. That thought just disheartens me more.

"Abby?"

My heart pulls a Flash and flies right out of my body and down the road, leaving me gasping.

"Are you alright? You look a little tired." Steve's actually standing near his mailbox, a handful of letters in his hand.

"Me?" I force a smile. "I'm fine. I was just distracted thinking about a case." Thank you brain, you've never failed me. You're my greatest blessing, as always. As an extra bonus, my body manages to rummage around and find a third wind, and I feel energized and ready to show him I'm not a complete disaster.

"Oh. Well, I was going to offer you some soda or something. But if you're in the zone, I won't disrupt."

"Yeah," I say. "I'm completely fine." Of course, my toe chooses that exact moment to find a half-buried rock, and I practically face plant into the gravel that makes up the boundary between the asphalt and Steve's front yard.

He's at my side a moment later, which I suppose is the next best thing to catching me. "I'm so sorry. In movies, the guy always catches the girl. If you could figure out how to fall a little closer to where I'm standing next time, I promise to do it right." He offers me his hand with a smile on his face.

"In movies, the klutzy female's usually a teenager." I groan as he pulls me to my feet. "Her knees don't creak and her back doesn't ache every morning."

His lips twitch. "Even so, try to follow the script."

"What does the script say I'm supposed to do next?"

He makes a hmm sound. "Let's see. It says you should

let me take you out on a date now that you've traveled across the country to be within easy driving distance."

"What exactly would a date here in scenic Daggett County entail?"

"Oh, there are plenty of options. Let me paint you a picture." Steve steps back a few steps and leans on his mailbox. "There's hiking." He holds up a finger. "There's a very nice shooting range that the county commissioners actually created a committee to monitor." He holds up another finger.

"That does sound promising."

He grins. "I wouldn't have taken you for a shooting gal. Good to know."

I scrunch my nose. "This shooting doesn't involve the death of small or furry critters, right?"

"Large ones are fine, but small ones aren't?"

"I'm not sure my aim would be good enough for the cute ones," I say.

"Interesting."

I hobble closer and shove his shoulder. "I'm kidding. I won't shoot anything other than a paper target, obviously."

"I figured." He nods his head. "Well, the hike and the range, and of course there's dinner, and if you want, a movie at either my place or yours."

My eyebrows shoot up. "At your place?"

He shrugs. "Can't fault a guy for dreaming big." The dimple is too much. I need to figure out something that can counteract it. Something powerful.

"Are those all of my options?"

"Well, if you're the one dreaming big, there's a pretty big deal coming up." He leans closer and drops his voice. "But I hear that the guy would have to ask you. We're kind of traditional like that out here."

"Is it prom?" I can't help my snark.

"Close." He likes to draw things out, clearly. "It's the annual Labor Day Parade and Daggett Daze Games. They run all Saturday, and there's a boat lights parade and fireworks at the end."

"I'm sure my kids won't mind sitting that out," I say. "If I tell them I'm going to go on a date instead."

He laughs. "I'd be happy to go as your town-appointed escort, including your children on all activities, of course. I think all the new people get assigned one."

"Not very romantic," I say.

"Ah, but the romantic part's saved for Sunday night." He wiggles his eyebrows. "The Flaming Gorge Yacht Club hosts a dance, and I happen to be a member."

"Aren't you fancy?"

"I think you'll find that there's only one horse doc around here."

"Only one?"

"And I'm him," he says. "In case that wasn't clear."

"Well."

"So is that a yes? Do people in Houston say 'well' when they mean yes?"

I laugh.

He pulls out his phone.

"What are you doing?"

"I'm checking Amazon for a Texan to English dictionary. Clearly we're having a language problem here. I can't tell what you're saying, even though I'm sure you're doing your best to accept my kind offer."

"Fine."

"That one I know." He grins. "And I would totally hug you right now, but don't take this the wrong way." He grimaces. "You're kind of sweaty."

"Whoa, so you're one of those guys."

He frowns. "What does that mean?"

"Ah," I say. "I bet it's the doctor thing. You're a germaphobe, aren't you?

He rockets off the mailbox and closes the space between us. "I'm not afraid of a little sweat." His arms wrap around my waist and yank me closer, until his face is hovering just over mine. "Especially not yours."

Is he going to kiss me? My heart flutters. My fingers tremble. My breathing's shallow.

He releases me. "You probably ought to head back."

What?

"Weren't you in the middle of a run?"

I nod, numbly.

"So far, Amanda has driven past twice. I think she's worried you won't be able to make it back home, but if that's not it, then she's probably going to put photos of us up on her social media." He eyes my pants. "Are those a fancy brand, by chance?"

She wouldn't dare.

"If she's worried, it's sweet. I do always have a handful of moms that show up the first week of school with work-out-related injuries. Actually, I'd be willing to do a full body exam right now, if you think you need one."

My cheeks heat.

But not in a good way. I haven't pulled my hamstring, but now that I've been stopped for a bit, I feel stiff and a little shaky.

This time, when Amanda drives past, she stops the car and rolls down the window. "Are you doing alright? Need a ride?"

I really, really hate to admit it, but. . . "Actually, a ride sounds good."

Steve's still staring with a knowing smile on his face when Amanda's car starts to move.

"Please tell me you didn't snap any photos of me for your social media," I say. "That is *so* not why I bought these clothes."

6

DONNA

When Beth was born, I was the world's best aunt.

I was a senior in high school, and I had the time and the energy to babysit, to play, and even to help with the miserable parts of having a baby. I changed diapers, I burped and fed, and I washed clothes.

Even after I left for Stanford, I spent all my breaks with her. I was blessed to watch her learn and grow and develop from a baby to a toddler, and from a toddler to a young child. That's about the time things went south for me.

But when I had a child of my own? That's when I became a lousy aunt.

It's awfully hard to be a good mother and a stellar aunt. You just don't have the bandwidth to ace both things. And lately, I've barely had the mental energy to be a moderately competent mother. I don't even want to think about the time I haven't spent on her.

So it's hardly Beth's fault that she and I aren't close. It's mine.

"Did you have fun?" We're less than a block from

home, and even on the brief ride between the old Brooks place and ours, Aiden fell asleep.

Beth doesn't turn to look at me. She keeps her nose pressed to the glass of the passenger side door. "It was fine."

"What did you think about Maren?"

"She's snobby."

"Izzy?"

"She acts even younger than she is."

"So none of the Brooks children met with your approval?" And now I sound like a matron from a Jane Austen novel. Sheesh.

"My approval?" She turns to face me now that the car has stopped. "Uh. Sure."

"Well, I won't be likely to be invited over again, but even if I am, I promise not to drag you along."

She frowns. "I mean, I'd go over again."

I do not understand teenagers. They're like aliens dressed as humans.

"Wait. Did you say we wouldn't be likely to be invited over again?" She scowls. "Why not? It looked like Aiden loved that cute little guy. What was his name? Abe?"

"Aiden and Gabe got along," I say. "It's just a hunch, that's all."

"Nothing in this family is a hunch." Beth squeezes my armrest harder than she should. "Don't lie."

"Look, I didn't mean anything. It's just that people in this town aren't always welcoming to outsiders and—"

"That's because there aren't any outsiders." She growls. "When's the last time someone new moved here?"

"Aiden and I—"

"Someone who didn't grow up here," she says. "You know what I mean. Manila's usually the land that time forgot."

She's not exactly wrong there. "Look, I've got to get Aiden in bed, and it's past time for you to be—"

"It's nine-forty-one on a Saturday night." She snorts. "I'm seventeen, not seven."

Duh. "Well, the Aiden stuff is still true."

"Whatever. You're as bad as Dad."

That one stings. No one's quite as bad as Patrick. "Look, that ranch has been in the Brooks family for a long time," I finally say.

"Okay. What does that have to do with us?"

"When Jed died, he left the ranch to them," I say.

"I know."

"Except, he had a stipulation, probably because they're outsiders. He said that it had to be worked by them for a year before they could inherit it."

"Right, Ethan mentioned it." Her face flushes when she says his name. The fact that I can see it, even in this low light, means she must really be. . . Whoa. Does Beth like Ethan? I mean, I know that when you're a teenage girl, crushes are natural and extremely common, but I didn't even consider it. It explains her interest in going back, and her feigned disinterest in everyone and everything else.

"Well, anyway, I'm not sure they'll really want to hang out with us, since they're not from here."

"Nice try," she says. "What aren't you telling me?"

She's too smart for her own good. "As part of my divorce settlement, I'll be coming into quite a bit of money, but that money is coming from the sale of real estate, and I'll have to buy more real estate with it as part of the terms of the deal. It's called a 1031 exchange."

"I still don't get—"

"I'd like to stay here, close to family, and the obvious place for me to buy is—"

"Jedediah Brooks' ranch." Beth's tone is flat. "Which means, they'd need to not keep it."

It's worse than that, but I don't elaborate.

"You want them to sell to you?" Beth frowns. "But Ethan wants to stay. He wants to keep the ranch."

"Something like that."

"I hate this crap." She folds her arms. "You're as bad as Dad. You took me there, knowing you wanted to kick them out." She hops out of the car and races up the drive-way, glancing back with a look of total disgust.

What she doesn't even know is that the Brooks family won't get the money. They wouldn't even have the ability to sell until one year after they came out initially, which would be next June. My clock starts ticking October 1, and I have six months to complete every part of the sale. I couldn't wait until June if I wanted to. If I don't complete the 1031 exchange in time, the Windsors get my entire divorce settlement back.

I'm pulling past the main house and moving toward the old farmhouse when I notice movement behind me. Patrick's waving. I grit my teeth and consider pretending I didn't see him. It's not like he'd risk coming into the house and having to deal with Dad himself.

But boy would I get an earful tomorrow morning.

I don't want to, but I stop and climb out. The only thing worse than this discussion I'm about to have with my older brother would be if he woke up Aiden and I had to deal with a crying kid *and* this conversation.

"How'd it go?"

I should've cancelled. When you're doing a bad thing, the last thing you should do is get to know the people you're doing the bad thing *to*. "They're nice people." I cross my arms.

"Who cares?" Patrick lifts one eyebrow.

"They're not ranchers," I say. "Is that what you want to hear?"

"I wanted you to find out whether they realized they'd already violated the terms of the will. I wanted you to find out if they have some kind of defense ready, some way they think they'll be able to hold onto the ranch even though they both left for more than the one-week vacation the will stipulates is acceptable."

"I think we should consider other options," I say. "The ranch idea was a nice one, but—"

"But what?" Patrick shakes his head. "The ranch is what I want. I don't want land down in the valley. I don't want land way out in Wyoming, either. This ranch is even contiguous across the back of each parcel, and—"

"Abigail Brooks is a lawyer, and not some slapdash lawyer who runs around throwing ridiculous claims at people and hoping for money. Amanda mentioned that she went to *Harvard* for law school, and *Princeton* for undergraduate."

"And you went to Stanford," Patrick says, "and look where that got you. She's probably just as incompetent."

I flinch, but hopefully he can't see it in the dark. "I'm just saying that maybe it's not as cut and dried—"

"You're still a softhearted baby, even now." He snorts. "You'd think that being left destitute by your husband and having a child to care for would have made you tougher." He leans closer. "Worry less about them and more about yourself."

Patrick used to pull beetles apart as a kid just to see what was inside. He shoved the small kids and laughed. He made me do his chores, and if I told Mom and Dad what he did, he'd destroy something valuable and tag it back on me. I learned at an early age to fear him. But in this instance, we're finally on the same team. I'm not sure whether that makes me happy or terribly, terribly

73

nervous. "I won't have the money until October first. I'm just saying, let's explore some options, let's see what other properties you might like. A stock yard, for instance. That might be—"

Patrick's lips are pursed. "I want that ranch."

I hate working with my brother. I *hate* it. But I don't need a large property of any kind. What I do need is cash, and every single dime in Mom and Dad's estate, as well as Dad's large life insurance policy, are all going to Patrick as part of the deal I made fifteen years ago. All I have to do to get my hands on most of it is use my divorce settlement money to buy this ranch, and then gift it to Patrick.

"We still have more than two months—"

"It's ironic that I didn't go to Stanford. I didn't go to college at all, but I would never have been moronic enough to sign an agreement in which my divorce settlement was the proceeds of a real estate deal, accepting all the burden of capital gains tax on an entirely depreciated apartment complex."

The Windsors are a little cash poor and real estate rich, so I didn't have any other options. Not with a spouse who was headed for jail, but I'm not about to explain that it's not really a divorce settlement. "All I'm saying is, give me a few weeks and listen to what I have to say. We can make a decision in the middle of September and still have plenty of—"

"Donna, stop." Patrick's enjoying this. "I spoke to a man named Leonard this afternoon. He was quite delighted to take my call," he says.

My stomach sinks. "Did you just call to make contact? Or—"

"His name is Leonard Nemoy, no joke. He swears that's the name on his birth certificate, only his last name is spelled with an 'e.' The quackpot practically begged me to send him a copy of the will in which Dad is named as one of the three men who will determine the fate of the ranch."

"But Dad—"

"Gave me his power of attorney," he says. "His daughter, after all, lived in California."

"Patrick, I know we agreed, but we—"

"The beauty of this is that *we* don't have to do a thing. The Institute of Research into Alien Life is the entity with standing to sue. That's what it's called, apparently, standing. Funny word, right? Anyway, they're practically chomping at the bit. Mr. Nemoy was quick to see how well our interests aligned. He'll even put an agreed sale price that's a little below market in writing, including all the equipment and both farmhouses, if I promise to do everything in my power to see that justice is done per the terms of the will."

In other words, my brother just cut another shady deal, this one behind my back. I should have known he'd do it. He'll refuse to allow this poor family to obtain their family ranch, so it will go to this alien group, who will probably end up selling it far below market rate. To me. The whole thing makes me a little ill.

"Mom?" Aiden's sitting up in the backseat now, no longer slumped sideways. "Where are we?"

And that's the reason why, instead of arguing with him, instead of trying to help those poor widows, I'm going to do nothing and hide behind my terrible brother.

For once, his beetle slaughter is going to help me, and I refuse to feel bad about it.

7

AMANDA

The ebb and flow of my life is a very funny thing. When I was a kid, it felt like I spent all my time waiting around for something to happen. Road trips were the worst of all. Sometimes my mom would say it was a three-hour trip to get somewhere, but I swear it felt like a ten-hour trip. I still recall one time where I desperately needed to go pee. It felt like I was dancing around in the back seat of the car for at least an hour, and my mom just kept saying we were less than five minutes from a bathroom.

Those five minutes stretched to what felt like five hours.

But when I was playing outside, riding my bike and kicking a ball with friends, three hours would pass in a snap. When my mom got home, my homework wasn't done, and I was completely grubby from all the fun.

As an adult, I'm more aware of how to measure and balance my time. After all, we have more guideposts to make things feel somewhat normal, even when boredom stretches and delightful experiences seem to zoom past. But no matter how I try to prevent it, my life is still punctuated by moments of absolute frenzy that never seem to smooth out, no matter how much I try.

It's probably my fault, if I'm being honest. I'm a chronic snooze button smasher.

Abigail, on the other hand, never hits snooze. When I finally drag myself out of bed and shuffle into the family room, Abby's already decked out in a workout outfit, her hair in a perfect ponytail, her pants matching the accents of her top immaculately.

Ethan's already gone, presumably mowing yet another gosh darn field. How they don't yet have enough hay for the winter, I may never understand. It feels like all he does is cut grass. Abby's other kids already have their hair done—braids for Whitney, a miniature version of Abby's perky ponytail for Izzy, and a precious little swoop of spiky hair styled carefully on the front of Gabe's head. They're all eating with their backpacks lined up against the wall in a neat line. They're all wearing shoes, and they look utterly serene.

My two girls, meanwhile, are racing around in a state of barely contained panic, just like their mother.

Emery's silently sobbing where she's crouched by the sofa. "I can only find one shoe."

"You have dozens of shoes," I snap. "Pick another pair."

She brandishes three shoes at me, and I open my mouth to tell her to just put them on already, when I realize she's holding three different shoes. One pink moccasin, one yellow Converse sneaker, and a single Nike Air. "Then keep looking. Geez. You aren't going to find anything while crouched on the floor like that."

"Mom." Maren's wringing her hands, and her face is bright red. "I have a zit, and *someone* lost my concealer."

I'd like to roll my eyes and tell her to deal with it. Zits

aren't the end of the world. But for a teenage girl in an unfamiliar school, they kind of are. "Just use mine."

"Are you kidding?" She clenches her fists at her side. "I don't have concealer, Mom. It's yours that's missing."

For the love.

Before I can even yell at Maren for losing my concealer or Emery for being a slob—they're way too old to be this scattered—Abby floats out in front of them. She tosses a tube to Maren, who snags it out of the air and races to the bathroom. Then she points in the corner, next to the tall lamp. "Emery, check over there."

My darling baby jogs across the room and clutches the carelessly discarded Converse sneaker to her chest like it's her long lost child. "Thank you, thank you, thank you."

Abby has to save the day two more times, but we finally manage to get the kids' stuff all pulled together just in time to make the bus.

Day three of my plan to become just like Abby? A complete and total failure.

Once everyone's gone, Abby disappears into her room to work, and I'm left alone out here with absolutely nothing to do. Well, not *nothing*, nothing. I pop online and check prices of ingredients for four different cookie recipes in Abby's cookbook. I add them up, and calculate a rough cost per batch.

Only then do I realize I should probably *make* the cookies and find out how many cookies each recipe makes, or there's no way to know my cost per cookie. Blerg. I pull up Netflix and start flipping through to find a show to watch in the background while I bake all these cookies. Only, once the show starts, I get so caught up that I forget about the cookies.

Then it gets a little boring and. . .I fall asleep.

A loud banging on the front door wakes me up just in

time for Abby to emerge from her room. "Is someone here?"

Uh, duh. That's what knocking on the door means.

"Were you sleeping?" She glances pointedly down at my chin.

I wipe my hand across it and. . .there's drool. I cannot catch a break today. The worst part about sharing a home with someone, especially someone like Abby, is that she's always there, silently making me look like a loser. I do what anyone would do, and make up a lie. "I didn't sleep great last night—"

The banging starts up again. "Abby?"

Oh good, it's for her.

"Jeff?" She jogs across the room and yanks the door open. "Is everything okay?"

He nods. "Fine, totally fine. But Kevin called. He's out with Ethan, or he'd be here instead. You guys planned out the place for the bathroom and the rough layout of the rest yesterday. He said if you're totally positive about it, one of his friends can come do the preliminary framing. He's on a huge job so Kev thought it would be weeks before he could do it, but he got the rest of this week off."

She swings the door wide open. "Fantastic. What do you need from me?"

"Not much. You and Kevin made the plans, and he has those. He just needs to sketch out the dimensions and then start framing it out. Plus, bonus, the framer's ex is dating an electrician, and she owes my buddy a bunch of child support, so her boyfriend agreed to come tomorrow and start the preliminary electrical. We'll just pay my buddy for both, apparently."

"Oh." Abby's eyebrows draw together, like small-town life is mostly unintelligible to her. "Alright."

"Don't worry—Kevin will be by later to make sure things are all in the right places."

"Awesome." Abby half turns and beams at me.

It *is* exciting. We were bummed to hear that, with the order in which things have to be done, it would be quite some time before we'd have any significant progress made.

Less than ten minutes later, the framer shows up. I'm in the garage with Abby to show him the wall we need to excavate and the new area we need framed, when my phone rings.

It's Heather, my supervisor at Lololime, the client who pays all my bills. "Hello?" I point at my phone and mouth 'Heather' to Abby. She waves me off.

"Amanda?" She always says that like there might be a frat boy answering my phone, or like I might be so hungover I can't recall my own name. I suppose in her world, that just might be the case.

"Yes, Heather, it's me, Amanda Brooks."

"Great. And you're not, like, milking a goat, or anything?"

"We don't milk our goats," I say. "No need to worry."

"A cow, then?"

"I don't milk anything."

"Great. Good. I imagine that with school starting, things have been hectic."

"They have, yes, but now the kids are in school, and I can breathe again."

"Wonderful."

"Yes, I think so. Breathing is somewhat critical."

"Uh-huh." She does not, nor has she ever, really gotten my sense of humor. Which is ironic, considering she's the one who pushed for them to bring my account under their umbrella.

I'm guessing I have ten or fifteen minutes until saws

and hammers start flying. "Heather, what can I do for you?"

"I forget how direct you are sometimes." She giggles. "Your East coast is showing."

If I was a little braver, I'd tell her that with that giggle, her Valley Girl was showing, but I don't have that kind of confidence. "Are you calling because I'm late on my post this week?"

This time, her laugh is nervous. "I mean, sure, yes, encouragement for my team is always something I care about. But I figured I'd take this chance to remind you how much your viewers love little peeks into your social life."

She means I haven't posted a Cowboy photo in a very long time. The comments on my last few posts became borderline icky, to be honest. It feels a little like, by sharing photos of a hot cowboy, I gave food to a Mogwai after midnight. My fans are all turning into gremlins, hungry for more, and they're never quite satisfied. "But you said you don't want photos of Eddy."

She clears her throat. "It's true that we don't feel Mr. Dutton is a suitable—"

"Dr. Dutton," I say. "He's a vet. Remember?"

"Sure. We don't feel *Doctor* Dutton is someone who would reflect well on our brand. But surely that area is just rife with handsome cowboys, no?"

Rife? Does she have one of those word-of-the-day calendars or something? "Uh, well, I did meet a new guy over the weekend." I'm not sure he could ride a horse, but he did have cowboy boots on, and his job is connected to cattle.

"Wonderful! Just wonderful!" She's tapping something —I wonder what it is. It could be fake nails on a table. Or a pen against the phone?

"He called me twice since Saturday. I couldn't call him back right away—"

"Obviously, but now it's Wednesday." Clearly, she does have a calendar. I should probably get one—maybe a word-of-the-day one. Ha.

"I'll shoot him a text and have something up by Friday. Would that work?"

"Tomorrow would be better. We have a staff meeting to review metrics on Friday. I'd love to be able to present how your clicks spiked when you posted about the new guy."

I suppress my groan. "Sure thing, boss."

She's so young, she doesn't even realize I'm being sarcastic. "Wonderful. Just wonderful."

"Did you need anything else?"

As if he was waiting for my cue, I hear a saw in the garage.

"Hello? Amanda?"

"I'm here," I say, "but we're doing a little bit of a remodel on the farmhouse. It's old."

Her squeal is worse than her giggles multiplied by her wonderfuls, times ten. "Amanda Brooks! You were holding out on me! My goodness! Your followers will go wild for this! Who doesn't love a good makeover?"

"But I'm not sure how that will tie in to Lololime?"

"Please. I'll get a new box of clothes out to you immediately. You'll be in the photos of course, or your precious girls can be. Post about the changes, but make sure you're in them. This is influencer 101." She huffs.

"Silly me," I say. "I can't wait. I'm so lucky to have you to help guide me."

"At least you appreciate it," she says. "Some people get snippy."

The saw is running again, and I can barely hear myself think. "Alright, well—"

"Yes, you better rush to get those 'before' photos quick!"

I do as I'm told, but the before photos are pretty terrible. It looks like a tired, rundown, somewhat filthy, big empty room with stained floors.

"Once I have this section framed out," the guy says. "I'll cut the window. Probably tomorrow."

Cut the window?

"It's pretty noisy," he says. "Do you know if Kevin ordered the window already?"

Ordered a window? "Uh, no. I'm not sure we even picked—"

"I found one online," Abby shouts from the doorway. "I sent you an email with a link. One of us can pick it up from Home Depot either this afternoon or tomorrow morning."

'One of us' is clearly code for me. Before I can suppress my annoyance that she's picking windows without me and then sending me like a delivery person to pick them up, my phone buzzes. It's Derek Bills. Apparently no one explained to him that you aren't supposed to act too eager. I texted him less than five minutes before.

SLAMMED WITH MEETINGS RIGHT NOW. MEET ON FRIDAY FOR BREAKFAST?

WHERE?

I'M MEETING A RANCHER NOT FAR FROM MANILA—IS THE GORGE ALRIGHT?

SURE.

"I'll go pick up the window now, I guess." Before I can even grab my purse, I hear a long line of swear words coming from the garage. Abby's as worried as me, and we both swing around the corner together.

Water's spewing from a pipe in the wall.

"What's going on?" Abby asks.

"That valve was leaking," the framer says. "I tried to tighten it up, but it broke."

I swear under my breath.

"You can say that again," Abby says.

Kevin bursts in behind us a moment later. "What in the holy—"

"Valve broke," Abby says. "We need a plumber immediately."

"Where's the main water line?" I ask. "If we turn that off, the garage won't keep getting wetter."

Abby darts out the door Kevin just entered through. I hope that means she knows where it is. I didn't even know you *could* shut off a water line before Paul died. Some things about my life really *were* better before he passed, I suppose.

Kevin whips out his phone. "Hey, I have an emergency." He pauses. "Nah, not animals. Plumbing problem. Kinda urgent."

"Who is that?" And why's he saying, 'not animals?' Yesterday he said his plumber was working down in Vernal for the next two weeks.

"I'm at Amanda's, yeah. Greg's down on that new build for like ten more days." He grunts. "Right." He sighs. "Sure." Then he hangs up.

The water pressure eases off, and water's only trickling out, and then finally it stops. I breathe a sigh of relief, but I still feel uneasy. "Kevin, who did you call?"

He turns to face me slowly. "Aren't you headed out to Home Depot?"

"It was Eddy."

Kevin's eyes widen and spins around to get away from me. "How hard did you twist that valve, man?"

He and the framer get to work, opening the garage door and sweeping most of the water right outside. It's gotten pretty hot in here, and both of them are working

84

with no shirts on. They're both young—way too young for me—but my readers might like a snapshot of the worksite. That's what I should be thinking about. Or maybe how lucky we are that hardly any of the central framework is up yet, so nothing was really damaged. Or I could be focused on how great it is that Kevin found anyone at all who could come change out this broken valve quickly.

Instead, my mind is spinning at the rate of nine million miles a minute. Because *Eddy* is coming over.

Which is stupid. I've avoided him for precisely this reason. He knows we can't date. I know we can't date. It would be bad for him to collapse back into the public view, and even worse for me to be affiliated with him. With his history (he struck someone with his car while high, and that person *died*) and my job (as an influencer, my reputation *is* my value), I really can't risk falling for him.

Not any more than I already have, anyway.

I force myself out of the garage where Eddy's coming and into the house, where I retrieve my discarded purse and trudge toward my car. I need to get the window, and I need to not be here when Eddy is. *Go, Amanda, go.* I climb in the car and throw it into reverse, and that's when the backup sensor picks it up.

Roscoe has crawled behind the car and lain down again.

He took to doing this after we came back—whenever he's not locked in the house, and I leave, he parks himself behind me. It's like he's terrified I'll never come back, so he wants to keep me from going anywhere. I shove the car back into park, climb out again, circle and grab his collar and do the hunch-and-walk-and-drag thing I always have to do to pop him back inside.

Only, that doesn't work this time.

I'm such an idiot that I didn't consider how he got

out. By the time I get back to my car, he's raced through the open garage door and leapt into his spot behind the back wheel. "Roscoe!" He huddles a little lower, but doesn't move. "I'm not leaving, boy." I huff. "I mean, I *am*, but I'll be back in a few hours."

His light brown eyes are so full of desperate love that my irritation evaporates. I crouch down at his side and pet his head. He immediately shifts to crawl halfway into my lap and nearly knocks me over onto the gravel drive. Seeing his opening, he starts to lick my face. "Hey. Stop." In dog language, that means, 'please, lick me much, much more exuberantly.' I finally stand up just to escape the zeal of his tongue.

One more drag-and-shuffle later, and I'm finally ready to go. "Hey, Roscoe's locked in the back and I'm leaving," I shout loudly, so Abby and Kevin will know. "Finally."

"Oh." That tiny word is only one syllable. It shouldn't be enough for me to recognize his voice, but it is. My head snaps up, and our eyes meet.

My eyelids flutter. Like, they actually *flutter*. What am I? A debutante? Maren, panicking about her zit this morning, was more composed than I feel right now. "I have to go buy a window."

"Okay." Eddy doesn't argue. He doesn't even chat. He just looks at me from the doorway, but a look from him, even without his double dimples showing, is practically paralyzing.

I make myself, through sheer force of will, move. My legs first, and then my arms so I don't look like a robot. "I mean, I'll be back."

"I'll probably be gone by then," he says. "It's just a busted valve."

Is that a quick fix? Why couldn't that stupid framer have wrecked something bigger? "I didn't know you were a plumber. Could you do the rest of the plumbing for us?"

The words just fly out, and then they keep on coming. "Kevin said the only plumber in town is gone—it's going to delay the entire project."

Eddy's brow furrows. "I mean, I have my practice—I just did plumbing work to pay my way through vet school."

Of course he did. He's smoking hot. He's kind as the day is long. He's the most gifted musician I've met in real life, and he's a veterinarian. On top of all of that, why *wouldn't* he be handy around the house? "I'm sorry. I don't know why I asked." Play it cool, Amanda. Don't sound so strung out. I mean, I know why. I'm just hoping it's not super obvious to him. "I mean, I know why." I need to stop talking.

Fix it, brain, fix it.

"Three times," Abby says from the hall. "That's how many times I've had someone walk in while I was showering this week." She laughs. "That's why we're all so desperate, but we'd never dream of imposing on you. Of course you have your own vet practice that keeps you busy."

"Please." Kevin ducks out behind her. "All the cattle are still up on Forestry Land. You're half bored, I'm sure."

Now that there are three of us begging, Eddy doesn't last very long. He certainly doesn't change his mind for me. It's much easier to drive away, knowing he'll probably still be there when I get back. And every day for the next few days.

The drive to Rock Springs is lovely, but since I've been quite a few times now, it doesn't hold my attention. No, that keeps drifting back to Eddy. An hour down and an hour back, thinking about his boyish grin, his silky voice, and his grass-green eyes. It's no wonder that when I arrive and march toward the garage, prepared to ask for help unloading the huge window box, I stop in my tracks, totally caught off guard.

I had, in my two hours of daydreaming, never thought about Eddy's glistening chest muscles, or his shockingly ripped abdominal muscles. Not because they're not worthy of *hours* of daydreaming, but because I'd never have dreamed they'd be quite this amazing.

The framer's working again, with Kevin assisting, and Eddy's working in between them, doing something with a large white PVC pipe.

None of them have shirts on.

All of them look pretty decent.

But those two young guys don't have anything on Eddy. How does he have time to treat animals? He must spend hours at the gym. "Hey, with the sun shifting, it's right in my eyes." He doesn't look up from what he's doing, but he hollers loudly. "Toss me my hat."

Kevin grabs it off the side of the sawhorse and tosses it to him. When Eddy puts it on, it's like some kind of gift. His face is partially obscured, but his body, glistening in the sunlight that prompted the need for a hat, is totally exposed. With the way he's angled, it's more like it's *showcased*. I whip out my phone without thinking and snap a photo.

As I edit it, it's clear that no one could tell quite who he is.

And Heather wanted a post ASAP. If I post tomorrow, there will be less than a day of interaction before her meeting. Before I can talk myself out of my rationalization, I upload the image and tag it. #HotCowboy #DownandDirty #FixerUpper #DoingalittleRemodeling #YesPlease and #GiddyUp.

My phone rings not five minutes later, and I just know it's Heather. Before I can come up with reasons to ignore her, I press talk. "Hello?"

"Mrs. Brooks?" The slow cadence of Mr. Swift is hard to forget.

"Oh."

"You were expecting another call, perhaps?"

"Not exactly." I have no reason to be guilty. I did exactly what Heather wanted. Sort of.

"I'm calling to inform you that I was contacted today by the Institute of Research into Alien Life." He clears his throat.

"Okay."

"That's the organization who will take under Mr. Jedediah's will, should your attempts to work the ranch for one year be deemed ineffective."

"What?" I'm confused. "Why would they call? And is that bad?"

"They seem to have come into the knowledge that both you and Mrs. Abigail Brooks began to work the ranch in June, and then left mid-July for a month, before returning in August."

"Uh, I'm still lost."

"I did try calling Mrs. Abigail Brooks."

Great. Now he's saying I'm too stupid to understand. "Can they, like, kick us out or something? Because we went home?"

He sighs. "The will specifically delineates that one-week vacations are acceptable, however, that implies that longer absences are not."

"Implies?"

"In my professional opinion, it's unclear."

"But we're actually related to Jed. Or, you know, our kids are."

"Mrs. Brooks, I'm merely calling to let you know that they informed me of their intention to file a petition with the probate court to make a determination of heirship."

That sounds bad. "Let me see if I can locate Abby."

"I left her a detailed voicemail and an email as well. I don't mean to bother either of you, and I'm not trying to be alarmist, but I thought you might like to know. I'll certainly keep you apprised as the situation develops."

Fan-freaking-tastic. "Well, thanks. We're happy to have you on our side."

"To be clear, I am not on your side." He grunts. "I'm on the law's side."

Thanks for that, Karl. Geez. "Well, I happen to believe that we're on the law's side."

"Your opinion is, sadly, irrelevant."

This guy's the worst. "Alright, well, unless you need anything else."

"No, our business is concluded."

Oh, I am not letting him hang up first. I rush to press the end call button, but he beats me to it. And another call manages to come in at that very instant. I accidentally answer it.

Today's definitely a bunchy, not-enough-time in-the-right-places, things-piling-up kind of day.

"Hello? Amanda?"

Oh, no, it's Heather. This time I don't manage to suppress my groan. "Yes?"

"Please. *Please* tell me that absolutely stunning specimen you just posted is *not* Edward Dutton."

"Uh."

"Amanda."

I thought my mom had a natural gift, given only to moms, to completely level me with just one word. Clearly, it's not limited only to mothers. "You wanted a hot cowboy, I gave you a hot cowboy."

"It's not just us being officious," she says.

She definitely has a calendar, and she's just rolling through this week's words all at once. I may not know what that word means, but I get her meaning. "I know."

"It feels like you don't really, though. So here's what I'm going to do. I wanted to avoid this type of nastiness, but Amanda, we are on your side. Trust me."

"Oh, I do." *Not.*

"I'm emailing you the dossier our investigator compiled on your Mr. Dutton."

"Doctor Dutton."

"Sure."

"Wait, did you say a *dossier*? Compiled by an *investigator*?"

"I understand that it's not really—"

"You're right about that."

"I actually convinced them to pay for it," Heather says. "I figured if we did a lot of digging and couldn't find anything bad, maybe you could go for it. After all, he is hot, and he's well educated. He could really help round out your page."

Well-educated—would round out my page? *Ouch.* "And?"

"But it's pretty bad," she says. "You'll see when you read it. Trust me. There's no way that you can date Doctor Dutton. No way at all."

"Should I delete the photo, then?"

"It's already getting a *lot* of attention, which is how I knew you posted it. I think you should leave it, since it's not enough for anyone to discover him. But, Amanda?"

"Yeah. I know."

"This is the very last one. Got it?"

It has been an absolutely miserable day. First, I fail entirely in preparing for my new business, taking a *nap* instead of working. Then I get yelled at for not posting enough. And then the valve busts, and then some alien people are trying to steal the ranch, and finally, my boss lays down the law on Eddy.

When she finally hangs up, my eyes drift upward and

lock onto Eddy's chest. It takes a full thirty seconds for me to tear them away. That turns out to be ridiculously embarrassing, because he's staring right at me.

He knows I was just ogling him shamelessly.

When he smiles a very smug smile, my heart contracts, and I realize that this part, the not interacting or dating or flirting part?

It's going to be way, way harder than I thought, and it's definitely the worst part of my day.

✴ 8 ✴

ABIGAIL

I am always calm. I am always collected. I am always a step or two ahead of where I need to be. I'm not the person who races to get things done last minute. I don't thrive on desperation forcing me to get something done. No, I'm the kind of person who would develop an ulcer in short order if I left things dangling on the bottom of my to-do list.

I'll work until all hours of the night to make sure things don't fall behind.

But lately, I feel stretched a little too thin, like too little butter spread over too much bread, to quote a very wise hobbit. Clearly working full time while helping with a ranch and managing four children in a new place, with a remodel thrown in for good measure, has been challenging.

Thanks to an internet glitch, and the joy of the time difference between Texas and here, I barely get my brief filed before the time clock rolls over. My fingers are shaking as the box pops up, indicating it was accepted. I save the confirmation and upload it to the firm document management system.

My phone rings just as I finish. "Hello?"

"Abby?" Robert Marwell sounds nervous. If I hadn't known him for twenty years, I might not notice. But I have, and he definitely is.

What's worse is that his concern was justified. "You didn't have to call," I say. "It was in on time."

He exhales. "Thank goodness. I checked online ten minutes ago, and the court still isn't showing anything as—"

"I know. Our internet here went down, and I had to boost the signal from my phone."

He groans. "Maybe next time, we don't cut it so close."

I don't remind him that I had the brief prepared last Wednesday, and I was merely waiting for his approval to send it. "I agree."

"The next—"

The whine of a saw in the background drowns out whatever he's saying.

"What was that?"

As if I needed another reason for the people at my firm to lose faith in my ability to work remotely and remain connected. . . "The farmhouse isn't very spacious," I say. "Or rather, it's fine, but it's not big enough for two families."

"You're remodeling?"

I ignore the note of censure in his tone. He sounds like that any time I say anything indicating we're planning to stay more than a few months. "It'll be hard to get a feel for whether this is a workable scenario without having enough space to coexist harmoniously."

"You don't both need to live in the same place," he says.

I've had that thought on several occasions, and I'm sure Amanda has too, but every time I think about moving out, that idea makes me more anxious. "It's not a major remodel, and we're not paying for it. Money left in the estate is covering the costs, and we're just converting the garage to add another bedroom, a bathroom, and a living area."

"*Just* two rooms and a bathroom." He chuckles. "Have you considered how miserable it'll be not to have an enclosed place to park in the winter? You're not in Houston anymore."

I had not given that much thought, and it now seems like a major oversight. "Of course we have. Robert, I'm not twelve."

"I'm aware," he says. "Actually—"

There's a beep on the other line. I glance at the phone screen. It's Karl Swift. "Uh, can I call you back? I've been waiting on this call."

He clears his throat. "Of course. It was nothing important."

I wonder, briefly, what he wanted to say, but my concern over the new development with the ranch is more pressing. "Thanks." I click the button to switch calls. "Hello?"

"I'm sorry it has taken me a few days to return your call," Mr. Swift says slowly. Everything he says and does is slow, so the three-day delay didn't even surprise me.

"I'm just happy to hear from you." Or at least, I hope I will be very soon. "You mentioned in the email you sent that the Institute Into Research on Alien Life, or whatever, is filing a petition of determination."

"Heirship, here, but that's correct."

"Have they absolutely decided to take such a drastic step? The will clearly gives us a year to comply with its terms, and we're in the middle of it."

"Their contention appears to be that, since you came in June, your year began at that point. The will mentions that you're allowed to leave for one-week periods of time in order to take a 'vacation' from the work, but that implies that anything longer would *not* be allowed. As such, an extended departure would be a violation."

"You think that, because we left for longer than a week, we lose the ranch?" I know it's not Mr. Swift's fault, but part of me still wants to reach through the phone and shake him.

"You were gone for a month." His voice is flat.

"Amanda was only gone for two weeks," I say. As if that matters.

"My understanding is that she's not doing much to help with the ranch." He sighs. "Either way, *something* would have to be done to address the extended departure. Perhaps the year should restart, or perhaps additional time should be tacked on the end. Or perhaps the stipulation has already failed. I'm not sure. As you know, when the four corners of the document aren't clear—"

"The parole evidence rule—I did attend classes during my first year of law school. But the will also appoints a panel of three people to adjudicate matters related to our compliance. Surely the decision about this would fall under their purview. I think we can and should avoid involving the court unless absolutely necessary."

"Are you saying we should pose this question to the three people appointed in the will? Would you agree to accept whatever they decide? It would have to be taken care of through some kind of binding mediation, perhaps."

Steve is one of the three. Eddy's another, though I have no idea how he and Amanda are doing, currently. She was certainly spending a lot of time staring at him longingly when he was working in the garage not long ago. The third was that terrible person Steve said wanted to purchase the ranch. A memory niggles at the back of my mind. He said the person who wanted to buy it actually wanted it. . .for his sister. That dislodges something. A red flag waves in my brain. "Mr. Swift, what did you say was the name of the third person? One is Steve Archer, one is Eddy Dutton. Who was the third?"

"Vernon Ellingson."

"And he has a son and a daughter, right? What's his daughter's name?"

"Donna."

Wow. Just, wow. A chill runs down my arms. "I just had her over for dinner." And now I'm wondering if that was a bizarre coincidence, or whether she came to do a little reconnaissance. "I need to talk to Amanda before I can even verbally commit to be bound by the decision of three people who may themselves be materially interested in the outcome."

Mr. Swift sighs. "I wonder whether Jed would rethink this provision today if he knew what a mess it would create."

"If he hadn't required us to be here, we'd probably have simply sold it." And that would have been a mistake, I think.

Maybe.

Some days, I miss my simple, well-ordered life back in Houston. Fewer animals to care for, no remodeling at all, and so much more consistency, for me and the kids.

But no excitement.

No new people.

I'd certainly never have met Steve. I still haven't decided whether that would be good or bad. He's texted me a dozen times in the past few days and called half a dozen more. I've avoided talking to him with carefully crafted short texts, mostly expressing that I'm busy.

It's not even a lie.

Work, kids, animals, a remodel, and now this. My

hands are *more* than full. Setting aside the question of whether we're well matched, I'm not sure I really have time for a relationship with anyone.

"Mrs. Brooks?"

I think he asked me something and I missed it. "Yes?"

"Talk to Amanda and let me know how you'd like to proceed. I believe the Institute is contacting a lawyer as we speak. I expect to hear from them quite soon."

"I will."

The only great thing about the time change is that I'm done with work earlier here than I ever was back home. It means a correspondingly early morning, but I'm usually done with work when the kids get home from school. I'm wandering outside to wait for the bus when Steve's white truck pulls up.

I hate how my heart sails into my throat.

And I love it, too.

I wave.

He parks next to my minivan and cuts his engine. He's wearing his usual plain, dark t-shirt that clings to his lean but muscular frame, and faded jeans. His boots are worn, but clearly high quality, his spurs clinking a bit with every step. I've never seen him without spurs, come to think of it, except when we saw him working at the hospital that one time. He didn't have boots on with his scrubs and white coat—maybe that's part of why he looked so strange as Doctor Archer.

"Everything okay?" I ask.

"I came to find out the answer to that myself." He looks around the ranch carefully. "You *seem* healthy."

"What?"

"Everything *looks* fine." He crosses his arms.

"We are fine. I never said any different."

"Just too busy to see me." Raised eyebrows belie the flat statement it sounds like. He expects an explanation.

"I said that we need to set up lessons."

"But we haven't. I was free today, and I thought I'd come see—"

"Maren and Izzy are trying out for cheerleading, and Emery's trying out for softball."

"So only Whitney and Gabe are here?" He sighs. "Without anyone to keep an eye on Gabe, we probably can't do a lesson for you and Whitney."

"How much time do you have? Maybe you could come back around five-thirty."

Steve smiles. "Why should I come back?"

"Then don't. You don't have to." This time, I'm the one crossing my arms.

He laughs. "Abby." He steps closer.

My stomach lurches.

"I meant that I could stay here and lend a hand—with whatever you need—while we wait for the other kids to get back."

I swallow.

"You've either been swamped, like you said, and you could use a hand, or you're putting me off. I came over today to find out which it is."

I can barely find the breath to speak. "Little from column A, little from column B. . ."

His hand reaches out, his fingers brushing lightly against my forearm. "We're back to the avoiding? I thought we pushed past that."

"It's *because* I'm so busy that we're back to it."

"You can't avoid when you're busy. You don't have time for it."

I sigh. "It was a fun idea this summer—"

"Wait, what was a fun idea?"

I feel my cheeks heat up. "Dating."

"Yeah, I knew that, but I wanted to hear you say it."

"You're twisted," I say.

He shrugs. "Apparently you're into that."

If I don't redirect him quickly, we'll head down some kind of flirty rabbit hole. "Steve. Focus. I don't have time to date someone right now. I'm a mother and a father both, and I haven't even gone back to Houston to actually pack and move our stuff. Coordinating with contractors to get the house fixed up and listed has been enough—"

He steps closer again, and I can practically feel the heat from his body radiating outward. "That's why I'm here." Steve squeezes my arm once and then drops it and strides right past me, heading for the side door into the space formerly known as the garage. They've removed the rolling garage doors, framed up the new wall and even applied the Tyvek, but they haven't finished taping or floating inside, and I'm not sure when the siding for the exterior will arrive.

Steve looks back at me and frowns. "It's supposed to rain next week."

"Which is why Kevin and Jeff and Ethan are frantically cutting as much hay as they can." I point at the garage. "That's the downside to having a general contractor who's also running the ranch."

Steve smiles. "What's going on in there, then? I hear a nail gun."

"Thanks to Eddy doing the drains and the water lines, we were able to get things set up for drywall, which is exciting."

"Let me get this straight. Amanda let Eddy help, but you won't let me?"

"First of all, Eddy and Amanda are not dating. He came to work as a subcontractor, nothing more."

"Sure he did." Steve lifts one eyebrow. "Then I'll do the same."

"Steve—"

"Listen, I'd be honored to be working for you. I'm not

sure I've seen a last-minute project come together this fast. . .well, ever."

My cheeks heat. "Thanks."

"You, Abigail Brooks, are a very capable woman. I am impressed."

Nate used to tell me things like that all the time. I'm not sure whether it's the deadline I nearly missed, the late nights, the early days, or the lack of any consistent compliments in over a year, but something horribly embarrassing happens.

I burst into tears.

Before Steve can react, I spin around and head for the front door. Let Steve see if he can lend them a hand. I'm going to hide in my bedroom. I'm yanking the front door open when he grabs me, his hand like an iron vise. I expect him to grill me about why I'm crying. I expect him to look hurt or confused. I know that's what Robert would be doing right about now, and maybe Nate too, if they were here.

But Steve just spins me to face him and wraps one arm around my waist, cupping the back of my head with his other hand and pressing me against his chest.

I knew he was tall.

I knew he was muscular.

Feeling that height and that strength is totally different. At first, it's foreign and strange and disconcerting, but I'm bawling so hard that I can't really shove him away. Eventually, I relax against him, and for the first time in two years, someone else is protecting me.

Which, inexplicably, makes me cry harder.

He doesn't ask me any questions. He doesn't try to talk to me at all. His arms hold me steady, and his chest is firm against my face. By the time I finally pull it together and straighten, the front of his shirt is soaked.

How embarrassing.

"That'll show you—don't call me capable."

Steve's lips twitch, and his arms don't loosen a bit. Which means we're still standing together, both his arms now around my waist.

"Sorry about the crying and the running."

He shakes his head. "Don't apologize. Even machines break down. You've been pulling a two-horse plow for years on your own." He ducks his head a little so that his eyes aren't so far above mine. "I'm offering to help. Let me."

"Hey, Abs, I have the samples—" Amanda pushes through the open doorway and freezes, her eyes widening as she takes in Steve and me and the hugging and the tears. "Um, uh, I mean. I forgot something." She turns and ducks back inside.

Before she can close the door, I shout. "Wait. Amanda." I step back from Steve and straighten my shoulders. "I'd love to see the samples."

She glances from my face to Steve's and back again. "Uh-huh." She extends them.

I snatch them out of her hand and look over them. "I think we should use this palest bluish grey."

She grimaces. "Really? I mean, yes, I know that's the safe call, but think this through. It's going to be a long, hard winter. At some point, we're going to be a little stir-crazy. Trust me—it happens in New York. Don't you think this seafoam color would be fun? It would brighten up the whole place, especially if we went with a white-wash theme otherwise and used only a handful of bright accents to pull the wall color."

I don't see it. At all. Our new game room will look like a beach resort. "Um, let's think about it a little more, then."

"We can't think too long," she says. "We need to buy

paint tomorrow, since Kevin said drywall is a day, and tape and float is maybe two."

"Amanda," Steve says. "How would you feel about holding down the fort for a few hours? I feel like Abby might need a break."

I splutter.

"I was already planning to pick up the kiddos. I'll just make sure to take Gabe and Whitney with me." As if on cue, their bus arrives.

They're giddy to see Steve. Gabe hugs him so tightly that we have to pry him off. "Mr. Steve!"

"Are we doing a lesson?" Whitney asks. "I really want to ride Dakota. I think I'm ready."

I laugh. "I'm not even ready to ride Dakota."

"Actually." Steve crouches down on the ground. "I was thinking of taking your mom to do something fun. She spends all her time doing things for you guys, and I thought—"

"You should take her for a playdate," Gabe says. "She never gets to go on any at all."

"I like that rebrand, young man." Steve stands up, his eyebrows rising suggestively. "How'd you like to come with me on a *play*date?"

I clear my throat. "Whitney and Gabe both have homework and—"

"Which I'm happy to supervise." Amanda's knowing smirk may be the worst thing about all of this. "Go ahead and *play*, you two."

Nope. Gabe's accidental phrase is the worst part. Definitely.

"I can't just—"

Steve looks me over head to toe. "Put on some boots and trade those slacks for jeans, and we'll be ready to go."

"What are you gonna do on your playdate?" Gabe asks.

"Since it's been a while, I thought your mom might like to go for a ride." Steve's grin is devilish.

"Oh, I bet she'd love that." Amanda bites her lip.

I am going to punch them both. "Wouldn't it make more sense to have the lessons—"

Steve takes my hand and gently shoves me toward the door. "Change. I wasn't thinking about a lesson. I was thinking of a trail ride."

In their typically exuberant fashion, Gabe and Whitney hound my steps, encouraging and chattering and cajoling. It's not like I can explain Steve's subtext, or Amanda's, so finally I just cave. How bad can a trail ride with Steve really be?

It turns out, pretty bad.

We've spent so much of our time together either with other people, including kids, or in places where other people could turn up at any point, that being alone with him in a car is. . .heady. And horrifying. And it makes me jittery.

Steve notices my hand bouncing around on the center console and reaches for it.

I snatch it back into my lap.

He raises one eyebrow. It's a clear message. *I know I make you nervous, and I have no intention of stopping.*

"Where are we going?"

"To my place," he says. "There's a beautiful trail that goes right past a creek that starts at the back of my property. It's why my mom and dad chose it so many years ago."

I realize that I know nothing about his parents. "Where are they now?"

"My mom passed," he says. "Cancer, unexpected, diagnosed late. She died fast. I thought Dad would follow her, he was so broken up. But then a lady from church sort of glommed onto him, and bam. Remarried a few months later. She relocated him to Idaho where her kids were so fast, my head spun."

"I'm sorry," I say.

"Don't be. Dad and I were never really close, and without Mom as a buffer. . ." He shrugs. "It's better, trust me. Violet's a great lubricant for our societally required interactions, and Dad gave me this place early. Said he plans to leave everything else to Vi, but he didn't want to leave me nothing at all."

"I'm glad you're okay with it." He says he's fine, but he sounds lonely. "No siblings?"

"Other than my sister?" He shakes his head.

I forgot his sister passed away. I'm an idiot. "I'm so sorry."

"Don't be. It happened long enough ago that sometimes I almost forget."

But I shouldn't. Not with my past.

"Please don't worry about it. You've had a lot on your mind."

Any apologies I offer will probably only make things more awkward.

"In any case, Mom and Dad always seemed mismatched to me. They married early, Mom was barely eighteen, and I'm not sure they were a good fit. Mom was always talking. Dad was always watching sports on television. Mom did all the hard work, but Dad did all the manly things."

"I wish I could have met her." I'm almost surprised that I really mean that. His mom sounds delightful, and frankly, insightful too. I imagine that's where her son gets it.

And we've already reached his place. The awkward tension evaporates the second Steve and I walk past his house, and I realize he really did intend for us to simply go for a trail ride. Watching Steve around horses is like

watching a celebrated artist paint. Or watching a professional athlete shoot a flawless three-point shot. He's so
comfortable with them, so sure of himself, that it's almost
a work of art to watch him move at all.

His barn is set up with two rows of ten stalls, most of
them the standard twelve by twelve foot setup. But the
four stalls at the very front are larger—quite a bit larger.
"How big are these?"

Steve's eyes light up. "A lot of folks go with ten by ten
stalls to save money, but the winter's long here so I went
with twelves. Sometimes the horses can't go out for
extended periods of time. I rotate them out into my
covered arena so they can move around a little more, but
it's hard. And as you know, I have my favorites. I decided
I could do eight stalls in this section, or I could do four
ultra long stalls. So these are twelve by twenty-four." He
slides the stall on the end open, and Leo, his stunning
palomino, walks toward us, whickering softly.

"If you're riding Leo, which horse should I ride?"

Steve halters him easily and hands me the lead rope.
"He's for you."

"Really?"

"I know he's your favorite. How could I fob someone
else off on you?"

Steve opens the stall next door and grabs Farrah—his
favorite horse, I'm pretty sure—a gorgeous reddish sorrel
with a blonde mane, a baldface, and bright, startling blue
eyes. "These two get along—thick as thieves."

"It helps that their stalls are adjacent, I imagine."

"It doesn't hurt," he says.

Steve finishes tacking up Farrah so fast that before
I've even finished hoof picking, he's moved to my cross
ties to help, and before I can object, he's saddling Leo up
for me.

I glance at my watch to see how long it took him—six

minutes start to finish—and that makes me wonder whether Amanda had any trouble finding the kids. And what she'll feed them for dinner. I started that chili. Maybe I should text her and let her know it should be ready any time. "How far is this trail?" If she lets it simmer too long, it'll burn. At the very least, it needs to be stirred.

"We'll be back before sunset," he says.

"I should hope so," I say. "It's not even five o'clock yet." Is it bath night for Gabe? I think it probably is. And the kids need to see the lunch menu so they know whether to pack their lunches. Did we run out of turkey? Whitney hates ham.

Steve hands me a bridle, our hands brushing. His fingers grab mine. "Abby, the whole point of today is to slow down a little. Let go of your fear that if you take a breath, everything will fall apart. You're not alone."

"I'm not that—"

His lips curl into a smile. "Alright, let's try this. If I can tell you everything you were just thinking, and I'm right, you will not think about the time or what needs to be done until I return you to your family."

I roll my eyes.

"You were worrying about the kids being picked up, about dinner plans, about homework, and about what needs to be done to get them ready for tomorrow, especially for Gabe."

My jaw drops.

"Abby, your kids are on the ball. They can handle things alone—but with Amanda there? They'll all be fine. I promise."

"I never agreed to your terms, and I—"

Steve presses one finger to my mouth.

My entire body pulses, and a shiver runs down my spine.

He leans closer, until I can smell his cinnamon gum. "Hey, Miss Lawyer, settle down." He picks up a bag, which came from I don't know where, and ties it to the side of his saddle. Then, while I bridle Leo, he bridles Farrah and tightens her girth again. "You ready?"

I don't dare argue. What might he do? Drag me against his body?

Kiss me?

My heart gallops away.

Do I want him to kiss me? What's wrong with me? I've thought this through a million times, and any way I look, I don't have time and I'm not at all ready for this sort of thing. I'm too raw and broken and weepy. I don't know why I've even thought about it.

Steve tosses his head my direction. "Need me to check your girth?"

I shake my head.

He turns and leads Farrah out the back of the barn, past the arena, and then he stops. "Ready?"

I tighten Leo's girth again, and then I check my stirrups. The old English "when you hold it out from the saddle, if it's the right length, the stirrup should fit right into your armpit" trick doesn't really work for Western. I measure to my armpit and then add another few inches. In my experience, that's usually pretty close.

When I swing up and over, just a moment behind Steve, my stirrups are perfect. Joking aside, it has been a while since I've ridden. Unlike the trotting and racing we usually do in the arena, Steve and Farrah set off at an easy walk, the same pace we held for most of the one actual trail ride I've ever done.

"Tell me about the plans for the remodel."

I launch into the disaster of the tile versus the carpet debate, and the mess we ran into when we planned the bathroom.

"In the end, we just flipped a coin," I say.

"And what won?" he asks. "Shower or tub/shower combo?"

"Shower," I say. "Thank goodness for that. I have the smallest child, and two combo tubs in the house is more than enough for me."

"Why did Amanda want one?" He smiles. "Sometimes she baffles me."

"Oh, me too," I say. "But in this instance, her reasoning was my strongest justification to argue. Apparently she loves baths, and her tub combo is far too small. She wanted to put in a Jacuzzi tub—in that tiny bathroom. Can you imagine? You'd be brushing your teeth over the tub!"

"We all want what we want," he says. "You'd have survived that, too." He has such a simple cowboy outlook —it's bizarre and refreshing at the same time.

"I suppose I would have." Why does everything in my life feel so darn important all the time?

"Some people go the other direction after someone passes, you know."

"Huh?" What does that mean?

"I'm just saying that for some people, when a loved one dies, they decide that no matter how much they do, they can never keep bad things from happening, so they kind of give up on trying."

And he's saying I went the other way.

I'm trying too hard.

I open my mouth to tell him where he can shove his judgey attitude. . .and then I realize that he's not being judgmental. He's saying it's good for me that I'm someone who still cares, but maybe I need to worry a little less. Some things might survive if I *don't* micromanage them.

He's probably right.

Our conversation moves easily then, just like the two

perfectly behaved horses on a trail Steve clearly knows well. Other than a few startled birds and one spook and dash that we quickly subdue, the ride is refreshing. Like a crisp slice of watermelon at summer's end. Like dipping my toes into a refreshingly cool pool. Like lying back and letting the fan cool me down after a jog outside.

It would be so easy to take this for granted. To take Steve for granted.

But if becoming uptight was a byproduct of Nate's passing, so was my appreciation for the small beauties of life. The lowering sun. The easy movement of our horses. The casual and comfortable conversation of two new friends.

And when we reach the small creek he promised, Steve stakes our horses and opens up the bag he brought. "It's just little sandwiches and some grapes," he says. "I wasn't sure if you'd even be home."

He planned this from the start. "You're sneaky."

"I'm optimistic."

But this ride cleared away the last of my crabby reservations. We eat. We chat. Our hands brush. Time freezes. And then expands. Contracts. Shivers. And after too short a time, Steve yawns. "It's probably time to head back."

Back to my life.

Back to shouldering the entire load.

I groan.

"Abigail Brooks."

My eyes turn toward his involuntarily.

He crawls toward me on all fours, his mouth open, just a little.

"Yeah?"

"You promise me something."

"Hm."

"The next time I call?"

I swallow.

He shifts just a little closer. His mouth hovers a few inches from mine. His eyes drop to my lips.

They part a bit, and I realize I was lying earlier. I definitely want him to kiss me. It's the thing I most desperately want. And I want our bodies pressed together like before, but I don't want to be sad. Or desperate. Just electric and terrifying and *right*.

"Promise me that you'll answer when I call you, from now on."

My brain is on vacation. He's talking, but the words are gibberish.

"Say yes," he whispers, his breath brushing against my face.

"Yes," I repeat, dumbly. Now kiss me, you big, burly man. Kiss me like you mean it.

The corners of his lips turn upward. Not into a normal smile, but into a smirk. A gloat. A cocky, masculine grin. "Abigail."

"Yeah." My voice is ridiculously airy, and I don't even care.

"We better get going, or we'll get home after dark." He straightens up and stands, leaving me on the picnic blanket alone. Practically panting. Like an idiot.

Steve's always happy, but he's in an absurdly good mood the whole way back.

You'd almost think he had actually *kissed* me or something, but *nooo*. The big dope is happy for no reason at all, as far as I can tell.

"You're supposed to be relaxed," he says. "Why do you seem crabbier now then when we left?"

I yank Leo's head back. He twitches his ear, as if to reprimand me. I pat his shoulder. "I'm sorry, boy."

"You're sorry?" Steve turns casually, as if he really has no idea what might be wrong.

I'm not sixteen. I'm not some debutante. I decide to tell him the truth. "You practically crawled into my lap back there," I accuse.

His eyebrows shoot up his forehead. "Excuse me?"

"You." I point behind us. "On that blanket. You crawled toward me, and your face, and your lips, and your hands." I huff. This is not coming out right.

"My lips?" He lifts one hand to his mouth, and by golly if I don't want to kiss him again. Right here. Even though he's almost ten feet away.

"I thought you were going to kiss me." I meant to berate him, but the words come out more like a sulky mumble.

Steve's huge belly laugh shocks me.

"Are you laughing at me?" I bump Leo with both feet and he shoots forward, edging Farrah aside and taking the lead.

"Do you know where you're going?"

I snap my head back and glare at him. "Do you mean in life, or just on this trail?"

His brow furrows. "Either?"

I urge Leo to walk even faster. As a perfect angel, he complies. Every second, my love for Leo and my disdain for his owner grow. I refuse to dignify that with a response.

"Abigail." Steve's voice is so close that I nearly jump out of my seat.

"Hey, that's not safe," I say. "You said we can't ride this close together."

"I know these horses," he says. "And they adore each other."

"Do as I say, not as I do, apparently," I snap.

"You really are crabby." His man-smirk is back.

"I think you're the one who doesn't know where he's going."

Steve's mouth hangs open for one beat, and then he says, "Abby, the last time someone tried to kiss you, you jumped into a lake to escape." He leans even closer then. "I can't wait to kiss you, but I won't do it until you're so desperate that you'll cling to me like a cowboy clings to his horse in a stampede."

I can't even meet his eyes the rest of the way back. If he only knew—I'd already have clung to him. How pathetic.

We're nearly to his house when my phone starts ringing. I pick up quickly, worried the rare reception will die off before I can find out who needs me. "Hello?"

"Mom?" Gabe is so bad at phones that I can almost see him, squinting at it.

"Yes, honey?"

"Are you coming home soon? Because Whitney's stories are terrible, and Izzy's a really bad prayer. She never even prays for me to sleep great with no nightmares."

I snort. "I'm almost back to Mr. Steve's and I'll come home straightaway."

"Okay. Hurry." He hangs up.

"That was Gabe?"

"Yep. He's always the one who needs me the most." I shake my head. "The little stinker."

"He's an adorable kid."

"I'm horribly biased, but I think he's precious."

"As an unbiased third party, I can objectively say that all your children are cute."

"Don't let Ethan hear you say that," I warn.

"With my luck, our kid would take after me instead of you, and he or she would be the only ugly one."

Our kid.

It's a good thing Leo's an angel, because hearing those words completely freaks me out. I spend the rest of the ride, the entire time we're tacking down, and the whole drive home hearing them on repeat in my brain. Our kid. Our kid. Our kid.

It was probably nothing.

Merely a turn of phrase.

Our kid.

People who are dating probably say things like that, and it's just been so long for me that I've forgotten. It's casual. Natural. It means nothing.

Or, possibly, it means that if we kept dating, and Steve and I got married one day, he would want me to have at least one more child.

And that, I can never do.

✼ 9 ✼

DONNA

My phone used to be the most exciting thing in my life.

Supposedly Charlie asked for my number so I could join their study group. He told me he'd call to let me know the time they were meeting. I stared at my phone for hours, waiting for him to honor his promise. He finally did, and my heart soared when that unfamiliar number popped up.

But now, my phone's essentially a torture device. Every single call brings more bad news. Unfortunately, the number calling me right now is one I know, and if I ignore it, he'll just keep calling and calling and calling. I step out of the receptionist area and duck out behind the school. If anyone asks, I'll say I'm taking an early lunch.

"Hello," I say.

"Mrs. Ellingson, it's Andrew Soco, the District Attorney assigned to your husband's case."

As if I didn't know who was calling. "Right."

"Do you know why I'm calling?"

"You want me to waive my spousal privilege and testify against him."

"According to my records, you met Mr. Windsor in college." His tone is flat. "At Stanford."

I don't reply. Talking just encourages him.

"You're quite bright," he says. "And you know that your husband is a genius—registered with Mensa and everything."

I don't argue with him. What's the point?

"He's going to get away with it," he says. "If you don't testify, all those people he robbed will never get justice. All that money he stole, it'll just be gone."

"It was HOA money that's missing," I say. "It's not like you're alleging that he robbed people's pensions." But I agree with him. Charles Windsor IV is a lousy human being, and he deserves to pay for what he did. It's just that I can't be the one to make him do it.

"He covered his tracks," Mr. Soco says. "But you must have known."

I didn't know a thing while it was happening, but I did see some things near the end that make a lot more sense now that I do know. "Mr. Soco, my position remains unchanged. My son and I moved to get away from everything, so I'd appreciate if you could stop bothering me."

"Mrs. Ellingson—"

"Mr. Soco."

"I know you're getting divorced. I know you're not happy with him. I know you want justice, too. I could get your accounts unfrozen, and I could make sure that the judge for the divorce knows the facts—and will side with you." He drops his voice. "We're not enemies, Mrs. Ellingson. We really aren't."

Except, we are. Unlike the naive idiot who started her education at Stanford, I've learned that no one is on my side. I'm all alone. I have to make decisions that make sense for *me* and no one else. "If you're through."

"We're running out of time," he says. "A month. That's

what's left before the statute of limitations runs and. . ." He growls. "We have one month to nail this guy. After that, he'll walk away. Is that really what you want?"

"I'm not in kindergarten," I say. "But it sounds like maybe you still are. Let me teach you something, Mr. Soco. Life isn't actually about what we *want*. That's a lie your parents fed you."

My hand's shaking when I hang up.

I know what I need to do, but it doesn't mean I like any part of it. Charlie should pay for what he did. He should be forced to return that money, and he should go to jail. It's just that my future, *Aiden's* future, matters more than justice or punishment or anything else in the world.

Since I'm not at home, I can't rummage through the box that has my important papers in it like I normally would. I can't read over the signed agreement that outlines the deal I struck. Touching it usually reassures me, reminds me what I'm doing this for. It's all for Aiden. It's all to keep him safe from people just like his dad. I wish I had other options, but thanks to the stupid, emotional, misguided decisions I made in my life up until now, I'm backed into a corner. I won't do the same dumb thing twice and let my heart wreck everything.

Without the document in my hands, I feel a compulsion to know that things are in order. I swipe through my contacts until I find the right one, and I press talk.

Julia picks up on the sixth ring, just before the call would go to voicemail. She *always* picks up at the very last moment, which makes me wonder whether it's just another of her never-ending power plays. "Hello?"

At least she's not saying *Bonjour* anymore. The two-year period when she answered every call with Bonjour made me bonkers. "Julia."

"What can I do for you, Donna?" Her forced cheer,

like she delusionally believes we're friends, always makes me wonder whether she has someone listening in on what she says.

"Mr. Andrew Soco called from the Prosecutor's Office. I thought it was a good reminder that I should check in and make sure our deal is in order."

"Of course," Julia says. "Everything with *your divorce* is proceeding just as we planned. The sale will go through in a week, and the funds will be in escrow with three weeks to spare—ready to transfer to your account the day after the statute—" She coughs. "The day after your divorce goes through." She can't say it's after the statute of limitations has passed, because that would be illegal.

"Would you mind sending me some paperwork to confirm that?" I clear my throat. "Not that I'm saying I doubt your word, or anything, but. . ."

Her laugh is like the shriek of a hawk descending on prey. "Not at all, darling Donna. You're just as bright as ever, and I understand your reluctance to trust us, given the circumstances."

"You mean, in light of the fact that your son turned out to be a criminal?"

She gasps, just as I knew she would. There are three things the Windsors never do: drink in public (you never know what secrets you might divulge), leave the house without being dressed to the nines, or speak any kind of unpleasant truth. "You know he's been falsely accused." She fakes a sob. "They can't find any evidence at all that he had anything to do with that nasty business. It's a witch hunt, start to finish."

I can't decide whether she thinks her phone has been tapped, a distinct possibility, or whether she actually just can't admit he might have done something wrong out loud. Either way, I can't help tweaking her a bit with information the state already has. "I don't think I'd call it a witch hunt. The funds disappeared only from accounts over which Charlie had supervisory control, and he fired two people who raised concerns about the anomalies in a ten-month period leading up to the discovery."

"Circumstantial evidence at best," she says. "I think you take delight in torturing me."

She's not wrong. "Send over the evidence that things are moving ahead," I say, "or I might rethink our bargain." Before all this went down, I hadn't ever hung up on someone in my entire life. Now it's becoming a habit. It feels good to press 'end' on the woman who has made my life miserable since the day after our wedding.

Beware of people who don't smile with their eyes, and who never have a hair out of place. I've learned that perfection in public often covers a very dark sky in private.

Now that I've stepped out for my lunch break, I find that I'm actually hungry. For all seven years of elementary school and most of high school, Mom made me the same exact peanut butter and jelly sandwich. I'm not sure whether it's fitting or depressing that I'm now making it myself and scarfing down the exact same meal as an adult.

When Mrs. Bluitt storms into the office, waving a paper in my face as if it's my fault her son can barely write, much less spell, I know the answer—depressing, squared. I'm just not sure, some mornings, how it happened. I'm thirty-six years old, almost divorced with a kid, and I have no college degree, no mother, and a dead-end job I hate. Which single decision led me here? Was it marrying Charlie? Could it be that simple?

I muddle my way through the rest of the day, alternating between being bored enough to do Sudoku and being harangued by parents with problems. I breathe a sigh of relief when the last kid has been picked up, finally, and I can walk across the street to pick up Aiden from an equally tired secretary at the elementary school.

"You still have three kids waiting?" I actually pity Alice. There are a few parents who are chronically late, and at the elementary school, you really end up babysitting them.

"Same ones as always." When she forces a smile, I notice her lipstick is smeared on her front left tooth. I consider telling her, but it violates my one rule: always do what's easiest for me. Old Donna would have braved the awkward conversation, more concerned about whether Alice might wish she'd known. New Donna knows that all that matters is herself—no awkward conversation for the good of anyone else is required.

"Ready, big man?"

Aiden's shoulders are slumped a bit when he stands up and trudges toward me.

I wait until we're outside and on the way to my car before I ask. "What's wrong?"

He shrugs.

"Honey?"

He shrugs again.

I stop walking and crouch down. "You can tell me. Is someone being mean to you?"

He shakes his head.

"Aiden Charles Ellingson." I still regret his middle name, but c'est la vie. "What has made my little baby so upset?"

This time, he doesn't answer. He just turns away.

My sweet little son is not like most kids, I've discovered. I don't have the luxury of backing off and letting him come to me in his own time. No, he's like a blackhead that, when you try to squeeze it out, sucks downward. If you don't apply maximum pressure and *force* his feelings out, he'll stay huddled down there forever, growing, festering, and compounding. "Aiden." I cross my arms. "We will stand here all day until you tell me what's wrong."

At first his lips compress. His eyes flash. But after a few moments, he realizes that I mean it, and he finally sighs in exasperation. Like always. "Nothing is wrong, Mom. I'm just invisdible. That's all."

"Invisible? As in people can't see you?"

He frowns.

"You're new."

"I know."

"It takes time to make new friends."

"It's been two weeks."

Well, a week and a half. "Look, Aiden, it took me months—"

"Kids aren't like that, Mom."

I realize that he's right. He made friends with his best friend back in California in twelve seconds, near a water fountain. He and Abigail Brooks' son Gabe hit it off immediately when he went over to their house for dinner. "What about Gabe?"

"Who?"

"The little boy we went to have dinner with right before school started."

"Oh, yeah. He's nice. He smiles at me in the hall. He's the only one."

Too bad Gabe's in the wrong grade. Although, it's unlikely he and Gabe will get along for much longer, anyway. Maybe it's good they're a year apart in school. I just can't understand why the kids don't adore my sweet, smart, helpful little baby. It makes me want to punch them all in the face. "Let me think about it, okay?" I squeeze his shoulder. "I bet Mom can think of some ways to make you shine."

"I don't want to shine." He pulls a face. "I just want

kids to give me a turn on the slide and push me on the swings."

"Duly noted."

"Huh?"

I encourage him along toward the car. "Never mind."

By the time we get home, he's telling me about his cloud project, and how they're gluing cotton balls to pictures. "I think I can bring it home next week."

At least his pouting and misery are temporarily forgotten.

My misery, as usual, is never ending. Patrick's waiting for me on his front porch when I pull in. He jogs toward the driveway, which is my signal to stop.

"Shouldn't you be harvesting hay?" I look at the clear blue sky. "I heard rain is coming." Once a rancher, always a rancher, I guess. I still follow the weather reports like a junkie waiting for payday.

"I had something more important to do," he says. "I met with my lawyer today."

I look around. "He came here?"

"No, idiot, I drove to Vernal, so it's a good thing I have people who work for me." Patrick's in fine form.

"I know you don't want to have to pay the nurse any overtime." Medicare will cover the home nursing costs while I work, but only up to forty hours a week. The last time we went over and owed an extra hundred and twenty dollars, Patrick lost it. "So unless you need something—"

He puts his hand on the door of my car. "I do, in fact, need something. Your signature." I have no idea where he was hiding it, but he pulls a thick stack of paper out and plops it in the space vacated by his hand, the pillar of my car door. I wouldn't know what it was called, except my car window got smashed a few years back and that featured prominently on the exorbitant bill.

"What's that?" I squint. Other than the signature

block and my name, I'm not sure what I'm looking at. "Or did you really think I'd just sign anything you dropped in front of me?"

He groans. "Everything is always so hard with you. I'm the one who talked to the lawyer, had him prepare this, paid for it, and then drove out to pick it up."

"What *is* it, Patrick?"

"Your affidavit, obviously." With his other hand, he proffers a pen. "Now, can you sign it, so we can give it to the alien people?"

"Why do you need my affidavit?" I ask.

"Did you think I told you to go over to their house for fun?" He leans closer. "You went in with a task, and you completed it. It's the first thing you've done right in quite some time. Now, finish it."

I snatch the paper away and flip to the beginning. Half a page is taken up with stupid legal posturing and names and wheretofores, but at the beginning of page two, it comes together. I look up at him, no longer surprised, but a little annoyed. "Dad's the one named in the will, right? And you're the power of attorney, so why do *I* have to be the one putting my name on a document like this?"

"The conversation they had was with you. You're the only one who can testify that they up and left in July and were gone for a month."

"Surely there are other people—"

He grabs the papers and shakes them. "Donna. Just sign."

Contacting those alien people was a terrible thing to do. Telling them the widows may not be in compliance with the will terms was a jerky move. But this? Using things I discovered by asking invasive questions in their home, where they generously invited me, without any knowledge as to why I was there. . . It feels gross.

"It takes two or three months, at least, to get something like this done," Patrick says. "You said you'll get the funds in a month, and if you don't use them to buy some property fast, you'll owe a lot of taxes."

Signing this is totally something Charlie would do.

"Think about Aiden." As if Patrick cares a lick about his nephew.

At the end of the day, I'm either a Charlie, or I'm an Abigail or an Amanda. It's time for me to stop worrying about right and wrong and do what needs to be done. Like Paul Newman said, 'if you're not sure who the sucker is, it's you.' And after almost fifteen years of being the sucker, I'll never be that way again.

I take the pen, and I sign.

AMANDA

I've always loved eating cookies so much that it never occurred to me I could screw them up this many ways.

"These are flattening because you must have used just a little less flour than the recipe said." Abigail reaches for the bowl.

I want to cry.

"Hey." She bumps me with her hip. "You're so smart—you'll be making these perfectly in no time."

Sure enough, after she's added a bit of flour, the next pan bakes perfectly.

It's only then that I remember the reason we had so many cookies last time is that I botched the recipe then, too. "What was I thinking?" I wail. "I can't start a company."

Abigail leans against the counter, licking her fingers. "Why *do* you want to start a company? Isn't your blog going well?"

It's not a blog. It's an Instagram account, but you know what? It doesn't matter. "It's fine," I say. "I mean, it's the same as always." I don't bother her with the fact that my fans will probably flip out when my #HOT-COWBOY is replaced with Derek.

"Fine isn't good enough?" She frowns. "What's up?"

"No, I mean, it really is fine, but the thing is. . ."

I can hardly tell her that I'm trying to live like she lives, and do what she would do. If I explained my plan, she'd probably laugh in my face. Abby's a top-rated lawyer. It took her years to work through law school, and years more of being an associate at a law firm. She did all that with kids, too. She'd never start a tiny company to make and sell cookies. No, she effortlessly makes perfect cookies in her free time. For fun.

I'm such a loser. What was I thinking?

While Abby washes her hands, her brow is furrowed. Clearly she's trying to make sense of me. It's hard for someone who's so perfect to grasp the underlying motivation of someone like me. That's my saving grace, the only reason she hasn't figured me out yet. She can't quite comprehend how pathetic I really am. "But if you—"

Misdirection is my only hope. "How'd the trail ride go with Steve?"

Her cheeks blaze red. Bingo.

"I mean, that's not like you, to just take off like that." A little bit of guilt can't hurt, either. Remind her that she owes me for helping out last night. Not that I had to do that much.

"He, um, right at the end of the trail ride. . ."

Oh, no way! "Did he kiss you?"

If it weren't impossible, I'd say her cheeks grow even redder. "He most certainly did not." She straightens up, drying her hands. "But he did say something. . .upsetting."

"Do tell." Who cares about the cookies! I can't believe I didn't ask her about this before.

"Well, Gabe called, and—"

"I'm so sorry. I didn't know—"

She waves me off. "No big deal, only what he said was kind of funny, and I said he was cute. Normal mom stuff, right?"

I shrug.

"And then Steve says, 'he's cute like you, but with my luck, our kid would probably look as ugly as me.'" She inhales and gulps quickly. Like a gust of wind hit her in the face or something.

I blink. "What?"

"Our kid," she says. "He said 'our kid.'"

"Oh. Like, he's already envisioning marrying you, or something?"

"I'm thirty-eight," she says, clearly exasperated with me. "Why would he say that?"

"Are we saying our ages?" I ask. "Because officially, I'll never admit that I'm forty-one."

"Stop," she says. "Be real for a minute. If your boyfriend of three minutes—"

"Whoa." I bolt up straight and step closer. "Is he your boyfriend? Did you guys define things?"

She rolls her eyes. "Amanda! Try to listen. No, we didn't talk about that."

Now I'm really confused. "So you didn't kiss, and you didn't talk about your relationship or decide you're, like, together, but he made a joke about future children and. . . Connect the dots for me. I think I missed something."

"You wouldn't care if your boyfriend, or your, whatever, your guy, commented on what your kids would look like?"

"First, Steve is not at all ugly." I frown. "So clearly, he was making a joke. He has to know he's stupidly good looking."

"Okay."

"And second, it was an offhand remark. He was just trying to be involved, and for someone with no kids, that's kind of impressive. Most guys I've met would be running for the hills."

I watch as Abby processes that, breathing in and out and nodding. Then she snaps out of it, her eyes widening, her nostrils flaring. "Did you set a timer for the cookies?"

It's hard keeping up with her, sometimes. "Uh, no." Actually, it's hard all the time.

"I think they're done." She spins around and hits the button for the light in the oven. Sure enough, she's right. When she pulls them out, they look *perfect*. She must have the nose of a bloodhound. A cookie-loving bloodhound.

"How do you do that?"

She shrugs. "Years and years of baking cookies."

"That's why you never set a timer?"

"Each batch of cookies bakes a little differently," she says. "It's safer to just be paying attention."

I can't even watch faithfully while my toast is in the toaster oven. "Well, for those of us born without a cookie-scenting superpower, I suppose good old-fashioned timers will have to do."

She laughs.

I grab the bowl and cover it.

"What are you doing?"

"I'll have to finish these later." I put the bowl in the fridge.

"Oh, no, that's a bad idea. First off, they'll dry out. Secondly, they'll pull the flavors from everything else in the fridge and taste a little funny."

I laugh. "Non-bloodhounds will be unlikely to notice. I'll take my chances."

And now she's silently judging me. "Look, I can't bake them now—I'm meeting Derek in twenty minutes."

"I wondered why you looked so dynamite." She beams

128

at me. "Good luck! Maybe he'll talk about your future children."

I chuck the oven mitt at her, but I miss.

Thanks to her, I'm in a good mood when I reach the Gorge for a date I've now rescheduled twice. Even though I'm five minutes early, he's already there, his head bowed over a laptop screen. The Gorge is hardly impressive outside, and inside it's even worse, like my grandma's old 1950s home. But the stone fireplace isn't bad, and the painting of the Flaming Gorge above it looks nice. It takes me a minute, but I frame up a decent photo.

With Derek's beautiful olive complexion and tawny golden eyes, combined with that silky black hair—people might not even notice the setting. Since he's looking at the computer and his face is occluded, I don't even have to get permission to post it. I go ahead and toss the photo up and tag it #WORKING #SMOKINGHOT #EYE-CANDYFORLUNCH and #GQ. It's not my strongest work, but Heather should be happy.

Because it's not Eddy.

That's my biggest problem with it, honestly, but I push that thought away.

"You made it." When he smiles, Derek's actually really handsome. He's easily as good-looking as anyone I ever dated in New York. It's not fair to compare him to Eddy—the only person I've ever dated who would have fit right in on any set in Hollywood.

"I'm so sorry for all the confusion," I say. "I've had a lot going on."

"Starting a new business is overwhelming," he says. "If you want to talk through any of it, I'm your guy. I've been there a lot."

"It's not only that. We're remodeling an old farm-house, plus my kids just started at a new school."

He freezes. "Who's *we*?"

I laugh. "Sorry. That did sound dodgy. I'm living with my sister-in-law. We're both widows. I can see where it might be a little nerve-wracking to ask someone on a date, find that she's a little hard to pin down, and then hear her talk about remodeling something with someone else."

He breaths a hearty sigh of relief. "Sadly, with the way my love life has been going the past few years, you having a husband or a lover or a side job as an escort would not surprise me."

"Sounds like your dating past has been as exciting as mine."

"I doubt you can really compare," he says. "There's a reason I've spent almost all my time starting businesses and then selling them. At least that's something I'm good at—and have some semblance of control over."

The way he keeps assuring me of his economic prowess is obnoxious, but. . .while he's here, maybe I should pick his brain. "I doubt much of your business venture experience will help me with mine. Have you ever tried to turn a profit on baked goods?"

The waitress comes and takes our order.

"Baked goods?" He glances sideways. "Make sure you strike up a deal with these people immediately. I've been eating here way too often, and let me tell you, they could use a little more variety."

I stifle a laugh. You never know who's listening. "I'm sure their food is wonderful."

"To answer your question, I've never owned a business in the food service industry, but I have learned that many principles are universal. For instance, if you start small, you'll never really get big." He shrugs. "Basic economics."

"What does that mean? I'm asking as a woman who's been making cookies in her own kitchen, so keep that in mind."

His sideways smile is killer. "There's nothing wrong with experimenting on a small scale. No one starts tinkering, or inventing, or manufacturing in a fifty-thousand-foot warehouse, but when you go in, go *all* in."

"Okay, put that in terms that make sense to me. Let's say my business model is to make cookies that cost me, without huge supply contracts, ninety cents to a dollar and ten cents a cookie, depending on the variety. What should I be selling them for?"

"It's good that you've worked out your basic costs, but keep in mind that economies of scale will jack with all that. And of course, as your supply costs go down, your management costs go up."

"Because I'll need employees."

"You should always be putting a value on your time." He stops. "You did calculate that into your cookie cost, right?"

Oh, boy. The rest of the lunch turns into an economics lesson, and I realize that I know next to nothing about any of this. He explains that my decisions can't be emotional ones, that I need to have a plan and regularly update it. He says that I should run everything past a partner, even if I don't have one, so that I'm getting at least two sets of eyes to spot possible issues. He even offers to help me along the way, until or unless I have a partner or a financial backer.

But eventually, the food is gone, the advice has tapered off, and I realize lunch is over. When he stands up to pay the check, I stand too and throw my purse over my shoulder.

One more thing on my list done—lunch with the good-looking stranger—and only nine gazillion more to go.

"Hey, are you alright?" His golden eyes show genuine concern.

"Oh, it's nothing." I paste a smile on my face.

"You looked pretty upset." Instead of walking toward the door, he pulls the chair out. "Don't make me sit you back down and grill you."

That actually makes me laugh. "Are you also a lawyer? Because that really reminds me of something my sister-in-law might say."

"Not even close to being a lawyer," he says, "but I started my life as a car salesman." He holds up a hand. "Before you start with the painful jokes, I know car sales-people can be annoying, but I also learned how to read people pretty well. Something's wrong, and I make it a rule never to end a date with someone I like if she doesn't look happier than when she arrived."

"Are you saying you'll take me hostage?" I arch an eyebrow.

His warm grin tells me that I may be rusty and half-uninterested, thanks to my preoccupation with the wrong guy, but I haven't completely lost all my skill at flirting. "Don't tempt me. I'm barely off probation."

"Please tell me that's a joke."

He sighs. "I do that—make questionable jokes a little too soon—but no probation at any point, ever." He holds up three fingers. "Scout's honor."

"Wow, you even did the fingers. I'm impressed." I straighten my shoulders and hold up my hand, three fingers saluting. "On my honor I will do my best to do my duty—"

"You must have brothers," he says.

"Two," I say. "Though now, they'll let anyone in."

"I miss the good old days," he says. "Where Boy Scouts meant only boys."

"Oh, no," I say. "Now that the meal is over, the true colors are coming out."

He shoves the chair back in and offers me his arm.

"That's what dating's about. You find out all my flaws and decide whether you can live with them."

I take his arm.

"For instance, today I've discovered you're quite adept at changing the subject when you don't want to answer a question."

I sigh.

"What had you looking so bummed?"

"Nothing, I swear. The date was great. It's just that talking to you helped me see that I'm in way over my head."

"You can call me anytime you need help." He reaches for the door.

But it opens before he can push it, and I'm suddenly staring at Eddy. As I'm leaving a restaurant with Derek. Again. This is starting to feel like the elevators in *Grey's Anatomy*.

I freeze, my brain realizing what I couldn't quite put into words during the lunch I just had.

One year for Christmas, I got a new bike. I could tell it wasn't *new* new, but it was new to me, and it was really nice. It had shiny chrome, a smooth purple seat, and perfectly round, perfectly serviceable tires. I was delighted to have that bike, and when I learned how to use it, it rode really well. The very first thing I did was ride it down the street to my best friend Rachel's house.

When she came to the door, she squealed. "Yes! We both got bikes!" I rode around the front of her house to meet her in front of her garage. There, leaning a bit on its shiny kickstand, was a cherry red bike. It had oversized wheels with pristine tread. It had a bell, and a basket, and beautiful fenders covering its tires. It had the kind of shine that practically put your eye out.

My bike was nice. I was lucky to have it. I really liked it, even.

Until I saw Rachel's bike.

After that, mine never really shone quite as brightly.

Eddy's like that cherry red bike. Derek was a great date—maybe the best guy I've been out with since Paul died. Kind, handsome, smart, and even funny. But compared to Eddy, he's just not shiny. It's not only about their looks, though that's the most obvious. It's also his type of humor. His timing. His charm.

It's hard to compete with a professional singer/guitar player who saves sick animals in his spare time.

And also, I've seen Eddy's stomach.

His perfect, rock-hard, eight-pack stomach.

I gulp.

"Amanda?" Derek's pulling on my arm.

While I gape idiotically at Eddy.

Who is grinning like the cocky rock star he is.

I lurch forward, nearly bowling poor Derek over.

"What would she need help with?" Eddy asks. "Because I'm from here, so she should try me first. I'm more likely to be able to help."

"If she had a sick dog, sure." Derek smirks, and it's not a great look for him. "I looked into you, Eddy. I hear you're the cow doctor around here."

"I am," Eddy says. "And you're here looking for long-term contracts with ranchers for some high falutin' beef company."

"We do partner with Jonquil," Derek says, "but I'm the Vice President of Processing and Supply for Highborn —a leather company. We've been so pleased with the quality of cattle in this area, and the quantity as well, that we're considering building a processing plant here."

Eddy frowns.

"I'd need to spend quite a significant amount of time here if we did," Derek says, "once it's established. While it's being built, I'd be here around the clock." He turns back to me. "In fact, I probably ought to look for a more permanent place to stay. Don't you think? Maybe you should help me choose a place."

"Wait, who decides whether to build a processing facility here?" I ask. "When will the decision be made?"

"I'm the one who decides," he says, "and I think I just did." He smiles at me. "Yep. I think it should be here."

Eddy snorts.

Derek narrows his eyes. "I'm sorry, did you have something to say?"

I place a hand on Derek's chest. It's not unimpressive, but it's not all flat planes and sharp lines like Eddy's was. Not that I should be thinking about that. I'm supposed to be heading off any unpleasantness before it can start. "Let's just go. Please."

Derek's still looking at Eddy when he swallows, but he nods sharply and turns away, thankfully.

"Hey, do you have a minute?" Eddy asks.

I glance pointedly at Derek, who's moving, still holding my arm. I trip along after him.

"It's about Roscoe."

I yank my arm free. "I'll meet you outside in a moment. I need to chat with him about my dog."

Derek frowns, but he doesn't argue. He even pushes through the door and lets it close behind him.

"That guy's a real charmer." Eddy's scowling at the door.

"I like him well enough."

Eddy laughs, all signs of anger gone.

"What's so funny?" I put my hand on my hip. "Eddy."

He sighs. "Nothing, just not as worried."

"Worried?" My heart contracts. "About Roscoe?"

"What?"

"Didn't you say you needed to talk to me about Rosc—"

"Oh!" Eddy slaps his forehead. "No, sorry. That was a lie to get him to leave."

"Edward Dutton!" I spin around and push on the door.

His hand grabs my upper arm firmly, but not too hard. "Amanda, just a minute, please?"

It's the please that gets me. "What?" I don't turn around. I don't look at his face. No matter what, it always softens me, and I'm officially annoyed.

"What would you need help with?" His voice is almost pained. "Are you alright?"

Oh, good grief. The plaintive note in his voice is my downfall. I turn back around. "I'm totally fine. We're remodeling, as you know, and the girls started school—"

"And you're starting a business?" Is that hope in his voice?

"Well, I'm trying the cookie thing, but it's harder than I thought, and the profit margin isn't optimal—"

"Is that what he said?" Eddy jabs a finger at the door, as if it's representative of the person who just walked through it.

As if on cue, a lady with a toddler walks through the door, and Eddy and I are forced to shift sideways. I wonder, vaguely, whether Derek's waiting on me outside, watching the minutes tick by, green with envy. Or pale with boredom.

"Did he tell you it won't work?" Eddy pauses. "Or is he saying he'll help? Because I'll help too. I may not be the vice president of anything, but I know everyone around here. I could go with you when you talk to them about selling your cookies."

"Actually, he said I need to think bigger—much bigger. He said the great thing about this area is that rent is cheap, and personnel costs are low. He said without much going on, I could likely find space and employees for a low price. He thinks I should go all in, once I have my recipes down, and—"

Eddy shakes his head. "This guy's a moron. You've never run a business, and you have no idea how well these will sell. Does he think you should just start making cookies and then hope to sell them?"

"Actually, he—"

"You should start small, and then slowly work your way up. You don't run before you can walk."

Great. Eddy thinks I should do the opposite of what Derek says, and apparently he also thinks I can barely walk. "I appreciate your input," I say.

"Amanda."

I don't want to look at him, knowing he thinks of me as some major loser who can't stand on her own and would never be wise to go big.

"I'm not insulting you." His tone is playful.

He knows me well enough to know what upset me. Sometimes I forget we've barely known each other for a few months—and had very few interactions, even in that time. He just always seems to get me without trying. "I'd better go."

"I know we can't. . ."

This time I do turn back.

"But I'm still your friend. If you need someone to talk to, or someone to help bake, or someone to help with anything, I'm not too important to do it."

It's hard, very hard, for me to turn around and walk through the door. When I do, Derek *is* there, but at least he's on a phone call.

"It is exciting. And yes, you're right, it will be a lot of work. Start working up the projections and send them for my review. I'd like to get this approved and moving." He pauses. "Yes, I will have to come back for that, but then I'll head back here. I do still need a few hundred head for this fall." He pauses again. "Yes, staggered, I know, and range raised."

He could be on this call for an hour, for all I know. I'll just text him. I move to walk around him.

When he notices me, his eyes widen. "I've got to go. I'll call you later." He hangs up.

"How's the dog?"

"What?"

He frowns. "Didn't he need to talk to you about your dog?"

"Oh, right, Roscoe. Yeah, he's alright. When I left for a while, he stopped eating, and Eddy wanted to make sure he was still gaining weight and eating well."

He rolls his eyes. "He needed an excuse, and he found one."

"We did date a few times," I say, "but that's all past, now."

"Which was your decision, clearly," he says.

"Well." The real answer is not mine to share. I decide to change the topic. "I didn't mean to eavesdrop, but did I hear you're looking for cattle?"

He blinks. "I am, yes. I've found quite a few, but Jonquil has a lot of requirements, most notably a zero-tolerance policy for any feedlots for their cows. It's part of the reason we need a processing plant out here. A lot of the local ranchers use a range over the summer, but they sell their cows as soon as they're back from the range to feedlots, and I can't buy them once they do."

Huh. "We do have a few hundred cattle," I say, as casually as I can manage. "Could you give us a good price?"

His jaw drops. "Wait, *you* have cattle?" He tilts his head. "I thought you said you were a social media influencer starting a cookie company."

"I am," I say. "But didn't you wonder what a social media influencer would be doing out here?"

He shrugs. "Moved to be near family?"

That's not entirely wrong. "Not the whole story," I say. "Suffice it to say we have cattle that haven't been, nor are they ever, kept on a feedlot."

"The slot I need filled is late fall. Could you keep them at your place that long?"

"I don't see why not," I say.

"Well, isn't this almost too lucky?" Derek's amazing smile is back.

But instead of enjoying it, I keep thinking of that shiny red bike that I'll never have.

❦ II ❦

AMANDA

I should never have insisted on picking the color scheme. I'm not the kind of person who usually demands that I get my way, but after that lunch where I thought I lined up an amazing deal for the ranch. . .and then Abigail had a million questions about the price per pound, and guarantees, and timing—I had all those fears dive bombing in my head, too.

It became horribly obvious that I know nothing about ranching, and nothing about starting a company, either.

When Abby said that the paint color I picked was too bright and it would look awful, I doubled down. I argued and I insisted and I complained.

And finally, Abigail Brooks, the most confident person I know, gave way to me.

I'm so happy she's working right now, and she hasn't yet seen the wall.

It's ghastly.

Everything she said was right. It's far too bright. It's totally a color you'd see at a beach resort in Miami. It won't fit the tone of the house. It'll overpower the rest of the room. Check, check, check, and double check. At least I can stop the painter from doing the entire room that color. I'm not great at Spanish, but I know that much. "Oh, no," I say. "No me gusta. Quizas debemos usar blanco para los otros paredes."

"I speak English, lady," the painter says.

And now I feel even dumber. "Um, so that works as an accent wall color," I lie. "But can we use white for the other walls?"

The English-speaking painter's expression is flat. "I don't have white paint."

"You have the ceiling paint," I say.

"It's matte, flat white." He's utterly unimpressed.

I sigh. "I'll go buy more."

He's just finishing the second coat on the back wall when I make it back. Luckily, the grocery store slash hardware store had satin finish eggshell paint. It's not going to be amazing, but better than four walls painted in slap-your-eyes-out aqua.

The kids aren't even home from school yet, and I feel the need to hide. I slink into the family room to look for my purse, since my keys live there, but Abigail catches me.

"That Derek guy texted me. He wants to talk about details in an hour. I'm meeting him at the Gorge."

"Okay."

"You're coming, right?" Abigail never dances around things.

"You know, I think I would only make it harder."

"Amanda. The only reason I'm meeting him at all is because—"

"The thing is, I promised Amanda Saddler I'd take her. . ." I look around the kitchen. There's a bowl of plums. "Plums. She said she was dying to have some, if we saw any good ones, and then—"

"I just happened to come back with some." Abigail

clearly suspects me, but she can't prove anything. "I'm not going to cut him some kind of deal because you think he's cute."

"And don't I know it?" Thank goodness for Abigail. I've never been more grateful to have her to run things. "Actually, maybe what I need is to have you help me with the cookie—"

"Amanda, you know I love you."

Do I? Does she? For some reason, that simple phrase kind of arrests me in place. Abigail Brooks, goddess walking among mortals, loves me? Amanda Brooks, who can't parent well, who has no idea how to run her love life or her business, and who is failing at everything, including imitating Abigail Brooks? I sigh.

"But I cannot take on anything else. Not another single project of any kind." Her shoulders are a little drooped, now that she mentions it. Is Abigail tired? I didn't think she ever got tired. I didn't think about her ever taking on too much. "And also, I love making cookies. That's my relaxation. I would never make them to sell. It would ruin something I love."

It had also never occurred to me that she might make cookies so often. . .because she enjoys it. What kind of person relaxes by standing up for hours and mixing things and baking things and cleaning up pans and bowls? There's definitely something wrong with her brain. The only reason I make cookies is so that they can get inside my belly. And now, to turn a profit, hopefully. "Well, don't let me keep you. I'm just grabbing my purse." I sling it over my shoulder and head for the door.

"And the plums, right?" Her cocked eyebrow tells me that my shabby excuse has been discovered.

"Right." I circle back to the kitchen and grab a few plums. She may know, but I can still pretend she doesn't.

My entire life has prepared me for this moment—clinging to something long past the time it really stopped working.

It's a relief to drive the mile down the road and pull into Amanda's drive. She has no idea I'm coming, of course, and I'm certainly not taking the plums in with me, but I know she'll welcome me anyway.

"Brooks? Is that you?" She must have been in the garden and heard me coming, because she's wearing her huge straw sunhat and coming around from the side of the house. Her grunty little pig is trotting along at her side, but he's not wearing a scarf this time.

"It's me." I climb out of the car, and the pig, who has largely ignored me up until now, trots over, its entire body jiggling as it runs.

For some reason, this time, it runs right up to me and sniffs my feet, whuffling and grunting. I've never been around a pig, and it makes me pretty nervous.

"Is it alright? What's it doing?"

"Jed," Amanda yells. "Come over here right now."

The pig ignores her, but when she pulls a clicker out of her pocket and clicks it, it lets out one last huff and turns.

"Do you have plums?" Amanda peers around me into the car.

"Uh, yes. I do, actually."

She shakes her head. "Jed's usually pretty well behaved, but he goes wild for plums, for some reason."

No wonder. I reach into the car and snag the three small plums I brought as my excuse. My lie turned out to be true, sort of. "He's welcome to these—"

The mostly black pig starts to shake and grunt wildly. When I hold them out to Amanda, he even hops toward them. It makes me very nervous. He must weigh a hundred pounds.

"Jed, knock it off, or I won't give you any."

Amanda takes the plums and rolls her eyes. "Did you wanna come inside?"

"You named him Jed?" I look at the pig, who isn't really very attractive, by my standards at least. "Were you not a fan of my late husband's uncle?" Jedediah Brooks is the man whose house we're living in—the man who left his ranch to my kids, if they work it for a year.

"Let's just say the pig reminded me of the man." She snorts and heads for the front door. The second we get close, a red bird starts to sing. "Hush, Arizona. I know her."

Amanda Saddler is, without a doubt, the strangest person I know. I follow her into the house, curious what new thing I'll learn next. "Sorry to just invite myself over."

She keeps walking, veering hard to the right to go into her kitchen. Once there, she grabs a knife and cuts the plum in half. "I know you want them all, but too many plums gives you diarrhea, you gross thing." She tosses the half plum to Jed, and he snaps it up, juice running down his face and onto the wooden floor. As soon as he finishes chewing, he sets to licking up his mess.

"I don't really need anything. I just came by because, well, I needed to get away from my house."

"I saw all the cars. Remodel? Is that what I heard down at the True Value?"

"Probably a dumb idea," I say, "but yeah. We decided that with six kids and two adults, we'd better make some extra room."

"About time. Jed refused to change a single thing in that house, the stubborn pig."

I'm seeing a little more why she named her pet after him. "Well, we're starting by adding the new space, and then after that, we'll fix up some things in the house, like updating the kitchen."

She smiles. "But it's exhausting. I know—I redid this place ten years ago. I swore I'd never do it again."

"Yeah, and instead of just me making decisions, it's me and Abby, and we don't always like the same things."

"You have someone, though. It's always nice to have family around."

Poor Amanda. She's the only one left of her family. That must be lonely. No wonder she dresses up her pig.

"That's not the only thing, though." She may be older, but she's a keen observer. "You've been remodeling for a while. Why'd you come today?" She pins me with the same stare she gave Jed when he was misbehaving.

"I'm fine."

"You can tell me, you know. I don't talk to anyone." She cackles.

"It's just that, I wanted to start a business, and it's a lot harder than I expected it to be."

"A business? Don't you do things online? Something with photos and selling stuff?"

I sigh. "Something like that, but that job interferes with my life."

She pulls the fridge open. "This feels like a two-drink kind of conversation." She plonks a handful of beers onto the counter. "Are you a regular or a lite gal?"

Ah, Amanda. Coming here was the right thing to do. Half a drink later, I've explained my cookie idea.

"But I don't understand *why* you want to make cookies. You make a great living with the internet photos, and even if you don't love it, why change horses now?"

"Well, they've started to try and tell me what to do."

"Like, telling you what to eat and how to dress?"

I'm almost embarrassed to say that they've done that all along. It sounds a little silly, when I explain things out loud. They shouldn't call me an influencer—they should call me *influenced*. "Well, that, and they started asking my daughter to pose for their stuff too—"

"Oh, that's a heck no."

"I did tell them that," I say.

"Good for you." She empties her second drink in one long pull and slams it down on the coffee table. "So stop pussy footing around it and tell me what the real reason is for the cookies."

I shouldn't tell her. She's from here. She knows everyone. She barely knows me at all. I have no idea whom she'll tell or. . . But in spite of all those reasons, I trust her. So I spill about Eddy. About how I like him, and I think he likes me, and she doesn't even interrupt and tell me he's a womanizer. She doesn't tell me it's silly, and she did know about his past already. How he was a big musician until, just before he turned 18, he got hooked on drugs, got high, and hit someone with his car.

He murdered someone.

The man turned out to be a serial killer, so they didn't press charges, but the fact is, Eddy has a past.

"And your shiny company don't want that to come out, right?" She may not understand anything about Instagram or influencers, but she's still sharp as a tack. "So you're starting this business, hoping you can bag that one and live how you want for once."

"For once?"

"Girl, you're pretty, you're smart, and you're talented. But you don't hide things very well. You don't talk about your husband as though you had a happy marriage. People don't just suddenly let someone else tell them what to do. I'm guessing you've been letting other people dictate your life for a long time, now."

My jaw drops and my mouth dangles open.

"Look, I'm not telling you want to do, and I'm beginning to think that's a rarity in your life."

Like a strobe light has gone off in my head, all of a sudden, things are clearer. Paul led me to this—not only by investing in risky, confusing options that expired after his death, unused. Not only by leaving us with no life insurance and no security, but also by the way he treated me during our marriage.

The way I let him treat me.

More than ever, I realize how important it is that I do what Abigail would do. She'd never let anyone push her around like I have. She'd never allow a company to dictate her future. She forges her own path, she makes her own decisions, and she's accountable to no one but herself.

"I really need this cookie thing to work," I say, "but all the advice I get conflicts. Eddy said I should start small, but this guy I met, this business guy, Derek, says I should go all in. He thinks I should rent a place and hire employees, and prepare for big business."

"Do you have savings, girl?"

I swallow. "A little."

"What's a little?"

"It was expensive to move out here," I hedge. "And my two girls were in private school for years."

"Do I look like someone who's going to judge you?" She peers at me, her face full of wrinkles from smiling. Her clothing's a mishmash of athletic gear and granny chic. She's been nothing but welcoming, supportive, and truthful in a way few people have ever been truthful around me.

"No, I guess not. I have about forty thousand dollars." Hey, I'm Amanda. I'm a forty-one year old woman with two kids, and I could barely buy a car with my savings.

I'm sure Abigail has a few million. Plus her house. Plus whatever her husband left her in life insurance. Ugh, I'm such a mess.

"That's more than enough," she says, "for you to do

what both of them say. You should start with something big enough to succeed, but small enough not to overwhelm or overextend yourself."

"Wait." What does this reclusive woman who lives in the middle of nowhere know about running a cookie business? Can she even bake?

"I know what you're thinking," she says. "Young people always underestimate how many things I've done in my lifetime. I look like a dried up old prune." Her laugh is wheezy.

"Not at all," I lie.

"But guess what? When everyone else was spending their money, I was sitting here in this house. It started to pile up, you know."

"Actually, I know very little about money piling up." I take a long drink. "But please do tell me all about how that feels."

"Well, I didn't like it a bit," she says. "So I decided to do something with my money. Every year, after I sold our cows off, I'd take the extra and I'd use it."

"For what?" I wonder—what did she buy? Does she have an attic full of Beanie Babies? Old baseball cards? Does she collect enormous diamonds?

"My favorite show was *I Love Lucy*." She grins. "Have you heard of it?"

I vaguely recall an old black and white show with strange hairstyles and a lot of slapstick humor. My face must give away my lack of knowledge.

"Never mind that then, but two characters, Fred and Ethel, were Lucy and Ricardo's landlords, and I always loved the idea of owning something and having someone else pay me for it." She beams.

"Wait, so did you buy an apartment complex?"

She rolls her eyes. "I'm not forty, dear. I'm almost ninety."

What does that have to do with my question?

"I started with a duplex, but by now I own half of Manila. I've been buying up lots all over the place for decades."

I can't decide whether she's serious or whether she's teasing me.

But she doesn't laugh—she doesn't even crack a smile. "I think you and I are in a position to help each other."

"How can you help me, exactly?"

"Your friend is right—you want to do this big enough that you're not trying to make cookies in a tiny old oven Jed never replaced. That thing's barely better than an EZ Bake oven—you know those boxes with the heat lamp kids use? Plus, if you try to do this at home, you'll annoy everyone in that house in short order."

"So you think I should rent a place from you?"

"Let me finish. Young people are always in such a rush."

A rush?

"That beautiful Edward Dutton is right too. You don't want to go into debt to try and start a company when you're not sure whether it will succeed. You should learn to walk before you run."

What's with people around here implying I can barely walk?

"I propose you take over one of my little shops, and you spend the money to remake it into a bakery by buying a nice set of commercial ovens and installing great countertops and whatnot. Probably put in a little shop window and some display cases. A table and chairs or two wouldn't be a bad idea, either."

"Okay."

"In exchange, I'll let you have it rent free for six months. That should give you enough time to really make a go of it."

"Rent free?" I can hardly believe my ears. "What's the catch?"

She shrugs. "No catch. What did I tell you when you moved back down?"

I can't remember.

"You came from New York where everything you might want is at your fingertips. Here, we don't have much, but we value what we have. You moved out here and took a chance on us? That makes you my family."

My own mother would never offer me free rent. She barely sends me a holiday card. Tears well up in my eyes—it's too much. I almost can't believe it.

"Before you get all weepy on me, remember this. I've seen a lot, and you know what? In sixty years of investing in this area, I've never backed the wrong horse. So if you have me behind you, that means you're already headed in the right direction."

I don't even bother trying to stop the tears after that.

12

ABIGAIL

I haven't agonized over what I would wear to an event since high school prom. Mostly because I'm sensible about this sort of thing and I never cared that much.

But also, having access to Amanda's closet is making it way, way easier to obsess.

"Tell me again why I shouldn't hate you?" Amanda arches one perfectly plucked and filled eyebrow.

"This was your idea!" I drop the dress I'm holding back onto the top of her bed and back away. "I'll just take this one off and—"

"Oh, stop. It's my way of complimenting you. I just hate that now, when I put these things on, I'll always remember how much better you looked in them."

"I'm surprised you can both wear the same things." Maren eyes me up and down critically from the corner of the room. I didn't realize she'd be part of the decision-making committee, but I'm not in a position to turn anyone away.

"Thanks for being willing to share," I say, "or I'd be going to this dance in a business suit."

"I can't believe that's all you have," Amanda says. "I suppose when you go back out to Houston to pack the house and bring things back, you won't need to borrow clothes anymore." She sounds almost wistful about it, like she's enjoying this.

"Not really. Back home I have more of what I have here. Business suits, jeans and t-shirts, and workout clothing. I still can't figure out where you ever wore any of this."

"My job was to see and be seen, and to make sure that everyone who followed my account saw me being seen."

That sounds *exhausting*, but it does come with a great wardrobe.

Amanda hands me the white lace sheath dress I dropped. "You literally can't wear this dress after this weekend since it's white, so go try it on."

"Mom, no one follows that rule anymore." Maren's staring at her phone, the picture perfect image of a bored teen.

I put it on like I've been ordered to, but it's so tight in the top that it feels like I'm toothpaste being squeezed from a tube. "This one won't work."

"At least show us," Maren says.

"Come out," Amanda says. "We've already proven that you can't be allowed to make this decision yourself."

I was ready to go thirty minutes ago, in a grey suit skirt and a red, white, and grey silk blouse. They said it looked like I was ready for court, not a date. They weren't wrong about that, but I can save us all a lot of time with this one. "Really, it's too small."

"Get your buns out here before I break in there," Amanda says.

I remind myself it's only Maren and Amanda, and I finally open the door.

"Oh. My. Goodness." Maren's eyes are round. I swear,

it feels like she'd sell me at auction if the bidding got high enough. "I mean, I knew they were bigger, but your boobs are *so* much bigger than Mom's."

"Yep, I hate you." Amanda stands up and starts gathering her clothing into her arms.

"I told you I can just wear the skirt and blouse. Steve won't care."

Amanda stops. "Um, no, you cannot wear that. Just, no. Not unless you're going to this thing to drum up business."

"Well, it's either that, or a pair of jeans and—"

"The dress you're wearing is *the* dress," Maren says. "That's what Mom's saying. It's why she's hiding the other stuff, so you won't try to change into one of those."

I look down at my mountain of cleavage and cover it with my hands. "Are you kidding right now? My *kids* are right outside."

Maren bites her lip.

Amanda just laughs. "You'd think from your reaction that an inch and a half of cleavage qualifies you for an adult film."

"I can't leave this room wearing this dress. I won't."

Amanda sighs.

"My chest got bigger with each kid and just never shrank back down," I say. "But that doesn't mean that—"

"Wait, are you complaining?" Maren asks.

"For the record, that's not normal," Amanda says. "Mine shrank back every time. The only change that stuck around was the newfound sagginess."

Maren laughs. "I know. I've seen."

Okay. "Look, I really appreciate what you're trying to do, but I'm going to just wear my grey skirt and—"

Maren whips out her phone and snaps a photo. She taps on her phone and a moment later, mine buzzes on the bed.

"What are you doing?" I put my hands on my hips and make my strongest I-am-a-scary-mother face.

"Look at the photo," Maren says. "If you still think you look indecent, fine. We'll give up. But I think it's your angle. You look down and all you see is an unfamiliar sight. But when we look at you, yes, you look curvy, but also you look classy and you look elegant, and you look amazing." She points at my phone. "Go ahead. Pick it up. Look at that woman, and pretend she's not you, and tell me what you'd be thinking. If any part of it is *adult film star,* we'll keep looking."

"Steve will be here any minute."

"Better hurry, then," Amanda says.

These two are the worst, but I pick up the phone. And I look, pretending it's a photo of Amanda, not me. And. . .they're right. I don't even see much cleavage. Mostly I see a horrifying amount of leg. I tug on the hem.

"See?" Maren beams. "I was right, right?"

"You did highlight how much shorter this was than I realized."

"Oh, for the love," Amanda says. "You're not going to argue a case before a judge. You're going on a *date.*"

"I won't enjoy myself in this," I counter. "Thank you for your help, but—"

The doorbell rings. Steve is five minutes early. Five whole minutes. Don't guys know that being *early* for a date is a cardinal sin? I should just tell him I can't go. I've changed my mind. I march through Amanda's door and toward the front door, ready to give him a piece of my mind, but Ethan has already opened it.

Steve's chatting with him, and then he turns and freezes mid-sentence. His pupils dilate. His mouth opens just a hair farther. And Ethan turns around to see what he's staring at and swears, loudly.

"Ethan Elijah Brooks."

My adorable son blushes bright pink. "Mom, you can't get mad at me." He looks me over head to toe and exhales. "I mean, I got no warning. None at all."

Steve's nodding. "I second that. No warning."

"You can't second it. He's not making a resolution in parliament."

Steve's still staring.

I snap at him. "That settles it. I'm not wearing this."

His eyes shoot upward to meet mine. "I'm just not used to seeing you look like you could walk off the set of, I don't know, *The Devil Wears Prada*."

Someone did a great job with his pop culture education, even if I still haven't found out whom I should be thanking. "I'm going to change into a skirt and blouse. I'll be right back."

Steve grabs my arm. "Oh, I think what you're already wearing is just fine."

Amanda beams at me from the doorway of her room.

If he really wanted to be helpful, Ethan could take my side, but clearly, he's useless. "Fine. Let me at least grab my purse and a sweater."

"No." Amanda moves in front of me. "Maren, go get her purse, but no sweater. You'll just wrap yourself up in it all night like a cocoon and you'll ruin the entire look."

"Oh," Steve says. "This is Amanda's dress. That makes more sense."

For some reason, that makes Amanda smile.

"That's why it's too small." I huff. "It's why I look so ridiculous."

"No one's thinking that," Ethan mutters.

"Oh, Mom!" Whitney's head is poking out from the hallway. "You look like a movie star!"

"Let's go," I say. "Quick, before anyone else sees me."

"I want a photo!" Whitney runs across the room and hugs me. "Can I get one?"

Twenty minutes and a hundred photos later, Steve and I are finally allowed to leave. "That will teach me to borrow something from Amanda," I say.

He opens the door of his truck for me. "I bet you look better in it than she does."

I slap his shoulder as I climb in. "Stop acting like a teenager."

"I'm taking the most beautiful woman in ten counties to a dance to show her off to every single person I know. And on top of that, she's also the smartest woman in the state." He leans in close to me, grinning. "Teenagers get a bad rap, you know? They just show their emotions in a way adults are afraid to do." It's probably the dim light, combined with the bright violet overhead lighting from his truck, but I can't stop looking at Steve's perfect teeth. And around them, his full, half-smiling lips.

Which reminds me of what he said a few days ago.

I won't kiss you until you're so desperate you'll cling to me.

My heart kicks it up a notch. I feel drawn to his mouth, like Roscoe to a piece of bacon. (Okay, like most anyone to a piece of bacon.)

Steve's eyes drop to my mouth, and the air practically quivers. Or maybe that's just my butterfly-filled stomach. And then he straightens, just like that. Like picking lint from his pants. Like flipping a switch. Easy. Barely an irritation.

At least I have a few breaths to calm down while he circles around to the other side of the truck. I thought he was kidding with his 'make you desperate' thing, but was he serious? Because it feels like I'm almost there.

I shake it off, though. That's insane. My husband died, and it didn't even happen two years ago. What's wrong with me? I shouldn't be thinking about kissing someone. I need to simply enjoy the evening, go home, and focus on what matters: work, kids, and our new home.

"What are you thinking about?"

"I finally chose a real estate agent," I say. "It makes the whole move seem real, somehow."

"What will you do when the house sells?" Steve asks.

"Do you mean, will I be sad, or will I do a happy dance?"

"I was asking if you'd stay in the farmhouse or find or build another place, but sure. Let's go with your thing."

"We're kind of stuck in the farmhouse, I think, unless Ethan wants to drive out to the ranch every single day. Speaking of, did you know your friend Donna's kind of a backstabber?"

His head actually whips sideways. "Excuse me?"

"Amanda and I met her at the school where she's working, and she acted like she and Aiden knew no one and had only been back for a short time. She sounded so. . .forlorn. . .that we asked her to come for dinner."

"Okay." He's agitated—I've struck a nerve by calling her a backstabber.

"Do you remember when I was slicing the brownies you brought? Remember all those questions she kept asking about our summer, like when we left, and when we came back?"

He shrugs. "Maybe?"

"It's possible that I remember things like that precisely because they remind me of work. But a few days later, she prepared an affidavit and sent it to the Institute of Alien Studies, or whatever it's called. You know, the people who'll take the ranch if we fail to work it for a year."

Steve actually stops the car on the side of the road, turns on his blinkers, and turns to face me. "She did *what?*"

"You heard me right. She's trying to get us kicked out."

"Why on earth would she do that?" Then his eyes widen. "Because she wants to buy it?"

I shrug. "Presumably."

"Wait, why would your leaving for a few weeks mean they get it?"

I fill him in on the vague wording in the will. "I don't think that a clause saying we are allowed to leave for one-week vacations was ever meant to be construed as a limitation on how long we can leave, but Mr. Swift disagrees."

"That's madness. Obviously Jed only meant for the ranch to go to them if you guys had no interest."

"Luckily it's not up to Mr. Swift. It's quite clear on that point. The panel Jed appointed exists for exactly this sort of thing, to determine whether we've met our obligations under the will."

"Eddy and I would never—"

"Patrick Ellingson is the third member of the committee, as I understand it."

Steve swears under his breath.

"I take it that's bad."

"He's got to be behind this. Donna would never—"

I hate to cut him off again, but Donna most certainly did do it. "Patrick couldn't have *made* her come that night. And he didn't sign her name on that affidavit, either."

"I wouldn't put it past him." He pulls out his phone.

"What are you doing?"

"I'm looking up the technology on skin suits."

I can't help my laugh. I put my hand on his arm. "Steve, either way, it will be fine. If we're not meant to have the ranch, then we won't have it."

His face turns toward mine slowly. "You're just going to give up?"

"Do you know me at all?" I quirk one eyebrow. "I never give up, on anything."

The corners of his mouth turn upward. "Oh, ho, ho. I have a feeling Patrick is in for a surprise."

"And Donna, too. I'm quite good at what I do."

"But maybe you should hold off on selling your house until you're sure which way it will go."

I've had the same thought, but I'm surprised to hear Steve say it.

"Or, maybe I'm an idiot for even suggesting that." His lips compress. "Go ahead and sell it now, while the market is hot."

"If we don't get this ranch, there's not much to keep us here," I say.

"I'm going to kill Patrick," he says. "If he wrecks this, I'll rip off his arms and feed them to Amanda Saddler's pig."

"Why the pig?"

"Pigs will eat anything."

"Ew, gross. That made me visualize." I slap his shoulder again.

This time, he catches my hand. "I'm only half kidding, and I'm not just saying that because I like you, and I *do* like you, Abigail Brooks. I'm also saying it because trying to keep a family from inheriting their family land is wrong. There's no way Jed really wanted it to go to some foundation, no matter how adamant he was that alien life exists. It was just meant to force you to put down roots here—to commit to being a part of the community. I'm sure of it."

"Well, let's hope we can convince a judge if it comes to that."

"We can." His eyes meet mine, and they're intense. More intense than I ever recall Nate being a day in his life.

I've been thinking of this man as a fill-in for my last

husband. But maybe that's been all wrong. Maybe I've been doing Steve a disservice.

"So you're going to list your house tomorrow, you said?" It's a recycled joke, but it does the job of breaking the tension.

"That's the plan," I say.

"And will the kids be sad?" His expression tells me what he's really asking. He wants to know whether I'll be sad.

"Yes and no." I think about how to explain this. "I'm sure you've lost horses you loved over the years."

Steve nods.

"If you had things that reminded you of them, you probably had mixed feelings about those things. Halters, maybe, or a particular stall?"

He nods.

"Our house is absolutely full of memories with Nate, and we all really needed that after he died. We needed to wrap ourselves up in the sadness of it all. We needed memories of good times, so that we could feel the depth of our loss."

"That's almost poetic."

"Buried under all my legal training is the soul of an artist."

Except he doesn't laugh at my joke. "I think that may be true."

"Oh, come on."

"I mean it, but go on."

"Now I'm not sure what to say." I force a chuckle. "But after a while, new memories replaced the old ones. We celebrated Christmas in the same house without Nate, and the memories of that replaced the ones that used to fill up that space." I sigh. "I'm wrecking this explanation. Maybe I should try and write it down—"

"No, I think I get what you're saying. My first horse,

Champion, was the opposite of a champion. He was stubborn, and he was lazy, and he was not keen on doing anything he wasn't forced to do." He shakes his head. "But that horse was perfect for me. It may not make sense to you, but he was like a babysitter in a horse body. He kept me from doing plenty of stupid things, including riding right off the edge of a cliff that I didn't realize was there." His eyes are almost unfocused. "Once, he kicked another horse that was trying to bite me. That horse—I may never love another horse quite that much. When he died." He sighs. "I couldn't put another horse into his stall for years. Finally, when that barn was falling apart, I decided to level the whole thing and build a new one. Not only because of that useless stall, but partly because of it."

Maybe he does get it. "We're all sad to sell the house. We may be devastated if it actually sells. I'm not sure. Sometimes grief clocks you sideways—in ways you just don't expect. But I think that we can sell the home, but retain our memories in it. It might even be kinder to me and the kids, to move forward without lugging around the sadness of overlaying those memories with new ones. Sometimes it feels like we're forgetting him over and over and over, like the simple act of living life is an assault."

Steve doesn't say anything else, but a few moments later, we're crossing a beautiful bridge with a soaring arch across the top of it. We've finally reached the Flaming Gorge Resort. The resort itself looks a little like a small apartment complex—the units all appear to be accessed from the outside—but the scenery around it, from the dam, to the pine trees, to the soaring sunset overhead, is breathtaking.

"I suppose this doesn't look like much to someone accustomed to posh places in a big city."

"This whole area is beautiful," I say. "I feel blessed to be here."

I don't wait for him to circle around to open my door —that always made me feel a little weird, for some reason —but he offers me his arm immediately after I emerge from the car, and I take it. The high heels Amanda insisted I wear with the dress are not stable in the best of places, and this parking lot is not entirely even to begin with.

"Thanks for coming," Steve says. "Prepare to be bombarded."

I'm not sure what he means, as we approach the main pavilion. The resort has put out a large tent, as well as a wide, flat dance floor. There's a buffet down one side, and tables at which to eat, and there's already a band tuning up on the other side of the dance floor. We've barely reached the tent when people begin to pop up in front of us.

I try to remember the names of all the people—many of which already know my name—but I give up after the tenth.

"Don't worry," Steve says. "You won't be quizzed on it later."

"That's a relief," I say. "You may not know this, but I'm almost thirty-nine. And that's when your memory just, poof. Disappears."

"Is that so?" Steve asks. "That explains a lot. For the past few years, I've just been making up medical treatments—so far, no one has caught on. But if they find out I'm forty-one..." He pulls a face.

I roll my eyes.

"I really am sorry for the eager people," he says.

"Liar."

Another couple arrives then, the guy going on and on about how confused I must be to have come with the Horse Doc. The woman looks annoyed. Steve finally steers me away from them. "I'd hate for her to pass out—haven't fed her yet."

"Are you sure she has room to eat in that dress?" The woman sounds as catty as she looks.

"Fine." Steve picks up a plate. "I'll admit it. I'm having a great time showing you off to everyone, including the people like that woman, Courtney Baldo. She's been that obnoxious since grade school."

She definitely overhead him. "Uh." I whisper, "She's right behind us. She can hear you."

"I was counting on that," Steve says. "If no one ever tells a spoiled brat that they're spoiled, how will they know?"

Courtney scowls, and pulls her husband toward the table at the far end of the room.

"In all honesty." This time, Steve's the one whispering. "It's been pretty lousy to come to these for the past, oh, decade or so. That comment she made about your dress was nothing to the kinds of things my friends have speculated about me."

I almost tease him about it, pressing for details, but the note of sincerity I hear underlying his statement stops me. I can imagine what things they might say about an older bachelor, and none of them are very kind. "I'm happy to be your armor tonight."

To my great relief, he finds us a table for two. He leaves for a few minutes to go to the restroom, but otherwise, he never leaves my side. There's no awkward conversation during our meal, and thanks to the tiny table, no one else interrupts us at all. As if he planned it, right as we finish our food, the dancing starts.

Steve stands up and offers me his hand.

"Wait, do you dance?" Nate was terrible. He had no moves, and he was strictly a bounce-from-foot-to-foot or shuffle-around kind of guy.

"I can't waltz or rumba or salsa, if that's what you're asking," he says.

"Then where are we going?"

"Out here, we don't really do much of any of that anyway."

"What do you do?"

He smiles. "Country swing, and baby, I'm good at it."

It's not a lie. It's not even lie-adjacent. I have no idea what I'm doing, but it doesn't matter. By the third song, I'm able to move when he tells me. It's a little like watching him ride a horse—the animal has no choice but to gracefully go where he leads. I should have known he'd be an excellent dancer.

After a half dozen more songs, I wave. "Water," I rasp. "I need water."

"You're so melodramatic," he says, but he's smiling.

"Parched," I say. "That's the word you're looking for." And sweaty, but I feel like the polite thing is not to draw attention to it. And at least I'm not the only one. The night air has cooled down significantly, and it washes over me like a caress as soon as we leave the dance floor.

"Ah, that feels nice."

"It is a decent work out," Steve says.

"That's why you wanted to come," I say. "You wanted me to see your moves."

"My mom didn't raise a fool." Steve's cocky grin is almost as hot as his dancing. Not quite, but almost.

"Is there anything you're bad at?"

"You can't set up lines like that," Steve says. "Not unless you want me to reply."

I run through a few terrible responses in my head and laugh. "I'm so sorry. I'm new to this, dating master."

"Ouch."

After we've both taken a short break, the people gathered around us start calling him back out. I don't even blame them. When a woman at least ten years younger than I am approaches us, Steve stiffens.

"Abby, darling, you have to spare him for a few songs. The rest of us are dying out there." She leans in like she's sharing a secret. "Do you know how many times my feet have been stepped on?"

Steve's arm circles my waist. "I'm so sorry, Amy, but Abby's a terrible introvert. She'd be terrified if I abandoned her." He pulls me back onto the dance floor before Amy can protest.

"Who was that?"

"Don't ask," Steve says. "Just know that some of my attempts before you were not well advised."

That's got to be the worst thing about a small town. There's no escape from things like that. I should remember that myself.

About ten or so songs later, my dumb heels have rubbed a blister on my heel.

"Are you alright?" Of course Steve notices right away.

"I'm fine," I say.

"You're wearing unfamiliar shoes." He glances down. "I notice when a horse goes lame. Did you think I'd ignore a person?"

I bite my lip.

"For a beautiful mother of four, it may be time to call it a night."

"Maybe," I say.

He leans down and takes my shoe off. Then he lifts my foot up and looks at the blister. "Yep, that's what I thought."

"What?"

"It looks uncomfortable." He hands me my purse and my shoe, and then he slides his arms underneath my knees and underneath my back and he stands.

"Whoa," I say. "I'm fine to walk."

"I know you are," he says. "But you see, this isn't about you. This is about the male need to protect." He grins. "You're smart, capable, and you probably make close to the same amount of money as I do." He sighs. "What else can I do to get your attention?" He whispers the next part against my ear. "Be a good sport and pretend to be impressed by how effortlessly I'm carrying you in your time of need."

"You're panting."

"Did you hear that I'm forty-one?" He wheezes. "And I'm doing an awful lot of talking."

"Are you sending me some kind of message?" I ask. "Do I need to lay off the cookies?"

He laughs. "Now who's being ridiculous?" He only sets me down for a moment while he unlocks his truck. Then he opens the door and watches over me as I climb in.

Before I can pull the door closed, he leans toward me, his face approaching mine slowly. I realize that it's finally happening. We ate, we danced, and he carried me out to his car, and now, he's coming in for a kiss. I lift my lips upward toward his, almost ready to cling to him like he said.

And he tucks a white stringy thing that's come out of the shoulder of my dress back underneath and steps back. "Thank you for coming with me tonight."

I blink a few times, and then I want to scream. Is he really never going to kiss me?

"You look flushed. Do you need some water?" His grin is practically evil.

He knows.

He knows I want him to kiss me, and he's still not doing it.

What is wrong with him?

What's wrong with me? I need to get it together. Tonight isn't about him kissing me. I should not be thinking any of these things. I buckle my seatbelt and try not to think about how he hasn't kissed me. Four dates, kind of, and no kiss. Does he not really like me?

"How was that, for a party thrown in an exceedingly tiny community?"

"I had a great time." I say that in as peppy a voice as I can, so he doesn't realize what I've been thinking about. "My thighs may not forgive me in the morning, but for now, I'm good."

"I bet you'll bounce back. I didn't start suffering until I actually turned forty. Now if I do too many push-ups, I get tendonitis." He grimaces.

"I know you're kidding, but there's not much difference between thirty-eight and forty-one."

"You're still young," he says. "That's all I'm saying."

That makes me think about what he said before. About kids. I should just let it go, but now that my brain has gone there, it's like a squirrel with a nut. I can't stop worrying over it.

"You got quiet."

"On that trail ride," I say.

"Yeah?"

"You made a joke."

"I did?" I can barely see that he's arched an eyebrow in the glow from the dash.

"You said our kid would be ugly."

"I'm sure your genes are strong enough to keep that from happening." His half-smile is back, that one dimple showing in full force.

"That's what I was wondering about. Were you serious?"

"Almost never."

"But do you really want a kid?"

"I love kids," he says.

"But, and I know we're like on step one." Before step

167

one, really. He hasn't even kissed me yet. "But if we date, and we like each other, and we move ahead, and one day we get married, would you want a child? I mean, we're old."

"Not that old," he insists.

And suddenly, I'm worried that Amanda was wrong. What if he does want a kid? "So is that a yes? You do want to have a child of your own?"

He shrugs. "I've always wanted a kid. Think back to before you had yours. Didn't you want to meet a child of your own?"

Oh, no. Oh, no, no, no. "Steve, I have four kids."

"I'm aware." He glances my way. "You seem to adore everything about being a mother. You're the best mom I've ever met."

"I do love it," I say, "but there's no chance I'll ever have another baby."

His face falls. "You can't?"

"It's not about 'can't' for me." I frown. "I *won't*. And if that's something that matters to you, it's probably better for us both to know that now."

Steve doesn't say anything else for the entire ride home. When he finally pulls up in front of my house, he says, "It's important to me. I guess I didn't know how important until you told me it wasn't ever going to happen for you."

My heart sinks, more than I thought it would. "Okay."

"I don't think we should make any decisions tonight."

But, if we're being honest with ourselves, it feels like maybe there isn't much of a decision to make. It's already been made.

13

DONNA

I've never been poor in my life.

My dad was always one of the most successful ranchers in the area. When I got accepted to Stanford, he sat me down and made a deal. He didn't want me to have to take out a truckload of debt, and he didn't want me trying to work part time while at one of the most competitive colleges in the country. The only thing worse to my dad than not getting into a school I wanted to attend would be failing after I'd gotten there.

But California's an expensive place to live, and Stanford isn't cheap either.

Dad offered to finance all the costs of my education, but to be fair to my brother who didn't even go to college, that money would be my inheritance. As an eighteen-year-old, that seemed like a brilliant idea. So while some of my friends were scrimping and saving and taking out loans, I merrily coasted my way through school with a flush bank account and a comfortable car.

Later on, lots of my friends were nearly broke as newlyweds. But Charles Windsor IV was a trust fund baby—so even before the business he started took off, we had plenty of money.

Which is why, at the age of 36, for the first time in my life, I'm poor.

And it really sucks.

It's one of the smallest problems in my life right now, but it's a persistent one. So when the secretary for the elementary school, Alice, calls to tell me she has a sore throat and offers me her part time gig at the Flaming Gorge resort, I thank my lucky stars that Aiden's useless grandparents have him for the weekend. I check in with Dad's nurse, get in my BMW, and drive over.

"Do you want to serve at the buffet?" A portly woman with dark hair stuffed into a hairnet asks. "Or would you rather be in charge of preparing things here and keeping the buffet stocked?"

It feels like the kind of question I ought to have some opinion on, but for the life of me, I'm not sure what's better. "Serve at the buffet?"

"Great." She hands me a hairnet. "Put this on."

"Wait, I have to wear a hairnet?"

"And that apron." She points at an ugly green thing that looks like an apron and coveralls had a baby.

"If I stay here and prepare things?"

She scowls.

"Then do I have to wear a hairnet and an apron?"

She shakes her head. "Just the hairnet." She glances at my clothes. "But I'd put on an apron anyway, if I was wearing such fussy duds."

But at least in here, no one will really see me.

As it turns out, I think I chose wrong. Preparing the food really means transporting food prepared in the kitchen to the buffet line, removing the empty containers, which are still messy, and lugging the full ones into place over the heating flame things. After about an hour of it, my arms are shaking.

A few weeks as a secretary at the high school has not prepared me for this in any way. I've probably never regretted taking my money for my last year at Stanford and using it to bankroll Charlie's business more. Well, maybe when I found out that his brilliant HOA management software was really set up to allow him to steal from people. I regretted helping him start it then, too.

I sigh and heft the last dish into place. Now that my cart is full, it's time to haul it back to the kitchen and load it up again. How can fewer than two hundred people eat this much food? As I push the cart around, someone catches my eye.

Most of the people here are wearing red, blue, green, or even purple. Jewel tones dominate the party, but there are quite a few that mix colors. Floral prints, even a few stripes.

Only one person is wearing white, and it's not just any kind of white. It's a stunning, fitted white lace sheath dress, and it hugs every curve the woman has. Her dark blonde hair cascades down over her bare shoulders, and red lipstick, combined with bright, fire-engine red high heels, bring the whole thing together. What bugs me the most is that I used to be someone everyone turned and stared at when I walked into a room, just like this woman.

Now I'm keeping my head down and hoping no one notices me.

I should just head back, but I'm not very visible in the back corner, so I watch as the stunning blonde woman starts at the buffet table. She even takes the food I'd have selected myself. Cornbread, mashed potatoes, the prime rib. I finally steal a good look at her face and I nearly knock one of the pans over.

I know her.

It's Abigail Brooks, the lawyer who's a mother of four. The woman whose life I'm busy trying to wreck, just to make mine a little better. Guilt is a sucky feeling. I shove it away as fast as I can. It's not like I'm stealing from her. The will had specific terms, and it's not my fault she broke them. Plus, someone like that will never be happy in a dinky little place like this. I'm probably doing her a favor.

Watching her makes me feel a little creepy, and I turn to escape before she notices me. Not that she'd ever recognize me, with my hair in a hairnet and this ghastly green blob costume. Unfortunately, when I turn and tug on the cart, my sneakers squeak on the rubber mats covering the ramp leading back into the kitchen.

The woman doesn't notice, but the man standing next to her does. I was so busy thinking about Abigail that I didn't even notice her date—Steve Archer. I drop my face immediately, but it's too late. His eyes light up in recognition. I really hope he doesn't say anything to me. It would be terribly awkward to have to chat with them here, especially since I'm guessing Abigail has already heard from Mr. Swift.

Steve walks away from the table with her, and I breathe a sigh of relief. I've nearly reached the door to the kitchen when I hear him.

"Donna?"

I freeze, but don't turn around.

"I saw you. I don't know why you're here, but I know it's you."

Caught. I finally turn.

"What in the world are you doing here—you know what? I don't care." Steve steps closer and lowers his voice. "Do you know what Abigail told me on the way here?" His sky blue eyes are usually light and dancing.

Right now, they're as dark as I've ever seen them, like storm clouds.

"I have a pretty good idea."

"So you did sign the affidavit." His shoulders droop. "I was sure it must have been put together by Patrick."

"You really think he'd forge my signature on a legal document?" I can't help raising one eyebrow.

"You don't?"

I suppose if he felt it was important, there's no telling what Patrick would do. In this case, however, I'm the one who masterminded the whole thing. "This one's not his fault."

"I don't get it. How often did we complain that there aren't any new people? That Manila—this whole county—is so painfully small?" His hands clench at his side. "I told her you were amazing. I called you my best friend in the whole area."

My heart shrinks a little bit, but that makes me angry. Why is my self-proclaimed best friend taking her side? "You barely know her. Why are you yelling at me?"

"I grew up with you, and I would never in a million years have thought you'd be this warped. Her husband died, Donna. I know yours left you, and I sympathize, but if you think I'm going to take your side on this? So that you can use your huge alimony payment to oust people who should have just been given that ranch outright, you're out of your mind."

"In case you forgot, you're not the only person making the decision about what happens to that ranch." I cross my arms, smearing creamed corn across the front of my green apron. It's really hard to act superior when you're dressed like a cafeteria lady who's down on her luck.

"Oh, I didn't forget, and you'd better believe I'm going home to read the terms of that will. I never really glanced at it—it never occurred to me that anyone I knew would be such a selfish, calculating monster that they'd try to steal from six little kids and their bereaved mothers." A muscle in his jaw pulses. "If you think I'm going to just stand around and watch you do it, you're insane as well."

"I'm sure you'll all try to stop me from buying the ranch legally." I try to toss my hair, which I definitely can't do while it's in a hairnet. "But don't kid yourself—I'm not stealing it. And those cute little kids don't deserve it any more than Aiden does. At least he's from here. They'll be better off back in Houston." My lip curls. "You're just mad that your pretty little date won't be here long enough for you to get her—"

Steve grabs my wrist. "Don't."

Someone behind me says, "I'm only going to ask you once to let her go, doc."

Both Steve and I freeze.

Steve turns first, his hand still wrapped around my wrist as tightly as a stainless steel handcuff. Thanks to Charlie, I know how that feels. "Will Earl. I had no idea you would be here."

"And I'd never have expected you to accost your friend, or the employees of any business, but here we are." Will folds his arms. "I'm going to count to three, and if you—"

Steve releases me and snorts. "You've got to be kidding me, Earl." Steve's probably an inch shorter than Will, but he's definitely thirty or forty pounds heavier than the lanky rancher.

"Oh, I never joke around when it comes to being a gentleman. It doesn't matter what's happened or what she was about to say. You should never lay a hand on a lady."

"Lay a hand?" Steve looks like his head is about to explode, and while I greatly appreciate Will being chivalrous, I would rather not see him be beaten to a pulp for his misplaced support.

"It was my fault," I say. "When you're a shark, you have to expect that some of the chum will get upset."

"Now Abby's chum?" Steve shakes his head. "Do me a favor, Will. Don't call her my friend ever again." Steve spins on the heel of his boot, his spurs jingling slightly as he storms off.

Will whistles low and long. "That was. . .intense. You alright?"

"No fights like the ones between former friends, I guess," I say.

"You're a shark now?" Will lifts both eyebrows.

"You either bite or get bitten." I swipe at the drying smear of corn chowder. "That's what I've learned."

"I'm glad I never went out to California," he says. "I hear there's way more sharks out that way."

I laugh. "Yeah, not too many in the streams and lakes around here. That's for sure."

"What did you do?" Will asks. "You don't have to say, but I'm curious."

"Maybe one day I'll tell you." But today? While I'm wearing a hairnet and rubber boots, an apron coverall and someone else's dinner on my chest? Pass.

Today could not get much worse.

Unless they stiff me for this job, I suppose. Geez, could that happen? It feels like if it can, it will. Maybe it's karma. I suppose I deserve whatever I get. As long as nothing blows back on Aiden, it's fine with me.

"Hey." Will steps closer. He could reach out and touch the chunks of corn dangling from my coarse green apron.

"I'm fine," I say. "Good to see you." What a lie.

"If I'd known you were back, I'd have brought you as a date."

What a hoot. As if I could afford a night out for fun. "I'm still married."

His eyebrows rise. "Where's your husband?"

"Rotting in a jail cell," I snap without thinking. Then I slap my hand over my mouth.

"Guessing most people don't know that?"

I shake my head slowly. "No one does, and he's unlikely to stay there, so if you could keep it—"

Will makes a motion across his mouth that looks like a zipper.

It makes me smile. Some things have not changed much since elementary school, and Will Earl is definitely one of them. Although he is taller. When he smiles back at me, I realize he has changed—he's much hotter. He's more confident. And he's looking at me like he wants to eat me, which is even more bizarre because I couldn't possibly look worse than I do right now. "Well, thanks for standing up for me."

His shoulders square up. "I swear, if that guy—"

I peel off my glove and toss it on my cart, then I touch his arm. "Steve wouldn't have hurt me, and he had a reason to be upset."

"One of these days, I'm going to make you tell me what's going on."

"I doubt it," I say.

Will's smile is as kind as it ever was. "How can I take your side if I don't know what you did?" It would be nice to have someone on my side, but if I told him the truth, he'd hate me as much as Steve.

But neither of them could ever dislike me as much as I hate myself.

14

AMANDA

If I hadn't been impressed with Abigail before, I'd definitely be fangirling over her now. "You got him to agree to how much?"

She smiles. "I did a little research first."

"You mean you called Steve?"

She shakes her head. "Not Steve. He's connected, but not in that world. No, don't get mad, but I called Eddy." Abigail wiggles her eyebrows. "And don't you know it, he was delighted to get me all the information on what Mr. Bills had agreed to pay the other ranchers, and the timing of when their cattle are going to be delivered."

"That was brilliant." Even if I'm not super duper pleased that Eddy's involved. "And?"

"I talked to Jeff and Kevin. They gave me information on a local feedlot, and I called them to get an idea of what cattle are selling for now, and what they usually go for in the early fall, versus late fall."

"They go for more?"

Abby nods sagely. "It's all a numbers game, right? Of course, the older the cows are the bigger they are, and the bigger they grow the more you pay, since you pay per pound. But also, the more you pay per pound, because it's closer to the sale time."

"Huh?"

"Well, the longer we have them, the more of their care and upkeep falls to us, so they obviously sell for more. And here's where it gets sticky."

"Okay."

"It's a balancing act, right? You take the total number of cows you have to feed, and then you calculate how much they need to feed them over the winter. We haven't harvested all our hay yet, but most of it, and the total tonnage of hay we're able to harvest kind of determines how many cows we can keep for next spring, and how many we should sell now."

"Now, meaning when they come back from the BLM land."

"Not Bureau of Land Management—Forestry land," she says, "but yes."

"And?"

"We projected the remaining fields, since they should finish harvesting in the next week or so, and then we calculated the number we want to keep for next year." She waves a paper in my face. It looks like a ridiculous mass of numbers to me. "This was the best idea I've ever had for convincing Ethan he needs to stay in college. He couldn't have done this without me, and he knows he needs to learn."

"Okay."

"And. . .we should have just enough hay to increase our total cows for next year by twelve, and sell Mr. Bills the cows he wants late in the season—beginning of November."

"That's better for us?"

"Oh, I convinced him we needed a premium amount to cover our additional hay costs." Abby's beaming. "And we got a dollar fifty a pound more than the going rate. In writing."

"That's great," I say.

She drops her elbows on the top of the kitchen counter. "I'll say it is."

"Why do we care, though?" I shake my head. "Doesn't all that go into the ranch account, other than our living expenses? And those alien people may get it all."

"I'm pretty sure we can use the surplus to remodel the kitchen." She taps her fingers on the counter. "Since we've used all the other money on the add-on."

"Ah, now I get it." This time, I'm the one who's smiling. "Nice work."

"Speaking of," she says. "Have you figured out exactly what it will take to get the place Amanda Saddler offered you ready?"

I dig around in my purse until I find the keys, somewhat ruining the flourish with which I meant to display them. "I just got these. I'm headed over now to check it out. Did you want to come?"

"I'd love to, but right now I have less than three hours to finish some document review and draft responses to the interrogatories."

Yeah, yeah, I get it. You're important, and I'm planning to sell cookies. "Alright, well, I'll take some photos. Maybe you can give me some feedback later."

"If you want my feedback, sure." Abby ducks back into her room.

I pull up the address on my phone and take screenshots of the map—you learn to do that kind of thing when your reception is notoriously unreliable. Although there's so little to Manila that I could probably stop and ask literally anyone where the Fine Features Salon used to be and they'd tell me. Apparently the previous owner retired to live near her kids in Orlando, Florida almost six months ago.

That does remind me that in another few weeks, I'll be looking for a new hair salon if I can't convince Abby to start doing my hair. Judging from what I've seen of Manila, I'll be driving into Vernal or Rock Springs for one. Remarkably, my internet signal stays strong the whole way, and I'm nearly there when someone on his cell phone walks right out in front of my car. I swear under my breath, but I don't flip him off. That wouldn't be ladylike.

Mom would be pleased that at least a few things she drilled into me stuck.

"Amanda?" The man looks up from his screen, and I realize it's Derek. Of course it is. The clueless guy who was almost just smashed to bits is another outsider, like me. He's probably just giddy that there's cell reception. One of my first orders of business at this new place will be getting internet installed. With any luck, that'll be done by, oh, next spring. Ugh.

I roll my window down. "Hey, Derek."

"What are you doing in town?"

"I thought you were gone."

"I just got back this morning." He lifts his phone. "I was actually just texting you."

"Oh. Well, I'm about to check out a little shop I'm going to rent." No reason he needs to know that I'm a charity case for a local real estate tycoon. "I'm hoping it won't need to be changed too terribly much."

"I'd be happy to check it out with you, if you want. I was just asking you to dinner."

"I can't do dinner," I say. "I've got a kid who has to be picked up from cheerleading and another kid who always needs about an hour of help with homework, but I'd love it if you came with me to scope it out. It's right there." I point about a block ahead of us at a little grey building with dingy siding.

"A new coat of paint would be a start," Derek says. "But then, that's true of every single store in this town."

I shouldn't laugh. It's my town he's insulting, but it's also not really. I mean, if I'm being honest, it looks a little shabby to me, too. "I'll jot that down on my to-do list." And now things are awkward. Do I drive the block and park, then wait for him to walk down? Do I offer him a ride for the two hundred feet between here and there?

"You go ahead," Derek says, as if he can read my mind. "You can go get the door open, and I'll stretch my legs a bit." His smile's actually pretty warm. If I hadn't seen that shiny red bike, I might really like him right now. My heart might be racing.

Only, it's not.

Stupid, unrealistic, demanding heart. Get it together. Like the guy who's a real possibility. The guy who's smart, generous with his time and advice, and clearly successful. Stop liking the local vet who has a shady past and a killer set of abs.

Oh, those abs.

"Amanda?"

And I still haven't put my car back into gear. I wave as I finally drive past him. At least the little shop has five parking spaces across the front. I decide to drive around the back for good measure, and I'm delighted to find that there's more than twice as much space back here. There aren't spots painted, but that's an easy fix. It's good to know that if we end up with quite a few customers, or if we have deliveries and whatnot, we'd still have plenty of room. I lock my car and circle around to the front. It takes me a minute to procure the key—I clearly need to clean out my purse—so I'm unlocking the door as Derek reaches my side.

"It's cuter up close."

He's right. The building has a small awning that's fairly neat for being abandoned. "A good power-washing and it might not even be grey."

Derek opens a water bottle I didn't even notice he was holding and chucks water at the side of the building. By golly, if it's not sky blue underneath a layer of grime.

"Holy cats, how did you know to do that?"

"I've rented a lot of buildings," he says. "It's dry out here. I imagine it gets dusty, and you'll likely need to plan on cleaning the exterior at least once a year. But the paint isn't peeling, and that sky blue is a nicer, friendlier color than a dull grey. Maybe you can put off painting."

I whip out my notepad and write down, "1. Power Wash Exterior." I stick my notepad back into my purse and try to open the door. It won't budge.

I pull the key back out, but before I can try it again, Derek gestures. "Let me try."

I step aside.

He grabs the knob, turns his body sideways and whams it with his shoulder. I'm expecting a big groan and a crack, but to my surprise, the door actually opens.

"You're a pretty handy guy to have around."

"I'm happy you think so." He steps through the door and flips a switch. Nothing happens, and it's so dark that I can't see much.

"This is annoying," I say.

"Eh, it's standard to cut the power while it's vacant." He flips on the light on his phone and starts to examine the place. Two seconds later, he's found some blinds, the paper kind that spool into a big roll, and he's lifting them up. The windows are dirty enough that it's not super bright, but at least we can see enough to find more windows.

When the third window's unveiled, dust explodes

outward in a cloud, as well as a handful of moths.

I freak out a little bit.

Derek actually leaps in front of me to block me before we realize it's only bugs. His laugh is nice—easy, calm, reassuring, even. "I should get bonus points for being willing to protect you, even if it wasn't necessary."

I straighten up, noticing for the first time that although he's not as tall as Eddy, Derek is still at least a pair of stiletto heels taller than I am. "Noted."

"Maybe write it down." He tosses his head at my purse, which is now in a heap on the dusty floor.

"If I can find my purse, under all the dust."

We spend the next few minutes trying to imagine what this place could look like.

"What's the budget for this?" Derek asks. "It's not divided properly for a bakery of any kind." He paces the length of the room off. "It's two-thirds front parlor, and only a third in the back is set up for storage and a break room. You'll need to knock out this wall." He whams on it. "It's not load bearing, and it's pretty thin. Should be easy." He circles and looks at plumbing. "You'll have to take that little kitchenette in the back and turn that into a full kitchen with multiple stoves." He sighs. "Are you sure there's not a place that's more suited to being a bakery?"

"My friend owns this, and I don't have to pay rent." I blurt it out before thinking.

"Oh." He smiles. "Well, that changes things. It's good to have a backer—I think you've found your first partner."

Huh. Why didn't I think of that? I kind of have. "Yeah, I guess."

"So your only expense will be the remodel?" He rolls up his sleeves. "Maybe we can do a preliminary sketch of what you'd like so that when you get a contractor in here, he can't push you around and badger you into just doing what's easiest."

Derek wasn't kidding. He does know his stuff. An hour later, we have a good idea of what I think I want. Enough room in front for a glass case, three four-top tables, one two-top, and a register. Then behind that, a big kitchen with at least two commercial ovens.

"Room for four would be better," he says. "If things go well, you'll want to have room to double your capacity."

"Really?"

"Always plan for success," he says.

I wonder what paying for someone to consult like him would normally cost. Sometimes being single works in my favor. "I really appreciate your help today."

"We're not done, yet." We go out the back and check out the connections and leads and cables. He makes note of an electrical issue and a possible plumbing leak.

By the time we're done, my list is pretty long.

"Are you sure you don't have time for food?"

I glance at my watch. "Oh, no. Actually, I need to leave right about now to pick up Maren."

"Maren?" He smiles. "That's a nice name."

"Thanks." I actually have ten or fifteen minutes, but I can't think of anything we could do in that timeframe that wouldn't be awkward, like the walk down the block to this little shop was.

"I'll head out, then. I'm staying right down the road." He heads for the front door and turns just as he's leaving. "By the way, you did not warn me that your sister-in-law is. . ." He pauses.

"What?" I ask. "What is she? I'd really like to hear. I'm always trying to figure out whether she's Mother Teresa, Wonder Woman, or, like, Janet Reno."

Derek's belly laugh is full and throaty. I quite like it. "Yes. I'm not sure I see the Mother Teresa, but a combination of Janet Reno and a blonde Wonder Woman is about right."

"She's a little scary." I shrug. "Maybe I should have warned you, but I wanted a good deal, too. And look, your money's going to a good cause. It's going to pay for us to remodel our little old farmhouse kitchen."

"Then I'll count it as money well spent." He walks through the door. "I look forward to many years of partnership ahead of us. This is a secret, but my management team approved my project, and we're going to be building a processing plant ten miles out of town. That'll bring another hundred and fifty or so employees to town—I think it'll be good for everyone."

I can hardly believe it. "A hundred and fifty more people? Plus their families?"

He nods.

"You're going to single-handedly double the population." I laugh. "I should get into residential real estate real quick."

He chuckles. "You and me both."

"I guess we'll be seeing you around," I say. "And I'm glad."

Two of his fingers brush his temple, and I realize he just saluted me. "Yes, you sure will."

It takes me a few minutes to lock up the front door, but I should be about five minutes early to pick up Maren, so all in all, a productive day for Double or Nothing. I realize I never locked up the back door. I'm fumbling with the key when I hear a loud growling sound maybe fifty feet away.

Oh. My. Word. Yes, there's wildlife on two sides of my new place, but I didn't really think there would be bears or anything. Would wolves come this close to town? It looked like there was a house with a huge yard behind me, but maybe it's abandoned. Maybe wild animals moved in, and now. . .I turn around slowly and see the largest dog I've ever slapped eyes on.

Or is it a wolf?

Its muzzle is peeled back into a snarl, and when I move away from the door toward my car, it snaps at the air. "It's okay, little wolf, creature," I say. "I'm nice, I swear." It snarls louder, and inches toward me.

I can feel my pulse beating in my ears, and my hands are shaking. Roscoe likes me. Why does this one hate me? I've never really been around dogs much, and I've never seen a wolf in my life. I'm not much of an animal person, and this is why. They're unpredictable, and they're scary.

I decide to try and let myself into the store and go back through the front. I can call Abigail and maybe 911. Is there a 911 operator out here? How can I not even know that?

My hands are shaking so badly that I can barely hold the key, but I finally force myself to turn around and try to slide it into the lock.

"Snuggles!"

Snuggles? Is someone calling for that horrible creature with the name Snuggles? They can't possibly be—but the snarling stops. When I turn around, slowly, like everything I've done since I first realized I wasn't alone, there's a man jogging our way. The dog has dropped to the ground and its ears are back, like it's in trouble.

"Snuggles, what are you doing out here, scaring this poor person—" The man cuts off, because apparently we both recognized each other at the same time.

"Eddy?"

"Amanda?"

"What are you doing here? And what in the world is that thing? Please tell me it's not actually named Snuggles."

Eddy clips a leash on the collar I didn't previously

186

notice around Snuggles' neck. "She's a wolf dog, half timber wolf, half malamute. There was a breeder around here for a while who would not stop breeding them, even though ninety-five percent of the people he sold them to had no idea what they were getting into. They just wanted a dog that would 'protect them' and was 'pretty like a wolf.'" He sighs. "I should probably have put her down when she came to me, but she's made so much progress in the past six months, I swear." He pats her on the head. "She just gets really territorial, that's all."

My heart is only now starting to cycle back down. "I noticed."

"What are you doing here?"

"I'm renting this space for my bakery, Double or Nothing Cookies." I grimace as I say it.

"Double or nothing? Are you making gambling cookies?"

I can't quite bring myself to tell him that I came up with the name when I almost ruined a batch of cookies by adding too much flour. "Hey, wait," I say. "Why are *you* here?"

"Uh, I live here." He points to the house that's mostly occluded by the trees. The one I thought might be abandoned. "I'm guessing Amanda didn't tell you that?"

She most certainly didn't, but now I'm understanding a little more, after all my gibbering to her about how I like Eddy but can't date him until my business is a success, why she offered me this particular place. "Tell me this," I say. "Was there ever a bakery in town?"

"Yeah, there was." He crouches down and rubs his hand down the back of Snuggles, who leans into his touch, like she's just your average, sweet little canine. "It was on the other side of the Grill, but the lady who ran it broke her ankle about two years ago and now she's living with her sister in Vernal."

Of course she is. *That* place probably has ovens and a little glass case already. I'm going to kill Amanda Saddler.

"It's pretty exciting you're actually doing this," he says. "I hope Amanda's giving you a good deal. She owns like everything around here."

"She's not charging me much," I admit.

"Perfect. But you'll have a lot of work to do to get this ready to be a bakery." He pauses. "Actually, you may turn me down, but I'd be happy to donate some time to help you get things off the ground. I'm good at plumbing, as you may recall, and I'm pretty handy with simple electrical as well."

I should tell him no. I should distance myself. I should shove Amanda's offer in her face and insist she rent me that bakery instead. "That would be amazing," I say.

Because when a shiny red bike is right in front of you, begging you to ride it, you don't say no. You get on it and ride.

"I'm so glad," he says. "I figured you'd turn me down."

"We can be friends, right?" I ask.

"Oh." His face falls. "Sure. Friends."

The only thing I can think about on my way to pick up Maren is an image of my dear friend Eddy, working without a shirt on in my garage. And working without a shirt on in my new shop. And doing other things without a shirt on.

I shake my head to clear it.

"Mom?" Maren's waiting on the curb. "Are you alright?"

"Of course, honey," I lie. "I'm doing just fine."

I really, really need this bakery to do well so I can stop worrying about my internet persona, because none of the thoughts floating around in my head are things a friend should be thinking. And I don't even want them to be.

❧ 15 ❧

ABIGAIL

When I lived in Houston, like everyone else, I would complain about the weather. Some days it would be eighty-two degrees when I woke up. That afternoon? It would be eighty-eight. And then between seven and nine o'clock at night, it would drop to thirty-two degrees.

No lie.

Texas weather is as fickle as Larry King with his wives.

But when I lived in Houston, the difference between eighty-eight and thirty-two was whether I turned on the air conditioner or the heater. Sure, I'd pile on a sweater and maybe even start a fire in our mostly-decorative fireplace, but my life remained essentially unchanged.

Not here.

A storm's coming. Soon. Ethan spent the past three days, and nights, alternating with Jeff and Kevin on the tractor. At night, they ride with a light. During the day, they ride half-awake. But this morning, they harvested the last hay field. What Ethan ought to do is go take a long nap. All three of them should. They haven't been inside more than a handful of minutes since we realized it was coming.

But none of them are sleeping today.

No, we're tacking up our horses, and because it's a Friday, Izzy is coming, too. We have three hundred cows to bring down before the weather hits.

"This is supposed to be the worst storm we've seen in at least five years," Jeff says. "And it's September." He shakes his head. "Mother Nature is ticked about something."

Just our luck that it's happening now, at the beginning of our tenure as incompetent managers. I want to call Steve to help. I pick up my phone about five times to text him and ask whether he's off work, but each time, I put it back down again without messaging him. After all, he's called me fifteen times and it's taken all that I had not to answer. We said what we needed to say, and unless one of his texts says, "I changed my mind! Your kids are just fine, and I don't want any more if things go well," then we don't have much else to talk about.

I can't tell whether being around him will really hurt as much as I think it will, or whether I just have no tolerance for additional emotional pain, given that my baseline has been so high for the past two years. Either way, it's smarter for me to hold firm.

"You're sure we'll be fine?" I ask for the fiftieth time.

Kevin smiles. "We have two days, yet."

"That's why we didn't get off those tractors day or night." Ethan rubs his backside. "Remember?"

I sigh. "Alright."

"Plus," Jeff says, "bringing the cows back is really easy. You'll see."

"The hardest part is that we'll need to break into two groups." Kevin points at Ethan. "You and I will be one, and Jeff will take the two girls."

"Sorry, Jeff," I say. "Clearly you drew the short straw."

He laughs. "Have you seen your son on a horse? I was rock, and Kevin was scissors." He's still laughing as he bridles his horse.

"Alright, if we're the better riders," Izzy says, "then I think we should be the ones who go up higher to make sure we have all the cows."

"Agreed," Jeff says. "We'll let Kevin and Sleepyhead there bring back the ones who are raring to come home and take care of any injuries and any strays from our neighbors."

"Strays?"

"We try to keep the herds separate up there," Jeff says, "but the cows are usually ready to come home in early September, so they'll start to get mixed up around now."

"Fabulous." I sigh. "How do we know how many we have, then?"

"Remember when we branded them, how we also put tags on their ears?" Jeff asks.

I nod.

"The tags are easy to see, although sometimes they go missing. But we'll look for the hot pink tags and count those. That'll give the three of us a good feel for how many we'll need to be looking for up there."

"What if we don't find them all?" Izzy looks like she might cry. "With the storm. . .will they. . ." She can't bring herself to say it.

"Some of them die every year," Jeff says. "Nature of the business, but remember that cows like to be in groups. They'll gravitate together. Some of our neighbors' cows end up with ours, quite a few, really, since we're at the base of Birch Creek, but some of ours will end up with theirs, and they'll let us know."

"Okay." Izzy's horse is bridled now, and Jeff checks to make sure her saddlebags are all secure.

He hands me a rifle.

"Uh, what's this for?"

"Do you know how to use it?" He tosses his head over at Izzy. "Either you or me has got to stay with her at all times."

"Wait, with a rifle?"

Jeff's lips are pressed flat.

"Coyotes, wolves, bears, even mountain lions," Kevin says. "They're all getting ready for the winter, and they can feel that storm too. They'll be restless looking for food and shelter."

Fabulous.

"Let's go." Jeff swings up on his horse and the rest of us follow his lead.

As we get near the fence line that separates our property from the Forestry land, I can see that they're right. The majority of the cows are already gathered there. Sure enough, our rough count is that almost two hundred and seventy of our cows, including at least eight bulls, are already down. Kevin and Ethan shouldn't have much trouble encouraging them to head home.

"Usually they'd want them in the far pasture first," Jeff explains as we move past the herd. "But this year, with the storm coming, we'll keep them close to the barn. The little ones won't survive in the snow, so we'll move as many of them inside as we can."

"What about the ones that can't fit?" Izzy's tender heart is terrified.

"Did you notice that cover we set up?" Jeff motions with his hand.

"The canopy thing?"

He nods. "It hangs off the side of the barn, and it's sort of like covering hay with a tarp, but with an added benefit that the barn blocks the wind."

"So they'll be alright?"

Jeff shrugs. "They'd probably be fine without it, but Ethan was nearly as worried as you."

I laugh. "I suppose snow isn't new to the cows up here."

"Not to the adults, no." Jeff kicks his horse and we take off at a pretty brisk trot. "We need to move. Can't waste daylight."

The worst part of our task is that once you find the cows, you have to keep them together while you look for the rest. But it's not nearly as bad as I thought it might be. We manage to round up sixty-four more cows in a matter of three hours. "Not all of these are ours."

"We'll call when we get back. I'm sure they'll come get them."

"Does that mean they left them all here?" Izzy sounds incensed.

"I'm sure they did. Them purple ones is the Ellingson cows, and they're used to us cleaning up after them. The blue and yellows are the Earls and the Coxes and that's why there's hardly any of them. They're a little more thorough."

"Are we the last ones to bring ours down?" Now I feel a little guilty.

"We're always the last ones," Jeff says. "We can afford to be."

That makes sense, I guess.

We find eleven more cows and a bull on our way back to the entrance, bringing us to a total of seventy-six stragglers.

"Not bad at all," Jeff says. "I imagine they're almost all accounted for."

"If we missed any?"

"Pretty good odds they'll turn up on this fence line in the morning. They don't like being left."

Even if he's lying, Izzy breathes more easily after that, and so do I.

Ranching's harder than I thought it would be, if I'm being honest. It's not harder in terms of the physical labor, but the emotional toll is draining.

"Think of 'em as delicious steaks." Jeff's suppressing a grin. "That helps."

Izzy chucks something at him.

"Hey, what was that?" I ask.

Jeff, apparently, caught it. "Granola bar. It's no steak, but it's not bad. Thanks."

We really lucked out with our ranch guides. Jeff and Kevin surely can't stay working for us forever, but I wish they could. When the barn comes into sight, I release a breath I didn't realize I was holding. A trail ride is one thing, but a trail ride with a storm hanging over our heads. . .and our instructor nowhere to be found? I had taken for granted just how much I trusted Steve to keep us all safe. Without him here, even with Jeff and Kevin, I felt frayed around the edges.

"Alright. Izzy, if you want to hop off—"

Maggie has been a champ all day, but she must hit a rock, because she stumbles. Izzy shifts backward to try and stay upright, but it's not enough. Maggie keeps rolling, right over on top of Izzy.

It feels like the world slows down. I leap off of Snoopy as fast as I possibly can and run toward Maggie and Izzy. Either Maggie's fall or my jumping around spooks the cows, and they start to run. Jeff was swinging off, but he gets back on and moves wide to keep the cows, who are now headed for a fence, from breaking back toward us and running over me and Izzy both.

By the time my eyes manage to find Izzy, she's already sitting up. "Maggie!" Her trusty little mare took off when the cows did, so hopefully she's also just fine. Snoopy, champion that he is, is following right behind me. When I stop to lean toward poor Izzy, he bumps my backside with his nose.

"It's alright, sweetheart. Everything is fine." I offer her my hand.

But when she reaches up to take it, her entire arm is coated in glistening red.

I like to think of myself as a fairly capable person. I manage crises for clients on a regular basis. When my husband got sick, and even when he died, I stayed as calm as I could, and I worked through things systematically. But when I see my daughter's skin flapping open the entire length of her forearm, something inside of me snaps.

I'm not sure what Jeff and Kevin and Ethan did in response to my shrieking. I'm not sure whether Snoopy stayed by my side or not. All I remember is taking off my jacket and wrapping it around Izzy's arm as tightly as I can, and then picking her up, my hundred and twenty pound daughter, and running with her toward the house. My only thought was getting to the hospital as fast as we possibly could.

But the distance between the back of our property and the house is much farther than I realized, and even adrenaline wears off eventually. My pace slows to a clumsy stumble. By the time I finally reach the house, shouting for Whitney or Maren or Emery or Amanda in intervals, there's already a white truck pulling into the driveway.

I've never been more delighted to see Steve Archer in my entire life.

"Steve!" My voice is ragged. I sound like I've got laryngitis, in fact. "Steve! My baby!" He doesn't simply stroll over to where we are. He runs, and he takes Izzy from me, my pale, sweet little girl. "Her arm. It's gashed." But the tears are back and I'm sobbing and I can barely breathe.

"You, sit. Right now." He points at the porch. "Give me some space. That's an order."

I don't even question him. I just obey. He sets Izzy on the wide, bottom porch step, and the strangest thoughts fly through my brain.

What if there's chicken poop on the step?

What if the bloodstains never come out of my jacket?

What if Izzy dies from blood loss, and then all I have left is this stained jacket? A jacket I bought when I was at Harvard and I've lugged around for years.

Why did I even bother going to an Ivy League school at all? If I'm this useless when my daughter is injured?

Why do things like this happen to my family?

"Abigail."

"Yes." I answer without thought, again.

"I want you to say the Pledge of Allegiance, over and over. That's what Izzy needs you to do. Can you do that for her?"

Of course I can. I can do anything she needs.

"I pledge allegiance to the flag of the United States of America. And to the republic for which it stands, one nation, under God, indivisible, with liberty and justice for all." He doesn't tell me to stop, so I say it again. "I pledge allegiance to the flag of the United States of America. And to the republic for which it stands, one nation, under God, indivisible, with liberty and justice for all."

I repeat it again, and again. It's for Izzy. I can do this all night.

It takes a moment, but I notice that Steve's talking to someone. "Yes. Bring it right away. It's in a blue box."

"What are you doing?"

"I need you to say the pledge," he says.

But something about that makes no sense. Why would my saying the pledge help Izzy? What could it possibly do? As if I'm coming out of a fog, I realize he was trying to calm me down. The more I thought about the pledge, the less I could think about what was worrying me. I stand up and walk toward him, my eyes scanning Izzy.

Her face is still pale, but Steve has clearly poured something over her arm, and it looks both better and worse. It's a terrible gash, running from an inch or so above her wrist to just below the inside of her elbow. It's jagged, and it's still leaking blood. A lot of blood.

"Is she—"

Just like Izzy before, I can't ask it. No one in our family can say the word 'dead' unless it's part of a joke. How pathetic.

Steve turns then, his face calm. "She's going to be just fine. I know it looks bad, and she has lost some blood, but that was quick thinking with the jacket. It always looks a lot worse than it is." He's watching my face for something.

"Okay. That's good news."

He smiles. "Yes. It is. Now, I have a question. I can take her to the hospital in Green River, but there's no plastic surgeon there. The closest plastic surgeon is probably in Evanston. That's quite a drive, but she'll be fine if I make sure it's got a good tourniquet."

"Plastic surgeon?"

"This is going to leave a scar," he says. "I'm pretty good at suturing, but a plastic surgeon might be better. Do you have a preference?"

I shake my head. "No, if you can do it, I'd rather you do it than that we drive her all over. For all we know, the one plastic surgeon could be on vacation, or he could be sick. Plus, there's a storm coming."

"Good. That's what I needed to hear." He holds out his hand. "Do you have the suture kit?"

Jeff hands it to him.

And I stand and watch as he injects my sweet little girl's arm with lidocaine and then sews it up. Izzy is an absolute champ. She whimpers a time or two, but only when she looks over at where he's stitching the injury.

"Alright." Steve turns toward me. "Did you want to take a photo before I bandage this up? A lot of kids are disappointed if there's nothing to document what it looked like."

"Yes," Izzy says, the color returning to her face, finally. "Please, Mom?"

Her energy level does it for me. My panic finally starts to recede. "Fine, fine." I pull out my phone, which is surprisingly, still in my jacket pocket, and luckily not on the blood-soaked side. "Does she really not need blood or anything?"

"A human can lose up to thirty percent of their blood volume and be okay." Steve eyes Izzy. "What do you weigh? A hundred and fifteen pounds?"

Her eyes widen. "A hundred and eighteen."

"You'll be fine. The way you look tells me that already. I doubt you lost more than a half liter, and you'd be fine up to probably double that." A half smile creeps up on his face. "Now, don't go donating blood anytime soon or anything."

"I won't."

Ethan comes running up. "Is she alright?" His eyes are frantic.

"She's fine," I say.

"What happened?" He looks like I felt.

"Maggie stumbled," I say. "No big deal, but I guess her arm hit a rock, so when she rolled over her—"

"She rolled over you?" Steve's voice is tight.

"Yeah."

"Izzy, can you stand up for me?"

Oh, no. "Is she okay?"

"Stand down, Your Honor." Steve grins at Izzy. "Your mom's a handful, huh?"

"You can say that again." Izzy's smirk helps a lot. It's the exact blend of mischievous and saucy that she always strikes.

Steve asks her to lift and lower her arms and legs, and he presses on her all over. Then he takes her pulse and checks her eyes and ears. Finally, he listens to her heart. "She's fine," he says. "I'm going to put her on antibiotics to be safe, but I doubt that gash will cause many problems. I should check it this time tomorrow, and then in a few days or a week. You'll want to keep the bandage clean and dry."

"Wait, are you leaving?" For some reason, panic sets in.

Steve's head tilts. "Don't you want me to go?"

"No," I say.

His lips curl up on one side. "Okay. Then I'll stay."

"You don't have to work?"

"I worked five in a row, finishing last night. This is my week off."

"Oh."

"Hey, can I change clothes?" Izzy asks.

"Of course," Steve says. "Go put your pajamas on, and use a damp towel to clean yourself off. I'll have to check my house. I think I may have some waterproof bandages."

"Is it normal for you to have, like, suture kits and stuff, just lying around?" Ethan asks.

"Well, in the emergency room, everything comes in

big kits. If I need one part of it, we have to open it, and then the rules say anything that's not used has to be thrown away."

"That's too bad," Ethan says.

Steve drops his voice. "I've never been a fan of following rules that don't make sense, but shh. Don't tell the lawyer that."

"Are you saying you brought all those supplies home from the hospital?" I ask.

"Technically, they were on their way to the trash," Steve says. "So I call it recycling."

Izzy heads for the door, and Ethan follows her inside.

"I should go get her something to drink, maybe?" I ask.

"Juice or Gatorade would be best." Steve shifts from foot to foot and his eyes drop down to his feet.

"Thank you for coming," I say.

"Jeff called me, and when he said Izzy was hurt—"

Steve—big, handsome, capable Steve—chokes up. Over my kid. "Thank you. So much. I'm not sure I've ever been that scared."

"It's hard to see people we love hurting," he says. "I get it."

And I guess he does. He must see hysterical parents every single day in the emergency room. "Well, I don't know what I would have done if you hadn't come."

He drops his arm over my shoulders. "You'd have driven her into Green River, and you and Izzy would both be fine. Wrapping her arm was exactly right, and it slowed the bleeding down tremendously."

"I swear I've never fallen apart like that."

"The times in life when we have no control are the very scariest of all."

"Why are you so smart?" I ask.

"Speaking of smart," he says. "I've been thinking about—"

I put my hand over his mouth. "Can we not do this right now?"

His arm loosens over my shoulders and his head droops. "I'm so sorry. Of course not. I mean, yes. Later. Whenever."

He follows me inside, just as I asked him to do, and having him around is like a balm. Gabe plays Uno with him, and Whitney joins in. By the time Whitney wins the round, Izzy has finished a Gatorade and she's perked way up. Ethan has taken a shower and no longer smells like cows.

Which makes me think that maybe I should be taking a shower, too. "I'm going to. . ." I point over my shoulder.

Amanda's car pulls up outside, and I realize I hadn't even thought about where she was.

"Where was your mom?" I ask.

Maren shrugs. "Probably at the bakery. I think."

When she walks inside, she's partially beaming. "When I went to Rock Springs, I really didn't think they'd have what I needed, but guess what?"

Everyone in the entire room swivels to face the doorway.

"They not only had commercial, true convection ovens, they had a set that are on sale, because a new model just came out. I know the kitchen isn't really ready, but I ordered them, anyway. They're delivering them tomorrow."

"Tomorrow?" I'm struggling to keep up. "As in, the day before the storm hits?"

"What storm?"

I swear, sometimes it annoys me that she pays so little attention to the ranch. We're all here to work it, per the will terms, but she acts like it's a backdrop for her photoshoots or something. "There's a huge blizzard coming," I say. "That's why we went a week early to bring the cows back."

"Oh. Well, good job. And I'm glad the ovens will get here before the storm. Can you imagine if they were coming in the middle of a snowstorm?" She laughs a little feebly. "I mean, obviously I know they won't really deliver them then. It would just be delayed." She looks around the room, notices Steve is there, and stiffens. "Is everything okay?"

"While you were out shopping, Izzy nearly died." Maren waits to see her mother's face fall and then turns on her heel and heads for her bedroom.

Some days, I think Maren's gotten a lot better. Some days, not so much.

"I am so sorry—what?"

Izzy and Ethan and Whitney all launch into an explanation, but I don't have the energy for it. I catch Steve's eye. "I'm going to shower."

"Is that an invitation?" He lifts one eyebrow. "Because if so, I'm definitely in."

I laugh. "Shut up."

"Can't fault a guy for having a dream."

I toss one of the throw pillows at him—it's right there in the name—and head for the hall bathroom. Walking to and from the bathroom to shower when people are here, that's a new low. This remodel can't be finished soon enough. Not that it'll give me an en suite bathroom, but at least I could go to the one in the back of the house. What happens if Steve needs to pee while I'm in there?

But my entire attitude is improved when I finally emerge. My kids are all healthy and safe. The storm is coming, but the cows are back here with us, too. And I no longer smell. Hallelujah.

I'm wearing pajamas and toweling off my hair when

Steve gets a phone call. I always thought he kept his phone on silent, since I've never heard it ring when he's around. Maybe he just doesn't get many calls.

"Hello?" He pauses. "Are you kidding me?" He pauses again. "Surely there's someone else you can call."

I walk over next to where he's sitting on the couch, a little nervous that I'm interrupting, but when he sees me, he shifts over and gestures for me to sit. "Who is it?" I mouth.

"Donna," he mouths back.

I can hear a high-pitched sort of screeching coming from the phone. And then a loud crash.

"Is she alright?" Poor Steve can't catch a break. First he's paged urgently to our place, and now Donna's got some kind of medical crisis, too?

"I hate to say this, but that's not a medical problem," Steve says. "With those symptoms, it's almost certainly a UTI."

Oh, no. Who at Donna's house is sick? Her husband?

"If Patrick's refusing treatment, they won't listen to me. He needs a culture before they can start him on the right antibiotic." He sighs. "Look, at the end of the day, they won't risk being sued for me or anyone else." Whatever she says this time, it makes Steve scowl heartily. "No. I won't even ask her, and you know why."

Me. She wants me to help with whoever this is. An elderly parent, perhaps?

Donna, the woman who's trying to take our ranch away, the woman who came into my house under false pretenses, pretending to be my friend, asked invasive questions, and then used our answers to harm us, that's who's calling to ask for my help?

"You reap what you sow, dear girl, and—"

I touch Steve's arm. "I'll do it," I say.

Because even though things were strange between us,

Steve didn't drag his feet. He sprinted. And when someone does something bad, it doesn't change wrong to right. Leaving this poor woman to deal with a sick and possibly dying relative alone? Any way you look at it, that's wrong. And if I actually tell her that it's what she deserves?

Then I'm no different than she is.

16

DONNA

I'm the kind of person who feels guilty when I kill a cockroach. I recognize that it's dumb—but guilt just doesn't listen to reason. I don't want big, nasty bugs in my house, and I know my best bet is to squish it, but after I do? I feel terrible for having done it.

Don't even get me started on how bad I feel about throwing away things I'm not going to use.

Sometimes I donate things I know no one will want, just so I don't have to suffer through the emotional guilt of thinking it's going in the trash. I blame my mother. She anthropocentrized everything. My stuffed animals fell off the bed keeping me safe from monsters. My pencil was sad when I didn't use it. Toys that were left in the corner and never used were pariahs. The *Toy Story* movies just exacerbated a problem I already had.

My brother Patrick does not struggle with this kind of thing at all. To him, it's simple. Our father was not a nice man, and now he's even worse. He yelled a lot, he hit us often, and he never made us feel loved. Now that Dad's mind has checked out for the vast majority of the time he's awake, Patrick really has no patience with him.

Which is why, when he gets sick and becomes even worse to manage than usual, Patrick feels no remorse about squashing the cockroach. "No." He folds his arms.

"I'm just asking you to help me load him in the car," I say. "Let Aiden stay with you for a few hours. I'll take Dad to the hospital, and I'll sit with him, and I'll file whatever forms they need. He has Medicare, so it won't cost much."

"You said he's running a fever, and he's more delirious than usual."

"And he screams whenever he goes to the bathroom," I say. "Something's definitely wrong."

"It's either something he'll get over on his own, in which case I shouldn't have to be involved, or—"

Dad starts shouting right then, as if to make his point. "See?"

Patrick frowns. "He's doing this a lot?"

"For more than an hour, every few minutes." Aiden covers his ears.

"I can't just sit here."

"If it hurts when he goes to the bathroom, it's either a stomach bug or—"

"It's when he pees," I clarify. I absolutely hate that Dad needs help to go to the bathroom, but helping him go is much less depressing than changing his diaper. I do that every morning already. I have no desire to do it all day long.

"Then it's definitely a urinary tract infection. I heard the diapers cause those sometimes."

Aging is not for the weak. "A few antibiotics will clear it up," I say. "I'll go grab my keys."

"No."

"Excuse me?"

Patrick shifts, blocking me from walking into my small kitchen. "You won't take him anywhere."

I shove him, but he doesn't budge. "Seriously, Patrick, move."

His chest swells and his feet widen, as if he's expecting me to rush him or something.

"If we do nothing and you're right, this will become a kidney infection. He could die of sepsis."

My older brother looks so much like my dad in this moment that I almost flinch. "No, he *will* die of sepsis. I'm counting on it."

"Are you kidding me?"

"Look, I know you're like a dog, but I'm not."

"You think I'm like a dog?"

"Dogs, even when you hit them, will come lick your hand and beg you to love them." His hands clench at his sides. "I'm no dog, and I never have been. Dad treated us like garbage, but I'm going to do him this one last favor. I'll let him die quickly instead of miserably dragging on and on like he has been."

I have two choices, here. One of them is to keep arguing with him while Dad shouts and yells in the bedroom. Eventually, Dad'll decide he can leave on his own, and he'll shuffle out, get upset, yell at me and Aiden, and Patrick will end up locking him up in his room. I'll have a huge mess to clean up in the morning, and Dad will probably get worse and worse, and possibly even die.

The other option is to tell Patrick I acquiesce, make him believe it, and do what I want once he's gone.

"Don't even think about calling someone to help you load him after I leave," Patrick says.

I swear, some days I think he's telepathic.

"I have a DNR and a medical power of attorney for him, and I sent a copy to Green River, Vernal, and Rock Springs."

He can't go a single day without reminding me that Mom and Dad picked him to handle everything. "What about the life insurance?" I ask. "If he dies now, our plan won't work."

"Please." He shakes his head. "We're the ones who have to fill out the forms to get that money, and we'll just wait to fill them out until after your divorce funds have come through."

He still thinks the funds are for my divorce. "Right. My settlement."

"Isn't it soon?"

"A few weeks, yeah." Two, to be precise. Two weeks from today, one of my major problems will be solved, and a few days after that, another one will wrap up—the dissolution of my marriage. Finally.

"It won't change a thing." Patrick narrows his eyes at me. "I want your word that you won't take Dad anywhere. I have his medical power of attorney, and I have the signed DNR."

And he plans to walk away while I sit here and watch Dad die? Uh-huh, sure, I'll go along with that. "Yes," I say. "I know Mom and Dad trusted and relied on you while I was off living my own life away from home. I get it."

"And you admit that I'm the one who makes these kinds of decisions?"

I grit my teeth, but I also nod.

"Good. I better not see your car headed down that drive."

I wait, dutifully, listening to Dad groan and moan, shout and yell, and cry out in pain, my resolve only strengthening. Wasting away is one thing, but I'm not going to let Dad die because Patrick wouldn't get him some antibiotics. While I'm watching Patrick's house, I do some research on DNRs, and it bears me out. They're do not resuscitate orders, not something that outright refuses all medical care. I really doubt Dad wanted this.

A small red car drives up in front of the main house

and I can barely breathe, I'm so full of hope that Patrick's leaving, but it's only someone picking up Beth.

But it's a Thursday night.

In the months I've been back home, Patrick has taken Amelia out to dinner over in Flaming Gorge every single Thursday night. With the storm rolling in tomorrow, I can't imagine they'll miss it. I certainly haven't seen them out working with our personal livestock, not that we have much anymore. Patrick's always been more of a four-wheeler rancher, and Amelia thinks the idea of having chickens "is absurd. And disgusting."

It makes preparing for snowstorms simpler, at least. And he had his ranch hands bring the cows back down last week, anyway. I'm pretty sure he goes first so he can steal a few of the other ranchers' cows, but I can't prove it. The brands should protect against that, but Patrick always slaughters a few cows for himself in the fall. I'm guessing he eats the extra ones he's grabbed himself.

Or maybe I'm too hard on him. Maybe he really is doing this to try and help Dad. It must be terrible not to be in your right mind most of the time. If he were able to make a meaningful decision, maybe Dad would want to reunite with Mom.

"Donna!"

It's rare that Dad calls for me by name, so it stands out from the more familiar shouts and moans.

I check Aiden first—he's watching television in my room, so I doubt he'll hear anything Dad may say. I walk slowly to his room and tap on the door. "Dad?"

"Took you long enough."

That's the most lucid he's been today. I push the door open. "Can I come in?"

"I've been calling for you." He's scowling, which is familiar. "I'm hurting. I'm hot and my. . .my—" he clears his throat. "My man parts are burning."

It sure sounds like a UTI. "I'm sorry to hear that. I'd love to take you to the doctor so we can figure out what's wrong. What do you think?"

He sits up in bed. "That's what I've been asking for. Geez, it's like you've got wax in your ears."

"I'm sorry," I say. "Patrick was here earlier, and he said you'd do better off staying here and resting."

"What does Patrick know? He's even dumber than you."

I wish I could pretend this is part of his dementia, but this is the first time in days he's sounded exactly like himself. "Let me see if I can find someone who can help me get you to the car."

"Help you?" He swings his legs off the bed, one slipper on, one slipper missing. "I'm a man," he thunders. "I don't need you to help me do nothing."

And then he stands up, on his own. That's almost a miracle in and of itself. It's something to do with the dementia, or maybe they're unrelated, I'm not sure, but he's been so dizzy he hasn't been able to stand upright without help for the past few weeks.

"Where's your car, wax ears? Or do you think I should walk all the way to Green River?"

He remembers where the closest hospital is. That's almost a miracle, too. "Dad, what year is it?"

His nostrils flare and he blinks. "What difference does that make?"

It's not like I thought he'd be able to answer, but acting upset to cover for his lack of knowledge is classic pre-dementia Dad. He shuffles toward the door, and I offer my arm. He bats it away.

The two men in my life are both jerks. No wonder I married a monumental loser. I follow behind him, hovering, while he moves toward the door. If Patrick shows up right now, I'll let him argue with Dad. Good luck.

Dad's actually doing surprisingly well. I thought he'd have lost more muscle tone, only walking assisted, but I suppose all the flailing around and kicking at me, and walking with my assistance, was enough to keep him upright. I glance out the window, and Patrick's car is still there. Maybe they aren't going out tonight after all. I'm not sure what he'll do if he sees Dad climbing into my car. I don't love the idea of Aiden riding with me the entire way, either. On his best days, Dad's a handful, and he doesn't watch what he says. He's not exactly the role model I was hoping would take Charlie's place in Aiden's life.

Dad's nearly to the front door when I notice movement through my front window.

Patrick and Amelia are finally leaving!

"Dad." I grab his arm. "Hang on."

"What?" He sneers. "Do I look like an Olympic medalist? I'm tired here. Don't yank on me, princess."

I think a lot of dads call their daughters 'princess.' They want them to be beautiful and feel adored. But that's not what my dad means. He only calls me that when he thinks I'm being high maintenance or unreasonable. "Hey, you haven't called me that in a long time. You really must be feeling better."

He swears up one side and down the other. "I don't feel better. I feel terrible, wax ears."

At least he's lucid. With no idea how long this will last, and in an attempt to distract him while Patrick leaves, I decide to go for it. "Look, Dad, I know I've been a huge disappointment, and that you and Mom felt like my education was a big waste of money, but I wanted to thank you for being willing to spend all of that on me. It meant a lot to me, that you'd support my dreams even though they weren't the same as yours."

Dad turns toward me slowly, his eyes watery, his age-spot-stained and knobby hands shaking. "It was a waste of money. You didn't even get a degree. Maybe you should be bawling me out for not knocking some sense into you."

Mom said Dad was proud that I got into Stanford. I always thought she was lying, but for the first time, I wonder whether it was true. I've spent my entire life reading between the lines, trying to interpret his meaning from under layers of vitriol and anger. But this time, I think that's his way of telling me that he was proud.

Until I dropped out, I suppose.

"I know I didn't graduate, and to you that seems like a failure, but I'm honestly happy I went."

"Is this where you spit out some stupid junk about how mistakes make us who we are?"

I laugh. "Hardly. I traded my entire inheritance for that education. Patrick's getting the house, the ranch—this house too, actually, and all the money, life insurance, everything. And you know what?" I shrug. "It was still worth it for me, because it's the only time you guys have actually let me make my own decision. I think it was your finest parenting moment."

"You didn't give up anything," Dad says. "You just spent my money."

Is he serious? Was he never planning to leave me anything to begin with? "I worked every summer," I say. "I did as much as Patrick did. I know without a degree, it feels valueless, but I learned a lot in college." And I've learned even more since. I wish my dad could admit, just once, that I've grown. That there might be some value in my life, but that's a hopeless wish.

"You got my brains, ya know. And then you wasted them."

I'm so shocked by his compliment that I nearly stop paying attention to what he's doing.

He turns back around and grabs the doorframe before

I have a chance to block him, levering himself toward it. His arm lifts and his hand comes down hard on the knob and, wonder of wonders, he actually gets it open.

I turn toward the front window, a little panicked, but Patrick and Amelia are gone. I breathe a sigh of relief as I hover next to Dad and help him into the passenger side of my car. "I need to get Aiden, Dad. I'll be right back."

He doesn't even argue with me, which is another small miracle.

I'm not normally a religious person, but with all the things that miraculously lined up for me—Patrick leaving just in time, Dad becoming lucid and walking to the car himself—I sort of figured everything would be fine. I'd get Dad the antibiotics he needed, and we'd both live to fight with Patrick another day.

I clearly underestimated my brother. I should have learned years ago never to do that, but here we are. "Are you serious?"

"Your brother called," the woman at the front desk in the emergency room says. "He said that under no circumstances are we to treat your dad." Her voice drops. "His lawyer called too. Said they'd sue." She picks up a stack of papers. "We do have the medical power of attorney and the DNR."

I slam my hands down on the counter. "But this man is sick, and he's standing right here."

Dad shakes his head. "I should've known better than to pick your brother. He's a cold-hearted prick."

Takes one to know one, I guess. "Hold on." I realize we're at Steve's hospital. Maybe he can help. My hand's shaking as I pick up the phone. It's not like we ended things well the last time we spoke, but what other choice do I have?

It's my dad.

You got my brains, ya know? It's probably the only nice

thing he's said to me in ten years or more. It makes my heart hurt even thinking about it. I wonder whether his parents expressed themselves well to him. Maybe his dad was worse—I never met my grandfather.

I have to at least try. I press talk. And then I wait. It rings, and rings, and rings. He's probably breaking a horse or preparing for the storm. I brace myself to get his voicemail when he picks up. "Hello?"

"Hey, Steve. It's me, Donna." I force it out. "I need a favor."

"Are you kidding me?"

"I wish I was. I know how you feel about me right now."

"Surely there's someone else you can call."

Pathetically, there's literally no one else. My brother wants our dad to die, apparently, and I'm not even sure he's wrong. "The thing is, my dad's really sick, and I'm at the ER where you work, and they won't treat him."

I'm not sure whether my dad heard me or whether something else set him off, but he stands up, wobbly-kneed and all, and starts to screech. "I'm in *pain*, you stupid morons! Can't you see that I need *help*?" He puts one hand under the end table next to the bench he was sitting on and flips it forward. A lamp and a half dozen magazines crash to the floor and Aiden starts crying.

It gets even louder as two nurses and a security guard approach, hands extended outward, faces doing their best to look soothing and also ominous. "Sir, we need you to sit down."

"He has a fever, and every time he pees he shouts at the top of his lungs, and when I checked earlier today, he would barely let me touch his stomach. I know he's sick, but they won't treat him because Patrick's the medical power of attorney and he's telling them he'll sue."

"I hate to say this, but that's not a medical problem,"

Steve says. "With those symptoms, it's almost certainly a UTI."

"I knew that," I say. "What I need is help from someone they'll listen to. Can you tell the nurses that we just need antibiotics?"

"If Patrick's refusing treatment, they won't listen to me. He needs a culture before they can start him on the right antibiotic." He sighs. "Look, at the end of the day, they won't risk being sued for me or anyone else."

"So you're saying I need a lawyer." I can't believe I'm asking this, but what else can I do? "I hear you know a decent one."

"No. I won't even ask her, and you know why."

"It's not like I know any attorneys—I might be able to dig up some information on Patrick's lawyer in Vernal, but he's not going to side with me. It's Patrick causing this problem."

"You reap what you sow, dear girl, and—"

I'm not sure why Steve suddenly stops talking. Until I hear her voice. It's soft, but it's clear.

"I'll do it," Abigail Brooks says.

I can barely believe what I heard. I can't bring myself to even confirm it.

"We'll be there in forty minutes." Steve hangs up.

"Ma'am, we have to ask the three of you to leave." The security guard is as old as my dad, or close.

"I appreciate why you're asking, but my lawyer's on her way." I cross my arms and glare at the guard and the nurses. "I don't suppose you want to make it easier on all of us and honor both the Hippocratic oath and the moral imperative that we all should do the right thing and treat my dad?"

It's a pretty tense forty-eight minutes, especially when Dad needs to go pee. The little girl who was in one of the stalls when Dad and I walk in shoots out like a mouse fleeing a barn cat when Dad starts moaning and whamming his hand against the side wall.

But true to his word, Steve does show up, and Abby's walking right next to him. Apparently it took her eight minutes to get dressed in that suit, and judging by the look on the nurses' faces, it was worth every second it took.

The old guard backs away slowly, heading for the door to the staff entrance.

Abby strides toward them like she owns the place, her head held high, her eyes alert, her hair pristine. Her black business suit molds to her body but isn't clingy. It's back-stitched with bright white thread, and her shoes are high black stilettos with white heels. She nods as she passes me, brushing past the nurses, and heads directly for the check-in counter.

"My name is Abigail Brooks, a lawyer with Chase, Holden, and Park. I'm here on behalf of Mr. Ellingson, and I understand that although he presented here in acute distress, you're refusing to provide him with the life-saving medical care he needs?" She lifts one eyebrow sharply. "Would you care to explain your actions?"

The ruddy-faced nurse was horrible to me, like I was a roadie she was ousting, but she practically trembles now. "Well—"

Abigail drums her fingers on the counter of the desk. "Oh, and I'd choose my words carefully. I have a sinking feeling that I'll be repeating them to a judge very soon in a wrongful death action."

The woman practically claws a stack of papers out of the way and clutches the power of attorney she printed off. Her mouth opens and then closes again, and she offers the papers to Abigail like a nun with a rosary.

"I hope that you're not holding up those pieces of paper as some kind of defense." Abigail snatches them out of her hands and glances at them. "I see that this is a medical directive, and it does list Patrick Ellingson, whom I presume you personally saw and can consequently attest was the person with whom you spoke?"

The woman blanches.

"Judging by how the blood just drained from your face, I doubt whether you actually saw and confirmed that the man telling you to let Mr. Ellingson here die was in fact his medical power of attorney. But let's assume for the sake of argument, that you did what you were supposed to do." Abigail drops the power of attorney on the desk. "You're not a lawyer, but that document, on the third line, says, 'if I become unable to make my own health care decisions, and that fact is certified in writing by my physician.'" Abigail looks around the room. "I don't see a physician saying that, and there's certainly not a certification attached, so. . ." She spreads her hands out. "I'm curious, when this poor man dies, what you'll be saying to the prosecution about the murder charges they'll probably bring."

"Mu-mu-murder?" The nurse shakes her head. "No, I mean, look, the man on the phone—"

"The man *claiming* to be Mr. Patrick Ellingson? Is that who you're referring to?"

She gulps.

"Go ahead. Tell me what you'll say."

The nurse looks past Abigail and waves at me. "Why don't you bring your father back here, honey. I'm sure we can get him taken care of right quick."

Abigail and Steve wait around long enough to make sure that they are, in fact, caring for my dad, but once we're put in a room, Abigail just disappears.

"Where did she go?" I poke my head out into the hall, but I don't see her.

"Has Aiden had dinner?" Steve asks.

"Uh, well."

"I had Cheetos," Aiden says cheerfully. Only then do I notice that both his hands and the front of his shirt are bright orange.

"It's been a really weird day."

Abigail breezes back through the door with a tray. It has three sandwiches, two chocolate milks, an apple juice, some Jello, and three saran-wrapped cookies.

"She suggested that you might be hungry," Steve says. "I offered to go ask the nurses for some of the on-call food, but we both agreed that she was much scarier."

"Terrifying." My eyes well with tears. "And I can't thank you enough."

My dad's lying back in his bed, his eyes closed for the first time all day. I'm not sure whether the antibiotics can possibly be helping this quickly, or whether he's just as relieved as I am that we're finally getting treatment.

"You're welcome." She sets the tray on the side table and ruffles Aiden's hair. "Now, they told me that you can't eat the cookie *or* the Jello until you've finished at least half a sandwich." Her face is utterly serious.

"They did?" Aiden's eyes are round.

Abigail nods. "And you've seen that this hospital means business. That guard is waiting outside to make sure you eat it."

I've never seen Aiden eat his sandwich that fast. "I ate it all," he says. "Every bite."

"Good boy." Abigail beams.

"We're going to head out," Steve says.

"Do you want us to take Aiden with us?" Abigail asks. "We can put him to bed, and you can swing by and pick him up later tonight or in the morning."

I toss my head toward the hall.

Steve and Abigail step out while Aiden's digging into a Jello cup.

218

I follow right behind them. "I just wanted to say how grateful—" My voice cracks on the word, as if I haven't already been embarrassed enough today.

Abigail puts one hand on my arm, just above my wrist. "I hope your dad feels much better soon. I'm sorry this got so nasty. Please call me again if Patrick tries something that ridiculous."

I didn't cry at my wedding. I didn't even cry when my mother died. I haven't cried a single time during the mess my life has become: not when my husband was arrested, not when I filed for divorce, and not when I brokered a deal with my in-laws to prolong my miserable marriage long enough that my crap-bag husband could get out of going to prison.

But now, I burst into tears.

"Hey, it's okay." Steve's awkwardly patting my back.

Abigail's face is crumpled up, like she really feels sorry for me.

When I called, I expected gloating. I expected a tongue-lashing. I worried she might come all the way here just to tell me what I already know, that I was getting exactly what I deserved. But instead, she's bringing me food for my son and offering to take him home and get him in bed. She's sympathetic and empathetic.

And I'm the worst person in the world for lobbing a grenade at this smart, generous widow and her precious little children.

It's all I can do to choke out the six words I have to say. "I don't know why you came."

A single tear rolls down Abigail's cheek. "We never know what burden someone else is shouldering. But if I've learned anything in my thirty-eight years, it's that we should always do everything we can to lighten someone else's load. Today I could help you, so I did."

My tears redouble, pathetically.

"Tomorrow will be better," she says.

"You help people whom you should hate," I say. "*Who are you?*"

"Hating someone is a waste of energy," Abigail says. "It hurts you more than anyone else."

I think about what she said while they process Dad's paperwork, and I realize that she's right. Hating Charlie only drags me down. Hating Patrick makes me miserable. Even anger at Dad holds me apart from joy.

The problem is, I'm not sure how to let go of any of it. That's something Stanford never taught. And most days, my anger, my hatred, and my frustration with the terrible state of my life is the only thing that keeps me going. I don't know who I'd be without it.

❧ 17 ❧

AMANDA

Kevin is a miracle worker. His electrician buddy actually finishes up everything I need—and because I went with pre-fab ones, Kevin's carpenter manages to install the cabinets, too. Which means that in only a week and a half, we were able to get enough things together that my new ovens can be installed when they bring them out today.

Of course, it's not like I've been sitting around, either. It took me an entire day just to get the place mostly clean. My right shoulder's still bugging me from spending all day sweeping and mopping and scrubbing, but hopefully the Voltaren will kick in soon. Tendonitis is the *worst*. Getting older stinks. My body feels like it's slowly falling apart, and unlike a car where you can replace parts with new ones, there's nothing anyone can really do about it.

Roscoe whines in the corner. I probably should have left him at home, but every time I do, Abigail tells me how terrible he is. "You need to stop crying whenever I leave." I crouch down and he hops up and races over, his ears back, and his big, puppy eyes pleading with me. "Oh, fine."

I let him lick my face sometimes when no one else is around. I know it's gross, but it makes him so happy.

"Alright, alright." I shove him back. "That's enough."

Except it's never enough for him. His tail is wagging and his eyes are pleading more than before.

"I already let you," I say. "Now I'm all covered in dog slobber."

My phone rings and hope rises in my chest. "Please be the delivery guy." I flip it over, but it's not. "Hello, Terrible Landlord."

"Stop calling me that," she says.

"I'll stop calling you that when I stop being annoyed."

"You're not annoyed. You're grateful."

"His crazy wolf dog almost ate me. Did I tell you that?"

She laughs. "Three times, now."

"And I'll tell you fifteen more," I say. "It's horrifying. You've probably never even seen a wolf dog."

"You're such a New Yorker." She chuckles. "I've seen actual wolves, you ninny. They don't have collars, and they certainly don't respond to *Snuggles*."

I never mentioned that name to her. "You talked to Eddy?" I can barely keep myself from shouting, and also asking whether he said anything about me, which is ridiculous. I've posted three more photos with Derek and my fans are finally coming around. I've been slow to get on board with this one, but I'm coming around too. He may not be a former rock star, and he may not have rock hard abs—more like a keg than a six-pack—but he's a good-looking guy and he really has been helping.

"Eddy called to thank me."

I can barely breathe. "For what?"

"For cutting you a deal on the rent." She coughs. "Does he know you're not paying any?"

I wrack my brain. "I told him I'm not paying a lot."

She exhales gustily. "Thank goodness. Did you know Eddy rents his vet clinic from me? I can't have people thinking I've gone soft."

I would never describe Amanda Saddler as soft, not if I wanted to go on living, anyway. "Is that all he said?" I hate myself for asking.

Even more when she cackles. "He told me that if I heard of anything that was troubling you to let him know. That boy does not like that you're shacking up with that leather and meat guy."

"Derek?" Her words finally register. "He said I was shacking up?"

"He said you were always with him."

This time I'm the one laughing.

"What's so funny?"

I'm lucky she can't leap through the phone to throttle me. She might do it. "Shacking up means—" I clear my throat. "Living with someone."

"Oh. Well, then he was upset you're spending a lot of time with him." She grumbles. "That doesn't sound nearly as rapacious."

I don't think she's using that word correctly either, but I'm not positive, so I let it slide. "Well, my bosses love Derek, and my fans are coming around."

"Well, if your boss and your fans like him, maybe you should shack up."

"Amanda, you know that I'm trying to start this business so that I can have the luxury of—"

"Be bold," she says. "Do what you want to do right now. Trust that it'll work out. That's what youth is about."

It's still funny to me that she's calling me young. I suppose it's all in the perspective. "I'm channeling my inner Abigail," I say. "She would never let go of one branch before she had a firm hold on another branch—or at least a sturdy vine."

"Are you calling Abigail a monkey?" She giggles. "I wish I'd thought to record that one."

"You're the worst."

The bell jingles on the front door. "Hey! I think those are my ovens."

"You're at the store now?" She practically growls. "Get home, girl! That storm is rolling in early."

"Oh, please, it's fine. It's not even snowing." I walk toward the front of the store, but it's not the ovens. It's just a package. "Hey, did you have something delivered here?"

"Me?" Amanda laughs. "I can't even remember my own address."

I don't believe that for a moment.

"Girl, you listen to me. You being a New Yorker, you don't understand our storms. You get home right now, and make sure your animals and your kids are safely inside. I want you close to a generator, you hear me?"

"We don't even have one," I say. "Only the tiny house does."

"Jed was the cheapest man I ever met." She sighs. "If you want to, you can all come up and stay with me. Jed would love the company."

"It's alright. We already talked to Jeff and Kevin. If the power goes out, we'll all take blankets and mattresses over to their house and have a sleepover."

"That sounds terrible. Good luck."

I laugh. She's not totally wrong. I wave at the mail lady and pick up the box. It's from a company called Gourmet Chic. It takes me a minute to find a razor blade —left by the tile guys, I think—but I slice it open. It's the cutest apron I've ever seen, with a double flared skirt, candy stripes going horizontal, and a bow tied on the side of the waist. It's retro and modern at the same time. Did I let something slip on social? Could this company be looking for a sponsor?

But how did they get my address?

I'm folding it up to set it back in the box, where hopefully it'll stay clean, when a piece of paper flutters to the floor. It says GIFT RECEIPT: THE CUTEST APRON FOR THE CUTEST BAKER. BEST OF LUCK WITH YOUR NEW ENTERPRISE. DEREK

I should've known. He's one of the only people who could have gotten the address. And sure enough, when I look at the label again, it's made out to CEO AMANDA BAKER; C/O DOUBLE OR NOTHING. How cute is that? See? He really is growing on me. I barely think about Eddy.

Or his abs.

Or his double dimples.

I almost never dream about him singing to me.

Or his hair as he does, falling down over his bedroom eyes.

Unfortunately, once I start thinking about him, it's nearly impossible to stop. I even try singing "*The Song that Never Ends*," but that doesn't make a dent. If something is more persistent than the song that never ends, it can't be defeated.

So I give in.

While I'm cleaning out the double refrigerator that came yesterday, I think about Eddy at the July Fourth dance. I think about Eddy catching my eye from across the room at the Grill. I think about him working in our garage without his shirt on. And I think about him offering to do anything I need to help with my shop.

Even the memory of him rubbing his terrifying monster's head is a fond one.

I'm definitely messed up. I wonder what a shrink would say about me liking the guy I can't have instead of the one who I can. What's wrong with me? Why do I spend my time liking the cowboy/vet/rocker/addict with whom I have nothing in common instead of the handsome businessman who sends thoughtful gifts and cute cards? A shrink would probably tell me it's because I don't love myself, so I can't love anything that's good for me.

Is that right?

Just as I finish the fridge cleaning, the bell jingles again, and this time it *is* the oven guy. "We better hurry," he says. "You're my last delivery, and I don't have snow chains."

Neither do I. "I'm with you. Let me know what I can do to help."

Luckily he has another guy in the van with him, and it only takes them about thirty minutes to get the ovens unloaded, and another thirty to get them all hooked up. "Alright, if you can sign here." He hands me a clipboard.

I almost just sign, but I think about what Abigail would say if I did that. Reluctantly, I force myself to scan the words, and I notice that it says they tested the ovens and they're both uniform and consistent in their baking temperatures. "Um, we didn't do any of this."

The guy takes the pen and marks that section off. He writes in, "Will return to level and check uniformity at later date if client informs us there's an issue."

"How will I know if there's an issue?" I point at the ovens. "How long does it take?"

"Lady, I'm not about to get snowed in at some startup bakery in the buttcrack of nowhere—"

"Manila," I say. "We're in Manila. It has a name, and it's printed right here on the slip."

"Fine, crazy pants, I'm not about to get stuck in Manila, because you're worried we're cheating you." He jots his phone number down. "Call me if this don't work, and I'll come back once the storm's past."

I glance out the front windows at the snowflakes falling, and I shrug. "Fine." I sign.

The men practically leap into their van and peel out. They're probably going farther than I am, though. I'm sure I'll be fine just to get home. I grab my keys and lock up, only to remember that Roscoe's locked in the back. He didn't like one of the install guys and he kept growling at him.

My hands are freezing from just a few moments outside as I unlock the door and make my way through the shop. Roscoe's whimpering. "It's fine, boy. I didn't forget about you." I almost did, but he doesn't need to know that.

He sticks to my side like glue as we head back out, and stays just as close when I lock the front door. I'm almost to my car when I hear a strangled kind of whimper from behind the shop. What in the world could that be? I think about Eddy's insane wolf-dog. He seemed to really like it. Could it be injured in some way? I think about locking Roscoe up, but I decide against it. I'm not sure *what's* making that noise, but it might not be a bad plan to have Roscoe at my side. He's pretty big for a border collie—over fifty pounds.

"Is it a raccoon?" I've always liked raccoons—even though apparently no one likes them around here. "They eat a few chickens, and everyone hates them. I eat chicken too, and no one hates me."

Roscoe turns his head sideways, like he's listening to me, but the closer we get, the rufflier his fur becomes until it's standing up in a weird ridge on his back. I've never seen him do that. "Should we head back to the car?" I'm less concerned about the whimper I heard, and more concerned about myself at this point.

He starts to growl then, a rumble that comes from deep inside his throat.

"Let's go back," I say.

But it's too late for that. There's an answering rumble in front of us. I look up from Roscoe and against the swirling snowflakes, I see a huge cat.

"You could take one of your online photos with me," Jeff said once.

"Please. I may be in Utah, but that doesn't make me a cougar." I paused. "Are there actually cougars here?" I thought I'd feel pretty dumb if there weren't.

"Not many, anymore, but if you ever see a cougar, don't run. Back away slowly." He then eyed me up and down and walked backwards with a goofy grin on his face.

Was he serious? Is that really what I should do? The car isn't very far away, and my desire to run is almost overpowering.

"Back away slowly," I say as if Roscoe can actually understand a single word. I take a step backward, my eyes on the enormous mountain lion with the bloody muzzle. I'm guessing that whimper was coming from its dinner.

Which I interrupted, like a New York moron.

I take another step, and realize that Roscoe isn't following me. The cougar isn't paying me any attention either. Its eyes are entirely on my sweet little dog. It's no dope—it knows I'm no threat.

"Come, boy. Back up with me, now." I take another step, but Roscoe doesn't budge. If anything, he growls louder.

Then he barks, loudly. And again.

I take another step back, partially involuntarily, and partially because I'm hoping Roscoe will eventually follow me. "Here, boy."

Instead of backing up, Roscoe advances, barking again, his muzzle lifted up to reveal his teeth.

The cougar doesn't like that, not at all.

It attacks.

Roscoe leaps forward, too, but he's so much smaller than the cougar, far less than half its size.

I'm not proud of this, but I don't try to defend him and I stop calling for him, too. I scream and run for the car. I fully expect the cougar to pounce on my back every single second, but if Roscoe's dying for me, I can't let it be in vain.

I reach the car door and I'm fumbling for my keys—my purse is miraculously still clutched in my hands—when I hear a gunshot. Then another.

When I spin around, I see Snuggles and Eddy.

The cougar's racing away.

And the little pile of black and white fur that's covered in blood on the ground isn't moving. I drop my purse as I race toward my little dog.

"Why didn't you call me?" Eddy shouts.

"I didn't—there wasn't time." Tears are streaming down my face.

Snuggles circles around behind Eddy, growling.

"Will the cougar come back?"

"I didn't shoot it," Eddy says, "but I don't need to. They know to run from gunshots. He won't be back."

"It was a he?"

"Way too big for a female."

I crouch down by Roscoe, and I notice that he's moving. His body is heaving up and down. "He's alive."

"He's wrecked." Eddy crouches down next to him, slides his arms underneath him gently, and scoops him up. He turns quickly and takes off for his house. "You coming?"

I almost couldn't hear him—he's not wasting any time. "Of course." I jog to try and catch up—a little worried about Snuggles, but mostly just terrified for brave Roscoe.

"I left him," I blurt. "He attacked that huge cougar and I ran away." My voice rises hysterically. "If he dies, it's my fault."

Eddy doesn't stop, but his voice is loud and clear this time. "You did exactly what you should have done. Roscoe attacked that guy to save you. If you'd stuck around, it would have wasted his actions."

He kicks his back door open—it must not have been fully latched—and sets poor Roscoe down on the kitchen table. Now that it's light enough to see him, my hands start to shake.

There's *so* much blood.

"Amanda, I need your help. I need you to focus. Can you do that?"

I nod.

"Can you?" He can't see me, obviously.

"Yes."

"Go through the kitchen into the laundry room and get me the big white caddy. It has a lot of stuff in it that I need. Then go and fill a pitcher with water. You'll find one in the second cabinet on the left, above the sink."

I do as he asks, but while I'm walking back with the pitcher, Roscoe whimpers and yips.

Snuggles growls by Eddy's side.

"Hush," I say without thinking. "Roscoe's a hero, and he's in pain."

To my surprise, Snuggles drops her head onto her paws and quiets.

"She likes you."

"Oh?" I know he's just trying to distract me. "You got that from the time she tried to eat me? Or just now, when she growled at my dog?"

He laughs. "Both. She didn't eat you. That's the first clue. And just now, she listened to you, obeying your tone."

I thought he was kidding, but now I wonder whether he's serious. "Is Roscoe. . ."

Eddy hasn't stopped moving. He was cleaning, he was injecting something, he was wiping and dabbing and pouring. Now he points at a lamp. "I need more light."

I drag it over next to the kitchen table and find a new plug. Once it's on, I make the mistake of really looking at Roscoe.

His stomach looks like raw hamburger.

"That cougar treated him like a chew toy," Eddy says.

"He's going to die."

Eddy freezes. "Have a little faith in me. I may not be a vice president, but I'm a mighty fine vet."

That's when I start to hope.

I fetch sutures. I hold the light from my phone. I rub Roscoe's head to calm him down when we need him to choke down some medicine. And then, once he's cleaned and stitched and bandaged, I sit on the floor and hold him in my lap until he falls asleep.

"What are his odds, do you think?"

"If he survives until morning?" Eddy sinks onto a kitchen chair. "Good. Pretty good."

"Is there anything we can do?"

Eddy shrugs. "We've done it. The rest is up to him."

Tears start to roll down my cheeks again. "Poor Roscoe."

When I glance his way, I notice that Eddy's crying too.

"Thank you," I say.

"This is why I became a vet, you know. Not so that I could vaccinate cows and grind down horse teeth." He wipes his hand across his face. "I did it because to these animals, we're family. They don't even think about it. They just act. If the humans I know were half as good as the animals—"

"I could never do what you do," I say. "I'd freeze up."

He shakes his head. "You were brilliant tonight. I've had a lot of assistants over the years—my sister included —and none of them were better than you. And it's your dog. In spite of being emotional, you were right there with everything I asked for the second I asked for it."

Eddy stands up and walks out without a word. Snuggles hasn't moved. I'm about to call his name, ask what he's doing, when he reappears with a large foam pad. He sets it next to me. "Let's transfer him here. You certainly can't sleep like that."

"How will we get him home?" I ask. "Can you carry him to the car? And once I get home, what should I do? Check on him every hour?"

Eddy tilts his head and lifts one eyebrow.

"What?"

His head slowly swivels toward the window. "Uh, Roscoe's not going anywhere right now, and neither are you."

I follow his gaze and see nothing but white swirls outside. I'm still staring when Eddy's powerful arms slide underneath Roscoe again, his hands grazing the tops of my thighs.

It shouldn't thrill me—not with Roscoe at death's door—but my body didn't get the message, apparently. I look the other way so Eddy won't notice that my cheeks are heating up.

His words sink in, then. I'm going to be sleeping here tonight.

With Eddy.

The second Eddy straightens up, I leap to my feet. "I have to call Abigail. She must be freaking out."

"I hope the phone lines are still working."

Panic sets in. "Will they not be?" I race to the floor by the door where I dropped my purse and dig around until I find it. I think about calling Maren, but in the end, I dial Abby.

"Amanda!"

"Oh, Abby, I'm so sorry."

"Are you alright? I've called you a dozen times. Are you stuck somewhere? Where are you?"

"I'm at Eddy's," I whisper.

"You're where?" Abby's voice is so loud I have to hold the phone away from my ear. There's no chance Eddy didn't hear that. "What in the world is going on? Did you decide to just ignore—"

"Abby!" I shout. "Abby!"

She stops talking, thankfully. Sometimes shutting her up is like trying to leap in front of a moving train.

"On my way to the car, Roscoe and I ran into a mountain lion."

"What?" This time her voice is so soft and so broken it twists at my wounded heart. "Are you okay?"

"I'm fine—Roscoe—" My voice just quits and I start bawling again.

Eddy takes the phone. "My dog, Snuggles, started to go berserk. I'm glad I grabbed my rifle—storms tend to really confuse all the wildlife."

"You shot it?" It's a good thing Abby talks loud, and Eddy's staying close to me, or I might not be able to hear.

"I shot the air, twice. It ran."

"Oh my gosh, Amanda's so lucky you were there."

Abby's right. I am lucky.

"Take care of her. And Roscoe, too, of course." She says something else, but it's so quiet I can't hear what.

"Prayers are a good idea. We'll know a lot more in the morning."

She's worried about Roscoe. Of course she is. I wipe my face on the sleeve of my coat.

Eddy offers me the phone again.

"Hello?"

"We're just fine here," Abby says. "Don't worry about us, promise?"

"Thank you." I've never in my entire life had someone else I could rely on like this—and right now, it feels like I have *two* people. "Tonight was a really bad night, but I guess the good thing about bad nights is that it shows you how many people are there for you."

"Maren and Emery send their love," Abigail says.

After I hang up, Eddy hands me a stack of clothing so large it looks like it could cover me three times over. "You should take a shower and get changed."

"Please tell me you have a generator," I say.

"Of course I do, and a wood-burning stove," he says. "But when it gets down below zero, it's still really cold."

"We need to keep Roscoe warm, though, right?"

Eddy points. He's moved Roscoe right in front of the stove in the center of the family room. His chest is rising and falling slowly. "Everything's going to be fine," he says. "This isn't my first injured dog, and it's not my first storm, either."

Which would be reassuring, if the storm was my biggest problem.

No storm, no matter how fierce, is ever going to pose a bigger threat to me than Eddy's handsome face. And it turns out, his earnest, concerned look is every bit as devastating as his smile.

I'm in so much trouble.

❧ 18 ❧

ABIGAIL

I spent a summer in Seattle, once. It was the only place I could find a clerkship, and I was convinced I wanted to be a judge one day. That long summer cured me of those notions, but it also taught me something. I had often heard the phrase, "When it rains, it pours." Seattle taught me that in some places, that's just not true. That summer it rained incessantly, but it almost never turned into what a Texan would call a downpour.

In Houston, when it rains, it really *does* pour.

I hadn't given that phrase much thought, other than in its application as a commentary on the weather. I knew it had another meaning—that when bad things happen, often other things pile on, but in my life, bad things mostly happened one at a time. I'd have a difficult pregnancy. Work issues would worsen. My child would be sick. Those things took place, but I never really felt like God doubled down on the trials in my life.

Even when Nate died, my friends and family supported me. My kids were practically angelic. When one side of my life collapsed, the other parts of the foundation stood firm.

But from the moment Mr. Swift informed us that the alien people were trying to take the ranch because we left for a month, everything in my life has fallen apart.

"I understand the trial starts next week," I say. "But I wasn't the one who dropped the ball to begin with."

"When we fired Bev, you said you'd step in."

"I was *told* that I'd step in," I say. "And I'm in the middle of a storm out here, something that's entirely out of my control, and I have kids and animals counting on me—"

"You think we don't get storms?" Lance asks. "Houston is the epicenter of storms. We get tornadoes, hurricanes, and even ice storms, but that doesn't mean we can fail to serve our clients." He grunts. "What did I teach you?"

"Our job is to inconvenience ourselves for the convenience of others," I say.

"Now don't just say it. Do it."

Ugh. Lance is the worst.

We now have more than six hundred cows on our farm—apparently when they count the total cows on a ranch, they count the mothers and bulls, not the calves, but *I* certainly count them—and we need to keep them safe. Plus the goats, the chickens we've come to love, and some guinea hens I tolerate. Then of course, there are the horses.

Ever since the numbing agent Steve injected into Izzy's arm yesterday wore off, she's been pretty miserable. Late last night, when I should have been downloading all the documents I'm supposed to review this weekend, I put everyone else to bed and curled up next to my biggest girl on the couch to watch *While You Were Sleeping*. We both needed it, but now I'm exhausted and I'm worried I won't get the documents downloaded before the internet cuts out from the storm.

"What's wrong, Mom?" Gabe's voice is trembling, and when I look over at him, so is he.

"Why do you think something's wrong?"

"You were yelling on the phone, and now your forehead's all wrinkly, just like it was before Dad died."

Oh, my heart. I sit down at the kitchen table and drop my face into my hands. "Everything's going to be fine, honey, I just need to get a lot of things done."

I need to prioritize. I pull out a blank piece of paper and do what I've always done. I make a list:

1. Download documents to review this weekend
2. Finalize animal shelters for storm
3. Repair the de-icer
4. Set up heat lamps
5. Run to feed store
6. Check generator
7. Weatherproof water pipes outside
8. Caulk windows
9. Replace windshield wiper fluid
10. Bring wood for fires onto porch
11. Prepare easy meals for power outages

Luckily, other than the chicken feed, I've grabbed the food essentials and whatnot already. I've barely finished the list and started the download of the proper documents when I hear clumping boots on the porch outside. A moment later, the door swings open and the big three kiddos plus Emery stomp through the door.

I'm not surprised when Maren ducks out of her room a moment later. I'm also wondering what's going on.

I turn around. "Is everything okay?"

Gabe's standing proudly by the front door, waving people through. "I tolded everyone how you needed help. We're all ready." He salutes me then, like a tiny general.

When I glance back at Ethan, Whitney, Emery, and Maren, they salute too, even Izzy with her bandaged arm.

"I know my mom's working a lot right now," Emery says, "and that means you're having to do all the stuff for us. So we want to help."

I'm not crying, but only barely.

"Are you making a list?" Maren leans over my shoulder. "I can carry the wood onto the porch. Do you want me to set it under the window?"

"I can caulk the windows and check the generator, Mom." Ethan's leaning over my other shoulder.

"How do you replace the windshield wiper fluid?" Izzy asks. "Do you have to suck out the old stuff?"

"Hopefully it's already low, goofball. Then we can just add the new stuff and it'll be fine." Ethan bumps her non-injured side. "Even gimpy, I bet you can do it. I'll show you."

"How do you know?" Izzy asks.

"I saw Jeff do it," he says.

"What about me?" Gabe asks. "I want to help."

"You and Whitney, clean the kitchen," Maren says. "No one's happy when the kitchen's a mess."

"I'll fold the laundry," Emery says. "I'm really good at that, because I'm good at fashion, so I pay attention to what clothes are whose."

Okay, now I'm crying.

"Mom, it's okay." Izzy hugs me with one arm, and Gabe faceplants against my side.

"Once we're done with those, we can go help you with animal shelters," Ethan says. "But maybe you go get the chicken feed first."

So that's what we do. I take deep breaths, and I download documents in between other tasks, and we all tackle it together. I'm nearly done with the document downloads, and we've finished with most everything else by three in the afternoon.

Maren's right, too. I do feel better now that the house

is clean. She went one step further and swept and mopped the family room and hallways. By the time I seal off the add-on area, which is making great progress, but not yet done, I start the download on the last batch.

I might actually pull this off.

Gabe climbs up on my lap. "Mom?"

I run my hand over his hair, which has fallen down over his eyes. "Yes?"

"Are you better now?"

"Thanks to you, yes, I am."

"Oh good." He leans his head against my chest. "Because I don't feel very good."

"You don't?" I've barely asked the question before he throws up, all over my chest, my lap, and the freshly mopped floor.

Apparently, when it rains, even when you manage to move past the initial downpour, it just keeps coming. Gabe starts bawling then. "I'm so sorry," he says. "I'm sorry."

I wrap one arm around him and slide the other underneath his knees and carry him into the bathroom. At least he weighs less than Izzy did, and he's not bleeding. By the time the other kids start to filter back in with reports that it's started to snow, I've bathed Gabe and cleaned up the floor, but I'm still covered in puke myself.

"Ew, what's that smell?" Maren's nose crinkles.

"That would be me," I say.

"Did you puke?" Emery asks. "Someone in my class puked on Wednesday, right on Mr. Bowman's shoes."

So it's going around. That makes sense. "It's just a stomach bug," I say. "And no, Gabe puked."

A terrible sound comes from the bathroom. At least this time, he's already in front of the toilet. "I'll be there in a minute, honey." I really wish I'd bought some Sprite and those little Lipton noodle soup packets. My mom always made chicken noodle soup, but I'm not that epic. The microwavable ones with the tiny noodles are my go-to.

"You should maybe call Mr. Steve," Izzy says. "Didn't he say he was going to check my arm anyway? Maybe he can tell you what's been going around."

He did say he was going to check on Izzy's arm, and if it's snowing, we're running out of time. Kevin said sometimes after a big storm, we're stuck for days before the snowplows can get everyone clear. Being up in the canyon, we're often left for last.

I didn't want to bother him, but I bet I have just enough time to head over to his place and have him check Izzy's arm. That really should have been on the list. As a mother, my emotions should never get in the way of what's best for my kids. Even so, my hands shake a bit as I dial.

"Hey, Abby. I was about to head over to your place. How does Izzy look?"

"She's doing pretty well," I say. "But maybe I should come to you. Gabe just threw up. I'd hate to get you sick."

"That's bad," he says. "Do you have plenty of Gatorade and crackers?"

"Crackers?" I ask. "Check. But we don't have soda or Gatorade. We're mostly water drinkers over here. Except I think maybe Amanda has some Powerade. She does posts for them sometimes."

"I'm closer to the store. How about I run grab some things for you, and then—"

"I'll meet you at your place to get it. You can look over Izzy then."

"Don't stress. I can come to you." He pauses. "Tell me your generator's ready. The weather reports are showing this hitting early, and much harder than they thought."

240

"The only place that has a generator is the small house."

Steve groans.

"It's fine. I talked to Jeff and Kevin. They said if the power goes—"

"It's going to, Abby. Count on it."

"We'll just all head over there. It's two hundred feet away."

"Isn't it a single bathroom?"

I swallow.

"If you've got one puking kid, I doubt it'll stay contained."

As if his words conjured it, Emery runs to her mom's room. A moment later, I hear the sound of retching coming from there.

"Pretty sure Emery just went down," I say.

I hear a car starting through the phone line. "I'm running to the store, and I'm going to get a ton of things. Load up whatever you can and come to my house."

"Wait, I hardly think—"

"I have four bedrooms, all of them with beds, and two and a half bathrooms. That's three times the toilets that you have at the little house." He sighs. "And Abby, I've got fluid bags and IV kits, and I'm afraid we might need them. The flu's really bad this year, and if you wait, I won't be able to get to you."

I think about poor little Gabe. If he gets hit hard, and I turn Steve down, it'll be on me. Or Emery. "Let me call Amanda," I say.

"I'm headed to you the second I'm done shopping," he says. "I'll load up anyone and anything you can't fit, including Roscoe."

"But our animals—"

"I'll stay with Jeff and Kevin," Ethan says.

I hate the idea of having Ethan separated from me during something like this. "What if you get sick?"

"Please." Ethan rolls his eyes. "Besides, I've been the most isolated of all—they're at school all day."

"You'll be all alone."

"I'm eighteen, Mom. It's fine. Please take them and go. You'll be doing me a favor. I really can't handle the smell."

Sometimes I think Ethan acts like a jerk to make things easier on me. "Fine."

I call Amanda to see when she'll be home, and what she wants to do. She doesn't answer. I try her again. And again. Four rooms. One is Steve's, that leaves us three. I'm gathering the sleeping bags and blankets we'd found into a stack, and pulling one out for Ethan, when my phone rings. Please let it be Amanda.

It's Steve again. "Okay, I probably bought too much food—I hope your kids like ramen and cold cereal—and I bought every single thing of Gatorade they had, except the orange and red. That stuff stains."

I laugh.

"I'm offloading it, then I'll be heading to your house. How's Gabe?"

"Amanda's not answering her phone. I'm nervous about that." I sigh. "Gabe's lying on the floor of his room hugging a bowl. Emery's puking in her mom's bathroom. Are you sure you want us to come to your place? I think we might be better off—"

"Freezing to death in your house because you don't want to all share one bathroom with Kevin and Jeff?"

"We have the fireplace," I say.

"I'm on my way. You can argue with me about it when I get there to pick you up."

"Fine."

"So you've told the kids and they're gathering their things?" he asks.

"Do you have stuffed animals?" Whitney yells. "What about any good movies?"

"If the internet goes down, movies aren't going to work," Maren says.

"They will with the old box movies we found," Whitney says. "Mom, what's it called? A VR?"

"A VCR," I say.

Steve laughs on the other end of the phone. "Tell her to bring it. This should be interesting."

"What?"

"Watching those old fuzzy movies on a huge TV."

"I've seen your TV. I imagine the VHS tapes will look just fine on it."

"You haven't seen the television I usually use."

"Huh?"

"I turned the biggest bedroom into a TV room, kind of."

What a bachelor. "I thought you said they all had beds."

"It does," he says. "A big king size bed, and a bunk bed. I said it's a big room."

This should be interesting.

"Look, the other bedrooms, mine included, aren't that big. But my barn has its own generator, and a bathroom in the tack room. I'll go sleep out there, and you guys will be fine."

"We can't kick you out in a storm to sleep in the barn."

"If I'm being honest, the barn's probably nicer than the house."

I did think that myself, the first time I saw his setup.

"Grab some clothing for her, and when Amanda calls, tell her to come straight here."

"She has Roscoe with her," I say.

"He can come, too."

"Fine."

"Good. I'm almost to your place."

I startle. "I better get going, then."

"See you in two minutes."

I hang up and start shepherding the kids around and stacking things in piles. Izzy, even with her bad arm, is pretty decent at bagging the stuff I grab. I didn't think to ask Steve whether he has a washer and a dryer, but surely he does. It's not nineteen-fifty.

Before I've even gathered Amanda's stuff, I hear the door. "Mr. Steve!" Maren sounds as giddy as Gabe and Whitney usually do, which is odd. I wish her mom would call me back. The snow's really starting to come down out there.

"Gabe's sick," Whitney says.

"I know," Steve says.

Kids are experts at stating the obvious. With Ethan and Steve helping, we gather everyone's things. I can tell Maren's nervous, and I'm sure Emery's a disaster. Normally I'd send Izzy to get Gabe while I dealt with Emery, but she couldn't possibly carry him right now. I'm standing in the hallway, unsure which poor, sick kid to get first when Steve touches my elbow.

"Hey, I'm going to get Gabe. I think he'll be fine with me, but Emery. . ."

"I'll get her," I say. "Thanks."

And he's right. Gabe collapses against his shoulder like a large doll, poor little guy.

"Thank you."

His head turns toward me for just a few seconds and he smiles. "Of course." In that moment, I wonder. Could this guy love enough that it wouldn't matter? Even if he had his own kids, would he still love mine? It almost feels like it.

But there's no way to know.

Once I've confirmed that my laptop and my external hard drive are all loaded—though how I'm going to review the virtual mountain of documents I'm on the hook to review this weekend, I have no idea—I head in to where Emery's crouched in her mom's bathroom. "Sweetheart?"

"My stomach still hurts."

"It's alright. I'll get you a bowl you can hold in the car."

"I don't want to puke in a car. I don't want to be sick." When she starts to cry silently, it breaks my heart. "And my mom's not here."

I wrap an arm around her tiny shoulders. "I know that, and I've been calling. I'm sure she'll be back any minute now."

Emery's face turns red. "I want my mom."

"I know." My heart breaks a little. How often in life do we want something desperately, and it's just not something we can have? I'm sure Amanda will be devastated when she finds out her little baby was hurting and she wasn't around. "I'm not as good as your mom, but I'm the fill-in you have." I tug just a little and she crashes against my chest.

After a moment, her crying subsides and she says, "Are we really going to stay at Mr. Steve's?"

"I know that probably seems scary," I say. "I've only been there once myself. But he's a doctor and has things you and Gabe or any of us who get sick might need. He told me he has nausea medicine, fluids if you can't keep things down, and plenty of stuff to drink."

"Alright."

"Once we're all there, I bet it feels more like home

245

than you think."

"Plus," Maren says from the doorway, "he has *three* toilets."

"Oh, good." Emery groans. "Because I may need to sleep in front of one of them."

"And since we don't have a generator here," Maren says, "it may get really cold, really soon."

"What if we don't lose power?" Emery asks. "What if Mom comes home and we're all gone?"

"I'll leave her a note," I say.

Before I walk out, I write a note for Amanda. I hope she's not upset about how I've handled things. The last thing I do before we drive away is to hug my big boy. "Be safe, please. You matter more than any animals. Remember that."

Ethan laughs. "We're going to be fine, Mom."

Poor Emery throws up twice in the bowl on the way to Steve's, bawling louder each time.

"I knew I should have ridden with Mr. Steve." Maren covers her face the entire ride.

Izzy doesn't say anything, but she looks a little queasy. We're pulling into Steve's drive when she asks, "Mom, what would we have done if we hadn't met Mr. Steve?"

I think about that for a moment. "I'm not really sure."

"Do you think God sent him to us?" Gabe asks.

Steve opens the door then and holds his hands out for Gabe.

"I think he did," Gabe says.

It's a little harder on this end, without Ethan to help, and moving people into a strange house, but Steve really did buy a lot of supplies, and seeing the stacks of them in the kitchen and the entryway reassures me. Between the things I packed and the things Steve bought—including two cases of toilet paper and a bunch of noodle packet soup—we're going to be alright.

I just wish Amanda would call. Every passing minute makes me more nervous. Steve never stops moving, from unpacking to unloading, to directing people into rooms.

"Izzy, I thought you and Whitney and Maren could share this room," he says. "Since so far, none of you are sick." He points at the first room off the family room. I duck my head through the door and see the room he was talking about.

"Cool!" Maren says. "How big is that TV?"

"It's eighty inches," he says. "When I bought it, that was the biggest size they had." He chuckles. "It's already old news, but it's big enough for me."

Maren tosses her bag on the king bed right across from the television. "I call this bed."

"I'll take the bottom bunk," Izzy says.

"Cool. I love the top bunk." Whitney's already scrambling up.

"There are three more rooms," Steve says. "You can split them up any way you want."

"I'd rather you not go to the barn," I say. "If we need anything, I'd have to tromp all the way out there."

He smiles. "I want you guys to feel at home. I'm not sure you will—Amanda especially—if I'm here."

"I need the bathroom." Emery looks pretty miserable.

I help her to the front bathroom, the half bath. "Can I just lie here?" she asks when she finishes puking.

"Sure." Steve's standing in the doorway. He hands me a blanket and a small pillow. "Wrap up with this, though. The floor's hard and cold."

Emery doesn't have the energy to argue, poor thing.

My phone rings, and I practically maul Steve to get past him and answer it. Thank goodness it's her. Finally. "Amanda!"

"Oh, Abby, I'm so sorry."

"Are you alright? I've called you a dozen times. Are you stuck somewhere? Where are you?"

"I'm at Eddy's," she whispers.

"You're where?" Why on earth would she be at Eddy's right now? Her kids are sick, and I'm preparing for this whole storm alone, and Gabe is sick, and I just want to reach through the phone and slap her. "What in the world is going on? Did you decide to just ignore—"

"Abby! Abby!"

Is she yelling at me? I swear, if this is because of that dumb cookie thing, which is doomed to fail, I'm going to be mad.

"On my way to the car, Roscoe and I ran into a mountain lion."

Ran into. . . "What?" I'm a horrible person. I was actually angrier with her than I realized, leaving me alone with all this with the storm coming. "Are you okay?"

"I'm fine—Roscoe—" She's crying too hard to talk. Oh my word. At least she's okay, but does that mean Roscoe's dead? I can barely form the thought. I have no idea how I'll tell the kids. They've already lost too much, all of them. I catch Steve's eye and toss my head at Maren. He understands, and leads her into the kitchen, asking her to help him get things organized.

Eddy must've taken the phone, but his voice is strong and clear. That's reassuring. "My dog, Snuggles, started to go berserk. I'm glad I grabbed my rifle—storms tend to really confuse all the wildlife."

"You shot it?"

"I shot the air, twice. It ran."

"Oh my gosh, Amanda's so lucky you were there. Take care of her, and Roscoe, too, of course." I can't believe I was angry with her, and she nearly died. "We'll be praying for her, and for Roscoe. Do you think he'll survive? Should I tell the kids?"

"Prayers are a good idea. We'll know a lot more in the morning."

Eddy must have passed the phone, because it's Amanda's voice again. "Hello?"

"We're just fine here," I say. The last thing she needs, if Roscoe's dying, is to worry about her sick kids, or the fact that they're not even at home. "Don't worry about us, promise?"

"Thank you. Tonight was a really bad night, but I guess the good thing about bad nights is that it shows you how many people are there for you."

She should know her girls will be just fine. If I were her, that's what I'd want to know. And that they love her, too, especially if she's scared. "Maren and Emery send their love."

I fill the girls in on the fact that their mom was in danger, but that Eddy heard the ruckus and kept her safe. I don't mention that Roscoe saved her, or that he's not doing well. We'll cross that bridge when we come to it. They have enough to worry about, being sick in a strange place and a storm without their mother.

I check my phone again once everyone's settled and everything's put away. As expected, a cell tower must have gone down, and it looks like the WiFi is out already, too. The last message I got was from Robert. HEARD ABOUT THE STORM. JACK AND I WILL DO THE DOC REVIEW. PLEASE BE SAFE.

Bless him. We may not be dating like he wanted, and he may have made some mistakes, but he's a good friend. I'm lucky to have him, too.

"Everything okay?" Steve asks.

I sink down next to him on the couch and turn the phone toward him.

He squints to read it and then meets my eyes. "That's good news, I take it?"

"The best." I close my eyes and lean back. "I was stressing."

He wraps an arm around me and squeezes my shoulders. "I hate that he's the big savior, but I'm glad it's a relief."

"Oh, the big savior today is definitely the horse doc. Have you heard of him?"

When I open my eyes, he's smiling, his one dimple showing. "I hear he's tall, smart, and strong. And that his abs could be used to wash clothing."

I bite my lip. "I'm not sure about that last part. I might have to check myself."

"Mom?" Izzy's in the hallway.

Steve and I straighten up so fast, we could be auditioning for the role of awkward teenagers on a first date. "Yeah?" I clear my throat. "What's wrong?"

"I think I—" and then my twelve-year-old pukes on Steve's floor.

A few hours later, once everyone and everything is clean, and everyone but us appears to be sleeping, I sit down again. "Okay, fine. I give up. You can go hide in the barn—if I were you, I definitely would."

Steve's laugh is tired. "I wouldn't dare leave you to handle this alone." He sits down next to me again, but this time, all our flirty energy has been depleted.

Plus, no matter how many times I've washed my hands, I still smell vomit. Steve's been elbow deep in all of it, cleaning, running laundry, holding Izzy's hair after redoing her soiled bandages, and they aren't even his kids. "You might be the best man I've ever met."

Even his smirk is tired. "One of these days, you're going to have to tell me the reason you're so opposed to having another child." His eyes meet mine. "Because I've never met a better mother."

19

ABIGAIL: TWO YEARS PRIOR

Hospital rooms are the most depressing places in America. They should be inspirational and calm and soothing. After all, they're supposed to be places of healing. But more often than not, they're places of sanitation and death instead.

The room we're in is clean and new and bright, but it's also clinical, spare, and utilitarian. The kids have provided things with which to decorate. They've drawn pictures and written letters, and I've brought box after box of things from home, but it barely makes a dent. Nate's favorite addition is the enormous portrait from our wedding, which is currently front and center, hanging right next to the television.

On the day our wedding photo was taken, we were both so very young, so fresh-faced, and so eager. It was the beginning of everything, of our cute and exciting love story. Now, the photo looks dated—faded colors, fussy flowers, and humorous hairdos. I really had no business getting married at the age of nineteen, but I was raised in a very traditional home. If you turn up pregnant and you love the father, you marry him.

I never once regretted the spur of the moment wedding, the groom, or the baby who was born seven and a half months later.

"You're just as beautiful now." Nate's fingers brush my cheek fondly.

I pretend they aren't trembling from that small exertion. I don't mention that he looks as if he's aged fifteen years in the last three weeks. Because to me, none of those things matter—except as harbingers of what's coming next. "You're such a liar." I shake my head. "I'm ten pounds heavier, fifteen wrinkles more wizened, and at least twenty stretch marks more weathered."

"You're ten times more capable, you're a hundred times more compassionate, and you're a thousand times more dear to me, for all those reasons." Nate's mouth is dry, and his voice rasps.

"Lie back on the bed." I fluff the pillow on the hospital bed behind him and press him back. "The kids will be here in less than an hour, and you need to rest before they overrun us again."

He closes his eyes, a smile spreading across his face. It does wipe him out when they come, but it also lifts his spirits like nothing else. "There's something we should talk about before they arrive." He sinks into the pillows I propped up and turns his head to face me.

"Okay." I wonder what topic we'll discuss today. Over the past week, as it has become increasingly clear that the surgery and chemo didn't do the impossible, we've covered exciting topics like retirement plans, life insurance information, wills, powers of attorney, and medical powers of attorney. He has recorded messages for each child, and I've scribed letters from him to be delivered at all their important milestones.

I try never to cry in front of him. His one request

from me has been that I enjoy the time we have, and that I don't spend a moment of it sad.

It's impossible to do, of course, but I try my best.

He's faking it too—there's no way he's really been happy all the time.

"What new and brilliant task will we tackle today?" I shudder to imagine what else he's come up with.

"I thought about writing you a dozen or so letters," he says.

I roll my eyes.

"Yeah, it felt a little cliché to me, too." He laughs. "And arrogant, in a way."

Cliché or not, a letter or two might be nice. "You decided to just tell me all the advice you'll have for me instead?" I reach for my phone. "Did you want me to record this?" I didn't realize how much I wanted him to leave me something as well, until the very moment it's happening.

He shakes his head. "No, this is a discussion we need to have. I've had a lot of time to think during the past few weeks. Time in the MRI and CAT scanner. Time while doing chemo. Time recovering from surgery. It's funny that now, when my time is so limited, I have so much of it that's filled with. . .nothing worth doing."

"Every moment we're together is worth sharing," I say.

His smile is kind. "But now I'm worried about you—and I want you to hear me out."

This sounds ominous, but what can I do? Argue with my very sick, very feeble husband? "Okay."

"You're going to be wrecked when I'm gone."

I stand up. I can't do it. "Stop."

His hand reaches for me. I can't walk out, no matter what crazy thing he wants to say. "Abs."

"Just, don't start telling me that I'll need to move on. Okay? It's too—" I choke up. "It's ridiculous." He's the only man I've ever really loved. We've been together since I was nineteen years old. "It's stupid."

"You're not even forty years old," Nate says. "You're every bit as lovely as you were when we married, and you're smarter, fiercer, even more impressive."

"Nate, I mean it."

"Sit, please."

In the end, I can't refuse him, not even this. Not even murmurs and blathers about me finding new love. It's nonsense, but maybe it'll make him feel better. "Fine."

"You're not going to think about this for months and months. You'll be drowning, I know you, with your head barely above water. You'll fixate on the very next task and then the next, until one day, they won't be quite as awful, or quite as overwhelming. And then one day, you'll realize you're not drowning anymore, you're just really, really sad."

"Nate." I'm not supposed to cry—I promised him, but how am I supposed to keep that promise *right now*? When he's talking about my future—the one he's not a part of anymore? "Please stop."

"You can cry. I grant you a reprieve, just this once."

Tears roll down my face, as if somehow I was just waiting for his approval.

"But it's important that you listen to what I'm saying, Abs, because when you do come up for air, when life starts to feel less traumatic, when you're able to operate without gasping, you're going to realize that you have too much to offer to spend your life all alone."

I've carefully recorded all his sage messages and advice for the kids. I've helped him craft the perfect words of congratulations for graduation and weddings, and consolation for breakups and failures. I've helped him think through the many things our kids may endure, and I've watched as he tried as best he could to offer his love and insight for those times.

But now he's doing it to me, and I am not okay with it.

"I love you so much, Abigail Wren Brooks, that I want you to live a happy life. The one thing I can't handle is the thought that you will be alone forever. I want you to find someone wonderful, and I want you to laugh and smile and dance and sing. I want you to celebrate and live and love. Promise me."

My tears are still rolling down my cheeks and my head throbs and my face is surely entirely blotchy. But I nod. "Fine. Whatever."

"But I have one request. A promise I want you to make to me in return for my blessing on literally anyone you choose. Anyone you think will make you happy, I give you my blessing to date and to kiss and to marry. Anyone you think will take care of you in all the ways I won't be able to anymore is fine."

To kiss? To marry? He's lost his mind.

"Abs."

He has a request? That I remarry? "What?"

"Promise me that you won't have any kids with him, whoever he is."

Kids? "I don't understand. Why would I—"

"You're not quite thirty-seven." His shoulders slump, and his eyes shift back to his lap. "It's a demanding thing I'm asking of you, but I have a reason—I'll explain. You'd be able to have more kids—your pregnancies were bearable and you're healthy."

I lean toward him.

"But no matter how great that man you meet *is*, no

matter how smart, or how kind, or how generous, he will love his own biological child more than one he's only caring for. He just will. And our kids will sense that. So I give you my permission—no, my encouragement—to date. To find love. To move on. But in exchange, I beg you for just one thing. Promise me that our four children will be your only biological children. Forever. Make sure they're never competing for time and affection with children from their *new* dad."

"No one could ever replace you." I grab his hand.

He takes my hand in between both of his and squeezes as hard as he can—it's so feeble. "Promise me? That you won't have any more."

"I won't have any more children," I say. "I promise that, readily. I love my four to Mars and back again, and I don't need or want any more."

He smiles then, and his entire face lights up. "Thank you."

A tap on the door draws our attention to the nurse standing there. "He needs his port changed. Didn't you say his kids are coming?"

"Yes, let's do that now," Nate says. "I'm ready."

He's entirely stoic and calm as they poke and prod and jab him, day in and day out. He's chipper as they administer drugs that are basically trying to kill his cancer before they kill him. And he's absolutely delightful when the kids do arrive—no sign whatsoever of the macabre topic he covered with me before they arrived.

As I watch him play with our children, as I think back to the nearly twenty years we've spent together, I realize that he's right. One day, I may want to find someone who can bring me a bit of the joy I've shared with him, but the thing I must keep at the forefront of my mind is that I can't ever do anything that might jeopardize my kids feeling as loved, as fulfilled, and as supported as they possibly can be.

That's my number one job, from this day forward. To make sure my children are as close to as whole and happy and healthy as they would have been if Nate had been with them their entire lives.

And I won't fail him. I'll keep that vow.

20

AMANDA

I cannot sleep.

I suppose I could blame the cougar. This whole thing really is his fault.

But I'm blaming Eddy instead. He, at least, is here, and being mad at him is a good idea. It keeps me from wanting to kiss him.

"We should both go to sleep," he says. "But first, I thought I'd tell you a story."

I close my eyes. Listening to his voice may be the most soothing thing ever. Maybe it'll put me to sleep.

"The reason I never told you about this before is because I thought it might make you sad."

I open my eyes to see what he's talking about, but he won't meet my eyes. "Okay."

"After Jed died, Kevin called me."

"About?"

He glances up, but then looks back down at his hands again. "Roscoe."

The hair on my arms stands on end.

"He was sick."

"What?" My heart stops. "What are you talking about?"

"Actually, sick is the wrong word. Kevin thought he was sick, because after Jed died, Roscoe wouldn't do anything. He moped around, listless. He lay on the porch in front of that door all day long, and all night long, too. He didn't play. He didn't race or jump or bounce. All the life just went out of him, and for a four-year-old border collie, that's abnormal."

I don't understand what he's saying. "But when I met him, he was fine."

"No, when you met him he *came alive* again. Something about you made Roscoe happy. Some dogs are happy to be around all people. Some dogs love kids and hate adults. Some dogs only like adults, and kids make them nervous. Like people, dogs come in all shapes and sizes—personality can differ even more than their physical bodies."

I swallow. "And you're saying that something about *me* changed him?"

"Healed him is probably a better word," he says. "Jeff and Kevin mentioned it right after you got here. They both texted me to say he had found a new person."

"I don't even like dogs," I confess.

"Maybe that's why." Eddy shrugs. "Either way, when you left? It was worse than when Jed died. Roscoe had found a way to trust someone new. . ."

"And then I abandoned him." My heart breaks. "I should have taken him with me to New York when we went back."

"It would have been much easier on him, even though he'd never been to a city in his life." Eddy runs a hand down Roscoe's black back. "You became his whole world, so when you left." He sighs. "He just gave up. He wouldn't even eat."

"Why didn't you tell me before?"

"I'm only telling you now because you look so distressed."

"How would this possibly make me feel better?"

Eddy rubs Roscoe again. "Hearing your voice is probably the best thing in the world for Roscoe right now, even better than the antibiotics I gave him, or the stitches I made to keep him put together."

"How could my voice—"

"Even with the pain medicine, he's in a lot of pain." Eddy pats his head gently. "Your voice is like home. If he keeps hearing it, he'll keep fighting to stay here."

I start bawling. In my entire life, no one has ever loved me that much.

Once, long before Paul died, when the kids were still quite young, I had a day where things seemed too hard. I lay down on the floor of the girls' bedroom, and I curled into a ball. I really thought that my little girls would come over and comfort me. Maren didn't seem to notice—she was too busy with her block tower—and when Emery noticed, my sweet, darling Emery who loves all things, she started poking me. "Mommy wake up. Mommy." When that didn't work, she slapped me. Eventually, she stood up and kicked me.

That's when I realized that while children may love you, they don't feel the way that a mother might, not really. And my husband was never very devoted or very dedicated either.

My parents—it's better not to even think about that. But this little dog? He quit eating when I left, and I didn't even know it. Eddy tried to convince me to sleep in his spare bedroom, and when that didn't work, the couch. But any way I moved the pad that Roscoe's laying on, I couldn't quite reach him from the sofa. So Eddy finally brought me a sleeping bag and a pillow and lay them down on the floor next to my furry number one fan.

But as soon as I fall asleep, I hear Eddy's voice in my head. *Your voice is like home.* I jolt awake, and I start over, telling him stories, singing him songs. And then I get sleepy again, and start to drift off, and then I remember something else Eddy said. *If he survives until morning.*

His odds are good, if he survives until the morning. And my voice might help him do that.

Around four a.m., Eddy's door opens and he emerges, rubbing his eyes. He releases the blanket around his shoulders so he can rearrange it, and I realize he's not wearing a shirt. My brain immediately shorts out.

"Why'd you stop singing?" he asks.

"Why are you awake?"

"I heard a noise."

"I'm sorry I woke you up."

"I had no idea you could sing. You're actually really good."

I stifle my laugh. "You said my voice might help him."

"Please tell me you haven't been awake all night."

"Says the vet, who has dedicated his life to saving animals, and not even ones that have decided you're the only person they love."

"Touché." He yawns, and then crosses the room to where I'm lying, one hand on Roscoe's paw. He sits down cross-legged next to me, the blanket spilling out around him, brushing against my leg. "We lost power. It wasn't your singing that woke me. It was the growling of my generator. It's right outside my room. I just happened to hear you when I woke up."

"Am I crazy? Is there really any chance this will help?"

"Are you still awake because of what I said?" He groans. "I'm so sorry. I shouldn't have told you that."

"He can't die," I say. "If there's anything I can do, I have to do it."

"Roscoe may not even be able to hear you."

"But maybe he can," I say.

Eddy grabs a pillow off the sofa and lays it down on the floor, yawning again. "Well, you take a break, and I'll do some talking."

"Nice try," I say.

"You'd rather I sing?"

Yes, actually, not that I'd admit it. "Roscoe doesn't love you. Your songs won't help."

He smiles. "That's true."

With his face directly across from mine on the floor, inches away, it's hard to remember why I can't touch him. Or kiss him. Or slide my hand underneath his blanket and touch—but I have good reasons. Like earning money and paying my bills and providing for my family. "You should go back to bed. You'll need to be in top form tomorrow to do all the vet things."

A whining sound draws my eye. Snuggles is standing just behind him, glaring at me.

"Uh, your wolf hates me."

"She likes you."

"You're clearly insane," I say. "She's staring daggers at me right now."

"Snuggles attacks anything she hates," Eddy says.

"This should reassure me, how?"

"You've been here for a long time, and you're still fine." He beams. "Now. Get to talking. Or singing, if you'd rather do that."

"I'm not doing any of that while you're in here." It's so dark that at least he can't see the heat rising in my cheeks.

"But it was so cute," he whispers. "Plus, think of Roscoe." When I still don't speak or sing or do anything other than glare, he says, "Please?"

As if she agrees, Snuggles drops to the floor with a whuffle, stretching and leaning up against Eddy's other side. I'm a little jealous. I'm maintaining a careful distance, but she's practically rolling all over him.

"He has to actually hear you for there to be any benefit," Eddy whispers. "You know that, right?"

"You're not playing fair," I say. "I'm stuck here, so you're supposed to keep your distance."

His hand reaches out and pauses, right in front of my face. "What about me," he says, "makes you think I'll ever play fair?" His fingers brush the hair away from my face and tuck it behind my ear. He bites his lower lip, his teeth gleaming even in the low light.

"I'm only here because Roscoe's injured and you're a vet."

"You don't think fate might have had anything to do with it?"

"Fate?" I can barely stop myself from laughing. "No way. A meddling old lady, maybe."

His eyes narrow. "What does that mean?"

"Amanda Saddler was the one who offered me that shop for free, and I should have known she had a reason."

Eddy's eyes brighten. "Why in the world would she offer you a shop right by my house? What reason could she have for that?"

I can hardly admit that I got drunk and blabbed about how much I liked him.

"Amanda."

I should never have met his eyes. Now that I have, I feel like I'm sinking. Even in the low light, they're so unbelievably green. His shaggy hair's falling over his forehead and blocking one of them, and it feels like a tragedy. I don't even think about it, my hand just does the same thing his did—reaches out to correct a wrong. The world needs to see both those eyes.

But instead of being polite, instead of maintaining some semblance of space between us, Eddy catches my hand before I can touch him. His fingers caress mine, and then shift. His hand's flat against mine until his fingers move just a little more and our hands are offset—and then he slides his fingers in between mine.

I can't help the sigh that escapes. It's involuntary.

"Did Amanda have a reason to offer you this shop in particular? Does she know we dated? And that now, we can't?"

I swallow.

"She must know you've been seeing that boring bank guy."

"He's not a banker. He's a vice president of—"

Eddy rocks up on his elbow, his hand releasing mine, and his fingers press against my lips. "Sh."

"What?" I ask, against his hand.

"Don't talk about him here, in my house. It's a loser-free zone."

"He's not a los—"

His hand disappears from my mouth, evaporates, is gone, and then is replaced by something so much better—his mouth. It's warm. It's firm, and it's an explosion of feelings and want and need. I'm already in his house, wearing his clothing, lying on his sleeping bag. And now, I finally have what I've been dreaming about for months.

The hand is back, gripping my cheek, dragging me closer, his bristly jaw pressed against me, and his lips moving against mine. He's not gentle. He's not calm. He's definitely not in control, and it's everything I hoped it would be.

It's a bonfire on a parched mountainside.

It's the beating of a thousand butterflies' wings.

It's a single glass of pure, clear water when I'm dying of thirst.

I need more than what I have, more than what he's giving me. I slide my hand around the back of his head and cradle the base of his scalp. He shifts, moving closer, practically crawling on top of me. His blanket shifts, and when my free hand braces against his chest, I feel nothing but smooth, hard skin.

His groan is like gasoline on an already raging fire.

I explode.

No matter the cost, no matter the risk, no matter the danger, there's no way I can't be with Eddy right now. It's been so long, I hardly remember what to do, but I have a feeling he'll be more than capable of filling in the gaps.

And then I feel something strange—wet and raspy, and persistent.

"Oh my—your dog is licking me."

Snuggles is wagging her tail as she enthusiastically licks my shoulder. When Eddy and I both freeze, she stops, looks from Eddy to me, and then yips once.

Eddy's groan sounds like it starts in his toes. "I should have put her down when I got her. It would have been better than *killing her now*."

She makes a strange whimpering, whining sound, and then proceeds to lick his face, too.

I can't help it. I start laughing.

And then Eddy starts laughing.

When I collapse backward on my sleeping bag, Eddy does the same, lying right next to me. When he takes my hand in his, my heart flips. When he presses a kiss to my forehead, my heart flops. "It's probably a good thing she was here." He sighs gustily. "I might have done something stupid otherwise."

"Oh, I definitely would have."

"You're too tempting, Mrs. Brooks."

I glance at his bare chest. "You're not so bad yourself, Mr. Dutton."

He ought to cover himself up. He ought to be shocked. Instead, a cocky smile spreads across his face. "I showed you mine."

"You have got to be kidding."

"Mostly." He still looks like a little boy when he grins like that. A very naughty little boy.

I shove him, and he reluctantly releases my hand and wraps the blanket around himself again.

"I don't regret it," he says.

"Regret what?"

"I've thought about kissing you every single day since we first met."

My heart flips *and* flops over that one.

"I've never regretted living my life, you know." He's staring up at the ceiling, so I do the same. "I regretted that someone died, and of course I wished I hadn't ever gotten high that first time, but I never wished I could go back and give up what I learned."

I'm not sure what to say.

"Until I met you."

Oh.

"It's funny. Back then, I always thought I got off too easy."

"You lost your record deal, and you lost your job, and you got sent home in disgrace. You were only seventeen years old."

"If I had known then what it would cost me, if I had any idea that the thing I wanted more than anything else in the world would be ruined." He shakes his head. "I'd shake my teenage self so hard."

This hurts. It might even hurt more than losing Paul did. He was my husband, but he never really touched my heart. Not truly. "You don't know whether you and I would even work."

"Oh, I think I do."

"You barely know me."

"You're stunning, and you're smart, and you're big-hearted, and you're a dreamer, and you're everything wonderful in this world, and you have no idea."

"Oh, please. You make me sound so cliché, like the teenage idiot who's perfect looking and amazing and everyone loves her, but she doesn't know she's beautiful."

"I'm sure you know you're beautiful to look at," he says. "It's your livelihood, after all. You don't become an amazing influencer who sells designer clothing without having a beautiful face. But that's not what I'm talking about."

"Huh?"

"You take great care with your appearance and it shows, but you've never been told your true value. You don't believe in yourself because the people who matter to you didn't believe in you." He pauses. "Don't take this the wrong way, but I'm guessing your husband was a sack of crap who never supported you."

"He earned a good living—"

"That's paying for you. Supporting you is telling you that you matter, that you're his everything. I don't think he did a good job of that at all."

I can't keep listening to this, not without breaking down and bawling again. I suppose I could probably blame it on Roscoe, but he'd know I was lying.

"Maybe you know more than I thought, but I'm not sure—"

"My parents have spent their entire marriage miserable." He turns toward me again, rocking up on one elbow so he can study my face. "It made me never want to risk something like that."

"Probably smart. I've only really known one happily married couple, and the guy died of cancer."

"Abby's husband?"

I nod.

"Well, much like your sweet dog there, I don't just take to anyone." His voice drops to a whisper. "But also like Roscoe, when I met you, something was different."

"What?"

"I'm saying, Amanda Brooks, that you're home to me. And it may take some time, but I will do whatever it takes until you feel the same way."

I can barely breathe—he shouldn't be allowed to say things like that. "It's not simple for me, Eddy." I feel like the wicked witch of the East, or wherever she was from. "Imagine if, to date me, you had to lose your job. And on top of that, you'd lose it while living in this tiny little place where there's literally no other way you could support your family."

"Gosh, you'd have to really trust the guy, huh? I mean, assuming he was a guy who made enough money to support you and said children."

"You're saying that, before I start dating someone, I should be willing to lose my job?"

"No." He sighs. "I'm not saying that. It's not reasonable."

I relax just a bit. "Thank goodness."

"But." He leans a little closer until his lips are right next to my ear. "I am saying that you could date me, in secret, for a while. And once you trusted me enough, then yes. You could pull that cord. And I'd keep you from hitting the ground, ever. Because unlike that first idiot you married, I'd support you until the end."

Date in secret? "Would I keep dating Derek? As, like, a cover?"

At first, I think the growl is coming from Snuggles, but then I realize it's her owner.

"I'll take that as a no."

"Maybe you should. I don't know. Having some kind

of believable cover is probably a good idea, but I might have to kill him. I don't share very well."

I can't even say I hate his reaction. At least he's consistent. "I'll think about it." And even as I say the words, I remember that kiss. "Maybe I should say I'll think about it constantly."

"You do that," he says.

A whimper from behind me shocks us both. I bolt upright, and he does the same a second later. Snuggles circles around and sniffs Roscoe, whose eyes are now open. He shifts and bats at me with one paw.

"He's moving," Eddy says. "That's great."

"Wait," I say. "Does that mean he's going to be alright?"

"We're not out of the woods yet," he says. "But it's a pretty good start."

DONNA

Aiden comes home with a fistful of papers every single Tuesday. It reminds me that we live in a world of multiple-choice questions.

Thomas only likes things that aren't orange. Does Thomas want to eat:

A: An apple

B: A mango

C: An orange; or

D: A carrot?

"But apples can be orange too." Aiden frowns. "And mangoes can be red. Or yellow."

"The apple on this sheet is red, though," I explain.

We've taught our children the same lie that was foisted upon us, that life has right and wrong answers. Sure, there *is* right, and there *is* wrong, but that's not true for every aspect of life. What Thomas wants to eat now may not be what he wants or needs tomorrow. Or next week. Or next year.

Sometimes the promises that we make are right when we make them, but as life changes, and as it changes *us*, those promises don't serve us anymore. That's when it's time to cut off things that don't help us, to eliminate things that don't keep us safe. It may be hard, or it may feel harsh, but it has to be done. I've been thinking about Abby coming to help me, over and over.

"Hey! Wax ears! Can't you hear me? Get in here!"

Dad's nurse rounds the corner, her bag in hand. "You said you don't have plans tonight, right?"

This new nurse is always eager for overtime—which would be nice if I ever had any place to go. "That's right."

"I've got an hour left after my break, but I figured I may as well haul all my gear out now." She pushes past me with her huge bag—I've never known someone who ate as many snacks as Rena does.

"I'm here, Dad. What do you need?"

He shoves a bowl of soup at me. "That woman is poisoning me."

Not this again. "Dad, she gets paid to take care of you. She has no reason to poison you. She told me herself that she needs this job."

Dad's eyes flash. "Are you calling me a liar?"

I sigh. "Not a liar, no. But I think you've misunderstood."

He stands up, his blanket dropping down to reveal grey sweatpants with a sagging elastic waistband. I could happily have gone the rest of my life without ever seeing my dad's shirt tucked into his tighty-whities. But no, I get to see it on the regular. "Get me something else." He doesn't wait for me to come and take the bowl. He just drops it, and potato soup splatters all over the floor, and the bedspread, and my shoes.

I've cleaned it up and am almost finished making him a ham sandwich when the nurse comes back inside. "Your phone's ringing and ringing," she says.

"No, that can't be mine." I feel for my pocket and realize I might not have brought it back in from the car. I consider handing her the sandwich to take to Dad, but that'll just result in more food being chucked across the room. Whoever's calling will have to wait a bit.

By the time I've convinced Dad that I had complete custody of the ham sandwich from its birth until its delivery to him, I'm ready to go back to work just to get away from him. "I don't know how you do it," I mutter on my way out to the car.

"I don't care as much," Rena says. "When patients are jerks, it doesn't hurt my feelings, cuz they ain't my family."

She has something there. It's much easier to ignore insults and criticisms and complaints when they aren't coming from someone who's supposed to love and support you, not that Dad ever really did that.

When I finally dig my phone out from where it fell between the driver's seat and the center console, I have four missed calls. That must be some kind of new record for me. One is from Patrick, and one is from his lawyer—probably more threatening messages telling me not to go against the terms of the power of attorney ever again. But there are two missed calls from an unknown number.

No message.

It's probably that prosecutor, getting creative. But I'm curious enough that I check the area code.

Houston.

I know exactly one person who lives, or, er, lived, in Houston.

And I owe her.

I wondered when she'd call me to ask me to spare the family ranch. I've been preparing what I'd say—how I could defend my actions and explain that it's not me, but justice that necessitates their losing that ranch. According to Steve, she hasn't even sold her house in Houston yet, so it's not like she didn't know there were risks to the prospect of coming out here. I can't feel guilty for doing what needs to be done, either. I review my arguments one more time in my mind, and with shaking hands, I hit 'call back.'

It only rings once before she picks up. "Donna."

"Is this Abigail?"

"It sure is—Abigail Brooks."

As if I know a lot of Abigails. "What do you need?"

"Well, that question could possibly require a very long answer, but I'm not willing to even try and answer that without some alcohol in me." Her laugh is forced. "And on that overshare, I called earlier to see if you'd have any interest in coming to a girls' night."

"To a—" I must have misheard her. "To a what?"

"Have you met Amanda?" She pauses, but when I don't respond, she plows ahead. "She's an older lady who's an absolute hoot, and she lives at the top of the canyon. Just up from us."

Amanda Saddler changed my diapers. I can't believe she's telling me where she lives. "Of course I know—"

"Great! So the thing is, we're planning to watch the new Julia Roberts movie at her place in about an hour. We're bringing wine and cookies, and she says she's providing sunflower seeds?"

"It's a Wisconsin thing," I say, "and it sounds like fun, but—"

"Don't say no without thinking about it first," Abigail says. "I know we didn't get off on the best foot. I know it feels awkward just to talk to me, but Gabe has been asking to play with a friend, and he really liked Aiden. You could bring him over here, then we can head up to Amanda's together."

I'm not sure why she thinks a few moments to think will change my mind—and then I glance over at Aiden. He's standing in front of the mirror in my room, making faces at himself. He's such a happy, good-natured kid. And he's been really alone since we moved back. Even in his own home, he can't act like a kid, because if he makes too much noise, it sets my dad off.

I may not really relish the thought of a girls' night with two women who are almost certainly planning to ambush me and either take their pound of flesh by attacking me, or convince me to recant my position and somehow stand on their side. But Aiden could really use a friend, and surely they wouldn't lie about Gabe wanting to play with him.

"Let me see if I can iron something out first." After all, I did just tell Rena I don't need her. She may already have come up with other plans.

"Oh, sure. No pressure, but I wanted to at least invite you."

"I'll text you and let you know."

I duck out of my room and ask Rena right away, bracing myself to hear that she's busy.

"Girl, I was hoping you had some plans. My car needs some work done."

Oh good. My paltry bank account is about to fund her new transmission. Maybe I shouldn't go. It's not like I have very much money, either.

"Mom!" Aiden hugs my leg—I didn't even realize he was within earshot. "Are we really going to see Gabe?"

Money's tight, but I can't even remember the last time I had a girls' night, and Aiden's only had one playdate in the past year. "Yes, honey, it looks like we are."

I text Abby back and ask what I can bring.

JUST YOUR SWEET LITTLE BOY. COME TO OUR PLACE FIRST SO YOU CAN DROP HIM OFF.

Yeah, she's definitely planning to ambush me, but that's okay. I've been preparing for this moment too, and if I didn't meet her openly, I'd probably get attacked in some sneaky way. It's always better not to be surprised. And I'm certainly not going to show up empty-handed.

I open the fridge and scan the contents for something I could take.

Hot dogs.

A third of a gallon of milk.

Moldy cheese.

She *did* tell me not to bring anything.

"Mom?" Aiden's already put his boots on—unfortunately they're on the wrong feet. "Can we go right now?"

If I were still living near a real city, I could swing by most anywhere and pick something up. But with the recent storm—the roads have barely been plowed. When I swung by the True Value this morning, the shelves were bare. Since they're probably going to lay into me anyway, I may as well give them something else to be annoyed about. "Let's go."

It takes some time to get out the door—scarves, coats, gloves—but eventually we get on the road, and it's clear enough, even on the bend leading up to Abigail's. Ready for a face-off or not, my heart races a bit as I walk with Aiden up to the front porch.

When the door swings open, I expect a kid to answer, or perhaps a passive aggressive mother. I do *not* expect Amanda to be carrying an enormous dog like he's a baby.

"That's why he loves her," Gabe says from behind Amanda Brooks' back. "Because she holds him like a baby."

"Sorry," Amanda says. "I was carrying him into the family room, but then I heard the door. . ." She turns and takes two steps to a large flat pillow in the corner. "Poor guy gets so upset if he's away from me for five minutes, but if any people show up, he gets upset that he can't see them." She gently sets him down, but he whimpers a bit anyway. "It's okay, big guy. You're going to be fine."

"What in the world happened?" I ask.

"Why's he all wrapped up?" Aiden asks.

"He saved my Aunt Mandy from a bear," Gabe says.

"It was a mountain lion," Amanda says.

Gabe sighs. "A bear sounds cooler."

"Actually, cougars are a lot more aggressive. Most bears will just walk away," I say.

Gabe scowls at me. "Fine."

"It was going to eat your mom?"

"My *aunt*," Gabe says. "My mom was taking care of me. I was puking my guts up."

"Sounds like you guys have had an eventful week," I say.

"The snow-in was long," Amanda says. "But we're all happy that the kids are better, and that Roscoe's steadily improving."

At the sound of his name, his ears perk up.

Amanda stands. "I swear, no one has been throwing up for more than forty-eight hours, though." She starts to tidy up the room, picking up shoes, jackets, slippers, blankets, and pillows, and I notice that Roscoe's eyes follow her the entire time.

Gabe and Aiden have already disappeared into Gabe's room.

"Did he really save you from a mountain lion?"

Amanda nods. "I was an idiot, I guess. I heard a sound as I was leaving the new bakery I've been working to open, and instead of just getting in my car to go home, I thought I should check it out."

Brave, actually. But once you've been here a while, you learn to leave nature sounds alone unless they're threatening your livestock. And unless you have a gun in your hand. "They don't often come into town."

"I think the storm threw a lot of us off," she says. "But Roscoe was not going to let it get anywhere near me. He leapt in front of me to stop it, and it used him like a chew toy."

"He can't walk?" I'm not a vet, but that doesn't seem very promising.

"His internal injuries are healing, including the messy lacerations Eddy sewed up, but he broke his leg, probably when he was tossed free." Amanda shakes her head. "It still makes me sick to think about it."

"Eddy was there?" I shouldn't be prying, but I can't seem to help it. I thought she was dating the out-of-towner. He seems much more her speed than a local vet, although Roscoe's lucky he was around.

"His house is right behind my shop, and his wolf-dog heard the fight."

That was lucky.

"If he hadn't fired his gun, Roscoe would've been eaten, I imagine."

And maybe Amanda, too. I can tell she knows it. "How does your boyfriend feel about it?"

Amanda's cheeks blaze. "He's not my boyfriend."

"I'm sorry," I say. "I've seen the two of you together a few times, and I just assumed. . ."

"Like I said, I was lucky he was close."

My brow furrows. "Wait, are you dating Eddy? I thought you were seeing the guy who's buying cattle. Bills, or something."

Her eyes widen. "Derek, right. I mean, I am."

I blink.

"Anyway, I bet you're ready to get out of the house of chaos." She drops down to her knees and rubs Roscoe on the head.

Amanda has always struck me as someone who would have fit in beautifully at most any Ivy League school. She's more buttoned up than a Stanford girl, but just as snobbish. Her dark hair looks perfect at all times, her outfits are utterly coordinated and could be sold to fund a full year of college, and her speech is usually fairly polished. So the last thing I expected was for her to shout for Abby like my mom used to call the farm hands for dinner.

"Abby! Let's go!"

"Did you, by chance, grow up with older brothers?" I ask.

"Two," Amanda says. "How did you know?"

"Lucky guess," I say.

"Alright!" Abigail breezes out of her room, wearing jeans that are way too cute for a mother of four. It also looks like she just got her hair done.

"How does your hair always look like you just stepped out of a salon?" I ask.

"She paid her way through college and law school doing hair part time," Amanda says. "And she's always done her own. Now if she can just find the time to do mine."

"That's why the back of mine never looks very good," Abigail says. "It's hard to get things right with just a mirror. At least I've improved over the years."

Is there anything she can't do? "Did you happen to make a triple layer trifle from scratch to take to Amanda Saddler's?"

Abby stares at me. "No, I barely had time to—"

"She's kidding," Amanda says.

"Oh."

"Are you going?" Emery pops out of her room. "I'll sit with Roscoe. He'll still cry, but it won't be as bad."

"It's like having a baby," Abby says.

"At least he won't wreck my boobs," Amanda says.

Abby laughs. "Let's hope not."

"I'll drive," Amanda says.

"Should I tell Aiden I'm leaving?" I look around.

"Izzy and Whitney will make dinner when they finish

with the horses," Emery says. "I'm sure Gabe will be fine with Aiden—I bet they don't even realize you're gone. But if there's a problem, we'll just call my mom."

"Are you sure?" I haven't really left him anywhere since they came and took Charlie and me and left poor Aiden with an officer he didn't know for hours.

"Sounds like you might need a night off more than even we do," Abby says.

I must—or I'd never have accepted their strange offer. What kind of people invite someone who's screwing them over to watch a movie and have wine? Not normal people.

Luckily, the drive to Amanda's is a quick one. Her house looks much nicer than the last time I saw it. There's a fresh coat of paint on the outside, and as we walk up onto the porch, the wood all looks recently replaced. When the door opens, I peer through at new-ish appliances, bright floors, and shiny countertops. It looks almost like a brand new home.

"Good word, you invited *her*?" the old lady asks. "I thought you said she's the one who sicced those alien crazies on you."

Abby coughs.

"I'm too old to beat around bushes," Amanda Saddler says. "I don't waste time either."

"She's the one who contacted them," Abby says. "But—"

"Then why'd you invite her? Are we supposed to yell at her? Or just quietly make her feel lousy all night?"

"Neither," Amanda says.

"Then why'd you invite her?" Amanda Saddler asks.

"I'd actually like to know that, too," I say. Since the issue was already raised.

"Did you really think we might invite her just to yell at her?" Abby asks.

"I don't know you real well," Amanda Saddler says, "but I feel like Amanda, here, might."

To my surprise, Amanda laughs as she pushes past her old neighbor and turns the corner into the living room. I walk along, since I'm not sure where else to go. Eventually I stop in the demarcation line between the kitchen and the family room.

Abby walks in as well, stopping in the family room. She sets the plate of cookies and a bottle of wine on the coffee table. "I'm sorry."

That's definitely not what I expected her to say.

"If I'd realized you were uncomfortable, I'd have brought it up sooner." She tilts her head just a bit.

"I think we could all use a glass of wine." Amanda walks into the kitchen and opens the right cabinet straightaway, like she's more than comfortable here.

They've been here for five minutes and they're, what? Besties with one of the toughest old ladies in town? Meanwhile, I grew up here, and now that I'm home, my closest friend is a nurse I pay by the hour to come over from Vernal and sit with my dad. This girls' night is not making me feel any better.

Amanda plonks the glasses on the coffee table and opens the wine. She doesn't wait—she just starts pouring.

"I've got a few more bottles when we finish that one," Amanda Saddler says.

It's probably a good thing. Unfortunately, I haven't even finished my first glass when Abby decides to pick up where she stopped. "When I was a little younger, and a little less. . .world-weary, I suppose you could say, I had a run-in with a very smart, very talented lady to whom I was very, very close. Instead of assuming the best things about her, I assumed the worst. My feelings were hurt, and I lashed out at her without thinking about her reasons or her situation." Abby swirls her wine. "It broke something that couldn't quite be repaired. I vowed *never* to do that again. So when Steve told me you needed my help, my initial reaction was to leave you to deal with any mess you made all on your own."

Amanda's staring at her wine. "That's what I'd have done."

"But I remembered that promise I made to myself." Abby sits down on the far end of the sofa. "I'm glad I helped the other night. You looked like you could use a friend or two." She sets her glass on an end table. "Besides. You didn't make us go home over the summer. We did that on our own."

"I did contact the alien group," I say. "If I hadn't, they'd never have even known."

Amanda shrugs. "Have you met Abby?" She snorts. "I'm not scared. They should be scared."

"Still. It's a fight I caused, and now that I know you better, I'm sorry I did."

"People matter more than all the other stuff," Amanda Saddler says. "It sounds like you ladies already know that, but if I've learned anything in the last hundred years, that's it. People matter more than any of the other stuff."

"Hundred years?" Amanda glances at Abby. "I'm not sure you can claim a hundred—even Gabe doesn't exaggerate that much."

"Exaggerate?" Amanda Saddler says. "That's just rounding, m'dear. Maybe they don't teach that in school anymore."

"Are we ever going to start this movie?" Abby asks. "Because I'm tired, and if we wait much longer, I might fall asleep."

"I'm the octogenarian," Amanda Saddler says. "If anyone's going to fall asleep, it's me." She sits down right next to Abby and takes a big gulp of her wine. "But let's get going." She picks up the remote. "Do tell us before we begin, however, why you're so tired. Could it be that hunky Steve Archer who's always mowing without a shirt on?" She whistles. "You know, he's looked that good for almost thirty years, now?"

Amanda busts out laughing.

Abby splutters.

I'm not sure what to say. I know Steve likes her, but I wasn't sure what their deal was.

"Oh, you're not going to share details?" Amanda Saddler leans forward. "As good as his top half looks, I've always wondered—"

Even though she's not drinking anything, Abby practically chokes.

"They're not together right now," Amanda says, coming to Abby's aid. "They've split over irreconcilable differences."

"Isn't that the phoney baloney line that movie stars use?" Amanda Saddler's eyebrows lift. "What's the real problem?"

It's like Amanda is Abby's bouncer. "I'm not sure that Abby—"

Abby's shoulders slump. "I don't want any more children, and he's set on at least one of his own."

"Oh." Even the old woman doesn't think of any way to laugh at that one.

The movie's a decent distraction—the writers didn't really strain any muscles doing anything unique or insightful, but the acting is great, and the leading man is as delicious as Steve Archer. Almost.

"I'm going to make some more popcorn." Abby ducks into the kitchen.

Before I've taken any time to think it through, I follow her. "I'll help." Help? With popcorn? You just kind of stick it in the microwave and hit 'go.'

Luckily, neither Amanda really seems to be paying

attention—they're too distracted by the on-camera chemistry, I guess. I don't blame them. But I haven't been able to think about anything but Abby, and how badly I wish I could find a way to pay her back somehow for her help the other night. And inviting me to dinner. And now for this. There's no doubt in my mind that Abby's the one who wanted me here.

Even though she's arguably the one I've most notably wronged. As I understand it, her son is the one doing all the ranching.

"Don't give up on Steve," I say, a little impulsively.

"What?"

"I know you said you're not dating, but if I were you, I'd give him a little more time."

"More time?" She looks terribly interested, so maybe I can help.

"It's just that, with his past, he clings to things like this. I mean, if you had an ex-wife like his—she was a real piece of work. That's all."

"Steve was married?" The popcorn in the microwave isn't popping anymore, but Abby doesn't seem to notice.

I lean down and open the door, catching it before it burns, thankfully. Now, if only that will distract her a bit. It didn't occur to me that Steve had left her *this much* in the dark. "Uh. Yeah. Maybe that's something you should ask—"

"To whom? For how long? When did it end?"

Hello, Pandora. That sure is a fabulous box. Why yes, I'd love to open it.

Shoot.

"What does that have to do with this? Did they lose a child?"

"Hey, wow, it looks like we're missing the movie in there." I wave at the family room enthusiastically. "Oh, look. They're kissing."

283

"Donna."

I swallow.

"Tell me."

"I mean, I think Steve might be the best—"

Abigail snatches the popcorn out of my hands and opens it, steam pouring out of the top. "Donna Ellingson, I think the best person to tell me what that meant is the person who said it in the first place."

"Fine, but you didn't hear this from me. Things between Steve and me are weird enough already, thanks to you." I drop my voice to a whisper. "He met his ex-wife Stephanie right after he graduated from medical school. They didn't get married until he was nearly done with residency, and she led him on a merry chase for those three years."

I can tell she wants to ask more questions.

"The reason this is complicated for him is that he and his wife had a little girl, only, after a year or two—I can't recall the details so don't press—she told him it wasn't really his. She left him, and took that little girl with her, thanks to a paternity test, and married the rich baby-daddy. So just like that, Steve lost a wife and a daughter. He moved back home then, and hasn't dated since, as far as I know."

Abby looks like someone slapped her. Color in her cheeks, and a dazed look in her eyes.

"Steve's a good guy. He's even a reasonable guy—just not on this issue. It may take him time to figure out that his ex was the problem." Or, in spite of my prior advice to take a beat, it's possible he won't come around at all. I hope for Abby's sake that's not the case.

AMANDA

"**M**y bad," isn't a phrase I heard much before I moved out here. Now I hear it all the time—clearly one of Emery's friends loves the phrase, because she has picked it up with a vengeance.

It's almost as if Utah is saying, "My bad," after sending that nasty storm. The weather levels out and the snow melts, and then day after perfect day rolls out ahead of us. And if that's not enough of an apology, Roscoe improves every single day, too.

Eddy comes by to give him a walking cast after ten days. He also spends nearly every late afternoon and evening helping me with finishing touches to get Double or Nothing ready to open.

The only days he stays away are the days I can't get out of doing something with Derek Bills.

Eddy presses a kiss to my forehead. "I hate that he's coming over here."

"We agreed this was the safest thing to do," I say. "If I can post photos of myself and Derek, then no one will suspect you are anything other than a friendly neighbor."

"I *want* everyone to know," he says.

"So do I," I say. "But I also want to save for the girls' college funds and be able to pay for food."

He rolls his eyes. "I hate this."

"My store opens tomorrow," I say. "Once it gets established, bye-bye fake dating."

"How can that guy be so stupid?" Eddy asks. "It's like he—"

The door jingles.

"What guy's stupid?" Derek beams at me. "You have the loudest voice of anyone I've ever met." He glares at Eddy. Their dislike is quite mutual.

"He's not loud," I say. "His voice just carries well." Maybe it's residual, from when he learned to sing to thousands and thousands of fans.

"Are you ready to go?"

"She's got cookies in the oven," Eddy says. "Can't you smell them? Or is your sense of smell as poor as—"

"I'm ready." I take my apron off and toss it at Eddy. "Remember our deal? You'd take them out and put them away, and in exchange you can take a dozen home."

Eddy's beautifully full lips compress into a tight line. "I never agreed to this."

I know he's not talking about the cookies—about which we definitely never spoke. But I also know that if I don't get Derek out of here soon, Eddy's going to punch him. I doubt Lolo will appreciate photos of Derek as much if he's sporting a black eye.

"I've been researching hikes," Derek says. "I'd love to get one in before the weather turns again."

The last thing I see as I walk out the door is Eddy, smirking. He knows me well enough to know that the only thing lower on my list of fun activities than hiking would be horseback riding. Or maybe scooping cow dung. "Uh, sure. Sounds. . .interesting."

I do manage to get a decent photo out of the whole thing, at least.

But the next day, when I wake up at four a.m. to make the rest of the cookies I need for our grand opening, my legs ache badly. Stupid Derek and his stupid hike. From now on, I'm sticking to my guns.

Amanda doesn't hike. Amanda doesn't bike. Amanda doesn't do anything that ends in a k sound. Except for bake, I guess. Huh. Although, maybe I should rethink that one. By the time Double or Nothing actually opens, my shoulders hurt, my feet hurt, my back hurts, and my arms hurt. On the bright side, it's no longer only my thighs making me miserable.

"You look exhausted." Eddy must've come in through the back door. His hands land on my shoulders and start to massage them. "Are you ready for this?"

For almost five minutes, I don't move at all. I just groan. "Thank you."

Finally, he stops. "It's go time."

A knot forms in my belly. "What if no one comes? What if, with such a small town, I don't sell *any* of these?"

"You have people waiting outside," he says.

"How do you know?"

"Because there were people waiting outside when I got home forty-five minutes ago."

"There were?" Hope soars inside of my chest.

"You're underestimating people's love for sweets. The only thing better than delicious dessert is a novelty that's also a delicious dessert."

"What if they hate mine?"

"Let's open the door and windows and we'll see."

I snap one photo of the glass display case and post it online before I can second guess myself—tagged #DOUBLEORNOTHING, #COOKIES, #NOMNOM, #BAKER, #NEWBUSINESSVENTURE, and

#CUTESTCOOKIESEVER. And then I square my shoulders and open the front windows and door.

To my great delight, there are dozens of people waiting outside. I sell out of three different kinds of cookies—the chewy delicious cowboy cookies, the simultaneously crisp and soft chocolate chip cookies, and the frosted sugar cookies, made in the shape of cowboy hats. On top of that, I get thirty-one orders for specific cookies—birthday parties, anniversaries, and even two holiday party orders.

And the biggest coup is that both of the local restaurants ask me to start providing them with a daily order of cookies.

All in all, it went better than I could ever have hoped.

When I finally lock the door and sink down onto a chair, I realize only two people are left. Derek and Eddy. Umm, #Awkward.

"Hey, Eddy, since you're still here, do you mind snapping a photo of my girl and me?" Derek grabs a Butterfinger cookie and a frosted lemon sugar cookie and wraps his arms around me from behind, holding both cookies up near my face.

Eddy grimaces, but he picks up my phone and unlocks it.

"Whoa. Isn't that Mandy's phone?" Derek stiffens. "How do you know how to open it?"

"He's been helping me a lot," I say. "Sometimes my hands are covered in cookie dough."

"It must be nice to have a job where you have so much free time on your hands," Derek says. "Or maybe it's not so nice when you can't pay your bills."

Eddy grits his teeth, but doesn't argue. "Smile."

I force a smile and turn toward Derek, hoping my fake smile won't look as canned if I'm not staring right at the camera. To my surprise, Derek, whom I have successfully avoided kissing until now, lays one on me.

Other than an exhalation of breath, Eddy doesn't say a word. But as soon as I stand up, shoving Derek back a bit, Eddy slams my phone down on the counter and darts out the back door.

Derek catches my hand before I can leave. "What's wrong with you?"

"Did you kiss me because you wanted to kiss me?" I ask. "Or because you wanted Eddy to see?"

He blinks, and for the first time, it occurs to me that I may be the only one who's always entirely aware of Eddy's presence. "What?"

"Did you really want our first kiss to be in front of someone else? Someone you hate?" I shake my head. "That felt weird."

"Every time I've tried to kiss you, you've darted away like a tiny fish." He frowns. "But tonight, you turned toward me, smiling, our faces right next to each other."

So it had nothing to do with Eddy. Until I made it about him.

Derek steps backward, dropping the cookies on the counter. "Apparently, though, there's a reason you've been darting away from me."

"It's not like that," I say. "Eddy's just a friend."

"And you're not supposed to date him," he says. "I know."

What? How does he know that?

"It's too messy to date your neighbor, and the local vet." Derek huffs. "Whereas you can date me and cast me aside if things get boring, and there'll be no awkward interchanges in a few months when I'm gone. Is that it?"

"Look," I say. "It's just that—"

Derek storms toward the front door. "I've been patient. I've been supportive. I've practically been a

289

saint." He jabs his finger in my direction. "You need to figure out what you want, and then let me know. I'm tired of this back and forth." He ducks out before I can even think about responding.

It must be some kind of indication of how much I like Eddy and how little I care about Derek that my only thought at that point is what I should say to Eddy. I lock the front door and practically sprint toward the back, hoping Eddy's not locked in at his place already.

I'm in luck. He's pacing back and forth in the parking lot behind my store. The second he hears the door, he stops and turns to face me.

"I can't do this," he says. "I'm going to beat that guy to a pulp or start drinking, and either one of those will land me back in jail."

Sometimes I forget he's an alcoholic. Even with twenty years sober, it's always a temptation. "I'm so sorry. I have no idea why he did—"

"You said you haven't kissed." He's pacing again. "The only reason I said, 'sure, keep dating that loser' is that you said you wouldn't kiss him."

I catch his arm. "I didn't kiss him, I swear. I mean, I hadn't ever. I think he did that because he'd gotten so impatient—"

"So you ended things?" His eyes are intent on mine—searching for the answer I haven't yet given.

"Not exactly," I say. "The thing is, there aren't many options out here for me to date. I mean, it's not like—"

"*You're dating me!*" he practically roars.

Snuggles leaps over the fence and races to Eddy's side, whimpering and yipping in response to his clear agitation.

"Girl." He crouches down next to her. "I'm fine. See? I'm upset, but I'm not hurt. You should not have escaped just because—"

"I get it," I say. "I know. I thought it would be easier for us if I had—but it's not working. I'll end things."

His shoulders relax visibly. His hand slides down Snuggles' head and back up to repeat the process rhythmically. "It's just that I like you *so* much. I know I'm the problem, and I know I can't really be angry about whatever you have to do, but boy, it's hard."

I step closer.

He stands up immediately.

Snuggles circles our legs.

I wrap my arms around his waist and lean my head against his chest. His lean but powerful, ripped chest. I never get tired of feeling him against me. I sigh, and his arms tighten and suddenly the world stops spinning. All the things I'm not sure about, they come into focus.

"Let's go back inside," he says. "I'll help you balance the till and get everything all sorted out. We'll see how well your opening went, and maybe if it's good enough, we can start making some projections on how much longer you need that Lololime account."

"It's a good plan."

His head lowers until his lips meet mine, and I forget about plans and balances and tills. I forget about cookies and my Insta account and the dog circling our feet. Even now, after dozens of nights like this, stealing kisses behind my shop, my heart still races when his mouth makes contact. My fingers still dig into his skin as if to say *mine*.

When he finally releases me, I ask the thing I've been wondering about. "Is this so good because it's a secret?"

"I don't think so," he says. "But the only way to know for sure. . ."

"Is to go public." A thrill runs through me at the thought. I *want* it as badly as he does, but it scares me still. I'm not self-sufficient. I'm not enough like Abigail. I'm still far too 'Amanda' for a move like that.

Which is why I need Eddy's help sorting through all the dollars and cents and calculating my waste, my losses, my expenses and my income.

"A hundred and twelve dollars?" I want to cry. "All that work, all that effort, and all I made tonight in profit was a hundred and twelve dollars?"

"That's actually pretty good for an opening date," he says. "Most people lose money across the board for the first month." He coughs. "Or five."

"Five?" Panic grips my chest. "I'm not even paying rent on this shop right now, Eddy. What about when I *do* have to pay rent? It's not like Amanda's going to let me pay nothing forever." I need a paper bag to breathe into. I have no idea why that would help, but it works in movies, right?

"Amanda." Eddy's tone is full of humor.

What in the world could he possibly find funny about this?

"Amanda Brooks."

"What?"

"This is like a pitcher worrying that their career is a failure after a single inning."

"Do I look like the kind of girl who likes sports metaphors?"

He laughs. "Sorry. Are sports metaphors like taking you on a hike for a date?"

I lean against him again. "Not nearly as bad."

"Phew."

My phone buzzes in my pocket.

"Your pants are vibrating."

"Probably my kids, wondering where I am."

"Why in the world does Steve want more?"

"You like my kids," I say. "Don't you?"

Eddy laughs. "I'm kidding."

"Do you want kids?"

He shrugs. "I'm not the one baking them, so I figure it's not really up to me."

"That's a non-answer if ever I heard one."

"I'd love a kid or two. Or I'm fine not to have any. I feel like, for some people, having kids is a Band-aid to cover an injury that won't heal, or to fill a void that can't be filled. If your relationship is great, whether you have kids or not, your love for that other person should remain the same."

Spoken like someone who's never had kids.

"Do you need to take that?"

I figured I'd call my kids back, but my pants are buzzing again. "I hope they're okay."

But when I pull my phone out, it's not the kids. It's Victoria Davis, Vice President in charge of Social Media for Lololime.

"You can answer," Eddy says. "Maybe you should. She's called twice."

"I'm not sure it was her the first time." But the call rolls over to voicemail and I can see that it was her—twice. I groan. "What in the world does she want this late?"

"Only one way to find out."

With plenty of dread, I press the button to call her back. "Victoria?"

"Amanda!"

She's not usually enthusiastic about talking to me. "What's going on?"

"I wanted to check in—I saw you had a major social function today. Is it true you're starting your own bakery?"

"It's only for cookies," I say, "but yes. That's true."

"Do you think a tiny place like Manila can really support a bakery that makes only cookies?"

I'm not sure how that's really any of her business. "Look, I appreciate you checking on me, but—"

"I hate to be a pain, but I feel I ought to remind you that if your ability to promote our brand or to build your own suffers as a result of outside employment, that constitutes a breach of our agreement terms."

"I haven't forgotten," I say. "In fact, just today I posted—"

"Yes, the cookies." Her tone is utterly flat. "But wouldn't a photo of you, with your boyfriend, for instance? Maybe holding cookies or something? Or kissing you? Wouldn't that be more interactive? Especially if he happened to be wearing a Lolo polo?"

My boyfriend. Holding cookies. Wearing a Lolo polo.

Derek was wearing a blue polo shirt I gave him. And he held cookies. And he kissed me.

It's too many coincidences for me to believe they're truly coincidences.

"Victoria, please tell me you haven't sent someone out here to follow me around." The skin between my shoulder blades is crawling at the thought. Eddy looks around too, as if he doesn't think I'm even a little bit crazy. "Or that you didn't put cameras in my shop." Because if she did that, she'll know all about Eddy.

Oh my word, would she do that?

"Oh, stop." She giggles. "Don't be ridiculous."

"Tell me how you know that Derek kissed me. Tell me how you know he was wearing a Lolo polo."

"Look, it's nothing nefarious like you're making it out to be. He's a friend of my husband, and he mentioned he was looking for a place to add a processing center for—"

"You *know* Derek?"

"He's a really good guy," she says. "I swear. And he really likes you."

I remember Derek saying that I'm not supposed to date Eddy. He played it off well, but. . .

"You sent him here? And you've been talking about me behind my back?" I can't believe what I'm hearing. "He reports to you on how I'm—how *we're* doing?"

"I'm going to say goodnight," Victoria says. "I feel like you need to cool off a little bit. We can talk tomorrow."

Even if she gives me a month, I'm not sure I'm going to cool off. Not about this.

❧ 23 ❧

ABIGAIL

When people come to me asking for my legal opinion, more often than not, what they really want is for me to agree with them.

"Don't you think this is a clear cut case of food poisoning?" they ask.

Or, "I should be safe to use this release form, right?"

If I had a dollar for every time someone asked, "Can you just review this document and make sure this will is alright? I found it on the internet and generated it myself."

They want me to tell them that their plans are correct, that their opinion is sound, and that they have the right to do as they please. If I disagree with them, that's when the guns come out and their fangs are exposed.

"But I *know* it was food poisoning."

"But that release *says* they can't sue for any of those things."

Or, "But the website promised that was a valid will for Texas."

Unfortunately, I was not born to be a yes man, nor

have I learned in my legal career that it's a brilliant plan. When I tell people what they want to hear instead of what they *need* to hear, they inevitably show up on my doorstep a few weeks, a few months, or a few years later, upset that I didn't prepare them for the failed attempt to obtain food poisoning compensation, protect them from a lawsuit, or ensure their mother's will protected them from losing the house to their sister.

No, the reason I'm paid the big bucks is to tell people things they don't actually want to hear. It's just not very fun for me.

As soon as Amanda comes to me, I know what she wants me to say. I just can't bring myself to say it.

The dust from the departing school bus is still settling around us on the ground when she says, "I'm worried."

"About?"

"Last night, Victoria called. She wanted me to post a photo Eddy had just taken—a photo of Derek kissing me."

"Wait, how would she know what Eddy did? Does she have cameras at your place?"

"See?" She shakes her head as we walk back up the driveway toward the house. "I'm not the only one who's paranoid."

"No cameras, then?"

She sighs. "She apparently sent Derek out here. She set me up without telling me she was setting me up."

"Like a blind date that you didn't know anything about."

"But creepier, right?" She climbs the steps of the porch, stopping on the top one. "Because he was someone she approved of, meant to replace Eddy. And then he was, like, reporting back to her on how things went."

"Not that she really needed him to—you post photos of everything."

I don't need to see her nostrils flare to know I'm saying the wrong things.

The second we enter the house, she rounds on me. "It's a major violation of trust. I mean, she's hand-selecting the people I date. It's as bad as. . .as bad as when she wanted to tell me everything to do and what exactly to post."

"Except she didn't actually tell you what to post or whom to date. And I presume that Derek actually likes you."

"Last night she called to tell me to post a photo of Derek kissing me. That's when I figured it out. And she threatened me about the cookie shop. She said if I can't do my job, that's grounds for termination."

"It is, though. I mean, that just makes good sense. If I was a doctor, and I started moonlighting as a waiter, and I missed or was late to shifts, they'd fire me."

"Well, that's true if you just started doing a terrible job or going late for no reason."

"Right, but seeing that you're starting a business?" I shrug. "If I were your boss, I'd want to check in and make sure you're not going to lose focus."

She plops into a chair. "For once, can you be on my side?"

I sit next to her. "I am on your side, 110%. If they cancel your agreement, no matter why they do it, even if it's totally your fault, I'm on your side. I'll argue and threaten and negotiate my very best."

"It doesn't feel like it." She looks at her hands.

"Being on your side also means telling you what you don't want to hear if it's true." I lean toward her, flattening my palms against the wooden table. "Amanda. What do you want me to say right now?"

When she looks up, her eyes are flashing. "I want to quit my job. I hate how they're always in the way."

"You want to burn the whole thing down, huh?"

She blinks and sits ups straighter. "No. I'm saying that—"

"You have been trying really hard," I say, "to create something new. Building something new is *hard*. It might be the hardest thing you can do. The vast majority of new businesses fail in the first few months—and almost all the ones that make it to six months are gone by a year. Why do you think that is?"

"What I'm saying—"

"You want me to tell you to just quit your job, because you have a new enterprise. But Amanda, I'm not going to tell you that. In life, the things that are worth doing are hard. And you don't get a medal for being dramatic or diving off a diving board. It's easy to blow something up. It's hard to rebuild. If you quit at Lololime, and you end things with Derek badly, where does that leave us? I just signed a contract with him for the majority of our feeders."

"Our what?"

"That's what they call the new calves that need to eat in order to get big enough to do something with."

"What does that have to do—"

"Amanda Saddler told me that you want to be like me. She said you're trying to channel your inner Abigail. Well, if you want my advice, if that's really what you want to do, then you need to dig down deep and do things you hate even when you hate doing them. You need to do the hard work that creates something new, even when you don't want to do it. And you can't give up because things are hard, because they will be really hard, a lot of the time."

Amanda and I talk for another half hour before I have to dive into a complaint that's due by the end of the day. I feel pretty good about the advice I give her. It's the same thing I would have told one of my kids. I mean, it's a great plan for her to quit doing something she hates, for her to free herself, but you walk before you run. She needs to get her new job off the ground before she cuts the safety net. If that means long hours and some irritating exchanges with overbearing bosses, well, that's what you do when you have kids. You keep that safety net at all costs.

Especially with the uncertainty about the ranch, she cannot be quitting her job right now.

Thanks to a stroke of luck in my researching and an old brief that covered a similar topic, I finish my complaint in record time. I ought to dive into answering the interrogatories that are due next week, but the painters are blaring a horrible mixtape or something, and it's a glorious day, and I haven't been out for a run in way too long.

So I tie up my shoelaces and I head outside. Now that I've been making a point of running when I can, I can easily run five or six miles. There's no need for me to pathetically slow to a crawl in front of Steve's house. In fact, maybe I'll head up into the canyon. When I reach the edge of the driveway, I mean to turn left and head out toward Amanda's, but my feet turn right. As if they have a mind of their own.

Which is stupid. There's nothing for me this way.

Yes, Steve was amazing with the kids. Yes, he's a doctor and he makes things that scare and overwhelm me seem like no big deal. Yes, watching him ride a horse is similar to how I imagine it would feel watching Van Gogh paint. And yes, I still dream about him without his shirt on, mowing his yard. When I'm asleep, and embarrassingly, even when I'm not.

No one our age should still be that hot.

And I've spent way too much time thinking about what Donna said.

I think she hoped it would change my mind. I think she wanted me to come to the conclusion that *of course* Steve needs a child. Of course someone who cares about him should be willing to provide what he *needs*. But it only made me more sure that, if he had a child of his own, he'd be fiercely protective and guard it with his every breath.

I admire that sentiment and in another life, that would have been fantastic.

But I already have four children over whom I watch and pray in exactly that way, day and night. I can't possibly risk them not feeling loved and adored and cherished and protected by any man I may one day remarry. I can't leave their happiness and well-being to chance, or trade it for the love and joy a future child might feel. It goes against every maternal fiber in my body.

Unlike Amanda, I don't have a safety net—not in this. If I keep spending time with Steve, I'll move from liking him to. . .I can't say it, even to myself. I'm too close already. I think about him way more than I should. I lament the time we don't spend together. My fingers itch to text or call him all day long. My mind moves to him at night, when I should be sleeping. Sometimes, even when I am sleeping.

I've even thought about what our son or daughter might look like.

No, if I keep moving on in the way I am right now, I'll fall, and nothing will catch me. I can't risk it. Maybe that's why my shoes turned me this way. Maybe they know that now is the time—while I still have the strength.

And if fate really exists, well, I haven't been sure until this moment, because as I pass his house, Steve's riding circles out in his arena. He waves at me, and within a few moments, he and Farrah are riding alongside me. "Hey, beautiful."

My breath catches.

"Fancy seeing you here."

"Hey, Steve."

"You've been avoiding me. Again."

I crane my neck to look up at him. The sun has crossed the center of the sky, and it's blocked by his head. It gives him a bizarre and almost other-worldly halo from this angle, like he's God's messenger or something insane. "Is this really how you want to talk?"

"No." He pulls Farrah to a stop. "Of course not." He wheels her around. "I'm going to shower. I'll catch you on your way back."

Great. He'll smell great and look even better, and I'll be five miles worth of stinky. Actually, maybe that's for the best. I rehearse my speech the entire way down and back to his house. And by the time I reach his mailbox, he's there. Just like he was that first day of school.

Except today, my legs are shaking for a totally different reason.

I've only known him for a short time, but my brain is already cram-packed with memories. The time he asked me out. The time he rode down in front of us at the rodeo. The hours he's spent teaching me and my children to ride. The trail ride. Our first date, when I fell into the lake and he jumped in to save me. The times I've practically begged him to kiss me.

Most memorable of all, the time he came and saved us in a storm, offering up his home and his expertise to keep me and my children and my nieces safe. He did it all without obligation, without exhibiting any frustration. We spent three nights in a row taking care of sick kids, and when we finally left, all of them feeling better, he had just started throwing up himself.

"Go," he'd said. "I'm a big boy. I can take care of myself."

But if what Donna said is true, he's a big boy with a

big wound, and he hasn't taken a risk on anyone since his ex-wife. Until now.

Which means he has no safety net, either.

"This isn't very fair," I say. "You showered, but I stink."

"Fine." He sighs, as if he's been quite put upon. "I would be willing to help you take a shower as well." He leans a little closer. "I could even scrub that spot you can't quite reach on your back."

"Steve."

"Usually I like it when you say my name." His grin is sad. "Like, when you pet a cat, and they arch their back like, 'oooh, that's the spot?' That's how I feel when you say 'Steve.' Usually."

"But not today?"

"No, that Steve sent a shiver down my spine, and not in a good way. Like someone walked over my grave."

"You don't have a grave," I say.

"Not yet," he says. "But it feels like there's something bad coming."

I sigh.

"See? Now you're doing it again. A soulful sigh."

"Stop."

"You can't dump me." He crosses his arms, the muscles in his forearms bunching. "We aren't even together. So why do I have a feeling that something is coming?"

"We aren't together," I say, "but you just did this incredible thing and we haven't talked about it, and you keep sending me flirty messages and calling and asking me to call you back with a sultry tone."

"Sultry?" His lip curls just a little. "What exactly does my sultry tone sound like?"

"I can't do it," I say. "I've given it a lot of thought." I exhale loudly. "A *lot* of thought. I like you, Steve, a lot.

Probably too much. And that's why I can't—my mind isn't going to change. If we had a baby one day, it would be amazing. I would love it to the moon and back—but I would love it exactly as much as I love my other kids."

"Great," he says. "That's what I'd want you to do."

"But you wouldn't."

"Huh?"

"You'd love your baby more than my other babies."

He holds up a hand. "Wait. You can't possibly know—"

"I'm not going to change my mind, and I know you well enough to know that you're not going to suddenly not want a child of your own." I have to get away from him right now. My one saving grace is that I have not a single memory of kissing him. But he's walking toward me now, his arms outstretched and I can't. If he wraps his arms around me—if he presses his lips to mine. . .

"I have to go."

"Abigail, you have done a lot of talking, but you haven't done any listening."

I wipe a tear away, and then swipe at another. "Donna told me, okay?"

His eyes widen and his hands clench at his sides. "What exactly did *Donna* say?"

My throat closes up and I can barely form the words. "She told me about your wife."

His knuckles are white, he's clenching his fists so hard.

"She told me that you had a child—"

"No."

"She told me that your wife took her away." And I remember then, when we first met, how I accused him of knowing nothing about teaching horseback lessons because he wasn't a parent himself. How much have I already hurt him, without even knowing it? "She told me that you will never be okay with not having a child of your own, one that no one can ever take away, and I get it."

More tears splash down my cheeks and drop onto my already sweat-soaked t-shirt.

"We're like some kind of Greek tragedy, and I've had enough tragedy already," I say. "More than I can handle. More than anyone should have to handle."

Steve finally reaches my side, and his hand hovers an inch above my face. "You are more beautiful to me for having experienced loss. We have more in common than you realize, Abby. And nothing is as simple as you're making it."

"But it is," I say. "I need this to be simple, because the complexity is breaking me."

When I run away, he doesn't try to stop me. He doesn't send me any more flirty texts or leave me any more sultry voicemails.

And even without seeing or hearing from Steve, I'm still breaking a little bit more every day.

24

DONNA

Aiden has finally learned to buckle himself into the car without any help.

"But, Mom," he says. "I forgot my lunchbox."

I roll my eyes, but I'm not really angry. This is what first graders do. I jog back through the side door of the garage and into my beautiful kitchen, with shiny granite countertops. I pull Aiden's new lunchbox out of the Thermador fridge, smile at the bright blue dog on the front of it, and head back to the car.

After I drop him off at school, I stretch in the car for a moment before heading back out. I ought to stop off at the True Value to pick up a few things before I head home. It's so nice not to need to work anymore. Not to be desperate for money. Not to be scrimping and saving.

I fill my cart with every single thing I want. Frozen pizza, organic milk, and the name brand cheese. For fun, I even grab a package of donuts. Who cares? I can afford it. And there's no one to tell me it's a bad call. When I pass a glass cabinet, my reflection reminds me that I've gotten my hair done recently—it's shiny and highlighted and perfect. I'm wearing nice clothes again—that are in season, not that anyone around here would know the difference.

Amanda Brooks would, probably. "Hey, Venetia."

I've known that kind face since I was very small. She beams when she turns to look at me. "Yes, dear?"

"Have you seen Amanda Brooks lately? I'd like to go see her—what things does she usually grab when she comes? Apples? Bananas? I want to take her something."

Venetia frowns. "Amanda Brooks?" She shakes her head. "She left, remember? She moved a year ago, when those alien people sued them and took Jed's ranch away." She tilts her head. "How could you have forgotten? You're the one who stole it from them, and then you gave it to your brother."

I blink. Is that right? Did I really do that?

"Yeah." Steve Archer's standing behind Venetia. "You did. You ruined everything."

"No," I say. "I mean, it wasn't my fault. They broke the rules."

"The only reason they lost that ranch was that *you* screwed them," Steve says. "You're selfish. You don't care about anyone but yourself."

My phone rings then. "Hello?" I'm desperate for anything to interrupt this conversation—no, this attack. That's a better word for it.

"Ms. Ellingson?"

"Yes, this is Donna."

"This is Alice, the elementary school secretary. Your husband, a Mr. Charles Windsor IV, is here, picking up your son."

I choke.

"I'm just calling you as a courtesy, as he's being taken out of school early."

"No," I say. "You can't let him take Aiden."

"He's his father." The note of censure in her tone is clear. "He has a right."

But he shouldn't be able to take Aiden. "He's a criminal. He should be in prison."

"It's your fault he's not," Steve says. "All your fault."

Venetia joins him. "It's all your fault. You're a failure. You're a liar. You're a terrible person who lets criminals go free. It's your fault that Aiden's with him right now, learning to steal and lie as well as his father."

I bolt upright in bed and wipe the sweat from my brow.

A dream.

It was only a dream. All the reasons I'm doing what I'm doing are still valid, and I still know it's the best decision for Aiden. Part of our deal, of course, is that Charlie won't get custody of Aiden. He'll only have supervised visitations. I breathe in and out, and then I breathe in and out again.

"Mom?"

Aiden's standing in the doorway.

"What's wrong, sweetie? Is grandpa yelling again? Did he wake you up?"

"No," Aiden says. "You did."

I'm taken aback by that for a moment. *I* woke him up? My dad screams at night when he has nightmares about the terrible things he's done. But I don't have nightmares —I'm doing what's best for my son.

"Are you okay?" Aiden pats my knee.

"I'm fine, hon," I say. "It's my job to ask you that kind of thing."

"Okay." He crawls into bed next to me. I don't encourage him to sleep with me—I want him to be independent and feel safe in his own life. I don't want him to need me. But when he curls up against me from time to time, I never turn him away. I crave the feeling of my baby, safe in my arms, even if it's only for a few hours.

But after he drifts off, I can't go back to sleep. I keep thinking about that dream.

I've been telling myself for the past year that if I can just wait things out, then I'll get what I need and everything will be fine. I know that poor, sweet Venetia, and smart, empathetic Steve won't harpoon me in the store. I know that it's not my fault that Abby and Amanda went home for that month. I know that Charlie won't be able to come steal Aiden.

But it's hard to shake the feeling that even when I've waited as long as I promised, even when I get money from Charlie's parents, even when I've run off the Brooks widows and I can buy the ranch and then gift it to Patrick in exchange for Dad's tax-free life insurance proceeds, even then, things won't really be perfect.

I climb out of bed, careful not to disturb Aiden, and read over the agreement I made with the Windsors. Just like I always do, I review every word carefully. It lays out the dates, the amounts and address of the apartment building they're selling. It has tax records attached showing that while it's a valuable piece of property, the capital gains tax will be quite high—because all the basis of the property has been taken over the years in depreciation.

I've done this dozens of times now—gone over the agreement terms whenever I start to worry that I'm doing the wrong thing. This is nothing new. But this time, unlike the other fifty times I've done it, I don't feel better, not really.

People matter more than all the other stuff. Amanda Saddler's words keep coming back to me.

Aiden matters. That's why I'm doing all of this. But when he's older, when he understands what happened in his formative years, and he asks me why I did what I did, what will I tell him? I'll have to tell him that his grandparents are scary. They're bad people, and so is his father, and in order to keep him safe, I had to become the same kind of scary person that they are.

Only, I'm starting to doubt whether that's true.

Abigail Brooks isn't scary.

I mean, she is. She terrified me, and she struck fear into the hearts of every nurse in that hospital.

But she's scary in the way an avenging angel would be scary. Righteous indignation. Terrible justice. The judge, jury, and executioner that keeps wicked people from harming good ones.

I, on the other hand, have become what I despise.

And one day, Aiden's going to see that. Or worse, he won't see it because I'm not teaching him any better. Am I failing him by trying to keep him safe? My mom was really religious and my dad always made fun of her for it. Watching her praying, and then watching my dad hit her, it was laughable really. There's a reason Patrick and I never went to church.

If God exists, wouldn't he have stopped Dad from hitting Mom—our devout, God-loving Mom?

Believing in God always felt like cheering for the losing team at the Super Bowl. A depressingly futile exercise.

But what if God only works through us? What if he's less worried about a few wins here and there, and he's really focused on helping us do those right things ourselves?

As the sun rises, for the first time, I look at that light spreading across the horizon, and I *hope* for things to be better tomorrow than they are today. I weigh the life I'm living against the life I want to have in the future, the person I want Aiden to discover that I am, and I realize that I'm on the wrong path.

I might be too late to fix it.

But I have to try.

I gather up all the documents I've kept hidden all this time. I kept them as collateral, as a way to ensure that the Windsors would keep their end of the bargain. But now, now they're my penance. They're my only way to get out of the terrible life I've made for myself.

When the nurse comes, I'm ready. I've fed Dad breakfast, ignoring his insults and his scorn, and evading the closed fist he uses to try and hit me when I don't immediately do as he asks. "You can't control me anymore," I say.

My dad has no idea what I'm saying, or even who I am, not this morning, anyway, but I'm not saying it for him. I'm saying it for myself. I drop Aiden off for school, and then I drive across the street and park, gathering up my documents carefully, and scanning them in one at a time, as I have a break between my daily tasks.

Finally, once they're all done and it's time for my lunch break, I dial a number I've dreaded every time I've seen it for over a year, now.

"Hello? County prosecutor's office."

"Is this Andrew Soco?"

"It is."

"I know we're running out of time, Mr. Soco, so I'm going to make this easy for you. A slam dunk, if you're a basketball fan."

"Mrs. Windsor?"

"Please call me Mrs. Ellingson."

He practically chokes. "Yes, ma'am, whatever you'd like."

"I'm about to email you a lot of files. I'll be able to describe these well enough to get them admitted as evidence, I'm sure."

"Mrs. Ellingson," he says.

"Yes?"

"This is the best news I've heard all week. No, all month. Maybe all year."

"I'm happy to hear that," I say. "Because I'm worried it's going to wreck my life."

"May I recommend you hire yourself a lawyer, though?"

"Am I in danger of being prosecuted too?"

"Not at all," he says. "But you do know there's currently a civil case pending against your husband as well, and of course, my guess is that your staying quiet had something to do with a deal regarding your divorce settlement."

I don't confirm or deny that.

"And now that you're testifying, you're probably going to need to renegotiate that."

A knot forms in the pit of my stomach. "Thanks for the advice."

"I'm happy to recommend some people to you," he says.

"Actually, I have an idea," I say. "She's not board certified in California. I wonder if that will matter."

"I'd definitely recommend using someone who is," Mr. Soco says. "But maybe she'll be a good starting point."

"Thanks."

"Let's set up a time to talk once I've gone over the files you're sending."

"I work all day long," I say. "Can we do—"

"You name the time, and I'll make it work."

Once I've sent the files, I only have about five minutes left of my lunch break. I think about putting it off, but that won't help me. And with the statute of limitation expiring soon, things are about to be happening quickly. I force myself to dial with trembling fingers.

"Hello?" Abby asks.

"Abby, it's me, Donna."

"Hello. What can I do for you?"

I know it's a common phrase, but I hope she means it. "I understand if you tell me to go jump in a lake. Really, I do. But I need help, and I don't have anyone else I can ask."

"Legal help?"

"Uh-huh."

"I have to warn you," Abby says. "My fee is quite high."

I should have known that. Obviously she's an excellent lawyer. "The thing is, my husband embezzled quite a lot of money, and now he's being sued for it." I fill her in on the rest as quickly as I can—divorce proceedings, my involvement in testifying against him, and the way I'm breaking the deal I had with his parents.

"Okay. Here's the tricky part." Her voice has dropped to a whisper. "If I bring a juicy case like this to my firm, well. I'm not a partner there. So I won't even get a cut of the profits." She sighs in an exaggerated fashion. "Honestly, between you and me, the best thing for me might be to do this for you pro bono."

"What's that?"

"It means to do it for free—my firm requires us to do some free work every year. And I'm always scrambling for something. You'd be helping me out, if I could write all this down as pro bono work."

She's a terrible liar. Absolutely awful. That should worry me, maybe, since she's a *lawyer*, which is basically a professional liar. But I can't worry too much about that when I'm busy bawling.

"Let's block off some time to talk about it this weekend, okay?"

"Thank you," I say.

"Of course. Remember, you're really doing me the favor."

I snort, and that turns into a loud and ugly sob. "Right."

"Donna." She waits.

"Yeah?"

"I'm proud of you."

I had no idea how badly I needed to hear those words —words neither of my parents ever said—until she said them. "Thank you."

"You won't have to do this alone."

If I was wondering whether I'd made the right decision—if any part of me was unsure, regretful, or having second thoughts, Abigail Brooks erases them in that moment. The woman who had done nothing to me, the woman I blatantly wronged, is helping me *again*, for free. And she's proud of me.

Amanda Saddler was right. People are all that really matters, and I'm desperate to become one of those people whom others care about. I will do it, I promise myself, one small step in the right direction at a time.

🦋 25 🦋

AMANDA

I always thought the WWJD wristbands and shirts and whatnot were a little silly. I mean, who knows what a perfect person who lived thousands of years ago would do? Or even if you know what Jesus would do, is it really a standard we could possibly meet? I mean, he was *perfect*, and we're not. So why bother trying?

I actually figured the What Would Abigail Do standard was more achievable. I thought that, with her living right here as my role model, I'd be able to make smarter decisions. I could parent better. With her help, I could make my new business work.

It *is* nice to be able to literally ask her what she'd do.

Except I hate her answer.

My fingers have been itching to terminate my Lololime account all day. No matter what she said about it being reasonable for them to send a good-looking guy my way. No matter what Abigail said about the day-to-day tasks being hard and only hard things being worth it, I just never want to have to deal with them again.

My expenses aren't really that high, especially right now.

Although, we could be kicked off this ranch at any time. That's a sobering thought. Thanks to Donna and her brother's interference, the alien folks really are trying to get us booted. And then I'd be right back to paying rent and utilities to live in an expensive apartment on the Upper East Side.

What I need to do is calculate just how much income I have right now without them. Then I can get a feel for how things would be if I did what I want to do. I'm not someone who uses paper very often, but this feels like something that needs to be done with an ink pen. After rummaging around in the kitchen junk drawer, and ignoring the eleven sharpies, three highlighters, and five dull pencils, I finally find a blue pen. Next up? I need to find some paper.

The junk drawer's a bust. I do find nail clippers, a few random coupons, lint, a nail file, a fuzzy toothbrush, throat lozenges, and some nasty Q-tips—all useless. The family room has nothing—partially because Abby compulsively cleans, and partially because no one uses paper anymore. My room's just as disappointing. And Maren's, and Emery's too.

I could definitely get paper from Abby's room—she's a lawyer—but she's not home and going in there feels like a big violation.

Do I dare rummage around in Ethan and Gabe's room? Gabe's always scribbling on something.

I pull out my phone and start to make my list of other sponsors on the notes app—but it's hard to toggle between my bank account and the list and I really want a piece of paper. So finally, I duck into Gabe's room. That kid is always coloring or drawing on something. Surely in his room there will be paper.

Jackpot.

Pictures hang on nearly every free inch of wall space.

Abby's always talking about how she needs to start disposing of them when he's at school. He'll never even notice if a few of them go missing. I pick one in the corner near the trashcan—I could say it fell in—and flip it over.

To my great dismay, there's already writing on the other side. Did someone else steal my idea? They're already using Gabe's paper. . .I focus on a few of the words.

Dear Amanda,

That catches my eye first, obviously. I mean, it's my name. Is Gabe writing to me?

Then I notice the word Clyde. It's not a common name, but I know it—it's Paul's father's name. Emery and Maren's grandfather.

It's a little hard to make out the entire letter, with Gabe's dark crayon picture on the back, but I focus and figure it all out.

D*ear Amanda,*

At first, I had a plan each night before I went to bed. I would wake up the next day, and I would put on my nicest shirt. The one with no stains at all. The one I wear to church each Sunday.

Did you know that after that day, after you picked Clyde over me, I refused to sit in our regular pew, just a row behind your family? I couldn't sit that close, and I worried that if we did, you'd glance over your shoulder at my brother and you'd smile at him, that knowing smile, and my heart would break right there in the middle of everything. Everyone would see it.

So I convinced Mom and Dad that sitting in the back, in the back left, was better. No one could tell if we were late. No one would notice if Clyde and I didn't comb our hair. It was quite a

317

coup for me, to convince Mom not to parade us right to the front anymore.

And like most of my ideas, it backfired.

I was simply farther away from you—but I still saw the sidelong glances you stole with Clyde. I still saw the

I t just cuts off there—which means there must be a second page. What else did he see? Who's writing this?

We're in Jed's house. It should have been obvious to me, but it takes my brain about three seconds to fully hit pause on the letter and engage. Clyde was his brother—and this Amanda person picked Clyde over him. Over. . .Jed?

And Amanda Saddler lives right up the road. She would probably have gone to church with them. I know she's been here for a long time.

Her pig is named Jed.

A chill runs up my entire body.

Was there some kind of great love story between Jed and Amanda? And how was Paul's dad involved? I'm absolutely dying to know. Without thinking of the consequences, I start pulling pictures down. Like some kind of bizarre treasure hunt, each drawing has the same handwriting scrawled across the back. A lot of them begin with Dear Amanda, but more than half of them are continuations of what I assume were other letters.

I could wring Gabe's neck for defacing the back of all these, although, like me, he was probably just happy to find some paper. When I get down to the True Value next, I'm buying all the notepads and looseleaf paper they have in stock.

The next three hours of my life is spent putting letters together like pieces of a jigsaw puzzle.

318

It's clear he never sent any of these letters. Many of them just stop, incomplete, and several show signs of having been crumpled up and then smoothed out again.

Why did he keep them?

More importantly, if he wasn't ever going to deliver them, why did he keep writing them at all?

I read snatches here and there as I matched them up, but I haven't sat down and read every one—mostly because they feel deeply private. Also, I want to read them in order, if I can. Can I justify reading them without asking Amanda Saddler about them first? Would Jed want me to show them to her now? After all, he was hardly young when he died. If he wanted her to have them, he could have taken them to her right away.

Finally, I find the second half of the letter I started.

urve of your jaw. The grace of your neck. The perfect fall of your hair across your brow. None of that changed.

It's just that I was farther from it.

Farther from you.

Just as I am now, still.

Day after day after day, just like the pew after pew after pew I put between us, time keeps rolling along between us, and my own insecurities keep destroying my plans to somehow bridge this gap. Each day I develop a plan for the morrow, and then, when it comes, I'm unable to take action. Sometimes I even put my nicest shirt on. I leave my room, and my mother looks at me like I'm crazy. "Jed, what are you doing? It's not Sunday."

I know it's not Sunday. That's a day to worship God.

But I spend the other six worshipping you, Amanda. Only you. Always you.

Actually, if I'm being honest, I spend all seven thinking about you. It feels like that's been my life's work. From the moment I first saw you, milking that spotted cow, until last week, when I dropped off your dad's plow and saw you working in the garden, you're the beginning and the end for me.

I'm just too cowardly to tell you.

It's not signed. The paper didn't run out of space, either. It just cuts off. As if that's the entirety of his reason: he's too afraid.

I don't even bother making a list of what my income is right now without Lololime. I know it's going to be a pathetic amount. I haven't been actively pursuing opportunities to represent other brands, and they aren't seeking me out. Most of my posts center around Lololime. It's what has naturally happened as I've let them take over my life. It's what I thought I wanted, to be honest. Instead of frantically trying to cobble together a living from dozens of brands, I've directed my focus on only one. It's certainly been easier to manage.

But it feels like they're taking away my choices.

I glance down at this letter again, and suddenly I just have to know what Amanda felt. Clearly this consumed Jed's life, but he never did anything about it. What about Amanda? Did she love him? Hate him? Have no feelings toward him at all?

The kids will be home in less than an hour, so I hurry. Boots, jacket, keys, and I'm out the door. I'm walking up her steps, her warning cardinal warbling, when she opens the door. "Amanda? I didn't know you were coming."

I realize that in my rush, I didn't bring the letter. "Uh, yeah. I guess I just had a question I've been thinking about a lot lately."

She waves me inside. "It's cold out there. I don't know why Arizona doesn't fly south."

"Cardinals don't move," I say. "They stay put, unless they run out of food and are facing starvation." I only know because I looked it up last time I was here. But now that I think about it, it's kind of like Jed, it seems. He loved, he suffered, but he didn't move. Consequently, he went his whole life not knowing how Amanda felt.

I wonder if his ghost is standing beside me, still desperate on the other side to know her answer.

"Well, come in."

I wipe my boots and slide them off by her door before going inside. I won't even consider tracking mud into her house—the idea of making this sweet lady clean because of me—no way.

"You thirsty?" Amanda's holding a glass and a mug, as though she's happy to make me something cool or something hot. She clearly comes from the old school version of hospitality. You offer people drinks. You make sure they're comfortable. It's just what you do.

I don't have time for all the pleasantries, though. Not today. "Did you have some kind of romantic relationship with Jedediah Brooks?"

Amanda drops the glass she was holding and it shatters. She's wearing slippers.

"Oh my word, don't move." It takes me a minute to find a broom, but once I get the majority of it cleaned up, I send her to the living room. Then I sweep again, and afterward, I vacuum for good measure. I feel like the harbinger of doom today.

When I glance over at her, she's sitting on the edge of the sofa where I left her, staring off at nothing. It's the opposite of the Amanda Saddler I know—an energetic spitfire who never stops going. I decide to heat up some water and make her some tea. I glance at my clock—kids will be done with school any time. I really need to get home.

"Amanda?" I hold out a cup of her favorite chamomile tea.

She starts. "Oh. Thank you."

"I'm sorry that I took you by surprise like that. I didn't mean to upset you." That might be a lie—after reading what I did, I just needed to know. I suppose dropping a glass and checking out may be a decent answer. He obviously meant something to her.

"You're living in his house. I suppose I should have known you'd figure out something. Did you find an old photo?"

I'm not sure what to say. Should I tell her about the letters? When I asked a simple question, her reaction was pretty significant. "Uh, yeah. Plus, you named your pig Jed. I've been wondering for a while."

She bobs her head. "It's an old story. Your question shouldn't have rattled me like it did."

"You dated in school, or something?"

She shakes her head this time. "No, nothing like that. Jedediah Brooks and I were born on the same day, in the same little hospital. Long before school even began, we were already best friends. We were practically inseparable all the way through high school."

"What happened in high school?" I ask. "Did you kiss?"

Amanda's eyes widen. "No, no. Never."

That's disappointing. Actually, it's downright depressing. *Never?* "What happened, then?"

"I noticed Jed's older brother, Clyde." She looks down at her knees. "Or rather, he noticed me."

Oh, no. "And?"

"I didn't realize that Jed liked me," she says. "Maybe that's a lie." She laughs. "I'm so old now, what's the point in lying to anyone else? Or even myself, anymore?" She sighs. "I was a fool."

"Did you love his brother, then?"

"I was infatuated with his brother. He was tall and

322

handsome and strong. He had two years on Jed, and it showed."

The handsome older man. I get it.

"There was a homecoming dance approaching—couples in this area had been made for decades at that homecoming dance. So when Jed asked me—Clyde liked to take things from his brother. I knew that. I *knew*, and I didn't think about it, not when he asked me, too."

I almost regret asking her. She looks distraught.

"I told Jed yes, initially. After all, who else would I go with? He was my best friend. I didn't even think anything about him asking me. But then, Clyde asked me too, and my heart fluttered, and my head swelled, and I told Jed I was going to go with him instead. I thought he might be annoyed, but he wasn't. He was livid."

"That's bad."

"He told me I had to choose. I could be his friend, or I could date his brother."

It's like a train is barreling ahead at me and I can't move out of the way. "You figured he'd cool off."

Amanda shakes her head slowly. "I knew Jed. He never cooled off. He was like that—he'd hold a grudge to the end. But not with *me*. I thought we were different, and I honestly, well. I guess to me, Jed, with as well as I knew him, he was boring. What I wanted was something exciting and new and shiny. So I told Jed to stop trying to control me, and I went with his brother."

"Did you regret it immediately?"

Amanda sighs. "Did you ever meet Clyde Brooks?" Her eyes are clear, but still sad.

"I did," I say. "He was a pretty tough old man."

"Everyone is, that grows up out here. But he was a talker, that one, could talk the ear off a mule. He was exciting and fun and he swept me off my feet. I think now, looking back, he just liked to take things away from other people. But he did take me away from Jed, completely. We dated for a year. My sophomore year of high school, and his senior year. Everyone assumed we'd get married."

"But you didn't."

"Clyde was never interested in marrying a local girl. He didn't want to stay here, in the middle of nowhere. He had a world to conquer, and he did it. I wasn't the right person for that, and he knew it. He broke up with me the second he left for college and never looked back."

"But what about Jed? You never kissed him?"

Her words are slow, clear, and profoundly sad. "He never even spoke to me again." I've never seen her this serious. I've never seen her this upset.

"He never *spoke to you* again? Like, not even a single word?"

"I think it started out as his way to punish me, but the more he saw me with Clyde, the more angry he became, and the more hurt, maybe. I tried to apologize to him at first, but Clyde would laugh so much whenever I tried that it made things worse." She sighs. "That year was exciting—it was everything I wanted at the time. But it's also my largest regret in life. Sometimes we think we know exactly what we want, but that thing we want poisons our life forever."

Now I'm glad I didn't mention the letter. How would she react if she knew Jed had been pining for her for the past sixty years?

"Is that all you came here for?"

I glance at my watch. "My kids are home—I really ought to go. I'm just trying to figure out what to do with my own life, and I'm struggling. I guess it was easier to focus on what happened to someone else."

"Amanda, I know you probably don't need this advice, but I'm an old woman, so humor me."

"Okay."

"You told me you're trying to live your life better—and your model is Abigail Brooks."

I nod.

"You couldn't have chosen a finer woman to copy. I mean, she's smart, she's a great mother from what I've seen, and she is generous. But I think your decision to try and do whatever she would do is nearly as bad as mine was to date Clyde."

Didn't see that slap coming. "What?"

"You can't live your life like someone else. You can try, but you're dooming yourself to fail. We are who we are. Your good things just ain't the same as Abby's. If you try to copy her, you'll fall short. You should be trying to do the things you're good at, and not worrying so much about the things you're bad at."

She started her advice by telling me that she also thinks Abigail is perfect, which just means that she thinks I'll never measure up.

What hurts the most is that I think she's probably right.

❧ 26 ❦

ABIGAIL

emodeling your home is like trying to control chaos. It can't be done, and I'm worried the attempt is damaging my brain. Remodeling a home with someone else whose design plans don't align with your own is like trying to manage a bunch of inmates in a psych ward without medication: utterly fruitless.

Also, there's a bunch of yelling.

"Lady, I don't know why you aren't happy. These is high end—it's an upgrade."

"I know there weren't many other options," I say. "I know we live in the buttcrack middle of nowhere." I breathe in through my nose slowly. "But surely you can see that this sticks out."

I wish we could use Eddy, but with the state of Amanda's business and professional life, it seemed safer to use a plumber we didn't have any ties to. I'm regretting that decision right now. The swan-head golden faucets on the shower and sink could not possibly clash any more than they do. "Are you sure you didn't get these secondhand, possibly from the demolition of a 1980s home?"

"Lady, I know you don't like them, but at least you can

turn on the faucet. Yesterday, your panties was in a wad because you couldn't use them."

"Surely they had something that might match all the hardware we found for. . .well, for everything else."

"Look, all you do is complain. I've done my job, and I'm going to see Kevin about payment."

"I won't approve these."

He storms off.

I pick up my phone and call Kevin—it goes right to voicemail. That likely means he's in one of the far pastures—the two we didn't get harvested before the snowstorm. When the snow melted so quickly, we decided to move the cows into them so that at least some of the dead grass could be eaten. I leave him a voicemail, explaining the bait and switch the plumber's trying to pull.

He is right about one thing. The assault on my eyes notwithstanding, it's nice to have a shower and a sink that actually work.

"Any word from the heater guy?" Amanda asks.

"Look at this!"

She ducks her head into the bathroom and gasps. "What in the world?"

"Right? It looks like it came from the Mr. T Collection." I groan. "And he refuses to change them out. Said he's already paid for them and now they've been installed, the store won't take them back."

"He had to have gotten them surplus," Amanda says. "It's got to be a lie. No way did he think that would go with the tasteful tile we chose."

I look around at the bathroom we finally agreed to do. White faux-wood slats on the ground and most of the shower. Blue glass tiles as an accent on the shower wall, the vanity backsplash, and in strips on the floor. It took almost three weeks for the tile to come in, but it was worth it.

"The new hot water heater's due next week?" she asks.

"Yep, and I'm telling Kevin he *has* to find someone else to install it. I'm not giving that guy another cent."

Amanda drops her eyes. "When are the painters coming to redo the game room?"

"I told them not to—I told you, I like it."

"You don't have to be polite," she says again. "I admitted that I was wrong. It looks terrible, just like you said it would."

"I think as an accent, that one bold wall is brilliant," I say. "You have a real flair for design."

"Ha."

"Hey, Gabe asked me something this morning—you weren't up yet. He says someone took all his art down. Ethan insists he didn't touch it. I checked the trash and couldn't find anything. I know they weren't amazing pictures or anything, but before I put the pressure on my kids about it, I wanted to see if you saw anything."

"Uh, yeah. Actually I have all of it."

I don't even know what to say to that. I gave her half the rooms, even though I have twice as many kids, and she. . . went into my son's room and took all his art down?

"I've been meaning to talk to you about it. I need some advice, actually."

More advice? She has been a black hole for advice lately. "Amanda, to be honest, I have no idea how to even manage my own life right now."

Her jaw drops. "You—what?"

I almost start to cry. I've been a hot mess ever since I broke up with Steve for the second time. I still think about him as much as I did before, which is stupid. "I hate my job now that all I do is grunt work. I have nothing to work toward." I hadn't even admitted that to myself until just now. "I'm totally and completely alone, and probably always will be." Now it's too late. I can't stop the tears. "And being a good mom means I have to walk away from the first thing that's made me giddy in—" I choke up. "A really long time."

"Steve." Amanda's eyes well up, too. Before I know what's happening, she's pulled me against her and her arms are wrapped around me tightly. "You're never alone, you know. That's why I moved back. Not because of Lololime. Not because my kids begged. Not because I thought I'd have a hot dating life." She inhales a ragged breath. "I moved back for you."

Something inside of my heart explodes. My own sister barely calls me. My mom and dad used to check in, right after Nate passed, but they're living it up in their retirement, and I can't blame them. They don't get why I came out here.

I wasn't really that sure.

It seemed like the right thing to do for Ethan, and Izzy and Whitney and Gabe were excited. It was a relief to get away from the constant memories of Nate, and the pain of making new memories over the old ones.

But I wonder if my real reason isn't the same as hers.

For the first time in a year, I didn't feel alone out here, with Amanda in the same cramped, old house. But with her trying to be like me, and asking me for advice. . .it has felt like I had seven kids instead of just four. It felt like I was dragging the whole world along behind me, and nothing I did was ever enough.

"I need a friend," I say.

"And I've been kind of annoying," Amanda says. "I've just put more demands on you. Help me make cookies. Help with my kids. Tell me what to do and how to live." When she finally releases me, tears are running down her puffy cheeks. "I'm sorry."

"I think you need to find a better role model," I say. "Aim higher."

She laughs then, and the incongruity between her tears and her laughter—something about it makes me laugh.

"I'm not even sure what's funny," I admit.

"Aim higher?" Her laughter escalates. "Wonder Woman isn't high enough. You're the perfect mom. The perfect lawyer. The perfect friend. You always do everything that needs to be done. You say the right thing, and you do the right thing. You put your kids ahead of everything else. Meanwhile, I'd probably already have *made* a baby with Steve, and be arguing with him over names."

The absurdity of her statement and the stress of the past few weeks crashes down and I descend into the same kind of unhinged laughter as her. "I'm sick of doing the right thing all the time," I confess. "I want to just say, oh well. Who cares about right and wrong and coloring inside of the lines? I want to just do what I want, and eat a vat of ice cream, and not go running, and tell my bosses they can suck it. I quit."

"But quitting is easy. The things that matter take hard work." When Amanda parrots my words back at me, I want to hit myself in the nose.

"I'm an idiot."

"You're a genius," she says. "But maybe you need to give yourself some cheat days. You can eat a big bowl of ice cream without losing all control, you know."

"What if I want to swap out ice cream for something else?" My mouth goes dry even thinking about it.

"You want to eat a big old bowl of hot horse doc, don't you?"

"It sounds disgusting when you put it like that."

"Oh, I don't think so." Amanda pokes my ribs. "I don't blame you at all."

I drop my face in my hands.

"Hey, come with me. I'm going to show you why I'm such a horrible monster who would steal a child's artwork."

I was about ready to snap her head off for that, but now I realize I should probably have given her the benefit of the doubt. As I follow her to her room to look at her stolen goods, I think about how far we've come. I despised her before—dreaded every interaction. I thought we had nothing in common, and that our goals weren't even similar.

I wonder how often we do that as humans, make assumptions without taking the time to look and listen. How many other people in this world do I write off without a thought—when maybe we're struggling through the same stuff? What if all our problems are just variations of the same themes? How much could we learn from each other if we'd stop screaming 'me' and start listening instead?

"Okay, so I know you were mad earlier."

"I wasn't—"

She holds up her hand and sits on her bed, picking up a stack of papers from her nightstand. "You were, and I'd have been furious too. But look." She pats the bed beside her.

I sit.

Instead of showing me Gabe's sloppy but vibrant pictures, she hands me letters—with pictures on the back. "What are these?"

She shakes her head. "Read them."

D*ear Amanda,*

. . .

331

I feel silly doing this. I should walk down the lane and knock on your door. But every time I think about doing that, I imagine how you looked—how I felt—when you picked Clyde instead of me.

Does it make me a monster, that I was happy when he left you behind? When I found out he was dating someone new, someone he'd met at school, my initial reaction was total joy. I thought about how exciting it would be the next time I saw you. Sure, maybe you'd cry. Maybe you'd even bawl for weeks.

But then you'd get over it.

You'd realize that you'd chosen wrong. My brother is fickle—my brother is unkind. He didn't know what he had when it was right there in front of him. He's the kind of person who always reaches for something else, something shinier, something new.

He's a fool.

Nothing could be shinier than you, and I've known it my entire life. Now you'll finally let go of him and look at me.

It just cuts off there, as if whoever was writing it just gave up. "Did Gabe draw on your old letters?" I sigh. "I'm so sorry. I had no idea." I hate it when I get upset for something that's my fault. "I'll have a talk with him right after school about not touching other people's things."

Amanda puts a hand on my wrist. "It's not me. It's another Amanda, and he didn't do anything wrong. Keep reading."

Dear Amanda,

. . .

Today it's snowing. It made me think about the time you taught me to make snow ice cream. I still remember the recipe. Eight cups of snow. A third of a cup of sugar, a teaspoon of vanilla, and a cup of milk. You mix it all together with a bit of salt and you pour it over the snow. Remember? I wonder how much we ate. Your mom got so mad when we used up all her vanilla. You told her it was because I was such a pig, and my mom whipped me for it.

It was worth it.

The smile on your face—I would endure any beating to see it again.

Sometimes, I lie in bed with my eyes closed and think about your smile. The biggest problem is that I haven't seen it lately. Has it changed? You're older, you're wiser, and you've changed. It breaks my heart to think about what other things may have changed, and I don't even know what they are. Why did I issue that ultimatum? I thought it would hurt too much to have you only as a friend, but watch you love my brother.

I'm an idiot. At least as a friend, I could still see your smile.

Sometimes I ask at the post office whether they've heard of any ranches going up for sale. I heard your mom wanted to move, and I'm terrified you'll leave. I should just walk to your house. Knock on the door. Ask if you're home.

I've been practicing jokes so I'm ready. Here's one I think you might like.

Why did the pig take a bath?

The rancher said 'hogwash.'

Okay, that was dumb. But sometimes you smile just because I said something dumb. Right?

How about this one? What did the mommy cow say to the calf?

It's pasture bedtime. Ha! I'm not sure that would work if I said it out loud. And if I'm being honest, I'm never going to mail this letter. And I'm probably never going to walk to your house, *either. Because I'm afraid that if I do, and you hate me, it'll ruin all my old memories.*

And memories are all I have right now.

L *ove, Jed*

W ait. Jed? I set the letter down and meet Amanda's eyes. "Jed? As in, the owner of this house?"

She shrugs.

"Dear Amanda? Like. . ."

She nods. "Saddler, yes."

I can hardly believe it.

"There are dozens of these. It took me hours to read them all. Plus, I'm not sure where Gabe was getting them from, but there may be more."

"I'm going to kill that little punk."

"In his defense, this house is sorely lacking in paper."

"It's lacking in everything," I say. "That's why I fly out next weekend to pack up our old house."

"I don't know what to do about all this," Amanda says. "I'm not sure whether to tell Amanda—"

"How do you know for sure it's her?"

"I asked her," Amanda says. "She admitted that Jed liked her, but she ended up dating his brother. That ultimatum he mentions—he told her if she dated his brother, he'd never talk to her again. And he never did."

"That's tragic," I say. "How depressing."

"You think it's better if we never show these to her?"

I see her dilemma, now. "We don't know how she felt, though, right? I mean, clearly his love was tragic, but maybe she never looked back."

"Oh, she dropped a glass when I asked about it and then sat off staring into space like a crazy person. She told me it was the biggest mistake of her life to have picked Clyde, basically."

"Clyde?" I shake my head. "I forgot how awful Nate and Paul's grandparents were at naming."

"Right?"

"I think," I say, "that we should show them to her. I mean, it's not like she has a heart condition or anything." I pause. Amanda knows her way better. "Or does she?"

"I'm not sure. She seems super healthy, and I haven't noticed any of those pill containers with like piles of pills per day or anything."

I flop back on Amanda's bed. "Are they all as pathetic as the ones I read?"

"Some of them are worse," she says. "Some are better. Some are really almost poetic. He was a weird guy, clearly, but he was a sweet weird guy."

"They lived their entire lives right next door, and they never told one another that they loved each other? How could that even happen?"

Amanda doesn't respond.

I sit up and look her in the eye. "What?"

"I mean, assuming we don't lose this ranch, and assuming you hold the line on this kids thing. . ."

"Wait, are you saying. . . me and Steve?"

She shrugs.

"That's crazy. We're not an epic love story. He's just a guy I met a few months ago."

"Okay."

"And it's not like I'm not talking to him."

"Which might make it sadder."

"Dating him more will just hurt us both."

"Oh." Amanda nods. "Sorry. I misunderstood. It looked like you were miserable now. My bad."

"My bad?"

"People around here say it. So sue me."

"You are on a snarky roll right now," I say. "Maybe I should sue you."

"It won't work," she says. "The woman I live with is a lawyer—a great one."

I roll my eyes.

"I think I'm going to tell her about these."

Which is her way of telling me I should reverse my position with Steve. "I made a promise," I say. "Would you go back on a promise you made to Paul?"

"Heck yes," she says. "Look, I get that our relationships weren't the same. You adored Nate, and Paul and I. . .things were rocky. Sharp rocks. But he's not here, and you still are. Life changes all the time. You can't be bound by things you thought were a good idea way back when." She picks up the stack of letters. "It's probably the only real lesson from all this. Jed made a promise too—he swore that if Amanda picked his brother, he would never talk to her again. She knew that, and she picked Clyde anyway. But Jed was a moron for sticking to that promise. Don't be like Jed."

"I think we need to think about this more," I say. "Don't show those to Amanda yet. I mean, what does she have to gain from knowing that he loved her, but also knowing he was too much of a coward to ever act on it? Should we really undo the decisions he made during his lifetime?"

"Maybe." Amanda's brow furrows, and she sighs dramatically.

I can't stop thinking about the letters—not all day, and not all night. I go over my promise to Nate, too. Over it and over it.

As a lawyer, my job is to help people make the best promises they can. I hold people to the promises they've made, too. Society only works when people live by the promises they make. And Nate and I both had good reasons when we talked about my future. We both agreed I shouldn't be alone, and that I should never let my own happiness get in the way of our children's well-being.

I still agree with all of that.

And one day, if Steve doesn't find someone else, and I don't find someone else, we'll be past the point where I could think about having more kids.

Then we could date and not endanger my children— not violate the promise I made to Nate. No matter what Amanda says, that promise does matter. Nate's and my history matters.

I'm not like Jed. I didn't issue some kind of childish ultimatum or act on hurt feelings.

"Hey, Mom." The kids pour through the door. "Hi, Mom!" "Mom! I'm home!" The smiles on their faces remind me of why I'm willing to make this kind of sacrifice.

"When's our next lesson with Mr. Steve?" Whitney asks. "I want to start getting ready for the rodeo. He said we could work on barrels."

"I think we'll take a week or two off," I say. "Wouldn't a break be nice?"

Whitney groans. "Take a week? Or two? Because that's not the same."

Kids are so melodramatic about everything. "Two, then." That should give me time to firm up my resolve.

"It could be snowing by then," Izzy says. "Why would we take time off?"

Ethan breezes through his bedroom door into the family room. "Mom and Mr. Steve are fighting again. Just let her put it off a bit."

"We have never had a fight," I say. "But I need a bit of a break. That's true."

"Breaks are stupid," Gabe says. "You should just talk to him until you can not be mad anymore."

Izzy drops her backpack on the floor. "What if I lose at the rodeo because I didn't get those lessons?"

I wave them all off and head back to my room so I can finish my work for the day. Amanda's letters and the remodel keep making me work late into the night.

But as I sit down to log my time from the work I did earlier, I think about it. My life is broken into these tiny pieces, and I'm paid by how much I spend on each task. I think about the next few *years* of my life, broken into tiny little bite-sized pieces, and how many chunks of time I'll miss if I just wait around for someone else who *gets* me to come along.

Steve is solid. Dependable. Smart. Kind. Generous. Loyal.

And he likes me.

So, he wants a child of his own and I don't. He never said he'd dump me if I didn't have one. And for all we know, we'll never get to that point. Am I stupid to be burning the house down over something that hasn't even been forced to the front? Did I do just what I told Amanda not to do? Skip the hard work and quit?

My hands are shaking when I leave my room.

They keep shaking when I put on my jacket and boots.

"Where are you going?" Ethan asks.

"I need to go to the store." It's not like I can admit that I was wrong and they were right, at least, not until I've found out what Steve has to say. He might wave me off the second he sees me coming. He may be sick of my yo-yo-ing and delighted that we're finally through.

"We need more milk," Izzy says. "I couldn't have cereal this morning."

"Duly noted," I say.

My heart pounds the entire drive to Steve's place. But when I park, I notice his truck isn't there. That's not promising. I poke around the barn, until his helper, Antonio, confirms he's at work.

I drive to the True Value, but instead of going inside, I decide to go for it. My kids don't have any meetings tonight. No one expressed distress about their homework —so I put my car into drive and head for the ER.

I almost turn around five or six times.

He's going to be busy.

What if he doesn't want to talk to me while he's at work?

Or even if he does want to talk to me, what if he can't? He could be buried under sick and dying people. What if my presence kills someone?

But there's always an excuse. Isn't that the moral of the Jed and Amanda cautionary tale?

So I keep on driving, my hands at ten and two, my brain whirling in little circles. No matter how many times I come back to it, I can't come up with a script for what to say. I have no plan. No roadmap. Nothing. I'm just driving toward Steve to tell him I want to drive toward him, and I don't want to take two weeks or two months or two years off.

When I finally get there, a young nurse with custom tailored pink scrubs and long, polished fingernails looks up at me, her eyes sizing me up and clearly coming to the conclusion that there's nothing medically wrong with me. "Can I help you?"

I'm acutely aware that I'm wearing jeans and a yellow t-shirt, and there's paint on my sleeve and probably in other places, too. "I'm hoping to talk to Dr. Archer."

She purses her soft pink lips. "He's taking care of patients."

"Can you please let him know that Mrs. Brooks is here, but that it's nothing urgent? I don't mind waiting."

"Ma'am, this is an emergency room. You'll be waiting a long time."

I think about texting him, but I figure that would be more likely to interrupt if he's doing something important. I wait, and I wait, and I wait, identifying paint on my shoes, on the heel of my palm, and when I go to the restroom, on my cheek. No wonder the nurse was so dismissive.

Eventually, my nerves get the best of me. What was I thinking, driving out here with no warning? Waiting in the emergency room, as just another patient to be seen? That nurse's glare was right. I duck out without even telling her I'm leaving. I'm nearly to my car when I hear my name.

"Abby!"

I turn around and see Steve in blue scrubs, his white coat open and blowing backward as he runs toward me. It's surreal—like a scene in a movie.

My pulse pounds in my ears, and embarrassment threatens to drown me. If he finally got my message, he'll know I've been waiting for a stupidly long time. "You can go back to work," I say. "I shouldn't have come." I open the driver's door on my minivan. I've never hated having it, but right now, it feels ridiculous. Did I think I was the heroine in some kind of romantic comedy? Heroines don't drive minivans with enough crackers on the floor to choke a small dog.

He doesn't head back inside, though. He doesn't even stop running until he's by my side. "No one told me you were here." His chest is rising and falling, and his cheeks are flushed. "Why are you here?"

This time, he looks me over, and it's as different from the way the nurse made me feel as night from day.

"Are you alright?" His eyes lock onto mine. "Is everything okay?" He releases my gaze to look over the car. "Are the kids hurt?"

I shake my head.

"Abby?"

I want to crawl into the car and disappear. There should be a new function for that. I'm sure I'm not the only minivan-driving mother who has ever needed that option. I'll have to send an email to Toyota. I bet they can work something out.

Steve grabs my hand. "Hey, are you alright?"

"I'm fine," I say. "Stupid, but otherwise, fine."

He frowns. "I can think of a lot of words to describe you, but stupid isn't one I'd use. Ever." His expression softens. "Why did you come?"

I glance back at the ER. "You can go back to work. It was a mistake. I shouldn't have driven all the way out here—"

"Bunch of whiny rich people today," he says. "No one's in danger. Except maybe that stupid nurse who didn't tell me you were here."

My heart starts to pound again, and I remember that I have no idea what to say.

"What made you drive all the way out?"

"I was wrong," I say.

"Wrong?" He's grinning now. "Wrong about what?"

"The kids need two horseback lessons a week," I say. "Every single week."

He blinks, the smile slipping away. "Uh. Okay."

"I told them they should take a break, and they didn't want to. That made me think about how I didn't want to, either."

"Take a break from lessons?" He's searching my face, and clearly still lost.

"You said you weren't going to kiss me until I begged for it." I swallow. "So this is me, begging."

The color leaves his face. "You—what?"

"I am an idiot," I say. "I thought that the promise I made to Nate—it made sense at the time. I mean, it still makes sense, but he didn't know you." I pause. This is coming out all wrong. What am I doing, talking about my first husband right now? "I don't know you that well yet, but every single thing I learn makes me admire you more. Humans make promises to keep themselves safe. They create contracts, they swear oaths. They want to predict the future, but we can't do that. Nothing anyone has tried can guarantee happiness."

"That's true," Steve says.

"But I'm happy when I'm with you," I say. "My thoughts jumble up, and my hands tremble, and I'm happy."

He takes my hands in his, and a zing shoots through my whole body, like he just shocked my heart.

"I thought that we were headed toward disaster and I should head it off before it happened, but leaving you has felt like a disaster. Like a train wreck, or a car crash, or a building collapse." I draw in a breath and try to collect my thoughts.

"You changed your mind?" He sounds so hopeful.

"I thought maybe you'd be sick of me, and all this back and forth." I squeeze his hands. "That nurse said you were busy. I felt so stupid, coming here, but time is precious, and I didn't want to waste any more."

"I'm not sure that was really begging." His voice is raspy and low. "But survey says. . .I'll allow it." His hands brace against my minivan doorframe on either side of my head, and his head dips then, lowering closer and closer and closer, and then his lips close over mine.

That zing from before is like static electricity to a

power surge. It's like a go-cart to a Ferrari. My hands release his and reach underneath his white coat to circle his waist, slowly.

He moans against my mouth and bites at my lips.

And I'm more lost than I've ever been.

Until the sound of a siren roaring yanks me back to reality.

Steve whams his hand against the car door. "Stupid sick people have terrible timing."

"I think the timing should probably be blamed on me," I say.

He softly kisses the side of my mouth. "I won't be blaming anything on you—not for a long time."

The drive home is much nicer, and much harder, than the drive to the ER was. But when I slide into bed that night, I don't have any trouble falling asleep for the first time in a very long time.

27

AMANDA

I never understood the draw of secret romances in television shows and movies and books. Who would want to sneak around? Who would want to lie to people they care about? Why not just come clean about who you're dating and deal with the consequences right away?

But here I am, dating someone in secret.

"Amanda?" Derek's voice is loud and a little aggressive—if I were a mountain lion, I'd probably run from it.

As a person, I opt for the next best thing. I duck behind the giant, metal trash dumpster.

"Amanda?"

I don't even breathe. I can't handle a conversation about this right now. I'll probably freak out on him, and it's not really his fault.

"I saw the lights on in the shop. You didn't answer the door. You must be out here, right?"

He may know I'm here, but he hasn't caught me yet. So, there.

"Amanda?" Eddy's head pokes out from the back door.

My head swivels around until I can see him, and I shake my head and wave.

But it's too late.

"She's out here somewhere, right?" The sound of footfalls tells me that Eddy has ruined my hiding spot. "What are you, five years old?"

I stand up and toss the bag of garbage into the dumpster. "I was resting."

"Resting? By crouching behind a dumpster?" Derek looks more disgusted by me than he is by the trash. "Raccoons rest in trash. I wasn't aware socialites from New York did as well."

"I was attacked back here," I say.

Eddy walks up beside me. "That's true. I saved her."

"Is that why you started dating and no one told me?" Derek's look of disgust only intensifies.

"Oh, no," I say. "We aren't dating. Eddy just came by to check on Roscoe's leg."

"It can come out of the cast, but probably not for another week or two."

"Where's Roscoe?" Derek looks suspicious.

I point.

Derek shuffles toward the back door, all glass, and presses his nose against it. Luckily for me, Roscoe really is inside.

"We need to talk," Derek says.

"We do," I say.

Eddy makes eye contact and shrugs. He's waiting for his marching orders, but Derek knows my boss's boss, so he can't stick around. One word from Derek and they'll know I'm not keeping my distance like I said. I toss my head at his house.

"I'll send you a bill later." Eddy grabs his bag and heads toward his house. "Make sure he's moving around as well as he can—his body needs good circulation to heal."

I'm perfectly cool. I'm perfectly calm.

Derek watches Eddy until he's gone. "I hate that guy."

"He's definitely an odd one," I say, speaking the absolute truth.

"He's a murderer," Derek says. "Did you know that?"

I've been trying to keep calm through all this—evasion and hiding aside—but that accusation really pisses me off. "Where on earth did you hear that?"

Derek frowns. "Victoria told me you know. You don't have to pretend."

Great. My hands fly to my hips. "Then what on earth are you doing here?"

"What does that mean?" He steps toward me proprietarily.

I shift backward, toward the door. "If you know that I know that you were a plant by my boss, some kind of bizarre set-up that she kept secret, why would you keep calling me and coming by? Take a hint, Derek, I'm not interested in boyfriends who spy on me."

"Spy?" His eyebrows shoot almost to his hairline. "What are you talking about?"

"Your dear friend Victoria tried to tell me who to date and what to wear and how to talk before. Did she tell you that? I told her I was terminating our contract—I quit. Did she mention that?"

He shakes his head.

"Guess it slipped her mind. Well, when that didn't work, she tried a nicer lasso. A silk one, in fact. A vice presidential, smooth-talking lasso. When I failed to do as she wanted then, she called to tell me which photos of us to post. That's when I about lost it again."

"You quit?" He doesn't look upset—he looks pleased.

"My sister-in-law convinced me not to quit immediately. I'm evaluating my options, though, and I'm not going to let anyone tell me who to date. Is that clear?"

His smile's almost naive. "Are you under the impression that I somehow answer to Victoria Davis?"

I'm confused. "Don't you?"

He laughs. "Her husband, who knows just how crazy she is and loves her anyway, suggested I check out a cow town his wife was talking about. He told me there was a girl I was supposed to meet if I did. He sent me a screenshot of your Instagram account. I thought you were awfully pretty, but I don't like being told what to do."

I'm lost, still. "Victoria knew about the photo of us kissing."

"I was upset that day. I called my buddy and asked him what he'd suggest. I kissed the girl I'd been dating in front of the guy who liked her—the girl I was head over heels for—and she freaked out, accused me of kissing her for the wrong reasons, and ran me off."

Oh. "I might have misread things a little bit."

"Finally some of this makes a little bit of sense." He shakes his head. "I leave tomorrow for a week of meetings. I wanted to try and see you before I did to figure out what the heck was going on."

"I thought—"

He waves his hand through the air. "Yeah, yeah, I got it. That I was some kind of puppet for your boss?" He snorts. "I really am a vice president, and I really am opening a processing plant out here. None of that was a lie. It just so happened that I met a beautiful girl who works for my buddy's super crazy wife."

"Maybe if you'd mentioned it upfront. . ."

"You've met Victoria," he says. "Would you use her as a recommendation? I figured if she thought knowing her would help, she'd tell you herself. I was struggling to keep your attention as it was. Trust me, this was not some kind of veiled attempt on my part to feed high-level information on a social media influencer to a sporting goods company that she works for. I figured if Victoria needed to know something about you, she'd just ask."

I get it. I'm small potatoes. Whatever.

"Well, have a great trip, and maybe I'll see you when you get back."

He steps toward me. "I really like you, Amanda. I'm not going to lie. I picked this spot for the plant because it was a good one, but there were two other places just as good. I liked *you*—that was the difference. But lately, it seems like everything I say or do is wrong. In my experience, if you have to work too hard for something at the beginning, it never gets easier."

I stare him down. "Are you. . .dumping me?"

"Not at all. But when I get back, if you're happy to see me? Great. I'd love to take you out for dinner. We could even drive an hour to Vernal and catch a movie. But if you're not into it, just tell me that and I'll leave you alone. I don't get off on stalking people, and I've hit my limit for tracking you down."

"Okay."

"Good." He doesn't even try to kiss me goodbye. He just stomps around the front to his car and drives off.

"That guy is the weirdo." Eddy climbs out of the bushes.

I nearly jump out of my skin. "You were hiding there? I saw you walk away."

"I'm a country boy. We can move quietly when we want to." He wraps his arms around me. "You think I was leaving you to chat alone in the dark with Mr. Stomp and Growl?"

"Mister what?" I laugh. "You're so cute."

"Cute?" His arms tighten around me. "I'm not cute. I'm ominous. I'm nerve-wracking. I'm a threatening, burly cowboy."

"I am so sorry," I say. "Your pretty face distracted me from all that other stuff, but I won't forget it again."

"My what?" He sounds genuinely shocked.

"You have to know you're a pretty guy."

He's still looking a little dazed, but irritation's creeping in. I duck out of his arms and rush toward the shop. "I have to lock up."

Eddy may be pretty, but he's also a lot faster than me. He races in front and blocks the door. "Did you just say I'm *pretty*?"

"What are you spluttering about? I can't be the first person to say that."

"I'm rugged." He huffs. "Handsome. Gorgeous, even. But not pretty."

I laugh. "Eddy, you are the prettiest man I have ever met in real life."

He looks hurt—like genuinely offended.

I press one hand to his chest. "I like pretty men. Did I mention that?"

"No one likes 'pretty' men." He's still scowling. "It's not manly. It's an oxymoron."

"Um, hello. Brad Pitt is beautiful. Robert Pattinson. Henry Cavill."

"You're naming handsome guys," he says.

"Travis Fimmel!"

"Who?"

"Who's more beautiful than the guy who plays Ragnar Lothbrok?" For the first time, it occurs to me that they always seem to cast beautiful men as Vikings. "Or the guy from The Last Kingdom. He's pretty, too."

"Ragnar? The guy with the tattoos and the scars and the beard?" He cringes.

"Oh my goodness—before he got all old and covered in gross stuff, he was just beautiful." I exhale. "These men are like works of art, and you could just stand right next to them and make them all look unkempt."

"I'm going on the record as protesting the word," he says. "But I'll allow the sentiment."

"You're almost too pretty to date," I say. "It's a good thing I have high self-esteem." Which is a complete lie. I have terrible self-esteem, which is why I know this is true.

"Huh?"

"It's hard to be the less attractive person in a relationship—people expect the girl to be prettier."

"Now you're being ridiculous." He opens the door and drags me through. "Now get your little duds and purse and whatever so I can take you back and make you dinner and kiss you silly."

"Maren texted—homework problems."

He groans. "Unfair."

"Sorry."

"Do her grades really matter?" He bites his lip and stares at my mouth. "I mean, does she have a lot of career aspirations?"

I smack at his arm, but he ignores me and kisses my anyway, his hands cupping my face, his mouth stealing my resistance. But he's a good person, and eventually he lets me go.

It helps that Snuggles is scratching at the back door. "Your dog is going to ruin my door."

"I'll buy you a new one."

"You'd better." I kiss him one more time—a short kiss this time—and then I reluctantly grab my purse. Eddy helps me load Roscoe into the car, and it's time to leave him again.

"I hate this dating in secret thing," he says. "I want to take you to dinner. *I* want to go to Vernal and watch a movie with you. I want to do all the things that Derek can, and more."

"The Vernal thing, we could probably do," I say. "Who would we possibly run into?"

My phone rings, and it's Victoria.

"That woman calls too much." Eddy leans against my car door.

"Hello?"

"Amanda, my husband just heard from Derek. You broke up?"

We did? "We were never together. We were only dating."

"That was stupid. You don't let a man like him get away."

"I'll take that under advisement." Abigail's method of speech is clearly rubbing off on me.

"You'll what?"

"Never mind."

"Look, I was planning something amazing for another one of our influencers, but now she's got a *boyfriend*." She says that like it's a dirty word. "And it occurred to me, since the Derek thing didn't work out, we could use the whole line-up for you instead."

"Uh. What are you talking about?"

"You've seen *The Bachelorette*, right?"

"I'm confused," I say.

"Just hear me out. You're not dating anyone, and you're beautiful. We have seven eligible men lined up, and they're all quite well off, and they're all willing to travel. We figured we could set you up on a few dates—featuring outdoor activities and our clothing line, of course—and we'll foot the bill. You'd get a lot of press for it, new followers, and some fun posts. We even thought we'd do voting by followers to pick a second round of dates— we're predicting amazing engagement. It'll be pushed as a small town Bachelorette."

I open my mouth to say no, but Eddy bumps me and gives me a thumbs up. Huh?

"Uh, I'll think about it?"

"Think fast," she says. "I need to cut the line on this or push it ahead tomorrow around this time."

"Okay. I'll call you in the morning."

After she hangs up, I drop my phone into the cup holder. "Why did you stop me from telling her no?"

"It's the perfect cover," he says. "If you date another local, I'll probably end up killing him. He'd surely be at least as annoying as Derek was, slobbering all over you."

"This will only buy us a few weeks," I say.

"My longest relationship before now was two months," Eddy says. "Let's take what we can get."

Two months was his longest relationship?

"And that was with a comb."

"Wow, you're a real catch."

"I wasn't—until you came along." He presses his hand to my cheek.

"But I'll have to travel to random places and hang out with these guys. You're telling me you won't care?"

"It buys you time to get Double or Nothing off the ground—that's all we're waiting for, right?"

"Or to find more sponsors from different areas, yeah."

"Do it." He steps back. "I'm not used to being a jealous guy—and having you date someone who lives far off and isn't a real threat sounds better than dating someone local."

"Alright."

I shake my head, but I do what he asks. I text Victoria and tell her I'm in. I hope this isn't a huge mistake. It feels like I've been making a lot of those lately.

"Hey." Eddy's hand is in his pocket, and he looks nervous.

"What?" I glance at my phone. "Did you change your mind? I should call Victoria if you did."

He shakes his head. "No, but I've been thinking about something. Who have you told about us dating?"

That question takes me by surprise. "No one." Is he upset? Will he read something into that? I guess I wasn't sure who to tell, or how they'd react.

"Good." He stares me right in the eyes. "For your sake, we shouldn't tell a soul. Every single person we tell, including Abigail and your kids, is another point of danger for you. If we want this to work, we can't let this out, not until you're ready."

I was not expecting that.

"I screwed up something huge once, and luckily, it only ruined my life. My parents were sad, they were hurt, but they weren't damaged by it." He pulls his hand out of his pocket and takes mine. "I can't handle it if my past hurts you. So we can't let anyone know until you're ready, okay?"

I know he's right—he's always right—but for some reason, nodding in agreement feels like the hardest part of my day.

28

DONNA

I'm sure it was hard for Abigail to line up childcare and get time away from work, but she never complains about it. She never even mentions it. She just shows up, like she said she would, on the day I'm supposed to testify.

With half an hour before I'm supposed to be sworn in, she sits in a seat next to me.

It's good timing, because they bring Charlie in at the same time. He's dressed in a suit and tie, and he looks much better than I remembered. His looks are like that. They aren't flashy or in-your-face, but they're rich, they're elegant, and they're surprisingly sharp. For someone whose memory always makes me shudder, the way he looks completely normal gets me every time.

His parents walk in right after him and sit just behind him.

"I need to get some air." I stand up and practically race for the hallway.

Mr. Soco's eyes widen, and he looks like he's about to follow me out. Abigail blocks his path, says a few words, and dashes after me instead.

"Is he worried I'm going to change my mind?" I ask.

"Without you to prove up those new documents, their case will fall apart," she says. "Of course he's nervous."

"It's a lot," I say. "With Charlie right there, it's just a lot."

"Because you remember your time together?"

I snort. "Hardly. Because his parents are there too— and they're the ones who were offering me big money to keep my mouth shut."

"You made the right call."

"Did I?" My heart's racing, and my hands are trembling, and I think about how many things in my life, and in Aiden's, that kind of money could change. "I thought I was past the point of backing out, but if they need my testimony that badly. . ."

"About that." Abigail bites her lip.

"What?"

"I understand a lot more of why you did what you did. I've been debating telling you this—maybe it will help."

"What?"

"The agreement you signed with Charlie's parents. . .it was illegal."

I blanch. Does that mean they could prosecute me?

"That's why I insisted that the lawyers include that clause—remember? The one granting you immunity, not just from embezzlement, but from any other charges for the specified time period."

I have no idea what she's saying. There was *so* much paper coming my way that I started skimming it.

"Look, the material point is, his parents never intended to give you any money at all. They were always planning to cheat you."

"What?"

"You agreed to the deal taking place *after* the statute of limitations had run—at that point, your leverage would have been gone. Besides which, if you took that agreement—that provided that you'd assert spousal immunity to hide evidence of wrongdoing—to any court in America, they'd never uphold it. Such a promise is illegal. Which means you'd have no recourse for them cheating you, and you'd face criminal charges if you tried to prove they had."

I can't believe it.

"I'm such an idiot."

"Not at all—they're just monstrously underhanded."

"So the 1031 exchange?"

"That's a real thing," Abby says. "But that was my red flag. Those don't work when the ownership changes. The existence of an unenforceable contract wouldn't preclude them from following through on their promises. People carry out illegal deals all the time. But the verbiage about the 1031, which was patently not an option under these circumstances, prompted me to investigate the whole thing—they never sold the apartment complex, and the proceeds are not in an escrow account. All of that was a lie."

A lie that I bought—hook, line, and stupid sinker. "I feel like a fool."

"You shouldn't. I led them to believe that after discovering they had lied, you took this action. They see you as stronger than ever before. But you should know that they will likely put up a tremendous fight during the divorce proceedings."

"He can't force me to stay married."

Abby's face is grim. "For Aiden."

The hits just keep coming.

Abigail hands me an envelope. "There is one piece of good news." She smiles. "Liars lie. It's what they do. As soon as they caught on to what he was doing, the government did what it does best—it froze your assets. Everything from checking accounts to real estate and investments funds. Every last dime is locked down."

"I'm well aware of that."

"But your husband was too smart not to have plans in place for that. His parents are paying for his lawyer—I was able to track that. When I searched under Aiden's name, however, several accounts popped up."

"What?"

"Since you have sole custody of Aiden currently, I strongly suggest that as soon as this trial is over today, we proceed with speed to the closest CitiBank and Charles Schwab locations. It's not millions, but I imagine that seventy thousand dollars and change will lighten the load you've been carrying alone."

I practically break down in tears and kiss her hands.

"After dealing with the criminal stuff," Abby says, "the divorce proceedings in a few weeks will be a piece of cake." She hands me another piece of paper. "I have a list of lawyers who come highly recommended by my friends to handle that part for you."

"No, I want you," I say.

"I'm not a family lawyer, and I'm not boarded in California."

"I can afford to pay you," I say.

"It's not that. I want you to have the best chance in the world—"

"Please stick with me," I say. "I'll hire one of them, too. But can you still help out?"

She sighs. "If that's what you want."

"It is. You're my good luck charm."

Her smile is rueful, but she wraps an arm around me and squeezes. "Everything's going to be alright. I really do believe that. Now you need to breathe in and out a few times. It's time to get that terrible jerk locked up for a very long time."

With Abigail at my side, the entire process doesn't seem quite as dire. I take her advice, breathe in and out, and march into the courtroom.

I don't have long to wait once the trial begins. I suppose being the prosecution's star witness has some perks—you aren't left hanging. "I'd like to call Donna Windsor to the stand."

It's all I can do not to flinch at the use of Windsor. I started going by my maiden name immediately when I went home, and I've already grown accustomed to it. Before they can swear me in, Abigail stands. "May I approach the bench?"

The judge glances toward Mr. Soco. "Who is she, and why is she here?"

"She's the witness's private lawyer, Abigail Brooks. You admitted her *pro hac vice* yesterday."

"Right." He waves. "Sure, approach."

Since I'm already sitting on the stand, I can hear what they're saying.

"As things have moved quickly," Abigail says, "I haven't had a chance to propose—"

"Things have been stalled out for over a year thanks to your client's refusal to testify." The judge steeples his fingers, the prominent creases on his face growing even more prominent when he scowls. "Consider your request carefully, counselor."

"I have given it a lot of thought," Abby says, seeming unfazed, "believe me, Your Honor. But my client has now waived her spousal privilege, and given up what could have been a sizable spousal settlement if she had held out and those funds had been released."

The judge leans forward. "Are you implying that there was some sort of illegal deal between—"

My stomach flips. What is she doing?

"Not at all." Abby looks cool as glass. "But as you

know, the state immediately froze all their marital assets, pending this action. She's been living on the charity of others for a year, with a five-year-old child to support. It hasn't been easy, and she did nothing wrong."

The judge sighs, but he's clearly less agitated. "What are you asking us to do?"

"I'd like you to issue an order to unfreeze half the assets and put them in an escrow account—she's been granted immunity as part of her testimony already, but I think you'll see that she's been acting in good faith all along."

"But a lot of her testimony is about things she's overheard," Mr. Soco says. "It's hearsay, unless it's against party interests."

"The reservation of a portion of the proceeds in escrow doesn't change whether it's against the relevant party interests," Abigail says. "The one speaking is the person against whose interest the testimony must be." She looks like she's teaching him about the ABCs. "Come now, Mr. Soco, surely this request is reasonable."

"It does feel a bit like she's trying to wiggle free and profit from her husband's wrongdoing," the judge says.

"None of the frozen assets are from any kind of embezzlement," Abigail says. "If they were, you'd already have a chain of evidence and you wouldn't need her testimony. No, I'm going to insist on this, or she's going to reassert her privilege." She folds her arms.

"Most of the proceeds are in retirement accounts," Mr. Soco says. "It's not nearly enough to make much difference in any case."

"So the prosecution doesn't object?"

"It's a peculiar way to strike a deal," the judge says. "This should have been worked out—"

"As you mentioned, it was all quite a rush," Abigail says, "because my client decided she was willing to make great personal sacrifices and take big risks to see justice served. If she keeps her mouth closed, she'd be sure to get her share."

"Fine." The judge waves them away.

"I don't want it," I say.

"Excuse me?" The judge is now staring at me, his eyes wide.

"I know what Abby's doing, and I appreciate it, but could you just put whatever funds you're talking about in escrow for my son? I want nothing to do with any money that comes from him." I stare pointedly at Charlie. "Whether he gained it through lawful employment or not, I don't want a dime."

Abigail covers her face with her hand, but she doesn't argue. The thing is, now that I've finally decided to do the right thing, I want to do it all the way. Taking any kind of money from my ex feels gross, and I'm done having anything like that in my life.

The testimony I give over the next few hours is hard —grueling, even—the cross-examination the worst of all. But at the end of the day, I can finally say that I stepped away from the cesspool I've been swimming in for years, and it's an unparalleled feeling.

"When will we know whether he's found guilty?" I ask.

Mr. Soco, briefcase in hand, is clearly impatient to get home. "A few days. We have more witnesses to call, and then they'll mount their defense." He loosens his tie. "I'll let you know if, for any reason, we need to recall you."

"Can you let me know the second the verdict is back?"

He nods. "I was impressed with your position back there—and I should tell you that I actually prevailed upon the plaintiff in the civil case to drop you from the suit. Anything you obtain in the divorce proceedings, for you or for Aiden, will be exempted."

Abigail isn't very chatty on the way back home, and I'm grateful for it. "Thanks for the ride."

"You did really well today," she says. "I was impressed."

"They say that no good deed goes unpunished," I say. "But today, hours after saying I wanted nothing to do with Charlie's money, the plaintiffs in the civil suit dropped me from the claim."

She smiles. "In my experience, sending good out into the world usually brings it back to you."

I'm surprised that's her position. From what I can tell, she's never done anything but good, and her husband died, and Patrick and I are trying to steal her ranch. "I'm really sorry," I say. "I know it's overdue, but I was wrong."

"I'm not upset," she says. "Like I said before, being angry only hurts the person harboring the anger."

"Did you learn that as a lawyer?"

She shakes her head. "As a mom."

I have a long way to go before I'll be ready to let go of my anger, but thanks to her, I'd like to try. "If there's ever anything I can do to set things right for you, please tell me," I say. "I'll do it. That's a promise."

✥ 29 ✥

ABIGAIL

When I was in high school, I worked hard. Harder than any of my friends, harder than my family—except for my sister, anyway— and I succeeded. Valedictorian, debate superstar. In fact, at the end of my senior year, I had earned a spot at the national tournament, and I advanced into finals. By then, they don't have a single judge making decisions about the winner. It's always a panel of judges that decides.

In that final round—the first two judges announced their winners. One picked me, and one picked my opponent. It came down to the last judge's vote.

Although he was impressed with my speaking, he voted for my opponent on a technicality.

That was the first time that I realized that my luck wasn't very good. It happened again and again of course— if there was a role luck could play, it worked against me every time.

On exams, if I had to guess, it was always wrong. In the grocery store, if I chose a line out of two that looked about the same, mine was always the slowest. The woman in front of me would break out a box of coupons. Or the computer at the register would jam. That's just how my life has always gone. While other people hope for the best, I have always planned for the worst. It's why I value contracts—rules and bounds that keep the parties in safe positions. Any protection that can be had, I utilize.

So when Steve asks me to go with him on a trail ride, I say yes, but I also check the weather. A thirty percent chance of rain.

To me, that means it's going to pour.

My luck is just never good, and I know this. That's why I pack a poncho. Two, actually, one for me and one for Steve. When I reach his place, the sky overhead is a beautiful shade of blue. There's a breeze, but for October, the weather's amazing. At least, that's what I hear.

"You look great," Steve says. "But then, you always do." He's beaming from ear to ear. It's the first time I've seen him since I met him at the ER, and I wonder whether things will be weird.

But they aren't. He walks me from my van to the barn, and once we're there, he asks me, "Did you want Leo again?"

"Who else?" I look down the rows. "Maybe Farrah?"

"For you?" He shrugs. "Any horse."

"I want Leo," I say. "I can't help it. I grew up playing with Barbies, and he looks like a Barbie horse." His gorgeous head's already hanging out of his stall. "Plus." I scratch behind his ears. Plenty of horses don't like it, but Leo definitely does. "I'm pretty sure he's in love with me."

"He was calling your name last night," Steve says.

I laugh. "It's hard for him—he's a younger man. He doesn't really stand a chance."

When I go to tack him up, Steve stops me. "I got some new gear for him."

"You did?"

He nods.

I've rarely seen a horse as beautiful as Leo. A dark golden coat, thick and shiny, and a long white mane—so thick I felt bad for him over the summer. It must be hot in the heat. Steve hauls out a turquoise saddle pad, and a shiny, new two-tone saddle—a chocolate brown and deep blue-green—with gorgeous Western swirls and curves. "That new saddle really is breathtaking. He looks like he should be on a movie set."

"He's wide here, thanks to all that muscle." Steve touches his withers. "It's uncomfortable for him unless he has a very wide tree. Since I was already ordering him something new, I figured I may as well get something that's nice to look at."

"You did a great job."

"Thanks." He grabs a matching bridle. "Here, I'll get it for you." He slides it on effortlessly, and buckles it too. Minutes later, we're leading the horses out, there are clouds overhead, and I hear rumbling in the distance.

"Are you sure we should go out?" I glance upward. "I'm not sure if I've mentioned this, but I don't have the best luck and the weather report says it might rain."

"It'll be fine," he says.

"But your new saddle might get wet."

"Life's about risks," he says. "I'd think you, of all people, know that as well as I do."

At least he can't say I didn't warn him. "Your call."

He takes me out on a different path than we took last time. This one heads up, into the mountains, not down into the valley.

"How many acres do you have?" I ask.

"I've only got forty," he says, "but like your property, it feeds into the forestry land. It's the reason Dad picked this spot way back when. He's always loved being out in the middle of nowhere."

I think about Amanda's recent run-in with the cougar. "Does it ever make you nervous?"

"All the time." He pats the gun on his saddle. "But if you give up whenever life makes you nervous, you never live."

He's right. I know that luck never breaks my way, but I keep on trying. I keep on living. "Did it annoy you?"

"What?" He turns backward in the saddle, trusting Farrah to follow the path.

"When I kept breaking things off? First to fly home, then because of, well, you know. And then again, after you came over and saved us when we all got sick?"

"I talk about horses too much," he says. "I wish I had a good example from the ER I could use instead." He thinks for a moment.

"It's alright. I like horses."

"That bodes very well for us," he says. "But here's the thing. Breaking a new horse, it's not that hard. You go over the basics. It's like teaching a kid in kindergarten. You teach him numbers, letters, and rules of the world around him. Kids that age want to learn, and colts are the same. They're excited, and usually, it's pretty simple."

"Okay."

He holds Farrah back a little now that the path has widened. Now that we have room to walk astride, we may as well take it. "But sometimes I get older horses. Horses who have bad habits. Horses who never went to kindergarten."

"Why do I feel like I'm the damaged horse again in this scenario?"

He laughs. "They aren't damaged. They've just been taught to deal with things in a certain way."

"Like, by running?"

"Some of them, yeah. Racehorses really only know

how to run. They weren't taught to be steady or calm. They weren't taught to be horses, really."

"I'm a racehorse, now?"

"You're a lawyer, and I think you'll agree that's worse."

My laugh startles Leo, who turns his head around to see me. "Calm down, boy. I'm fine, you're fine, we're all fine."

The clouds up ahead rumble.

"See? I told you it would rain. Whenever I'm around, bad things happen."

Steve looks up. "A little rain doesn't scare me. You can't have a rainbow without getting a little wet first."

"You're saying all the back and forth was worth it—"

"The second you came back to me, yeah." He smiles. "The funny part is that I was preparing what I was going to say to you."

"Oh?"

"I let you say your thing," he says. "But now it's my turn."

"What?"

"You'll see," he says. "Up ahead."

Oh, no. I knew I had bad luck. I think about the things Steve could be planning to say. We're on a special trail ride. He bought new gear for Leo. We're going. . .somewhere. He has something to say? None of this is going anywhere good. I'm happy to date him—and I think we can work through things together. But if he proposes right now?

Yeah, I'm going to run. Again. And I may never stop or even turn back.

Plus, I'm pretty sure you can't ever really recover from someone proposing and someone else saying no. With the clouds threatening above, and my stomach tied in knots down below, it's hard to appreciate the beauty of the trail around me. Eventually, though, Mother Nature gets my attention. Deer graze in the clearing to the left of us. Birds warble as they stop for a break on their way down south. Chipmunks chatter at us as though we're the usurpers, and I suppose we are.

"We're here." Steve stops up ahead in a clearing—surrounded by evergreens. There are cardinals in the branches. There's a white rabbit on the far end that disappears as we approach.

It's as close as I've ever been to stepping inside a Disney cartoon. Which means something equally bad is about to happen to balance all this preciousness out. I can practically sense the rainstorm right now. "I packed a picnic."

"You made food?"

"Correction," he says. "I bought food. If I'd made it, you'd be sadly disappointed with a ham sandwich and carrot sticks."

"I don't mind either of those things."

"Well, I went the extra mile and picked these up earlier." He pulls a bag off his saddle and unfolds a blanket. Then he sets a few paper-wrapped packages on top of it.

"Thanks."

He's right about the food—he really did go the distance. "These sandwiches are really delicious."

"We may not have high-end food options, but we know how to make a great picnic. Egg salad, coleslaw, and brownies. These we can do."

"Thank you," I say.

"Now, I get to say what I was going to say to you, if you hadn't shown up to surprise me that night."

"Okay." If my voice is a little unsteady, well. I doubt Steve noticed.

"You told me that Donna told you about my ex."

I nod.

"I owe you an apology for that. The entire town

knows about me and Stephanie. You've been more than upfront about your past, and I hid mine."

Until that very second, it hadn't even occurred to me that I felt betrayed—that it upset me for Donna to be the one sharing that information. I'm not even sure how to respond. "Uh. Okay."

"You don't have to accept my apology right now, but know that it's genuine. We can talk about her, or about the past, as much as you'd like. You aren't the only one with ghosts, and maybe I let them cloud my view a little too much."

"It's okay," I say. "It's not like you demanded anything."

"The decision about whether to have children—it's delicate at the best of times. And for me, it's even more emotional. I'm not sure any dad has ever been more excited to have a little girl. When she was a year old, and my wife told me she wasn't mine—" He chokes up. My big, strong, tough cowboy actually can't finish.

I reach out and take his hand.

"That was harder than losing my sister. That was harder than losing my wife. That was the hardest thing that's ever happened to me."

"I'm so sorry," I say.

"I didn't believe it," he says. "This is embarrassing for me to say, but I actually freaked out on the judge. I shouted and screamed at the final divorce proceedings. I told him that I knew the paternity test was wrong, and that Livy was mine." He closes his eyes. "Getting tossed in jail was a new low for me."

Horrific. I wish I'd been there for him—not that I could have helped.

"I always swore, after that, that if I ever remarried, I would insist on having a child right away. I wanted one of my own—one that no one could take away from me."

It makes sense, honestly. Especially for someone who's as good with kids as he is.

"But I never trusted anyone enough to risk that again. I never met anyone whom I could *dare* to have a child with. Until I met you. Someone so bright, so beautiful, and so good that she helps people who have wronged her. Someone who always thinks before she speaks. Someone who lost a person she cared for, and still fights to uphold the promises she made, even though he's gone." He leans toward me. "Abigail Brooks—"

Please don't propose. Please don't propose!

"Can you ever forgive me for putting my own needs ahead of yours? For letting you fret and worry and suffer because it took me so long to say that none of that matters?"

I blink. "Huh?"

"It should have taken me less than five minutes to realize that, if things work out for us, your kids will be my kids. Having a biological child with you won't change my past, and it won't change who you are. I *see* you, Abby. I know you're good and kind and true. Whether you decide you want more kids or whether you never do, I will love you just the same. It's *you* that I love and trust, and it's that trust that will keep me safe and bring me joy. Not the security of having my DNA inside some child."

He stares at me then, and the rest of the world drops away. When it starts to rain, I don't even care.

When we hop on his horses and canter practically the whole way back, it doesn't bother me. In fact, it's fun. It's an adventure. Even though the thing I worried would happen *did*, it wasn't bad with Steve at my side.

"That dumb rain." As we reach the barn and finally get under cover from the stupid sky, Steve stops me. "I wanted to show you this before, but by golly, you were right. It did rain."

369

"What did you want to show me?"

He takes Leo's reins and shifts me around to the other side. On the back side of the bridle, in beautiful ivory backstitching, it says, "Property of Abigail."

"I have my own bridle?" What a sweet gesture.

"You have your own *horse*—here on my property. I sent his papers off already. He'll be yours officially in a matter of days."

"What?"

"I know that the ranch is up in the air. Your job isn't what you'd hoped. Your kids are navigating new things. But one place in this county is always safe for you, and that's right here with me. If you're sick, if you're scared, if things go sideways, you and your family are always welcome here."

"Are you saying he's mine, but I can't take Leo back to the ranch with me?"

"Oh, you absolutely can." He cups my cheek and presses his lips to mine. When Leo bumps us, he finally releases me. "But I'd rather you keep both of your favorite men in the same place. It'll be easier for us to ride together this way."

"Fine," I say. "If that's what you want. I'll do it."

His single-dimple grin is everything to me. Even more beautiful than Leo, the first horse in the world that has ever really been mine.

Tacking down is usually the worst part of a ride, but not this time. I'm putting away my very own gear for my very own horse. And when I dry it off and slide the saddle into place, I notice there's a placard above it already. Abigail Brooks.

"What if things go well?" I ask. "That says Brooks."

He winks. "I'm always happy to upgrade."

"Ha."

The rain has already stopped as we walk hand in hand

from the barn to Steve's little white farmhouse, but the car that pulls up in front of his home has water beaded on the windshield. Apparently it's still raining in whatever direction it came from.

"Who's that?" I ask.

Steve squints. "No idea."

"I'd better head back anyway," I say. "I've got a few urgent deadlines looming."

"You always do." He presses a kiss to my forehead. "Finish them quickly, and maybe we can all eat dinner together. You, me, the kids."

"I'd like that." I try to release his hand, but he won't let me.

"Five more minutes."

I roll my eyes.

The car engine cuts off, and the door opens. A beautiful woman steps out—she looks at least five years younger than I am. Maybe ten. She's thin, with a fitted black sheath dress that hugs all her curves. Unlike the dress I wore on Labor Day, you can tell she didn't borrow this. She wears it with confidence, like the four-inch heels that round the whole thing out.

"Steve." She doesn't say his name, she purrs it.

The hand that wouldn't loosen before completely drops mine. "Stephanie?" His hands both ball into fists at his side. "What are you doing here?"

"I tried calling, but you didn't ever call me back."

"That's the beauty of a *divorce*," he says. "The other great thing is that I can say, 'Leave and never come back,' and you have to do it, or I can call a sheriff."

"Don't be ridiculous." She glances my direction. "Or is this whole show for her benefit?"

Steve's head snaps toward me. "Don't you talk to her, and don't even say her name." He steps toward her. "Just go."

"Silly me, I thought you'd be delighted. You were so upset when you thought Olivia wasn't yours."

"Stephanie, I don't know how I could be more clear. You aren't wanted here—please leave."

"Mom, who is that?" A little girl's head pokes out from the open driver's door. "Why did we stop in the middle of nowhere?"

"Livy?" Steve's entire body tenses up, like a bird dog sensing a duck.

"Olivia," she says. "No one calls me Livy anymore."

Steve swallows.

I've never wanted to slap someone in my life more than I want to slap this woman. Why is she bringing this little girl here? She's clearly almost Whitney's age. Steve hasn't seen her in years, from what I understand. It's terribly inappropriate.

"Give Mom a minute." Stephanie closes the door, almost on top of the little girl's face. "Look, as you can see, there's not much time. My husband discovered I lied to him and he divorced me, and thanks to the stupid prenup he made me sign, I was left destitute."

"What?" Steve's clearly reeling. I don't blame him—so am I, and it's not even my life or my child.

"Olivia is your daughter," she says. "She always was—I paid the testing center to say she was Antonio's, so that he'd marry me."

"You're a consummate liar. Why would I believe a single word you say?" Steve asks.

But the little girl has opened the car door again, and now that I take a moment to look at her, it's plain as the nose on her face.

Literally.

This little girl is the spitting image of Steve. She looks nothing like her mother. "I assume you'd be willing to undergo additional paternity testing," I say. "Which

372

would be conducted independently, at a facility of our choosing?"

"Butt out, lady," Stephanie says. "This doesn't concern you."

Steve grabs my hand and tugs me to his side. "Actually, whether any part of this is true or not, you may as well know. This is Abigail Brooks. She's my girlfriend, and she's also my lawyer. You can expect all communications from me to be made through her from now on."

What, now?

At least Stephanie looks as shocked as I do, judging by her spluttering.

I knew something bad was coming. The day was just going far too well, and that rain just wasn't enough.

❦ 30 ❦

AMANDA

It takes all morning to iron out the details of the stupid Bachelorette thing. I never should have agreed to do it. Eddy's right though—no one will ever imagine I'm dating him with all this going on.

"I'll send over the contracts from the network as soon as they arrive." Victoria's practically bubbling.

"Remember—no more than one day a week—eight hours."

"I'm aware," she says. Then she hangs up.

"I can't believe you're doing this," Abigail says. "I mean, you already spend too much time on Lololime, if you ask me. You seem to hate it. Now you're adding television crews?"

"They're giving me another fifty thousand dollars just to do these segments," I say. "It's more than fair. Plus, this kind of exposure is going to grow my following quite a bit."

"Which would matter," she mutters, "if you wanted to keep doing what you're doing."

"They've said I can mention my cookies," I say. "And who knows? Maybe I'll start shipping them."

"Yes, I do hear that shipping fresh cookies from the middle of nowhere is a very lucrative prospect." She rolls her eyes. "Have you even calculated how many cookies you'd need to sell to make up your Lololime salary?"

She's such a buzzkill. "I don't need that much money, not while I'm living out here. What would I even spend it on?"

"Fine, fine, I'm done harping. But come to me if they try and send over anything we haven't already discussed."

I'm smart enough now to know that I should go running to her in the event of anything unexpected. I open my laptop in my room and check for the documents. They haven't come through yet, but I ought to make sure the printer's on and running. It finally arrived from Amazon—along with reams and reams of paper. Poor Gabe won't need to draw on the backs of letters, and I won't have to spend an hour searching for paper.

Which reminds me of my dilemma. Abby thinks we should let sleeping dogs keep sleeping—she doesn't think we should tell Amanda. But as someone who's already keeping a big secret, I'm sick of lying to her. I've almost mentioned the stupid letters a dozen times. After staring at the computer for ten minutes, waiting for my documents, I make an impulsive decision. I grab the stack of letters, which we've now all read a few times, and I put them in my purse. Good thing I have a mom purse, or they'd never fit. Then I head out to my car.

And Abigail doesn't even notice, so she doesn't stop me. I drive to Amanda Saddler's immediately so I don't lose my nerve. I checked last week—she doesn't have a heart condition or anything else. She's 'healthier than an ox,' in her words.

When I pull up, before the stupid cardinal has outed me for being here, I hesitate. I'm bright enough to know that my reasons for telling her are selfish. I'm struggling enough to keep my own secret—divesting myself of hers will be a huge relief.

But am I possibly hurting her because it's easier for me?

I'm still staring at my steering wheel when Amanda taps on my window. "Hey. You."

I jump.

She opens the door. "You communing with your steering wheel? Or did your car break down?"

I shake my head. "Neither. I came because. . ."

She laughs. "It's alright. I don't mind." She spins on her heel and walks toward her front door. "Come on, then."

What in the world?

By the time I go inside, she's making tea already. "I wondered when we'd end up here."

"Here? Where are we?"

"We're in my kitchen, obviously," she says. "But I figured at some point you'd need money. Did you fire Lololime? Are you finally dating your Prince Charming?"

"No," I splutter. "I don't need money. It's nothing like that." I'm a little hurt she assumed we'd end up with me begging her for money. What happened to her saying she never backs the wrong horse?

She pauses, her hands clasped around her favorite mug. It says, *I'm just a girl who loves pigs. And tea.* The little pink pig on it looks nothing like Jed the Pig, but I've never pointed that out.

"Look." I glance at the living room. "Can we go in there?"

She shrugs, and precedes me into the family room.

Now that I'm here—committed, my purse clutched tightly in my hands—I have no idea how to tell her the truth. "It's about Jed."

"Jed?" She holds out her hand and makes a clicking

376

sound with her tongue. He trots over and plops down on the floor near her feet.

"No, not that Jed." My throat closes off.

"Jedediah?" Her heart is in her eyes. Gosh, I shouldn't be here. Abigail was right. "What about him?"

"So it's a strange story," I say. "My nephew Gabe—actually I should explain. Our house has no paper. Like, none."

"What are you talking about?"

"Gabe has been drawing—like seven-year-old boys do. He's always making pictures."

Amanda has never looked more confused. Is there something I could say to get out of this? To make an excuse and leave? But I can't think of anything. If I were Abigail, I probably could, but I'm not like her. I'm not quick on my feet, and I fumble over my words all the time.

Finally, I just pull the stack of letters out of my bag—most of them defaced on the back, but some of them clean, saved just in time from becoming a canvas for juvenile artwork. "He found an old stack of letters, and he was coloring on them. But if he wasn't, we might never have found them." I moved most of Jed's things out to the barn when we moved in. "I'm sorry about all the drawings."

Amanda blinks at me a few times, then she focuses downward and picks up the first letter. They aren't dated, but we put them in what *felt* like the right order.

She doesn't speak to me for a few moments. Then those moments turn into more. Eventually I stand to leave, but she grabs my wrist. That's when I realize she's quietly crying. "Please stay."

I sit.

And I wait.

She keeps reading until the very last letter has been read. Then she sets it down, stands up, and pulls me into an embrace. It feels like she's hugging me with every ounce of strength she has. She's still crying, but it's a quiet sort of sorrow. No heaving chest. No ragged breathing. Just tears, rolling down her softly wrinkled face.

"Thank you," she says.

I didn't expect gratitude. Sorrow? Anger? Frustration? Yes, all of those things, but not gratitude.

"We were such fools," she says. "If either one of us had—"

And now sobs wrack her little body. She clings to me now like I'm the harbor in a terrible storm and she's being tossed out to sea. I hug her back this time, finally sure what I ought to do.

After quite some time, she releases me and straightens. "Thank you so much for bringing these over. I'm sure it was hard to know how I'd react." A smile breaks out across her expressive face. "Is that why you asked about my heart?" She laughs. "Oh, dear girl, you're a treasure."

"Well, I just wasn't sure—"

"The answer to love is always yes," she says. "It should have been yes in my lifetime." Now her laughter sounds a little unhinged. "Think of all the time we wasted. That's time we'll never recapture, all because of our pride, and a stupid misunderstanding."

"I'm so sorry," I say.

"Even so, that can't be helped, and what you've brought me is a gift. Knowing you love someone, but never knowing that they loved you back, is an exquisite torture. It kept me from living, and it kept me from loving. But now, knowing that he felt the same." She sighs. "It's like a balm on my old, withered heart."

I'm so glad.

Her bony hands reach out and grasp my shoulders. "But you? You're young. You're beautiful. And you're so much smarter than I am. You get in your car, and you drive over to that young man's house and you kiss him right on the mouth. You hear me?"

I know I promised to keep it a secret. No one can know—everyone's a risk. I agreed with that decision, and I still do. But in this moment, I have to tell her. I can't keep this secret anymore, not from her, not from someone who was so damaged, who was destroyed, by hiding feelings. "We're dating," I say. "It's a secret, because of, you know, but we're dating and it's. . .it's bliss."

She beams.

"I know it's stupid, Abigail would never do it—she's too sensible. She would never ram her heart against a brick wall like this, but—"

"It's what makes you who you are. It's why he loves you." Amanda takes one of my hands in both of hers. "It's your strength, my dear."

"How can doing something stupid be a strength?"

"You seem to be confused." Amanda's eyes are still full of unshed tears. "Weren't you listening the other day? Abigail is beautiful and smart and very organized. She's solid and dependable." She laughs. "When I told you those things before, were you really listening?"

"Of course I was." I snatch my hand free. "I know that I'm none of those things. No matter how I try, I'll never be like her. That's what you said."

"You idiot. You're as blind as I was." She stands up and points at me. "You're brash, and brave, and unfettered. You're impulsive, and you're kind, and you're bighearted. Those are your strengths. You already do put people ahead of everything else. You do the right thing, even when it's terribly stupid and it hurts you. You love boldly, even though you've been hurt. And you may not always know the right thing to do or say, but you don't hang back and say nothing. You brave your way forward, doing the best you can." She sits down again and leans toward me. "I never had children. I was too idiotic to build the life I should have had with Jed. But if I had a daughter, I'd want her to be just like you, Amanda Brooks, not like picture-perfect Abigail."

Something inside of me cracks open—like a floodgate has released and the river's finally flowing outward. My own mother has never told me anything half so nice. Paul certainly never approached that kind of praise.

I've spent my life knowing all of the ways in which Amanda Brooks is lacking.

But Amanda says those weaknesses are also my strengths. Maybe that's what Eddy sees in me too.

"Don't sell yourself short, my dear." Amanda stands up and walks into the kitchen, resuming her initial activity of making me tea. "I was telling you this before, but you didn't listen. You can't be someone you aren't. All you've needed to do all along was embrace the beautiful parts of who you already are. That's how you'll really shine."

That's all I've wanted all along—to shine.

EPILOGUE: DONNA

The drive home is a long one. I'm a little embarrassed to have fallen asleep. When I wake up, Abigail looks just as she always does. Polished. Polite. Perfect.

I yawn and wipe the corners of my mouth.

Yep, I was drooling.

"Sorry," I say. It feels like I'm always saying that to her.

"I'm glad you got some sleep. I'm sure today was harrowing—both in preparation and in execution. I hope you'll be able to sleep better at home from here on out."

"I'll be a lot better once the verdict is in and the divorce is final, too."

"I bet," she says. "Not much longer, now."

"Thanks again for all your help."

"Did you mean it, earlier?" Abigail's hands are held perfectly at ten and two, her eyes on the road. Even so, something about the way she's sitting, about the tone of her voice, warns me: she's nervous.

"What?"

"You said that if there was anything you could do to help. . ."

"Absolutely, I did," I say. "Did you think of something?"

She swallows. "I know your brother Patrick is prickly. I know he's hard to live with, and that he's in charge of care for your father while you're doing all the actual day-to-day work of it. I imagine that's already a pretty uncomfortable situation that you find yourself in."

She came to my rescue the last time he tried to bully me, so it's no shock she's familiar with all that.

"Does he know that you've testified against your husband? Does he know that your deal to get the money from the Windsors has fallen through?"

I sigh. "Not yet. I figured I'd wait to tell him until after I was done testifying."

"That's already going to be rough. I hesitate to add to it."

"As you said, it's already going to be rough. If there's *anything* I can do for you, please tell me what." I wish I could look her in the eyes. "I would give anything to fix the damage I've caused."

Her lips tighten.

"I'm not kidding. If I were a lawyer, if I could think of a solution myself, I wouldn't hesitate to put it into action."

"Do you know whether your brother plans to proceed with buying the ranch, even without the money from the Windsors?"

I sigh. "He does. I'm not sure why he's so keen to do it —he'll have to take out a loan, at least until my father passes away and he can claim the life insurance money."

"Perhaps that's why—the ranch numbers don't work if you're paying a large note, but if it's free and clear, it's not a bad investment."

"It's hard to always know what Patrick wants. I think

maybe he just wants to have the biggest ranch in the area. Pride has always been his downfall."

"The thing is, Jedediah's will doesn't name your brother as part of the three-person panel," she says. "It names your father."

"But he's got a power of attorney," I say. "That's why Mr. Swift is using him."

"Before, you were the one buying the ranch, but if he's interested in buying the property directly instead, that's a pretty significant conflict of interest," she says.

"Huh." I hadn't even thought of that, but having the person who plans to buy the ranch from the alien people be the one who decides whether they get it is pretty shady.

"I think, if you pursued it, the court would appoint you to take your dad's place on the council of three, and they're the ones who decide what happens with the ranch. They determine whether we've met the terms."

"Are you asking me to rule in your favor?" They really did leave for a month. I didn't make that part up. But I think about the injustice of it all. Jed is those children's great-uncle, and instead of just giving them his land, he put all these rules on it. I can't even imagine if my dad left his property to some alien foundation instead of me or Aiden. It would be terrible. "I'll do it."

Abigail shakes her head. "I'm not asking you to rule in our favor. I want you to be just, and I want you to be fair. I want you to read the will and think about what Jed wanted and make a good decision. I just don't think your brother will be capable of doing that."

She may be unwilling to ask me to do it, but that doesn't mean—

"I can tell what you're thinking, and I don't want you to give us the ranch if, in your opinion, we've violated the terms. I'm not just saying that. Are we clear?"

Abigail is a strange kind of person, but that may be why I respect her so much. She clearly means it. "Yes, you're clear." But then it hits me—I may have something else that could help. "It might be hard to prove that Patrick's an interested party," I say. "He's sneaky with stuff like that. Only." I sigh. He will never forgive me for this. "But he already executed an agreement of intention to purchase or something like that with the alien people."

"If you could get your hands on a copy of that," Abigail says, "that would give us a real chance at a fair decision."

"I'll figure something out."

"But this is going to upset your brother really badly." Her hands tighten and lines appear beside her eyes. "Your life has been hard enough lately. I'm hesitant to ask you—"

"It's alright," I say. "This mess is all because of me."

"Are you sure?"

"I'll figure out how to get a copy of that sale thing, and you draw up whatever else you think I'll need. It's about time Patrick and I had a little head-to-head. After the last few weeks, I think I'm finally ready."

And no matter how ugly it gets, for once, I'm squarely on the right side.

** I hope you enjoyed the Vow! I'm hard at work on The Ranch, so that should be out before you know it. But if you don't want to WAIT for more writing from me, you can check out Finding Faith right now, FOR FREE on all platforms. It's a little more romance focused, but it has the same family and friends and real life that The Bequest and the Vow have. You might just love it! <3

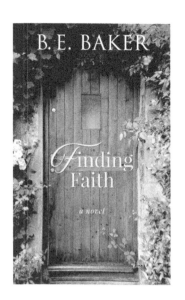

B. E. BAKER

Finding
Faith

a novel

ACKNOWLEDGMENTS

Always first and foremost, I have to thank my husband. He's an unfailing supporter, a true friend, and the best partner in the world. You inspire all of it, and you're there for all the highs and the lows of writing and publishing. Thank you for putting up with my nonsense.

My kids—I shamelessly stole you for this series, and I'm grateful you don't seem to mind. You are also unbelievably supportive. I love that you come beg me to send you the advance copy the second it's done. Thank you for loving my journey into these fictional worlds.

My parents and extended family: you put up with a lot. I'm sorry to put you through it. I love you for accepting it.

My editor Carrie, you're the BEST for your last minute help. I'm sorry I always impose so badly. My cover artist Shaela, thank you for making my ideas come to life and giving my baby a beautiful face.

My FANS/READERS. THANK YOU. Your reviews, your comments, your messages, they are everything to me. Without you, my stories would have no point. Thank you for your unfailing support and for sharing my stories with your family and friends. I hope you see yourselves in these pages.

ABOUT THE AUTHOR

Bridget's a lawyer, but does as little legal work as possible. She has five kids and soooo many animals that she loses count.

Horses, dogs, cats, and so many chickens. Animals are her great love, after the hubby, the kids, and the books.

She makes cookies waaaaay too often and believes they should be their own food group. In a (possibly misguided) attempt at balancing the scales, she kickboxes daily. So if you don't like her books, maybe don't tell her in person.

Bridget is active on social media, and has a facebook group she comments in often. (Her husband even gets on there sometimes.) Please feel free to join her there: https://www.facebook.com/groups/750807222376182

Disavowed (5)

unRepentant (6)

Destroyed (7)

The Birthright Series Collection, Books 1-3

The Sins of Our Ancestors Series:

Marked (1)

Suppressed (2)

Redeemed (3)

Renounced (4)

Reclaimed (5) a novella!

The Anchored Series:

Anchored (1)

Adrift (2)

Awoken (3)

Capsized (4)

A stand alone YA romantic suspense:

Already Gone

Made in the USA
Las Vegas, NV
29 January 2024

85058366R00236